THE GIRL FROM *Oto*

AMY MARONEY

ARTELAN
PRESS

Artelan Press
Portland, Oregon
ISBN: 978-0-9975213-0-6
eBook ISBN: 978-0-9975213-1-3
Published by Artelan Press
Portland, Oregon
http://www.amymaroney.com/

For Jonathan Scott Maroney

"The past does not exist. There are only infinite renderings of it."
— Ryszard Kapuściński

CONTEMPORARY CAST OF CHARACTERS

HISTORICAL CAST OF
CHARACTERS

Elena de Arazas......*Nomadic healer in the Pyrenees mountains*
Ramón de Oto..*Baron of Oto in Aragón*
Marguerite de Oto........*Baroness of Oto, originally from Béarn*
Their children:
Miramonde (Mira)
Pelegrín
Alejandro
Johan Arros..........*Monk at the monastery of San Juan de la Peña*
Béatrice of Belarac..............................*Abbess of Belarac Abbey*
Carlo Sacazar..*Merchant of Aragón*
Flora Sacazar...*Carlo's wife*
Amadina Sacazar...........*Carlo's sister, abbess of a convent in Nay*
Jorge de Luz.............................*Patriarch of a family in Ronzal*
Thérèse de Luz..*His Béurnuise wife*
Their children:
Arnaud
Tomás
Luis
Beltrán Fivalas...*Ramón de Oto's steward*
Sebastian de Scolna..*Painter and pilgrim*
Gonzalo Fernández de Córdoba..........*'The Great Captain,'*
Spanish military leader

PROLOGUE

Summer, 2015
Pyrenees Mountains, France
Zari

SILVER THREADS OF RAIN twisted down from the dark sky. A chaotic wind swirled around Zari, shifting and billowing from all directions, tugging at her backpack with invisible fingers. She stabbed at the slick trail with her trekking poles. It took all her concentration to stay upright.

At the edge of a broad meadow, she watched massive gray storm clouds curl in on themselves, gather speed, silently collide. A blaze of light ignited the sky above the mountains. Counting the seconds until the rumble of thunder began, she eyed a nearby pine forest. The lightning was still miles away. If it got close, she would take cover in the sheltering edge where the trees met the meadow.

A spike of adrenalin took hold of her. She was no mere observer. She was part of this great spectacle, a bit player in a dazzling show of power. Wading through the tall grasses, she let their waterlogged heads tickle her palms. A dark trail in her wake charted her progress. She would mark off the entire meadow this way, stride by stride, searching for a story written in stone.

On her third traverse of the meadow, she stumbled and fell. Heaving herself up, she untangled a kink in the chain around her neck and tucked the shell back in place at the base of her throat. Another flash of lightning. For an instant, the sky turned a bleached bone-white. The boom of thunder that followed reverberated in Zari's chest long enough to scare her.

She had not taken five more steps when she saw them.

Rows of half-sunken stone slabs jutted out before her like shards from a giant's pottery collection. Sinking slowly into the earth, corroded by wind and rain and ice, they offered themselves up to her. Foundation stones. Evidence.

"I knew it was here!" she shouted, waving the poles in the air.

She turned a slow circle, imagining the buildings that once spread across this land, protected by a high stone wall, by the sharp spires of iron gates. She saw a church with a soaring bell tower, a bustling kitchen, a garden filled with vegetables and herbs. In the murmuring wind, she heard the voices of long-dead women and children.

Then a dark shape materialized across the meadow. A tall figure moved toward her through the grass. A man. She stood mesmerized, vaguely aware of the crackling sky, the growl of thunder. She could almost see waves of sound rippling through the heavy wet air.

He walked quickly, cutting through the raindrops with long decisive strides, narrowing the gap between them.

Zari swallowed.

She took one step backward and tightened her grip on the poles.

BOOK 1

Ab initio. From the beginning.

1

Autumn, 1484
Castle Oto, Aragón
Elena

LIKE THE BREATH OF an angry god, the wind streamed over the mountains from the north and slammed into the castle. The balcony shutters bucked and heaved, straining against the iron latches that held them in place. To Elena's ears, the sound was the hollow clacking of bones.

Wind goes where it wants, she thought, finding the source of a draft with her fingertips. She closed her eyes and imagined herself in the forest, where brittle leaves swirled in unruly flocks and golden-eyed owls blinked in the high branches of oaks.

A faint moan rose from across the room. Elena straightened up, squared her shoulders. The sooner they got on with it, the sooner she could escape these walls. She rolled up a small woolen rug and wedged it against the base of the shutters, muffling the rattle. Then she padded across the thick Moorish rugs to the great bed and pulled aside the drapes.

The young woman lay curled on her side. In the candlelight, it was difficult to pick out details, but Elena had dressed and undressed this body so many times that she did not need the aid of the sun to understand the predicament. The woman—still a girl, really—was built like a snow finch. Her belly was far too large for her bony frame. For months, Elena had traced its bulbous arc with her fingertips, measuring the swell of it, prodding the taut skin. The likely explanation was not a giant, but twins, and for a first birth that often meant catastrophe.

She dipped a cloth into a copper pot of water that sat on the floor by the bed. With practiced movements she bathed the woman's pale limbs, smoothed back her tangled hair, massaged lavender oil into her skin.

"My lady, the baby can't wait any longer."

Silence.

She raised her voice. "Lady Marguerite! There's more yet to do. Rouse yourself!"

"Why do you shout at me so? Will you not let me sleep?" Marguerite turned her head toward Elena, her eyelids half open.

Elena felt uneasy, looking into those eyes. They were silvery green, like the hide of a tree frog, and the black lashes that framed them were spindly as spiders' legs. Perhaps it was this contrast of light and dark that made them so unsettling. Or the long, slanting sweep of them. Or their size, for they seemed much too large for the woman's angular face. Whatever it was, there was something more feline than human about them, and Elena had never been fond of cats. She looked away and put a hand on the distended belly.

"If you wish your baby to die, by all means sleep." Something hard—a knee? A foot?—pressed against her palm with urgent, fluttery movements. "If you wish your baby to live, then push. Now make your choice."

The glowing eyes found hers. A pale slender hand slipped into her strong brown one. The young woman on the bed took a deep breath, set her jaw and bore down.

The night was half gone when the baby was born. She squirmed and flailed her limbs, gulping air into her lungs and pumping it out again with wild shrieks. Elena cleaned her, swaddled her and thrust her into her mother's arms.

Marguerite bent her head over the baby. "A girl. God help me."

The newborn quieted and stared unblinking at her mother. After a few moments of utter stillness, she opened her tiny red mouth and began rooting for a breast.

"She will be called Miramonde," Marguerite said softly. "One who sees the world."

"How much can a girl see from behind a wall?" Elena asked.

Marguerite shook her head. "She will not be caged. When she is old enough, she will learn the ways of the mountain people."

Elena stared. "Who will teach her?"

"You."

Words of protest rose up in Elena's throat. But before she could speak Marguerite convulsed in pain again.

"Ah—I thought as much," Elena said, careful to keep a neutral voice. "Twins."

"No," Marguerite moaned. "That cannot be. What if it is another girl?"

"Then we'll be doubly grateful to have a plan in place."

When the second baby slid out of his mother's womb, Elena held him aloft so Marguerite could see what she had birthed. He was a tiny, red, crumpled thing, smaller than his sister. Elena rubbed him briskly with a piece of clean linen and blew on his drowsing eyelids until he opened his mouth and emitted a faint wail.

"An heir. My husband will be pleased."

Marguerite's voice was low and rough, but whether that was due to emotion or exhaustion, Elena could not tell.

"If he survives the war," Elena said.

"Talk like that can get you whipped. Have a care."

"Who is going to hear? Your father-in-law is bedded down with his favorite wench, and the steward's lame back has made a thief of him."

"What do you mean?" Marguerite's bloodshot eyes flickered to the door and back.

"Poppy milk. He's got your mother-in-law's bedtime habit now. Head lolling on the cushions, drooling. 'Tis not a pretty sight."

Another gust of wind barreled down from the high peaks, and the shutters struggled against the rolled-up rug. Thump. Thump. Thump. Elena hurled an irritated look in the direction of the balcony and got back to the business of cleaning and swaddling the boy. She tucked him under his mother's arm and led his pursed red lips to her other breast. For a time, they listened to the babies nursing and the soft thumping of the shutters.

"In the space of a moment, you have slandered my husband's parents and their steward. I have seen serfs lose their heads for less damning words," Marguerite said finally. "I placed all my trust in Brother Arros, bringing you here. I wonder now why he places his trust in you."

Elena shrugged. "I'm a creature of the mountains. Never learned to talk like a lady."

"You can start by biting your tongue. There are no secrets in this place."

"Tell me, my lady, if there are no secrets in the house of Oto, why am I here? We'll fail before we even begin."

"I order you to cease your prattling and your impertinence grows."

"I've simply asked a question, my lady," Elena shot back. "A fair one."

"Our plan will succeed. It must. And now you'll do your part to keep her safe."

A tense silence settled over them until the baby girl fell asleep. Elena plucked her out of her mother's grasp and wrapped her in a length of soft wool.

"When all is said and done, you've two healthy babies," she said. "And one of them a son. The luck of that."

Marguerite closed her eyes, one hand on the necklace at her throat. "Yes. The luck."

There was a stable boy Elena trusted, whose mother she had healed from illness on two occasions. She drew her cloak shut to conceal the sleeping baby swaddled against her chest. Bending over the boy's nest in the straw, she gently woke him and asked him to fetch a certain horse that she knew to be steady and calm. He readied the mare and helped Elena into the saddle. She squeezed his hand in the dark.

The horse clopped down the stone alley to the castle gates. The guards were not surprised to see her; she often came and went at odd hours.

"Good evening, my lady!" called one. "Look at you on that fine horse."

"I'm not one to put on airs, you know that well enough," she said in as light a voice as she could muster. "Even poor mountain folk like me are given a favor now and then."

The men unlatched the heavy iron crossbars and the great oak doors swung open.

"Are you not afraid of wolves and bears?" the other guard asked.

"Those creatures fear the moonlight. Puts them under a spell, it does."

He snorted. "The beasts outside these gates fear nothing but fire and iron."

She forced out a laugh and prodded the horse forward. Behind her, the crossbars clanged shut. She turned her head and spat. An urge rose up in her to yank the horse's nose due west and gallop hard all the way to Basque country, to the edge of the world where the rivers flowed into the sea. Instead, she dug her heels into the horse's belly, guiding it deep into the mountains. There was no point wasting her thoughts on idle fantasies. She would not betray a promise.

The horse followed the moonlit trail across streams and through stretches of forest until it shambled to a stop at a fork. The baby took a shuddering breath and started to wail.

The swiftest way into Béarn was the road to the right, which snaked down into a narrow valley where the yellow glow of a campfire was visible. This time of year, mule trains plied the road constantly, taking wares from Aragón to the market towns in the north. She did not like the idea of encountering the makers of that fire, especially with a shrieking baby and whatever Lady Marguerite had placed in the leather pouch she carried.

To the left, the steep path led to the valley of Ronzal with its cluster of stone cottages. Elena squinted into the night. The moon was playing tricks on her, dappling the grass and trees with smears of silver light that moved and twisted in the wind. The baby's cries hammered into her skull. Every wolf and bear for miles must be aware of them by now.

She made her choice.

The rhythm of the horse's steps soon put the baby back to sleep. Overhead, the moon slid to the top of the sky. Her muscles were stiff with cold when they arrived in Ronzal, on the south-facing edge of a valley in the shadow of the mountains. In the moonlight she spied a thin column of smoke rising from the chimney hole of the de Luz family's home. Before she even dismounted, Jorge opened the door.

"What brings you here at this hour, my friend?" he called softly.

"Come in, come in," his wife Thérèse said quickly from behind him. "You're always welcome here."

Jorge helped Elena off the horse and clapped a hand on her shoulder. For the first time in months, she felt the knot of worry in her chest ease. By the fire, she hastily untied her cloak and pulled the baby free.

"Would you share your milk?" she asked Thérèse.

Thérèse laid her infant son on the bed and took the baby girl in her arms. She fingered the soft wool wrappings and glanced up at Elena.

"No peasant child is garbed in wool this fine."

Elena felt her throat tighten. She kept silent and rubbed her hands together before the fire while Thérèse settled in a chair with the girl at her breast.

Jorge returned and latched the door. "The horse wears the brand of the Otos." He crouched by the fire and threw a log on the smoldering embers, poking it with his dagger. "First you go live on the doorstep of your great enemy and now you steal his horse. You court death, Elena."

"I hate that I've drawn you into this. After all the kindness you've shown me."

Jorge's eyes were on the infant at his wife's breast. "Where will you take that one?"

Elena deliberated a moment before answering. "Belarac."

"What will a child do there? The place crumbles into dust. I should know—we're bound to them and they to us, and little good has come of it in my lifetime."

"The new abbess has stars in her eyes, that's what." Elena's voice was bitter. "Stars and gold. When your men take the flocks down the mountain come autumn, go with them and see for yourself the changes that are afoot. Could be Ronzal's fortunes will rise with Belarac, if you're cunning about it."

"But what—"

Thérèse stopped him with a look. "Let her rest."

At dawn, Elena said her goodbyes and guided the horse along the rough, winding path to the pass. Overhead the sky was a dull gray. Fog swirled through the notch that was the passage to Béarn, obscuring the ridges and deep valleys that lay to the north. The horse stumbled down slopes of shale, its hoofs scraping and clattering over the rock. Elena gripped the saddle with her thighs, one arm encircling the baby, her muscles aching with the effort to stay upright.

Finally they slipped below the tree line into a pine forest, the silence pressing down on them like an invisible cloak. A lone crow followed them through the pines to a beech grove, scolding them with harsh, accusing cries. Elena vowed to herself that if its rasping woke the baby she would decapitate it with a well-aimed rock. But the girl slept through the journey, oblivious.

The light of day had been nearly snuffed out when she saw the dark outlines of the abbey jutting into the purple sky. The baby began to wail. Elena dug her heels into the horse's belly and it cantered through the narrow valley, kicking up dirt clods in the fields that radiated outward from the abbey's high stone walls. At the gates, she pulled the frayed rope that hung from the battered iron bell.

In a moment two shrouded figures appeared. One led the horse to the stables, the other motioned to Elena to follow her through a vast courtyard laid with dark cobblestones. The bell tower topped with its iron cross loomed overhead. She quelled a desire to run for the gates by biting her lip hard enough to taste blood.

Inside the battered oak doors, two nuns waited. One of them reached for the baby. Elena stiffened.

"What do you mean to do with her?"

"The wet-nurse awaits," the woman said. "Poor thing, she's so hungry."

Elena worked the infant free from her wrappings. Her hands trembled. She gave her head a quick shake, attempting to clear the worry from it. Shouldn't she be pleased to be done with this fool's errand? Yet something within her hesitated. For some reason she couldn't fathom, she hated the idea of handing the girl over.

"Take the child then," she said gruffly, "before she kills herself with all that screaming."

The chapel bell awoke Elena at dawn. A young nun led her through the dank corridors to the abbess's residence. She padded past tapestries on the walls and heavy oak furniture that glistened with beeswax. Wasn't this the way of things, she thought, rolling her eyes. The rest of the abbey reeked of poverty and ruin, but the abbess had made sure her private quarters were comfortable.

Béatrice sat unsmiling behind her wide oak desk, her thin frame nearly swallowed up by her black habit. Her finger, when she pointed at a chair, put Elena in mind of a bird's claw.

"Your journey must have been difficult," she said. "Sit."

"On the contrary, crossing those mountains is no trouble to me. I've known the way far too long." Elena remained upright, though every muscle in her body was knotted with pain from the journey. She retrieved the pouch from her pocket and handed it over.

"God protected you and the child from the dangers in those woods," Béatrice said, weighing the pouch in her hand. "Our prayers were answered."

Elena wanted to say that God and prayers had nothing to do with it, but she held herself in check.

"And Lady de Oto?" Béatrice asked. "The birth of her child was not too difficult?"

"She suffered, but not more than any woman bearing twins."

Béatrice drew her eyebrows together in a frown.

"The girl was born first," Elena said. "Her mother calls her Miramonde. Second came a son. His father will name the boy when he returns from the southern wars."

"A son. How fortuitous."

"If you say so."

"Ramón de Oto has an heir. Surely you see the value in that."

Elena shrugged. "'Tis none of it my concern."

Béatrice's lips compressed into a thin line. "Belarac once gave you sanctuary when you had nowhere else to go. And as for that family—you now live within their gates. Your every move is at their mercy. I would say that makes them very much your concern."

Elena said nothing, just pulled up her sleeve and held out her scarred arm.

"Oh, God save you. I've told you before, Belarac is not to blame for that."

"No—Ramón de Oto is."

"You were both children," Béatrice said, standing. "He is grown now, a warrior. One day he will be a baron. A spat with a kitchen waif does not warrant remembering for a man such as he. So put aside your fears."

"You misjudge me, Abbess. I don't fear the man. I despise him. And his father before him. The lot of 'em, in truth. I hate the house of Oto."

"Ah. Thank you for that point of clarification. And now I have things to attend to."

Elena did not turn away. "The girl must never learn who her people are."

"Of course. She will simply be known as an orphan who boards here."

"Another thing. She won't be shut up in here whispering prayers all the year long."

Béatrice stiffened. "That is enough impertinent talk from a mountain woman. For now, all the girl needs is a wet-nurse. I believe we can agree on that count, at least? In any event, I will decide how she spends her days."

Elena shook her head. "No. Her mother decides. She wouldn't have named her Miramonde if she wanted her locked inside these walls rotting away."

"What do you mean?"

"Miramonde—one who sees the world."

"How interesting that her mother would ascribe such power to the name of a girl. Is there a letter from the lady to this effect, or have you become her mouthpiece?"

"What I am is a messenger, and if you wish me to deliver more gold into your hands, you'll do well to heed my words."

Elena wheeled on the abbess and stalked out the door.

2

Autumn, 1485
Abbey of Belarac, Béarn
Béatrice

BÉATRICE STOOD JUST OUTSIDE the gates and watched the shepherds and flocks make their descent down the steep slope into Belarac's sheltered valley. The discordant rattle of iron bells reverberated in her ears. She squinted against the sun's glare, tracking the movements of a sinewy man who separated from the group and made his way through the orchard to the abbey.

"I am Jorge de Luz," he said to her, bowing. "I speak for the shepherds of Ronzal." He had thick black hair and a short beard, and his Béarnaise was flawless.

"You are not Aragónese?"

"My wife comes from Béarn. She taught me the local tongue."

"Ah." Béatrice looked past him at the milling flocks, the heavily laden pack mules, the golden dogs with their spiked collars. Her eyes lingered on the shepherds. In their flax blouses, wool vests and black felt hats, they looked like prosperous peasants, a far cry from the filthy pagans she had expected.

"Welcome," she said. "There is much to discuss. Will you return this evening to the abbey after your work is done? You and all of your men? For supper."

He looked startled. "Aye, if that pleases you, Abbess." He tipped his hat at her and turned away.

A table was set in the warming house next to the gates. When the men filed in, their hair and faces were dripping with water from the stream. The servants spooned a thin gruel into bowls and poured beer into ceramic cups.

"The crops here are not what they used to be," apologized Béatrice. "We do not get much meat or fish either."

"There's a bit more time before winter is upon us," Jorge said. "We'd be happy to hunt and fish for you these next few weeks."

"I did not realize that shepherds are also hunters."

"We do what we must," Jorge said. "All of us are handy with a bow and a knife. We're no strangers to axes either."

One of the shepherds, a bony man with a jutting nose and eyes fixed in a dark scowl, began to talk rapidly in Aragónese.

"What does he say?" Béatrice waited for a translation.

Jorge silenced the man with a fierce look. "We're grateful to you, Abbess, for honoring the ancient agreements," he began tactfully. "Our animals can't survive the snows in Ronzal, and we're lucky to have this valley for refuge. The problem is, in winter there is so little fodder for our sheep here that we're forced to butcher them and sell the meat."

"You still earn income that way," she pointed out.

"A thirst for our wool grows in the north—and merino wool fetches a much higher price than meat. That's hard to take for the men."

"The plague very nearly drained all life from this place, and it still suffers," she said. "You've seen how many cold hearths there are in the village. With so few peasants to work the fields, we are limited in what we can grow." Her eyes flicked back to the scowling man. "Does your friend offer any ideas to solve this problem?"

"His ideas sound more like insults," said Jorge, smiling wryly. "But I've an idea. In our valley, younger brothers and sisters must leave and find their own way. Why not point them to Belarac? The empty cottages in this valley could fill up with families again, with the brothers and sisters of these men. Then you'll have strong hands to work the fields and plow and harvest, and we'll have more fodder for the flocks come winter."

"But they would lose their freedom. Mountain shepherds are free men, are they not?"

Jorge nodded. "There is no lord who rules over us. We are governed by the peace accords, the *fueros*. The house of Oto can't touch us, nor can any other noble."

Béatrice stiffened in her chair. Her mind darted to the copper-haired baby asleep in the nursery.

"What about the kings?" she asked.

"The kings of Aragón honor the ancient agreements. Everyone honors the agreements—except for the sheep ranchers of Jaca and Zaragoza."

"What do you mean?"

"Come summer they send their flocks to the high meadows. Sheep pour into our valleys like a flood. They want us out, want all the grass for themselves. We've been willing to share, but their numbers keep swelling. The conflicts grow uglier with each passing year."

She barely heard him. The word 'Oto' rumbled through her mind like a thunderhead, drowning out all sensible thoughts. With great effort she willed her mind away from the girl Miramonde, forcing herself back to the conversation at hand, to the dark-haired men across the table.

"It is interesting that you say the demand for your wool grows. Meanwhile, the abbey's own flocks bear coarse wool that no merchant worth his salt will buy. I have a proposal of my own for you. We are better served slaughtering the animals we own and replacing them with your merinos. How much does a merino sheep fetch at the livestock market in Jaca? I will pay for the flock in gold."

She thought of the sack of coins Elena had brought from Marguerite de Oto. It was still half full.

Before Jorge even finished translating her words, the men exploded in high-volume Aragónese, shouting over one another in an effort to be heard.

Jorge stood, his arms outstretched, and let out a single, ominous "Ah!" Silence fell over the group. The tall, sharp-nosed shepherd who had spoken up in the beginning folded his arms over his chest and stuck his chin out at a defiant angle.

"The men disagree about that idea," Jorge said. "They've heard that in Castilla, if any man sells merino sheep out of the kingdom, his life is forfeit."

"This is not Castilla," Béatrice said. "Your sheep have overwintered on these lands for generations. Merinos journey back and forth from Aragón to Béarn each year unharmed, and so do their shepherds. You just finished telling me the peace agreements are honored by the kings."

"Still, some of the men are uneasy about the idea of selling sheep. Even if we agreed to it, I'd not want to write a note of sale on parchment."

Béatrice stared at him, speechless.

"Yes, I can write." There was a trace of impatience in his voice. "The council of families in each valley keeps records about livestock, grazing agreements, disputes. Those who sit on the council must read and write and work figures."

"Do you keep records of the number of fleeces you sell, the price you are paid for them?"

"Of course."

"In your record book, then, the merinos that grow fat on my crops will be listed as your possessions. But half of them will be the property of the abbey, and proceeds from the sale of their wool will be split between us. Privately. If you agree, your plan to populate our village with the spare brothers and sisters of Ronzal shall be done. What do you say?"

Jorge regarded her for a long while. He pointedly refrained from translating her last words, one hand held aloft to ward away the glares and disgruntled sighs of his men. Finally he spoke.

"We are in agreement."

Béatrice looked around the table in wonder. She had been expecting a pack of heathens clothed in filthy animal skins. She was wrong on at least one count—the clothes they wore were not what she had expected. And if they were heathens—well, God save them. As long as these men proved valuable to Belarac, how they worshipped was of no importance.

The following day she spent hours in the library poring over the abbey's record books. Her eyes scanned rows of numbers until she was caught up by an entry that looked nothing like the others: "Manuscripts, books, and sundries. Sold to Carlo Sacazar, merchant of Nay." She squinted. *How* many ducats were these items sold for? The numerals were blurred by a stain.

She brought the record book to the cellaress, Sister Mathilde, who was counting ceramic jugs of grain by torchlight in the stone cellars.

"Sister, what is this?" Béatrice hoisted the book into the shifting circle of light cast by the torch. "Here. This reference to books and sundries, and Carlo Sacazar."

Mathilde peered at the text. "Ah. Yes, the wool merchant of Nay. Always smiling, I remember. He came here with his sister.

Though *she* wasn't much for smiling. Looked as though she'd drunk sour milk, to my mind." She turned her head, distracted by a scuttling sound emanating from a dark corner. "The rats are at it again. What happened to that blessed cat?"

"Never mind the cat or the rats," Béatrice said. "What do you remember?"

"They came here—oh, it was long ago. The mother abbess was near the end, I remember. Begging your pardon, but some of us thought she was not right in the head in her last years."

"And?"

"And—" Mathilde hesitated, clearing her throat. "She—well, it pains me to say it. She sold most of the books in the library to them. For quite a tidy sum, if I recall. Two bags of coin, they gave her."

"Two bags of coin for the contents of our library? And it has all gone to the home of a wool merchant, you say?" Béatrice was incredulous.

"He bought them for his sister, for she's an abbess as well. Built her a fancy convent in Nay, is the story. The abbess before you didn't care for books. But I suppose that's obvious, given that she sold them all away."

Mathilde lobbed a piece of cork at the shadows. Whatever skulked there fell silent.

"Ah! That's better." She smiled in satisfaction.

Béatrice shut the book and turned away without another word.

The next morning, she composed a letter to the merchant Carlo Sacazar. She assumed a pleading tone, offering to travel to Nay and meet with him to discuss the return of the volumes to their spiritual home at the abbey. She carried on at length about the books' importance to the future survival of the institution, to its identity, to its moral strength. Her confessor, a bishop in Pau, would be much aggrieved to learn of the sale of Belarac's spiritual property, she added. Of course, she hoped she would not have to take the matter up with him.

She knew, no matter what kind of man Carlo Sacazar was, the implication that a bishop might intervene would force him to at least acknowledge her request. In truth, her goal was twofold. Yes, she desired the return of the books. But more than that, she wanted to learn how the wool trade in Nay functioned.

She dipped her quill in ink, thinking of the path that had brought her here to the edge of the wilderness.

If her father had his way, she would have been married off at twelve to a squire or a knight-for-hire like himself. He spent most of her childhood fighting for foreign nobles in distant lands. When she was seven, he sailed away from Béarn on a ship to Castilla. He was gone for three years. When he returned, scars puckered the skin on his face and he walked with a limp. He no longer held his arms out to Béatrice and her two sisters so they could run to his embrace; instead he obsessed over their futures. Within a few years both of Béatrice's older sisters were wed, one at fourteen and the next at twelve.

Her mother, blessed woman, had talked him into allowing her to enter the convent of Aldefount in the north of Béarn. Instead of paying a dowry to a husband's family, the silver went to the convent. And when her father died, with no son to carry on the family name, their modest manor house surrounded by wheat fields was turned over to a male cousin. Béatrice's mother died an unwelcome guest in her own home.

Béatrice, with her calm, practical nature, had proven herself worthy of the religious life. She rose quickly through the ranks of well-born sisters at Aldefount and was elected treasurer—the youngest woman ever to hold the rank, the abbess claimed— because of her intelligence and her immunity to the caprices of others. She had no use for mysticism and was unmoved when other sisters claimed to have heard the voice of God during trances or in their dreams. Béatrice found peace in the long hours of silent prayers, the measured pace of life counted out by the chiming of bells, the arc of the sun, the waxing and waning of the moon.

But now, that existence was over. Though her family's fortune had run dry, somehow a thread of value had attached itself to her bedraggled name again. It seemed her family was last of a line that traced back to the founders of a convent in the wild Pyrenees called Belarac, a place that had survived plague and poverty and famine. A place whose charter decreed that the abbess be a descendant of the convent's founding family.

She signed her name on the letter and sat back, waiting for the ink to dry. Twisting the gold ring off her finger, she stared at its face, at the simple sheaf of wheat that was her family herald. She would stamp the wax seal with her ring and send the letter out into the world, but the truly audacious thing was that she would follow it out of these gates, would ride back down the mountain road to Nay with no authority from anyone but herself.

Her father would roll in his grave to learn this, she was sure. He had paid good silver for his youngest daughter to live out her days safe behind a wall. And here she was, about to pass through the gates and travel in search of wealth just as he had. The difference was she wore no armor, nor did she wield a weapon. She was only a nun, after all—a nun who dared to enter the world of men.

Fate was not always kind to such women.

3

Spring, 1486
Nay, Béarn
Béatrice

BÉATRICE'S EYES FLITTED BACK and forth, taking in the luxurious details of the convent's entry hall. The pink marble floor gleamed underfoot. On a side table, beeswax candles burned in fat silver candlesticks. She spied the stone likenesses of a man and a woman carved above a doorway. They both had round faces and docile expressions, their lips curling up in faint smiles.

Amadina Sacazar descended the polished marble steps, following Béatrice's gaze with her heavy-lidded dark eyes.

"That is my brother you admire, Abbess," she said in thickly accented Béarnaise. "Our benevolent patron Lord Carlo Sacazar and his wife, Lady Flora."

She ordered a servant to take Béatrice's cloak and satchel to her room, then waved her through one of the doors leading off the hallway. Inside, torches burned in iron sconces along both walls, and a large fire blazed in the fireplace. Twelve identical oak cabinets lined the walls, each one filled with books. The center of the room was dominated by four long oak tables surrounded by high-backed chairs. A leather-bound record book lay open on the polished surface of one of the tables.

"That record book lists what my brother purchased from your abbey," Amadina said. "Once you have found the books in my cabinets, I will mark them off."

Béatrice looked at the silver candlesticks on the tables, the portraits of saints that hung in gold frames above each cabinet. There was more wealth visible in this room, she realized, than existed in the entire abbey of Belarac. When she turned back to the door, Amadina was gone.

Crossing to the first large cabinet, she pulled out a book. On the spine was the seal of Belarac—an ornate B superimposed over a cross. She felt a leap of excitement and gently laid it on the table.

By the time supper was ready, she had found nearly one hundred books. A servant led her to a private dining room where Amadina and her brother, Carlo, waited. At the sight of Béatrice, Carlo strode across the room and bowed to her, his two forefingers joined as if in prayer. She bowed her head in return.

Béatrice had never seen such fine clothes on a man. He wore black wool breeches with blue silk stockings, a velvet vest over a linen blouse, and sleeves that were set with an alternating diagonal pattern of blue and black silk. The pointed toes of his black leather boots gleamed with oil. Several of his fingers were adorned with gold rings.

"Please, join us." He nodded in the direction of the dining table.

Béatrice was slightly unnerved by the seating arrangements, which had Amadina and Carlo seated at either end of the long table, with her directly in the middle. The siblings' patter commenced at breakneck speed, helped along by copious servings of wine. Their conversation ranged from gossip about people back home in Zaragoza to complaints about the weather in Nay and the dismal lack of choices in the weekly food market.

Two servants kept their cups full and deposited platter after platter of food on the table. The bread was white and fine. There was a type of dry, thinly sliced ham Béatrice had never seen before, as well as hard cheeses unlike any she had ever tasted. There was salted fish marinated in oil, and olives, and plates of tiny fried peppers sprinkled with great flecks of sea salt.

She realized the Sacazars, who had gone silent, were staring at her.

"This is a welcome change from our diet at Belarac," she said, feeling foolish. "I am most grateful."

"Good, good!" Carlo's smile reappeared. "We are happy to host you. How do you find our convent? Is it to your liking?"

"I find much to admire in it."

"What you will not find here are vulgar goings-on," Amadina said. "In my house, piety and propriety reign."

Carlo nodded. "My sister is a fine abbess. She follows the wishes of her majesty Queen Isabella to the letter. Our queen, quite rightly, desires all religious houses to once again be places of quiet contemplation, prayer, and reverence rather than boarding houses for the wealthy."

"This is Béarn, not Aragón," Béatrice said. "I respect your desire to carry out Queen Isabella's wishes, but the fact remains that many religious houses would cease to exist without boarders." She sipped her wine.

Amadina's face grew red. "What you will not find here are women with private parlors entertaining visitors at all hours of the day or night," she said hotly. "We observe strict rules of silence, obedience, and prayer. My brother is an abbot, too, you know. He presides over not one, but two monasteries. He has imposed Queen Isabella's philosophy at those places as well."

"It is my duty to help her majesty bring back the proper decorum to these places," Carlo said. "Do you know, before I took over the monastery of St. Christine, there were women living in the dormitories with the monks?"

"That is not the first such instance of impropriety in a monastery," Béatrice said.

"Impropriety is one thing," Carlo said. "Violence is quite another. Some years ago, a monk was murdered in the chapel at St. Christine's. And the murderer was never brought to justice. The brute may still walk among us today." He placed a spoonful of salted fish on a slice of ham and deftly rolled it up.

"A horrible travesty, is it not?" Amadina asked, stuffing a pepper in her mouth. A spray of juices dribbled down her chin. She snapped her fingers at a servant, who rushed over and blotted her mistress's chest with a towel.

Suppressing an urge to laugh, Béatrice feigned intense interest in a platter of cheese tarts.

"With the moral decay all around us, your strict regimen of prayer and reflection is all the more impressive," she said once she had regained her composure.

"There is ample time for work as well. Every sister in the place is spinning and weaving from dawn to dusk, save for prayer time and meals, of course. I oversee the work to ensure the nuns are as industrious as God intends." Amadina's dark eyes glittered.

Béatrice imagined her patrolling rows of silent nuns as their fingers flashed, working their distaffs and threading their looms.

"They must produce a large quantity of cloth," she said.

"I would better call it a torrent of cloth," Carlo said. "Or perhaps an avalanche." He glanced at his sister, who preened at the compliment.

Dessert was served, a cream tart layered with caramelized almonds and apricots, set upon a crust of ground pistachios.

"I remember the first time I ate this." Carlo shoveled in a great mouthful. "I was with our grandfather, meeting the Moor who transported our wool to the coast. Grandfather told me it was time I made myself useful." He laughed. "I was no more than eighteen. We went into the office of Ebrahim Mosequin, and a servant brought us slices of this very tart. It was a specialty of his family."

"Why did you transport your wool to the coast?" Béatrice asked.

"The Italians wanted nothing to do with our wool until the wars between England and France strangled the English wool trade. Suddenly, our wool became fashionable in Florence. My father made a fortune sailing his fleeces across the sea. He struck up a great friendship with a Florentine wool merchant—so great, in fact, that I was named for the man."

"Do you still travel to Florence?"

"Oh, no. The plague, you see. Not to mention delays at the harbor, fires on board, storms, shipwreck, pirates, wars, spoilage of the wool." He waved a hand in the air. "Too many headaches. Now I bring my wool from Aragón across the Pyrenees and finish it here." He drained the last of his wine and gestured to a servant to refill his cup. "My fabrics are in high demand in Paris, and that market never stops growing."

"Your success is impressive, sir."

"Do you forget my brother is an abbot twice over, and titled?" Amadina cut in.

"My apologies, Lord Sacazar." Béatrice imagined the pile of gold he had exchanged for his titles.

"Think nothing of it. Yes, my business grows by the year. But there are limits, there are frustrations, which I never foresaw when I established myself here."

"Such as?"

"There is little riverfront property in Nay. But a waterway is necessary for both washing and dyeing. If I could eliminate the wool washing stations on the banks, I would build more dye houses along the river, and our production of finished fabrics would soar." He signaled to the servant for another slice of tart.

"So if you had another source of washed wool—"

He nodded, beaming. "Ah! Your mind works like that of a merchant. We are not so different, you and I."

Béatrice stared at him, a plan forming in her mind.

On the road back from Nay in the rattling oxcart, her eyes fixed on the long train of mules roped nose-to-tail before her, she sifted through possibilities.

There was a derelict building, perhaps an ancient chapel, that stood on the banks of the stream in the valley of Belarac. Perfect, she now saw, for a wool-washing station. The fact that she knew nothing about washing wool did not perturb her. She would tap the experience of the monks at the monastery of San Juan de la Peña who bragged of their wool washing station every time they passed through Belarac to points north. There would be expenses, of course. But come springtime, God willing, she would receive another installment of gold from Aragón in payment for raising the unwanted daughter of the Oto family.

The unfortunate truth was this: Miramonde de Oto—a girl not yet two—held the fortunes of Belarac in her tiny hand.

The mule train rambled slowly south into the mountains past rushing streams and cool forests, its progress marked by the creak and clatter of hooves and equipment, the grunting of animals, the shouted instructions of men.

Béatrice gazed ahead, stiff-backed on the oxcart's hard bench, oblivious to everything but the words that throbbed in her mind.

Please, God. Keep Miramonde alive.

4

Autumn, 1486
Castle Oto, Aragón
Marguerite

T HE BALCONY SHUTTERS FLAPPED against their latches as if a great bellows blew on them, startling the boy awake. Marguerite dropped her embroidery and reached for him. "Pelegrín," she whispered. "Do not fret, my son."

He was old enough to walk, but she could not bear the thought of him toddling away from her. So she kept him tightly swaddled and ignored his squirming protests. When her husband was away, which was often, she insisted on Pelegrín spending his days and nights at her side. The idea of him sleeping in some cold dark chamber with only a wet-nurse for company was unbearable.

She pulled a sachet of dried lavender from the small oak box she kept on a table next to the bed and tucked it into Pelegrín's wrappings. The scent of lavender always calmed her, and it seemed to have the same effect on her son. Memories of her mother always crowded her mind when she inhaled the herb's sharp, pleasing scent. She leaned back with her eyes closed, remembering.

In the gathering warmth of a late summer morning in her ninth year, she had waited in her brocade dress and velvet sleeves, watching the stable boys hitch mules to a cart and saddle the horses. Four knights milled about in the courtyard. The dull clatter of hooves on cobblestones echoed off the high slate roof of the house. A rooster crowed.

Leather trunks containing her dowry clothing, jewels and linens were lifted one by one into the cart. Marguerite's father picked her up and placed her in the saddle of the little black horse that belonged to her sister. Her own horse had a sore on its back that would not heal. Settled into the saddle, she glanced up. Two small, ghostly faces peered out from a window. Her brother waved. Her sister, who was more peeved that her horse was leaving than sad at Marguerite's departure, stuck out her tongue.

Her father stepped back and her mother approached. Marguerite bent down to hear the whispered words: "Be brave. Make the Béarnais proud." For the last time, she breathed in the scent of the lavender oil her mother always dabbed on her neck.

Marguerite's memories were interrupted by the sound of sandstone roof tiles tearing loose and careening off the tower onto the balustrade below. She flinched, opening her eyes. Her father-in-law the baron, urged on by the steward, had chosen a bad day to ride out from the castle. He was always stirring the pot, the steward, striding the halls barking orders, his iron keyring jangling at his hip. She had gleaned from eavesdropping that all the servants despised him. They complained that he never bothered to question the veracity of incriminating rumors and frequently invented them himself. This time, he had reported an incident of theft by serfs who worked the land a morning's ride away. So he, her father-in-law and several other horsemen had gone to investigate the matter.

A banging commenced that was nothing like the random smashing of roof tiles. She thrust Pelegrín into the arms of a maidservant and threw a cloak over her shoulders. In the corridor, the commotion was loud. Someone was thumping on the doors to the great hall.

She descended the stairs and ordered a servant to unbar the doors. Two of the gate guards stood at the doorway. One of them shouted something at her and hoisted a bulging sack in his outstretched hand. A roof tile smashed on the cobblestones behind him.

"Come in out of the wind." She waved them inside.

"The baron and the steward and their men, my lady," he panted. "The serfs rose up against them. Murdered their masters, the lot of them! They left this at the gate."

"Murdered their masters," she repeated, her eyes on the sack. A few dark drops leaked from it and spattered on the stone floor.

The men stared at her, waiting. She dragged her gaze from the blood on the floor and took a deep breath. Whatever happened, the horror she felt must not show on her face.

"There is no time to lose," she said. "Go to the armory and tell the knight on duty to come here at once. Then light the beacon to alert our allies to this danger. We will send out a party at once to deal with this uprising. And tomorrow we shall send another party to carry the news of these murders to my husband in the south."

"But my lady—" began one of the guards.

"Do not question me," she interrupted, her voice like a whip. "Go at once!" She pointed in the direction of the armory, willing her hand not to tremble.

Marguerite hauled a copper urn from the foot of the staircase to the entryway and heaved the sack into it. She called for a servant to fetch linen and water and wash away the dark smear of blood on the floor. When she turned, she spied her mother-in-law at the top of the staircase. In silence, the baroness tottered unsteadily back into the shadows.

"Wait," Marguerite called up to her.

But before she could climb the staircase, a knight from the armory pounded into the great hall.

The moment the castle gates slammed shut behind the horsemen, Marguerite hurried up the stairs to the baroness's chamber. The door was locked. She slipped into the room through the cramped servants' quarters next to the bedroom, a candle in one hand.

Her mother-in-law lay on the bed, her clothing in disarray. The glass bottle of poppy milk was clutched in one hand; in the other was a dagger. Marguerite pressed her ear to the woman's chest. There was no heartbeat. She snatched up the dagger, but the blade was clean. Whether the baroness had meant to stab herself or not, the poppy milk had finally stopped her heart. Marguerite stuffed the dagger and the empty bottle in her sleeve. She would do what she could to protect her mother-in-law from the gossips who lurked in every corner. For a moment, she stood with her head bowed, listening to the rattle of the shutters.

The thought occurred to her that she was the baroness now.

She strode to the door and jerked aside the heavy iron bar. A wide-eyed servant boy stood in the corridor.

"Go check the beacon and keep it fed with fresh wood," she ordered him. The boy turned, but not fast enough. "*Run.*"

Marguerite and a priest laid to rest what remained of her father-in-law in the chapel. She washed her mother-in-law's body with lavender water and covered her with a drape of silk. Only then did she return to her chamber, wrench open the shutters and charge her lungs with gasps of frigid air. Standing on the balcony, braced against the wild onslaught of the wind, she reached for the gold chain at her throat, for the small ivory shell that dangled from it. The scent of lavender still clung to her hands. The scent of her childhood.

The necklace had been a gift from the only person who showed her a measure of kindness on that long-ago journey from Béarn to Aragón in the summer of her ninth year. After her entourage climbed through the mountains to a wind-scoured pass and descended into Aragón, they stopped for a night at the monastery of San Juan de la Peña.

The kind smile of Brother Johan Arros, who alone among the monks spoke fluent Béarnaise, was the only thing that kept her from dissolving in tears. In the monastery's royal pantheon, he had showed her statues of Aragón's dead kings.

"Go ahead," he said. "You can touch them if you want."

Marguerite traced the outline of a king's nose with a fingertip. It was cool and smooth under her touch. "Who is this?"

"King Ramiro. He was the first king of Aragón."

"Who is the king now?"

"King Juan."

"Is he a good king?"

"Of course, dear girl, of course."

"Brother Arros, are the barons of Oto buried here?"

"No, my dear, they are buried in the chapel of their own castle, where you will soon be living."

"Are they good people?" She waited for his broad smile, his words of affirmation.

Brother Arros hesitated a moment.

"As much as all God-fearing people are good people," he said soberly.

He knelt. His blue eyes had lost their lively twinkle. He fished in a pocket and pulled out a scallop shell fashioned from ivory, strung on a fine gold chain.

"When you wear this necklace, know the saints are looking after you." He pressed it into her palm. "Lady Marguerite, you are always welcome here. If I may ever be of aid to you, it would be my honor."

Marguerite slipped the necklace over her head and the scallop shell settled against the bones of her chest. A pit of dread took root in her belly at that moment.

It lay coiled within her still.

She had rubbed the ivory shell between her thumb and forefinger so often since that day, it now shone with the brilliance of a precious jewel. Brother Arros had been true to his word. He had not forgotten his promise.

A hawk circled overhead, rising higher and higher until it was a dark speck against a dull gray sky. If only she possessed the hollow bones of a bird, if only she had a secret pair of wings—she would leap off this balcony and skim over the mountaintops to Béarn, to her sweet girl. But she belonged here, with Pelegrín. She had entrusted Miramonde to the abbey across the mountains, and she would cling to the hope that the girl thrived there.

Be brave. Make the Béarnais proud. The refrain had given her strength when she first stared into the unreadable dark eyes of Ramón de Oto, the man who would become her husband. It thrummed in her head the day she bled for the first time and knew she would soon wed him. It rose unbidden in her whenever she felt a pang of loneliness, of homesickness, of fear, of pain, and most of all, resolve. And today, on this day of horrors, it flowed through her mind like the pounding waters of a glacier-fed stream, once again her only comfort.

"Baroness?" a maidservant called from inside. "Baroness?"

The word descended on her like a stone.

5

Spring, 1487
Zaragoza, Aragón
Ramón

BARON RAMÓN DE OTO looked through the pile of letters that sat waiting for him in the front hall. The Zaragoza house had been shuttered for a year and the air had the stale smell that he always associated with the place. It was his least favorite of the Oto family's holdings. The home had come into their possession generations ago, after the previous owners, wealthy wool merchants, were entirely extinguished in the course of one week by the plague. Their faces were carved in stone over the front door. The round face of the wife was placid and gentle, while her husband had a hawkish nose and a stern expression. Ramón had forgotten how much the man's proprietary air annoyed him.

It had been a long time since he set foot here. He had spent most of the last several years fighting the Moors in the south and launching raids into the French-occupied north. But now that his father was dead, Ramón had to assume the position of representative at the interminable council meetings of the sheep ranchers. For the sake of his family, for his young son Pelegrín, he was determined to plumb the inner workings of the wool trade and profit from it.

Frowning, he pulled the red wax seal off a letter on the top of the pile. Carlo Sacazar had invited him to dine. The merchant family was an old one, whose rise to prominence as a sheep-raising, wool-trading force in Zaragoza was unmatched. The Sacazars had always been suspicious of the Otos for taking possession of their neighbor's home all those years ago. But since there was no will and no heirs to dispute it, the Sacazars knew better than to stick their noses in the business of a powerful noble family.

He called a servant to his side. Despite his aversion to the merchant class, he would accept the invitation. Studying the enemy seemed a prudent first step in his effort to understand the world of wool.

Sitting at Carlo's gleaming oak table, Ramón arranged his face into a blank mask. His eyes slid around the room. The stonework surrounding the hearth rivaled anything he had seen in the finest Moorish palace. The silver on the table was as fine as his own, and the smooth, rose-colored stone floor, laid with hand-hooked Moorish rugs, was more splendid than any surface in Castle Oto.

"Pink marble," Carlo announced, grinning at Ramón in an entirely too familiar way. "Imported from Italy."

Ramón did not return the smile. "Your family has done well."

When the servant approached from the left with a pitcher of wine, he made a hissing noise and struck at the boy with his hand. The boy jumped back, terrified.

"Servants approach me from the other side. Is that clear?"

"Yes, my lord," the boy said.

Carlo's brow furrowed. "Forgive us, my lord."

"It is forgotten." Ramón raised his cup in salute.

Carlo followed suit. "It is my pleasure and privilege to have a representative of another great family at my table this night. It is about time we shared a meal, in my opinion. May I express the deep sorrow of my family at the passing of your parents, God rest their souls. And may I wish your son and heir a long and happy life, with many brothers and sisters to follow."

Ramón acknowledged Carlo's niceties with a solemn nod, and they both sipped. The wine was excellent. A servant laid a platter of trout between them. Ramón examined it and made a slashing gesture with one hand.

"I do not eat trout. Remove it at once."

The servant rushed forward and took up the platter.

"How unfortunate that our cook chose to serve trout tonight," Carlo said. He made a tut-tut noise, clicking his tongue on the roof of his mouth. "Yes, yes, remove it all. I will not eat what my guest will not eat."

In fact, Ramón loved trout. But he knew that Alfonso, King of Castilla for a brief moment in time a few years ago, had his royal career cut short by a meal of poisoned trout. In all likelihood, Carlo Sacazar did not plan to poison him. Still, it never hurt to be cautious.

The next platter that emerged from the kitchens contained steaks fried in onions and garlic. Both men dug into their slabs of meat enthusiastically.

"Is this one of yours?" Ramón asked, brandishing a chunk of steak on the tip of his knife.

"Yes, we are proud of our beef." Carlo chewed so vigorously that pink juices leaked from the corners of his mouth.

The two men discussed wool prices, weather, the Moorish wars in the south, and the problem of predation on livestock by bears and wolves. When the meal was finished, Carlo's intent became clear.

"Your father likely informed you that both our houses share the services of a Moorish family who transported our wool to Tortosa for generations."

"Yes, the Mosequins?"

"They have been ruined. They were caught out as heretics. Someone saw the old man Ebrahim praying the way they do. On his knees, on a rug. That is the rumor, anyway. And you know the punishment."

"Burned at the stake, I assume?"

"The old man, yes. The rest have fled to Granada. They have family there. It's where they all go now. They have nowhere left, I suppose."

"They knew the consequences," Ramón said, shrugging.

"My father considered them friends." Carlo signaled to a servant to pour more wine. He pushed a plate of honey-soaked almonds across the table to Ramón.

"That was a different time. No point dwelling on the past." Ramón ignored the sweets.

"Without them, we've lost our wool transport to the sea. They were the best in Zaragoza, and trustworthy. Our families both relied on them."

"We will find a new agent. It is simple enough."

"With all respect, Baron, it is not simple. There are only a few other wool transporting outfits in Zaragoza, and none of them have any interest in working with us. I've already inquired."

"It will be a different matter when I inquire, I assure you. I intend to increase my production of merino sheep and ship more wool east across the sea."

Carlo opened his mouth, then shut it.

"The Florentine market is not what it once was," he said after a moment, his mild gaze never leaving Ramón's face. "But if you discover a way to accomplish your plan, I will be the first to congratulate you."

Leaning back in his chair in the chapter house of the church where the brotherhood convened each Easter, listening to the sheep-breeders arguing about poaching and territorial disputes, Ramón realized that Carlo Sacazar was right. Things had changed. The royal agents monitoring the meeting weighed in annoyingly on every little issue. Rights and privileges that used to belong to noble families now belonged to the royals. The only favor anyone was interested in currying was that of Queen Isabella. Even though King Ferdinand was the one from Aragón and she was Castilian, everyone knew she held the royal purse strings.

Equally bad was the confirmation that the Italian markets had dwindled to nearly nothing because of the plague. Florence was a city of ghosts, the sheep-breeders said. Even if Ramón could find an outfit to pole-barge his wool along the River Ebro to the coast, the Italian merchants whose ships once moored at Tortosa were nearly all dead. His wool would rot on the wharves. Rats would carry off tufts to make nests; the grease in the fibers would go rancid in the summer sun.

He worked the muscles in his jaw. When he flicked a glance across the table, he was irritated to see Carlo's face plastered with smugness. No one in the room, save the royal agents, spoke more often or more confidently than he.

Ramón wished that his father had spent more time instructing him in the ways of business. But whether he was raiding the French invaders in the north or fighting in the endless series of battles against the Moors in the south, his entire life had been dedicated to war. For the first time, he did not know what to do.

After the meeting, Carlo led him to a small square adjacent to the church. They stood watching twilight descend over the city. An icy wind was blowing from the north. Instead of turning his back to the wind, however, Carlo let it scour his face. He opened his arms and smiled.

"Feel the shock of it. Most men think of such a wind as a curse, but not me. It is a blessing, because God has seen fit to shower the Sacazar family with good fortune from the north."

Ramón felt a shudder of impatience run through him. He despised men who played games with words.

"It amuses me to think of this as a trade wind," Carlo went on. "Oh, I know it is far from warm and leagues from the sea, but a trade wind it is just the same." He thrust a finger straight into the path of the wind. "Over the mountains. That is the place to sell wool. I already do. I transport it by mule across those mountains and sell it on the other side."

"You do business with the French?" Ramón put a hand on his sword, closing his fist reflexively around the handle. The unyielding coldness of the metal pressed through the leather of his glove.

Carlo shook his head. "I sell the wool in Béarn, not France. I never set foot in France, I assure you. No reason to. But if the French want to buy my wool, why not?"

"As a matter of family honor, I would never do business with the French. Our family holdings in the north are overrun with them. But Béarn—that is a different matter. My wife is from Béarn. So were my mother and grandmother."

"Ah! Then you are well suited to do business there. As long as the English and the French are at war, the trade routes for English wool will suffer and our merino will be in demand all over Europe. The future lies to the north, I promise you."

"A man's promise is of little use to me. But I will consider your words," Ramón said, bowing slightly. "Good evening." He strode away across the darkening square, one hand still gripping the hilt of his sword.

The plains that flanked the southern foothills of the Pyrenees were damp with mist. The horsemen traced a path across a field of low shrubs tipped with blue flowers, threading their way around jumbles of rock the color of old silver. They crossed a shallow stream. The clatter of hooves on stone filled the air, but Ramón ignored the sound, his mind churning with thoughts of Carlo Sacazar.

What rankled him most was Carlo's assertion that he would gladly do business with the French. Clearly the man, as a member of the merchant class, had no personal stake in the issue of raiders from the north. The Otos, on the other hand, had a castle and lands in the northern territory of Cerdagna which had been stolen by the French when Ramón was a boy. One of his fiercest desires was to reclaim that property.

Joining the main road, the horsemen cantered toward the mountains, kicking up a spray of mud behind them. Ramón caught sight of a flock of sheep in the distance. Again he thought of Carlo and wondered if the sheep belonged to him. The idea struck Ramón that Carlo might be wealthier than he, and a scowl settled upon his face. The merchant class was unencumbered by the responsibilities of the nobles to their king and queen. If Carlo had to take up arms in the holy wars, his coddled existence would be quickly snuffed out. But for now, despite Ramón's aversion to the man, it would be wise to heed his guidance when it came to the business of wool.

At least he had one trump card up his sleeve: The Abbey of Belarac. It lay on the ancient pilgrimage route that passed between Aragón and the market towns of Béarn. His family had been patrons of the place long ago. He remembered visiting there once as a child, but the connection between his family and the abbey was severed soon afterward, when the plague swept through Belarac. A letter from the new abbess came shortly after he married Marguerite, pleading for the house of Oto to renew its patronage. His father had shown no interest, and Ramón himself told Marguerite to write a letter of refusal. Then he forgot the matter entirely. Until now. Perhaps some use could be wrangled from the abbey after all.

He glanced at the sky, marking the path of the sun with his eyes, estimating the distance that remained. In a few days he would see Belarac for himself, and he would have his answer.

6

Spring, 1487
Abbey of Belarac, Béarn
Béatrice

THE CHILDREN SHRIEKED WITH delight, chasing a blue
butterfly through the plot of bare dirt in the infirmary
cloister. Béatrice smiled in satisfaction, ticking items off
a list in her mind. By the end of the week, the garden would be
entirely planted in herbs, beans, peas, carrots and greens. She
had asked two villagers to dig up wild rose plants from the slopes
overlooking the valley and deliver them to her today.

Miramonde de Oto, called Mira by the residents of Belarac,
ran among the other children. Leaping with one hand outstretched to ensnare the fluttering butterfly, she tripped over the
hem of her skirt and fell face-first in the dirt. As far as Béatrice
could tell, the mishap had no effect on the girl, who jumped up
and resumed her pursuit of the butterfly at once. But that was
Mira. Her tolerance for discomfort was unlike that of any other
child in Béatrice's experience.

It was time for the next delivery of Oto gold from the mountain woman Elena, payment for the care and feeding of the girl. Yet the spring rains were behind them, the crops had been planted, and still the woman did not come. Béatrice tried not to worry. After all, it had been a harsh winter. Perhaps snow still covered the pass.

The sound of a man shouting invaded her thoughts, and she walked quickly to the abbey gates. A wild-eyed villager grasped the iron rungs.

"Horsemen approach, Mother Abbess," he cried. "Be on guard."

Béatrice heard the far-off thrumming of hooves on the hard-packed dirt road. Many hooves, from the sound of it.

"Tell all the villagers you see to go inside their homes and bar the doors, do you hear?" The man wheeled and sprinted away.

She put a hand on the iron keyring at her waist. A young nun who had become her assistant of sorts, Agathe, had followed her to the gates. Béatrice found her voice.

"Sister Agathe, gather the children. Tell everyone you see to go to the chapel. Sisters and servants alike. Go!"

Agathe hurried away. The sound of hoofbeats was louder. Béatrice stood back, her eyes on the stone wall and the sharp spires of the gate. Was it high enough to keep marauders out? She swallowed and closed her eyes for a moment.

"Mira!" she heard a girl call. "Where are you? Mira!"

Béatrice whirled. One of the novices who cared for the children was darting this way and that in the courtyard.

"What is the matter?" Béatrice asked, listening to the clatter of hooves in the distance. Were there three horses? Ten?

"Mira is hiding. I don't know where she is," the girl said, her blue eyes wide with fear.

"Go to the chapel. I will find the child." The girl hesitated.

"*Go.*"

The girl ran off.

The horsemen were nearly at the gate.

Pounding rose in her ears like thunder. She turned to face it. There was a blur of color, dust rising from the road, the stamping of hooves, the glint of armor. Béatrice took a step forward, then froze, staring at the banners carried by the horsemen. Her legs felt weighted down by lead.

A man on a great black horse pulled off his helmet and gazed around impatiently, one hand on the hilt of his sword. He wore a suit of red leather armor with a mail shirt underneath. His bearded face was lean and dark, his mouth a wide red slash, his eyes shaded by thick brows.

"Mother Abbess," he shouted. "The house of Oto calls." His deep voice had an Aragónese lilt to it.

Several of the other men laughed.

At that moment a child's giggle broke out behind Béatrice. The high, clear sound of it floated over the gates. Mira de Oto appeared at her side. Her slanting gray-green eyes were fixed on the horsemen. Béatrice bent down and snatched her up.

"My lord. Please forgive us—we are not prepared for your visit." She craned her head, searching in vain for a litter bearing other members of the noble family. "Do you bring your lady wife? And the Baron and Baroness?"

Béatrice pressed Mira's face into her shoulder. She felt the thumping of Mira's heart intertwine with her own heartbeat, and her nostrils filled with the acrid odors of horse dung and sweat. The girl struggled to free herself.

"I am the baron now, Abbess," Ramón said. "Pray for the souls of my parents. My father was betrayed on his own lands, and the shock of his murder killed my mother." He tossed his helmet to a squire as he dismounted. "Their deaths grieve me more than I can say."

At the sound of his voice, the girl stopped squirming. Her small body relaxed against Béatrice's chest and she turned her head, listening.

Ramón walked to the gate and thrust out a hand, rattling the rungs. "I have not ridden across the mountains simply to share the news of my parents' death, Mother Abbess. I have come to make amends and soothe an old hurt. Our family once patronized this place. Though my father let the connection lapse, I vow to do better."

"Yes, my lord—forgive my confusion. I thought, when my letter to your family went unanswered, that—"

Before she could complete her sentence, Mira pulled the cap off her head and flung it on the ground, revealing her long coppery hair. Béatrice froze in horror.

"Surely there is more for me to see here than a child from your nursery," Ramón said in exasperation. "Or shall I begin my inspection with her?"

His men laughed again.

Béatrice felt her knees nearly give way.

The baron's men were ensconced in the warming house next to the gates, tearing into a spread of beer, bread and ham. She had sent the oldest and least attractive servants to tend them. Mira was whisked away to the nursery. Ramón de Oto showed no sign of recognition at the sight of his daughter. And why would he? As far as he knew, she had never existed. The thought calmed Béatrice's mind. Her racing heart slowed.

After he ate his fill, the young baron strode out of the warming room, the heels of his dusty black boots clicking on the stone pavers. Béatrice was waiting for him at the gates.

They strolled through the fields and orchards. She was rightly proud of the progress the villagers had made in the valley, taming the brambles, tilling and replanting the fields, stringing up frames for the hops. Slender shoots of new green wheat shimmered under the noonday sun and neat rows of hop vines twined up alder frame poles, snaking along the flax ropes that connected them. Surely this display of organization would impress him.

"Wheat and barley—but not as much as I would like to see. And hops. You brew beer on rather a large scale for a convent, I would say." His deep voice with its rolling R's had a disdainful edge to it.

"We trade beer with neighboring landholders in exchange for grain and straw to feed the sheep during winter," she explained.

"Bartering is one thing. Gold is another. How do you earn income?"

"We draw a small amount of income from several sources. Our record books will show you how we have fared since I took the helm of this place."

She thanked God that she had burned every one of the letters sent by Marguerite de Oto, and her stash of Oto gold was hidden in a place unknown even to the cellaress. The record books showed no mention of that transaction.

Ramón surveyed the far hills, his eyes on the cluster of stone huts and willow pens that housed sheep during winter.

"Where are your flocks? This valley bursts with crops, but I see no sheep."

"The shepherds sheared them, then herded the flocks to the high meadows. We shall take the fleeces to market in Nay come June."

"Nay, is it? I know a merchant there. My flocks in Aragón are large, but the demand for wool comes now from the north, not across the eastern sea. Perhaps some of my animals could overwinter here. The valley is plenty large enough for my purposes. The beasts could be sheared here as well, and the wool transported to Nay for sale at market."

His brown eyes swiveled over the fields and orchards, assessing, calculating. When they settled on her face, the skin on her neck prickled. He was the most intimidating man she had ever encountered, but she kept her voice steady.

"We would be delighted to accommodate you, my lord."

A servant opened the tall iron gates and the two of them passed through to the courtyard. An enormous pile of rags by the warming house door caught Ramón's attention. He stopped in mid-stride. "Even a place as downtrodden as this should be kept tidy."

"When we are not hosting visitors, the warming house is a workshop of sorts. The nuns are making paper from linen, my lord. It is a technique invented by the Moors."

"It is a common technique. Our family uses nothing else for correspondence."

Béatrice felt a stab of irritation at his condescending tone. "I am from the north," she said. "Linen paper of this quality is not common there, so we have developed a trade in it. It is a modest addition to our income, but every bit helps."

"Indeed. So—you build wealth with beer, grain, paper, and wool."

"Yes." She hesitated. If she was going to ask for more, now was the moment. "However, my lord, this is just a beginning. If we had a wool washing station, we could sell wool that is ready to be spun and finished. The merchants of Nay desire it, and they say it is coveted by merchants as far away as Flanders."

"They say, eh?" Ramón scoffed. "I could swear I heard the exact words from Carlo Sacazar."

"I am also acquainted with Lord Sacazar. There is no one more schooled in the wool trade than he. Why not benefit from his knowledge? After the shearing, we could wash wool for you, then sell it in Nay. You would scarce be involved. Of course, we would need funds to construct the wool washing station."

He thrust a hand under his cloak and pulled out a leather sack. "There is talk of another war with the Moors. One day soon I will be called to battle again by Queen Isabella. The matter could take years to resolve." He tossed the sack in the air and caught it. The jangle of coins rang in her ears. "This is more than enough to build your wool washing station. But my flocks will take precedence over your scrubby Béarnais sheep, do you understand? I possess the finest merinos in Aragón. I will be comparing the income you report to me with those of other sheep-breeders in the region who sell their wool in the north. I expect higher returns than any of them. Is that clear?"

She bowed her head. "Of course. Thank you, my lord. Your generosity will not go unnoticed by God."

"Nor the Queen. Before I leave here, you will write to Queen Isabella to report on my generosity."

She hurried to keep up with him. His legs were impossibly long. He stopped and turned to face her, leaning so close she could smell his bitter sweat.

"The Queen must know every detail of my piety. In fact, let us proceed to the chapel, so that I may confess to the priest. You will note that in your first letter."

"Our priest is indisposed, I regret to say."

"Is he ill?"

"No more than any elderly man. He says the mass and hears the confessions, I assure you."

The priest was snoring off last evening's wine, his mottled red skin the evidence of a life spent inebriated. Béatrice could have written to her superiors in Pau long ago and requested a replacement. But the efficacy of a chapel vicar was far down on her list of priorities. And a new priest could disturb the order of things at Belarac. She would not tolerate the introduction of an unknown male into the world she was crafting here, not now, not yet. The thought, in truth, frightened her.

"Be that as it may." Ramón paused a moment, his eyes boring into hers. "If you fail to do as I order, I will see to it that every bishop in Béarn is informed that you preside over this place like a queen yourself, without oversight of a capable priest. I certainly see the benefit in it. Free to lead as you wish with no interference from a man of the cloth. The punishment for such audacity would be quite severe, I imagine. Excommunication, at the least. Or perhaps they would make an example of you— and burn you at the stake." His words thudded like axe-blows in her ears.

She opened her mouth but before she could speak he thrust the leather sack in her face.

"I care not for your reasons and excuses," he said. "All that matters is your allegiance to my wishes. So?"

"Yes." She grasped the sack with both hands to stop her fingers from trembling. "I swear to do as you ask."

7

Autumn, 1487
Castle Oto, Aragón
Elena

ELENA'S BARE FEET MADE no sound on the stone corridor's floor. When she rounded the corner she was caught up short by the sight of a thin man holding a half-naked girl by the hair. The girl was crying, crumpled in the pool of her skirts, her bare breasts exposed in the torchlight.

"What's this?" Elena's voice rang out. "Let the poor girl go."

The man turned to her, startled. He was dressed more richly than a guard and wore a red leather patch over one eye. His lank black hair spilled down his shoulders.

"Did you dare to question me?" His words sliced the air, hurtling past her ears like arrows.

He loosed his grip on the girl's hair and closed the distance between them. Elena took a step back. Was this the baron himself? Ramón de Oto? She cursed her impulsive tongue and shifted her weight forward, balancing on her toes. He was not

as imposing as she had imagined, the baron. But then, she had
not seen him since he was a child. Time, it seemed, had not
been kind to the man. Perhaps there was a measure of justice
in this world after all.

The slap he gave her resounded with a crack. She staggered
back, then righted herself.

"Speak your name, woman!"

"I'm Elena, my lord." She swallowed hard.

He reacted as if she had administered the slap to him, not
the other way round.

"Do you mock me?" His nostrils flared. "I am the steward,
stupid woman, not the baron."

The fear drained from her. So this was the new steward, the
man who had taken a lance in the eye for Ramón de Oto on
some southern battleground. She straightened her shoulders.

"Why is the steward abusing one of his master's servants, then?"

Without speaking he stepped forward again and hit her across
the face with the back of his hand. This time he drew blood. She
felt it trickle from her lip. Beyond him the servant girl gathered
herself and crept away into the shadows.

A door opened behind her. The steward stared past her shoulder, the imperious smirk vanishing from his face.

"Can I not have a few days' peace after my long journey?" The
voice was deep and tinged with annoyance.

"My lord," the steward said, bowing his head.

Heavy footsteps sounded in the corridor and a man stepped
into her line of sight. He was tall, broad-shouldered, his bearded
face marked by prominent cheekbones. His dark brows were
drawn together in a frown. His brown eyes ran over the length
of her body and settled on her face.

"What's this about?"

"I am Elena, my lord. Sent as a help-mate for the baroness by—"

"Yes," he interrupted. "I know who sent you."

He turned to the steward. "Beltrán, I will only say it once. This woman is not to be harmed. If any wrong comes to her I shall hear it, and the perpetrator will pay with his life. Is that clear?"

Beltrán looked from Ramón to Elena and back again. She watched incredulity flicker across his face, followed by a ripple of anger. Slowly he dipped his head in a nod.

"Yes, my lord."

Elena regarded the exchange with bafflement. Here she was, confronted by the sight of her ancient enemy, and by some madness he had shape-shifted into her protector. She held her head up, feeling the baron's eyes upon her, waiting for a flash of recognition to pass across his face. In an instant, she was sure, his lip would curl in a sneer. He would point a finger at her and say: *I know who you are.*

Nervously she glanced around, listening for some sound, some clue to explain his behavior. Perhaps it was a trick. Perhaps his guards massed even now, waiting to drag her into the dungeons.

"My wife awaits your return," he said curtly. "Go to her. She will see your wound is taken care of."

"Yes, my lord."

She took two steps back, bobbed a curtsy and ducked away, one hand cupped under her chin to capture the blood that leaked from her mouth.

8

Summer, 2014
Oxford, England
Zari

THE COBBLESTONES ON THE broad courtyard fanned out before Zari like rows of crooked teeth, snagging the wheels of her suitcase with their ancient pocks and fissures. She followed Vanessa through a broad oak door into a corridor where a whisper of cool air offered respite from the heat. Removing her sunglasses, she sensed movement in the shadows ahead. An elderly man stumped out of the gloom, the soles of his polished loafers slapping gently against the stone floor.

"Good afternoon," Vanessa said, inclining her head toward the man in a polite nod. Her black-and-white striped jersey dress and wine-colored platform wedges looked wildly out of place in the medieval setting.

"Good afternoon, Miss Conlon." His tone implied that this was, in fact, an afternoon from hell.

Zari aimed a broad grin in his direction, hoping to startle him into a smile. Instead, his disapproving expression was replaced by a look of befuddled panic. Blearily, she recalled the chocolate bar she had consumed on the bus from the airport to Oxford.

"Do I have something on my face?" she asked Vanessa, touching her fingers to her chin and examining them.

"Just the wrong set of chromosomes." Vanessa threw a glance back over her shoulder. "He's one of the dinosaurs. Spends most of his time drinking tea and reading newspapers in the fellows' lounge. He was on my hiring committee, so it's possible that he likes my work. But the more likely story is he was bullied into recommending me by a quota-wielding administrator."

She waved Zari through a door and pointed up a curving staircase.

"I booked you and Aggie into the last available double. It's been refurbished with new furniture and mattresses. Though I must warn you we've had a few claims of ghost sightings in that room."

Zari slipped the strap of her messenger bag over her shoulder and heaved her suitcase up the slippery stairs one riser at a time.

"Ghosts? Good. I'd love to meet one in person. I spend most of my work life chasing them."

Vanessa sorted through keys on the lanyard around her neck and unlocked a door at the head of the stairs. "You've come to the right place, then."

The room was an unassuming space painted white, filled with basic pine furniture. Zari deposited her suitcase at the foot of one of the twin beds, unable to contain a tremendous yawn.

"The only way to fight off jet lag is to stay in motion until the natives go to bed." Vanessa opened the windows one by one. "If you fall asleep now, you'll be knackered tomorrow."

In the adjoining bathroom, Zari splashed her face with cold water. She blotted her skin with a towel and appraised herself in the mirror. Dark shadows lay under her eyes and her skin had the yellowish-green tinge that it took on when she went too long without sleep. Ugh, she thought. Maybe that poor man *was* scared of me. She pulled her mass of brown curls into a knot, swabbed her face with powder, and rummaged in her toiletries kit for a stick of deodorant. Then she flicked off the light. There was only so much damage control to be done after nearly 24 hours of travel.

"Can we visit the painting?" she asked. "That should keep me awake."

Vanessa jangled her keys. "You're in luck. I've been granted clearance to our high-security underground archives. Follow me."

Vanessa led Zari down a flight of dimly-lit stairs to a basement that was scented with the faint aromas of damp stone and stale tobacco. Her long, silver-streaked dark hair twitched back and forth as she walked.

"High-security archives?" Zari asked. "It smells more like a smoker's lounge down here."

"Ha. The women's toilets used to be down here, back when all the upstairs loos were men-only. No, what you're smelling is the result of late-night shenanigans involving cigars and whiskey, I'd imagine."

They cut through a narrow hallway. Vanessa unlocked a door and pressed a light switch. The walls of the small room were lined with metal shelving and rows of shallow drawers. After consulting a note on her mobile phone, Vanessa tugged a drawer open, slid out a rectangular box not much bigger than Zari's suitcase, and placed it on a metal table. With two sharp clicks, she unclasped the latches and opened the cover.

The painting was small, its decoratively carved wooden frame riddled with scratch marks and gouges. The woman in the portrait, shown from the waist up, was pale and fine-boned. Her dark auburn hair was mostly hidden under a pearl-encrusted cap. Her black dress was nipped in at the waist, her neck concealed by a ruffled Elizabethan collar. One eyebrow was slightly raised. There was a curl to her lips that could either be interpreted as a smile or a sneer—Zari couldn't decide which. It was this ambivalence, she realized, that made her eye want to linger on the woman's face.

"I like her," Zari said.

"Do you? I don't think she likes us."

"Can you blame her for looking grumpy, with that corset on?" Zari put her mobile on flashlight mode and leaned in. Close up, the surface of the painting was dull and the colors swirled together in a muddled haze.

"Poor thing's been in a box for a year awaiting restoration, ever since that flap about her origins." Vanessa slipped on her reading glasses and bent over the painting. She glanced back up at Zari. "There's an empty spot on a wall upstairs that's been missing her terribly. Banished to the basement over a few letters—it doesn't seem right."

"You know the whole story, then?"

Vanessa nodded.

"I don't know what the restoration will prove." Zari regarded the painting again. "But this certainly looks like the work of Cornelia van der Zee."

"Too bad she didn't sign it."

"She only signed a few of her paintings."

Zari ran through the facts in her mind. Until last year the painting was believed to be the work of Flemish artist Cornelia van der Zee, its subject a French noblewoman named Marie de Béart who lived in the early 1500s. But a batch of 500-year-old letters tucked away in a Parisian attic resurfaced and put Marie de Béart's birthdate much later than had been assumed. According to those letters, she would have been a little girl at the time Cornelia van der Zee painted this. The dates just didn't add up.

"If this isn't Marie de Béart, who is she?" asked Vanessa.

Zari shrugged. "I'm not ruling out the possibility that she *is* in fact Marie de Béart. The writer of those letters may have been misinformed about the date of her birth. Two numbers might have been transposed by accident. The letters may have referred to another child altogether."

"Ah. Discounting a primary source. You're a bold one." Vanessa pulled her glasses off and eyed Zari. She was a woman of quick, birdlike movements. When she distilled her energy into a focused gaze, it was almost unbearably intense.

"It's a leap of faith to take any one source as gospel," Zari said firmly. "History is not that simple."

"Magna Carta, then," Vanessa said. "A load of rubbish?"

"I'm not suggesting we take snippers to the whole fabric of civil society. What I'm saying is, we have to work with an unreliable archive. It's full of holes."

"You're talking to an Irishwoman. I know all about silenced stories."

The copper-haired woman stared up at them from her wooden box. There was a trace of defiance in her eyes. She seemed tensed, ready to spring.

"From my perspective, it doesn't matter who this woman is unless her identity proves that Cornelia van der Zee painted the portrait," Zari said. "There are only seventeen Van der Zee paintings left in the world, as far as anyone knows. If this one is dismissed, we're down to sixteen."

"Here's hoping for your sake that it proves to be a Van der Zee, then," said Vanessa. "Solving a 500-year-old mystery would be quite a career boost." Again, those dark eyes searched Zari's face.

"I can't claim credit for anything the art conservator discovers—the restoration of paintings is a totally foreign world to me. All I can say with certainty, looking at the painting now, is that I understand why it's been attributed to Van der Zee."

Zari could have spent another hour with the portrait, but

Vanessa was eager to escape the stale air of the basement. Back above ground, they skirted the edge of the commons, passed through a long corridor and entered a high-ceilinged room where rows of polished wooden tables fitted with brass reading lamps stretched out before them. An oversized painting of a Tudor-era woman in a fur-trimmed dress hung on a stone wall. It was surrounded by a dozen or so oil portraits of red-cheeked men garbed in riding boots, white breeches and military jackets.

Zari's eyes widened. "A rose among thorns."

Vanessa smiled. "She's Catherine of Aragón, Henry the Eighth's first wife, back in her glory days before Anne Boleyn bewitched her husband."

"What a mess marrying him turned out to be," Zari said. "At least Henry just divorced her. Anne wasn't so lucky."

"Chopping off his wives' heads proved so much more efficient than divorce."

Zari contemplated the ruddy male faces staring down at them. "Are these her bodyguards?"

"They're the alumni of Fontbroke College," Vanessa explained. "Four centuries of them, enjoying immortality on these hallowed walls. What's the saying? *Ars longa, vita brevis.* Life is short, but art lasts."

"Where are the portraits of women alumni?"

"Fontbroke College has existed for five centuries. Most of that time it was entirely a world of men. The college only started hiring women faculty and accepting female students 50 years ago. You see why it's so important that our girl in the basement is freed from her box."

There was something new in Vanessa's tone, a weariness perhaps. Zari glanced at her sideways. Sorrow had crept over Vanessa's face, pulling her mouth down at the corners, muting the brightness of her eyes. Zari quickly looked away, feeling like an intruder. It was startling to see a hint of vulnerability lurking under Vanessa's breezy confidence.

"A portrait of a woman, painted by a woman," Zari said after a moment. "That's rare in itself for the era. And even more so here. No wonder you want her back on the wall."

Zari lay in bed past midnight staring into the darkness, her exhausted body and wired mind locked in a battle of wills. Jet lag always played out like this. Every molecule of her body was leached of energy, yet her mind flexed and hummed with stream-of-consciousness mania. Combing through memories, she replayed her departure the previous morning from California.

She and her mother had hurtled down Highway 101 in the ancient Toyota truck, Tibetan prayer flags flapping crazily in the cab behind them and the faint aroma of overripe banana emanating from somewhere under their feet. The sky was just beginning to lighten and the Golden Gate Bridge was empty of tourists.

"Look, Zari!" her mother said in delight. "No fog this morning. The sun is blessing your journey."

Zari stared groggily out the window toward the east. The sun shimmered above the undulating hills across the bay, scoring the water with pinpoints of silvery light.

"What did Gus and I used to call that—when the sunlight hits the bay? Waterfire?"

Her mother laughed. "Yes. You were such creative little spirits."

For a moment, as she contemplated the thousands of miles of land and sea that separated her from home, Zari's eyes welled with tears. She felt fragile, like thin glass about to crack. What was she doing in England? Who did she think she was stumbling around Oxford with her American accent? She couldn't even wash her hair properly. She had washed it with conditioner by mistake and then used all of her shampoo to get the conditioner out. Now she lay with her hair in a loose wet tangle on the pillow beside her, too exhausted to comb it. How could someone this inept possibly imagine herself traveling all over Europe conducting postdoctoral research?

She forced herself to do a round of deep breathing. In for four counts, hold for four counts, out for four counts. Her racing thoughts eased. Self-flagellation is a classic sleep-deprivation move, she reminded herself. Don't buy into it. Just sleep. She shut her eyes and counted backward from one hundred, just as her mother had taught her. Counting sheep never worked. Where did that even come from? It seemed like a lot of effort, imagining a sheep, ticking it off, conjuring up another, ticking that one off. It was so much easier to just count numbers. One hundred, ninety-nine, ninety-eight, ninety-seven, ninety-six. Before she reached fifty she was asleep.

9

Summer, 2014
Oxford, England
Zari

ARI STOOD IN THE reception room, wine glass in hand, gawking at the soaring wood-paneled walls and diamond-shaped windowpanes. She had slept through the night, showered again, downed a 'flat white'—which as far as she could tell was a latte, but somehow better—and today the world seemed a place of wonder, full of navigable challenges. She had given a talk on female patrons of portrait artists in Renaissance-era northern Europe and attended various presentations by other researchers. And here she was at the 'drinks reception,' not only still awake, but, as her brother Gus would say, on fire. A second wind was kicking in out of nowhere.

She looked down at her orange jersey dress, black sandals, and the crystal pendant that dangled from her neck, a going-away gift from her mother. Conducting a quick fashion check of the other women in the room, she saw that most of them were clad in neutrals. She craned her neck in search of outliers and spotted a polka-dotted wrap dress in turquoise and white, a deep purple tunic and, across the room, a sunflower-yellow blouse.

Her mental inventory was interrupted by a man with artfully arranged, thinning sandy hair and a body composed of long limbs and a reedy trunk. One of his hands clutched a half-full glass of white wine, the other was extended toward Zari.

"Herodotus Butterfield-Swinton," he said. "Medieval arts."

She shook his hand and quickly retrieved her own. "Herodotus? The ancient historian?"

"Ah—you're American," he observed, nodding sagely. "I was named for him, yes. Though I'm mostly called Dotie. Easier that way." His eyes traveled to her chest and telescoped back up to her face.

A current of annoyance rippled through her, but she kept her voice even. "Why Herodotus?"

"My father was translating Herodotus's *Histories* when my mother was carrying me. It seemed appropriate to name his first son after the man who wrote the words he was living, eating, and breathing. History is in our blood, one could say." He burst into a hearty laugh.

She forced out a polite chuckle.

"But you've not told me your name." Dotie sidled closer.

"Zari Durrell. I've got a postdoctoral fellowship with the Institute of Northern European Portraiture at St. Andrews. I'm here for the conference—and to study a painting."

"Ah! How nice to put a face with the name. I hear you've come to resurrect Cornelia van der Zee from obscurity—though our own portrait's reputation is a bit bedraggled of late."

He had a hard time keeping his eyes on hers. They kept zooming in on other components of her body. She fought off an urge to cross her arms over her chest and instead assumed a wide-legged power stance.

"You're familiar with the story?" she asked. "The Parisian letters?"

"More than familiar. It was I who brought them to the attention of the dean. They surfaced at a conference I was attending at the Sorbonne, what was its title—'*In the Sphere of the Personal: Letters of the Renaissance.*'" He paused to sip from his glass.

"So do you reject the idea that the portrait was painted by Cornelia van der Zee, based on those letters?"

"There is no denying the painting looks like her work, of course. And its subject resembles Marie de Béart rather eerily," he said. "But the entire provenance of the painting is in question now, don't you see? It's begun to reek of inauthenticity."

Zari was momentarily paralyzed by an inappropriate desire to laugh.

He rummaged in a pocket, pulled out a card and extended it to her. "I curate the Fontbroke College art collection, so I'll be in close contact with the conservator as the analysis of the painting progresses."

"Do you know who's funding the restoration, then?"

He shook his head. "Anonymous benefactor. But I suspect he is a descendent of either Cornelia van der Zee or Marie de Béart. That's the only reason a private donor would put up the cost of restoration for a 500-year-old painting by a minor artist like Van der Zee."

"He? So anonymous is a man?"

"What?" A small frown furrowed Dotie's brow. "Er—no, I sup-pose it could be a woman. In any event, the cost of a restoration can rise to 20,000 pounds or more."

"Only a blood relation would be motivated to pay that much, then?"

"Of course. There's no other logical explanation."

Zari opened her mouth to speak and shut it again. What would she gain by suggesting that logic might have nothing to do with it? That there was also tremendous power in the desire to solve a mystery—to reveal the secrets buried under layers of paint? To her, curiosity was an equally valid motive. But she was a junior academic, an interloper in the rarified world of Herodotus Butterfield-Swinton. It was wiser to stay silent—for now.

Dotie plucked a full glass of wine off the tray of a passing server and deposited the empty one in its place.

"Dotie!" Vanessa said, appearing at Zari's side. "Look who you found."

Dotie nodded curtly in Vanessa's direction and saluted her with his glass. "I must excuse myself, ladies. Lovely speaking with you, Zari."

He made off for the opposite side of the room.

"That was a quick exit," Zari observed.

"Dotie and I—what is the term you Americans use?—we agree to disagree. Quite often." Vanessa's eyes followed Dotie across the room. "It's a bit like modern-day jousting."

"His name can't possibly be real."

Zari found herself squinting at the shadows where the walls and ceiling met. Were cameras filming this? Was she an unwitting participant in some mocking reality show about the upper echelons of academia?

"Oh, his name is real," Vanessa said. "And how he loves to hear himself say it."

"Maybe he thinks it's a magic spell."

"Or a curse."

"Apparently I'll have ample opportunity to discover what makes Dotie tick, because he's involved with the restoration of the Van der Zee portrait." Zari couldn't hide the disappointment in her voice.

"Don't fret about that, Zari," Vanessa said. "His duties as curator are far eclipsed by his responsibilities as a professor. I should know. When we prepare for conferences like this one, he's always after me to carry out the administrative details he'd rather not deal with. Believe me, chatting with art conservators is at the bottom of his to-do list—and I would be happy to remind him of it."

A tall, blue-eyed woman with her hair twisted into a bun approached. "For the record, Zari," she announced, "Dotie's off limits. He's married with children."

"Aggie!" Zari enveloped her in a hug. The rush of gratitude she felt upon seeing a familiar face was startling. This was the first time she had seen Aggie in person since they met two years ago at a conference in New York, but they had kept in close contact through e-mail and video calls. It had been Aggie who convinced Zari to apply to the University of St. Andrews for a fellowship, Aggie who put her in touch with Vanessa Conlon, Aggie who offered to house Zari in her flat in St. Andrews. Without Aggie, Zari knew she would not be here.

Vanessa kissed Aggie's cheek. "The Scottish textile maven is back. Oxford missed you."

"Getting here was a bit dodgy," Aggie said, grinning. "I got caught up in a swarm of rather large American tourists coming across the bridge."

"Yesterday I was publicly shamed on that bridge," Zari said. "A man in a Hogwarts outfit yelled at me for taking a photo of a group of little Harry Potter clones."

"You thought Harry Potter was fictional?" Aggie threw a knowing look at Vanessa. "Yanks really are naive."

"It's good to have some new blood here," Vanessa said. "This conference tends to attract the usual suspects." She pointed across the room at a round-bellied man with a shock of gray hair, holding court with a bevy of younger colleagues. "There's Aggie's arch-rival," she said, leaning close to Zari with a conspiratorial air. "He's been parading around the room passing himself off as *the* expert on Scottish textiles of the Renaissance era."

"I'd be happy to go a few rounds with him, even with his Oxford pedigree," said Aggie. "Just let me sharpen my tongue." She took a swig of wine.

"The University of St. Andrews is nothing to sneeze at," Zari protested. "You've got quite an impressive pedigree yourself."

"Oh, but Zari." Aggie shook her head soberly. "This is Oxford. The universe of Oxford. No other institution can bestow the same burnish of prestige."

"We look mortal on the outside," Vanessa said, tapping the side of her head. "The gold is in *here*."

"You make light of it, Vanessa, but the universe of Oxford must be a lonely place for a woman at times," Zari said. "I'm sure Fontbroke College didn't exactly crawl with mentors when you were first hired."

Vanessa nodded. "Some of the dinosaurs had a hard time with me at first. Irish, and female, and calling myself an expert on the history of my own people."

"A triple threat," Aggie said.

"A trifecta of uppityness," Zari said.

"I thought they would welcome the addition of an actual Celt to the ranks of their Celtic experts," Vanessa admitted.

Aggie clucked her tongue. "The innocence of youth."

"They didn't know what to make of me." Vanessa's voice took on a low, dreamy cadence. "My family came from an island off southern Ireland where the women harvested kelp and the men were at the mercy of the sea, fishing for mackerel and lobsters, even taking seals when they could. My grandmother was born there, along with her nine brothers and sisters. She was trundled off to the mainland to work and never went back. She kept their stories alive, though—tales of sea maidens and kraken, and kelp goddesses and the like. So naturally, when I was adrift in my early days at Fontbroke College, I didn't have to dig too far into my memory bank for a mentor. Eilish, her name was. Covered in scales, her hair made of kelp—and she carried within her the power of the sea."

Aggie's shoulders started to shake with laughter.

"Jesus, Mary and Joseph, I'm dead serious." Vanessa glared at the empty space just beyond Aggie and let out an exasperated sigh. "For the love of God, back me up on this, Eilish!"

All three of them burst into laughter. The knots of people clustered nearby grew quiet, and Zari felt the weight of a dozen pairs of eyes upon them.

"To be fair, I've found real allies here in the boy's club," Vanessa said finally, collecting herself. "They're not all dinosaurs. Eilish has gotten me through some dark days, though, I won't lie."

Zari raised her glass. "To Eilish, then. And all the other women, real or imagined, who have helped us along the way."

10

Summer, 2014
Oxford, England
Zari

O N THE LAST DAY of her stay in Oxford, Zari got up early, careful not to wake Aggie sleeping in the narrow bed next to hers. Pulling a curtain back, she was confronted by the horrified stares of gargoyles perched outside on the rain gutter. A lone student sat in the sun on a stone ledge overlooking the grassy courtyard, texting. Beyond him, a few shadowy figures moved between the columns in a vaulted corridor.

Slipping out quietly, she made her way to the street entrance of Fontbroke College, waved a greeting at the porter who stood guard at the gates, and wandered downtown. Through the plate glass windows of a bakery, she saw rows of diminutive square cakes each bearing a line of script written in frosting. *Thank you for looking after the children. Thank you for feeding the fish.*

Thank you for looking after the rabbit. These must be made to order, Zari thought. Because how many people were going to need a rabbit-sitter? Maybe Oxford was awash in rabbits.

She passed under a tiny enclosed bridge fitted with diamond-paned windows that connected two buildings. Consulting her mobile for directions again, she strode down a small alleyway and emerged in a square lined with identical sand-colored stone buildings. She searched for a doorway emblazoned with a placard that read 'Dorrington-Moore Institute. Under 24-hours surveillance.' There were faces carved in stone over the door; one a dour man in a flat cap, the other a jowly fellow who looked vaguely like Benjamin Franklin.

She stared at the door, hesitating. Could this really be an art conservation laboratory? It looked more like a museum. Checking her calendar, she confirmed that this was the correct address; moreover, she had an appointment here in two minutes. She stepped forward and rang the doorbell.

When Zari was buzzed in and ushered by a receptionist to the main workspace, she was confronted by the collision of two worlds. Daylight filtered in from skylights on the vaulted ceiling. Opposite her, 500-year-old oil paintings— looking forlorn and bedraggled without their frames—were suspended from clamps on giant metal easels. Sleek machines sat on rolling tables and a bank of cream-colored cabinets lined a wall. The atmosphere was softened by the calming strains of a Baroque cello concerto emanating from hidden speakers.

A man seated by a metal trolley laden with jars of liquids and gels got up and extended a hand.

"Zari? John Drake."

He was not much taller than her, maybe in his mid-forties, with a face like a lump of clay that a sculptor had taken an initial fierce pass at, then abandoned: Broad cheekbones, a prominent nose and deep-set eyes behind wire-rimmed spectacles. He wore sturdy black leather boots and had what looked like a miner's lamp on his head. As they shook hands, Zari caught a faint whiff of citrus.

"Fashion-forward headgear, isn't it?" John pulled the contraption off his head, ruffling his short dark hair. "Tool of the trade. We do a lot of squinting in this business."

"I'm sorry to interrupt your work."

"Don't be. The break is welcome." He gestured to her to sit.

Zari settled in a chair. Above them, rectangular lights were suspended from the ceiling by rubber-coated wires that led to a control panel on the wall.

"Do those go up and down?" she asked.

"Yes. This is all about proper lighting. It's tedious work, interspersed with the occasional blaze of discovery."

"I'll keep my fingers crossed for that blaze to flare up while you're restoring the Van der Zee painting."

John smiled slightly. He took off his glasses and polished the lenses with a square of white cloth. "A fellowship with the Institute for Northern European Portraiture. That's quite a coup for an American just out of the gate."

"The topic of my dissertation was female portrait artists in Europe from the Renaissance through the Golden Age. It was a natural progression for me to go deep on Cornelia van der Zee—I'd already built the foundation with my doctorate."

"Ah—that puts things in perspective. Oxford's your first stop, I gather?"

"Yes. The Renaissance arts conference brought me here. For the next year St. Andrews will be my base. But my research will take me on the road quite a bit."

"I know there are a few Van der Zee portraits in the U.K., but where are the rest?"

"They're scattered in museums all over Europe. And a few are in private collections. I've gotten permission to see the one in Scotland this fall, and I'm waiting for approval to see the others."

"Best of luck," he said, replacing his glasses. "How can I be of help? You said you had some specific questions for me?"

The first notes of Vivaldi's '*Four Seasons*' began filtering through the room.

"To be honest," Zari admitted, "what I'd really like is a crash course on how the restoration process works."

"Come to my lecture in London next month at the National Gallery," he suggested. "It's about the conservation of paintings."

"There's a Van der Zee at the National Gallery I have to see anyway. I'll time it with your talk."

"Excellent. If you like, I can give you a quick primer now."

John led her to a machine that looked like it had been borrowed from a hospital's ultrasound imaging clinic.

"First we do the non-invasive work. We'll use x-rays and other imaging to see under the layers of paint, and what we find there will guide the restoration. Depending on how many layers we find, we'll do chemical analysis of a cross-section of the painting. That shows us, layer by layer, the origin and age of the pigments. If some of the layers prove to be newer, we'll remove them one at a time until we get at the original paint."

He went to a row of tall metal frames and pulled one away from the wall. The Fontbroke College portrait had been removed from its wooden frame and was gripped by rubberized clamps in the center of the metal structure.

"Oh—she's here!" Zari went to stand at John's side. "Looking a bit out of her element."

"They look like they've lost a limb, coming out of their frames," he agreed. He pressed a button on the wall and a light descended from the ceiling.

"Here." He handed her a headlamp.

The woman's hands, which had been half-obscured by the frame, were now fully revealed. One held a pendant that dangled from a gold chain around her waist. It was in the shape of a circle, overlaid by a cross. Where the two lines of the cross intersected lay a smaller circle. In her other hand, the woman held a book with a drab brown cover.

"Is that a letter on the spine of the book?" Zari asked.

John pulled on his headgear and switched on the lamp.

"Looks like a 'B'," he said.

Zari hugged her arms to her chest. "Talk about instant gratification."

John smiled, revealing a slight gap between his front teeth. "I'm glad somebody is getting a thrill out of this. Maybe you're in the wrong line of work."

"Do you think the black background could be hiding something?" Zari turned back to the painting. "Like that copy of the *Mona Lisa* in the Prado museum, in Madrid."

"There was a bit of a media flurry about it, I remember," he said. "They removed the black paint and found a landscape underneath."

"Right. Suddenly the painting wasn't just a ho-hum copy—it was work created in Leonardo da Vinci's studio."

"Maybe even done by the master himself, or so the theory went," John said. "That's a high bar to set, I'm afraid. There's little chance we'll uncover anything that glamorous."

Zari's face reddened. Why had she even brought that up?

"On the other hand," he added kindly, "I have learned to expect the unexpected."

She threw him a grateful look. "Whatever you discover, can you share it with me—along with an explanation of the technical details?"

"Of course. I'll start with this: the book she holds was likely red, not brown."

"How can you tell?"

"The artist probably used cinnabar, a mineral that makes a red pigment called vermilion, to paint it." He trained his headlamp on the woman's hands and the slim spine of the book. "When vermilion is exposed to air and light over time, it can change color quite drastically—it can even go black under certain conditions. We'll know if this is the case when the pigments are analyzed."

"So even before you peel back layers, what *you're* seeing is not what the artist saw."

"Exactly. Keep that in mind when you're traveling around to study these portraits."

"What else can you do to figure out what's really under there?"

He waved an arm at the machines across the room. "The x-rays and images called infrared reflectograms show us any underdrawings. And we can determine the age of the wood panel as well, using a technique called dendrochronology. There are loads of methods these days to uncover clues about old paintings. The days of 'gut plus experience' are over, for the most part. By that I mean when art experts identify paintings just by examining them. Ever since these technologies entered the field, it's been astounding how many paintings have been proven forgeries, fakes, or complete mysteries."

"The benefactor is a private citizen, right? Why would anyone other than a descendant of the artist or the subject pay for this, anyway?"

John looked at Zari sideways, amused.

"You've been talking to Dotie Butterfield-Swinton. He's always quick to pounce on a theory and promote it."

"A theory? So you don't know who the benefactor is either?"

"When someone hires me on the condition of anonymity, I listen. That's why I still have a job." John pulled off his headlamp.

"I understand. It's just—what if it turns out this portrait isn't Van der Zee's work? After pouring money into its restoration, wouldn't that be a blow?"

"That's the risk of looking beneath the layers of paint, Zari. Whatever is hiding in this portrait won't be a secret much longer."

11

Autumn, 2014
St. Andrews, Scotland
Zari

O N THE MORNING OF her appointment to see the only Cornelia van der Zee portrait in Scotland, Zari was hunched at her desk, organizing her teaching notes for the week, when a thin man with a swirl of white hair appeared through the glass wall in the corridor, flapping his arms and striding vigorously back and forth. He wore a pair of red polyester slacks, a white shirt with lapels that reached halfway down his chest, and a cream-colored cable knit cardigan. After his third pass, during which Zari got a glimpse of his patent-leather zip-up ankle boots, Aggie popped her head around the edge of the doorframe.

"Och, Zari—you've got that deer in the headlights look about you."

"Just trying to make sense of things," Zari said cautiously, her eyes on the man in the corridor.

Aggie lowered her voice to an exaggerated whisper. "That's Professor Emeritus Richard Crone, just back from Italy. He splits his time between Scotland and Sicily."

"I know. I met him at a faculty meeting yesterday."

"Did you know he wrote two books on Western art 40 years ago?"

Zari shook her head, watching him flap by again.

"You probably used them in an Art History 101 course in your early days at university," Aggie added.

"But what is he doing?"

"The arms, you mean? He does it to keep his circulation up. A 'healthy habit,' he calls it."

They watched him bustle down the corridor, jabbing the air with his fingertips, dressed like an extra from the set of a circa-1978 B movie.

"A researcher in my graduate program in California used to water the office plants with his urine, and then got offended when we asked him to stop." Zari pushed her chair back. "He thought he was performing a public service, infusing the sun-starved plants with life-sustaining chemicals like sodium and potassium. It was our intolerance, not his pee, that was the problem."

They watched Richard Crone march back to his office, chest puffed out like a peacock's. His flared slacks rubbed together with each step, emitting a gentle, rhythmic swish that trailed him down the corridor.

"Pee in the plants," Aggie said. "I'm fairly confident that would not be allowed here. Richard is distracting, but he's not disgusting."

"Richard is quiet, entertaining, and wears sustainably sourced clothing. Let him flap away to his heart's content, I say." Zari stood and pulled on her long down coat, rummaging in the pockets for her gloves and hat.

Aggie surveyed her, nodding in approval. "You ditched the hoodie and the puffy vest. For a Californian, you're dressed properly."

"If I play my cards right today, I might be allowed to study the portrait longer than the thirty minutes I've been promised. I've got to make a good impression."

"Private collections," said Aggie. "I feel your pain."

"I had to make a real pest of myself to get the owner to agree to this visit."

"I don't doubt it. You Yanks are so pushy."

"I didn't pull out the pushy card," Zari protested. "I resorted to bribery instead."

"Oh?"

"I found out she likes Oregon pinot noir, and I found a purveyor of said wine in St. Andrews." Zari hefted her messenger bag. "There's liquid gold in here."

Aggie laughed. "Brilliant! When you get back tonight let's open a bottle of liquid gold ourselves and do something about your room. You take the concept of living out of a suitcase a bit too literally."

Zari grinned. "Think of it as the minimalist look."

The wind bit into Zari's face, so cold and damp it felt as if it had been skimmed off the surface of the North Sea. The sky was molten lead. Tattered leaves hung from the branches of the street trees. Some of the streets in St. Andrews had no trees at all, and she was still not used to the monotonous gray of cobblestone streets flanked by stone buildings with no layer of green to soften them. Only now was she beginning to appreciate the redwoods, oaks, manzanitas, bays and eucalyptuses that bore silent witness to her life in California. How lucky she had been to grow up sheltered by such an extravagance of trees.

When she entered the bus station, a fine spray of rain had begun to fall. Zari's mobile buzzed. She fumbled for it in a pocket.

"Zari, my love!" It was her mother.

"Mom! I was just thinking how grateful I am for trees, and home. I miss you."

"Sweetie, Scotland is known for its treelessness. I could have told you that."

Zari felt a surge of annoyance. It was a huge achievement to have landed this fellowship, yet her mother could not get past the fact that it was so far away. The actual details of Zari's work didn't seem to interest her as much as the logistics of her daughter's life.

"What are you up to?" her mother asked.

"I'm off to see the lone Cornelia van der Zee painting in this treeless land."

"Mmm. How's Aggie?"

"Great."

"Did you give her the necklace?"

Zari's mother had made Aggie a long silver chain strung with a cluster of blue crystal beads.

"She loves it."

"Did you tell her about the energetic properties of the crystals?"

"Yes," Zari lied. She knew that the farther away she got from California, the more likely she would be to encounter outright mockery and disdain of her mother's world.

"Honey, I have a few minutes before Obsidian picks me up, and I wanted to check in."

"Obsidian?"

"The guy I met at the silent meditation retreat this summer. He lives in Montana. He's in town for a few days."

"What's his real name?"

"Who knows? He thinks my real name is Portia."

"Your real name *is* Portia."

"It hasn't always been, though."

"Mom, you changed it a lifetime ago. You haven't been Patricia since you were a kid."

"Anyway, he's a photographer. *So* much fun. And hot. I forgot how much energy younger men have—"

"I don't need to hear the gory details," Zari said, wincing. "Wait a second. How do you discover someone is fun and hot at a silent meditation retreat?"

"Obviously you've never been to one," Portia said testily. "Wise ass."

"Sorry." Zari riffled through a mental list of her mother's various freelance ventures. "How's the pet sitting business, Mom?"

"Fine, with the usual exception of Taffy. It should be illegal to spend that much money on a dog. He eats salmon I could never afford—and I now have to wear him in a baby sling on walks, because he has issues around other dogs ever since the neighbor's chow bit his ear through the fence. How that even happened is beyond me. Luckily it wasn't on my watch."

"How's Gus?"

"That's the reason I'm calling." A worried note crept into her mother's voice. "Will you check in with your brother? He's got a hamstring injury so he can't exercise, Jenny's been traveling a lot and the kids are driving him nuts. He's being stoic but I know better."

"No exercise? That's not good." Zari felt a seam of anxiety open up in her stomach. She took a deep breath, her eyes tracking the approach of a bus. "My ride's here. Don't worry, Mom. I'll call him tonight."

12

Autumn, 2014
St. Andrews, Scotland
Zari

THAT EVENING, AFTER TREATING herself to a taxi from
the bus station, Zari dragged herself up the five flights
of stairs to Aggie's flat. It was dark and cold inside. She
switched on some lights, changed into sweats and a long cardigan, turned on the wall heater in the kitchen, and poured a
glass of sauvignon blanc. After rummaging in the pantry and
the refrigerator, she assembled a platter of sliced apples, wal-
nuts, and crumbly cheddar cheese and settled in at the rickety
pine table with her sketchpad and charcoal pencils spread out
before her. She carefully pushed aside a pile of Aggie's work
folders, atop which lay a black-handled magnifying glass with
a thick, heavy lens.

When Aggie came home, she made a beeline for the refrigerator and poured herself a generous glass of wine.

"I don't know why I agreed to be in a book club." She flopped down in the chair opposite Zari. "I never have time to read the books, but I skim them and act as if I have. Then I've no idea what anyone's talking about." She peered at the sketchpad, which was open to a drawing Zari had made of an old woman in a Chanel suit. "That's pretty good," she said, sipping her wine. "Lady Muck, is it? Looks as if she's got a pickle up her arse."

"My hostess this afternoon. Her name's Saundra Gordon-Fitzhughes. Patron of the arts, Scotland's only owner of a Cornelia van der Zee painting, and world class snob." Zari smudged two dark lines under Saundra's eye with a thumb, giving her a bleary expression. "She doesn't think much of Americans. I felt like a bull in a china shop in her home, tiptoeing around antiques, porcelain vases and blown-glass bowls."

"Did you get anything good for your research?"

"She had a copy of the painting's provenance. An ancestor of hers bought it from a French art dealer in the nineteenth century. Before that it was in the possession of a French family for nearly three hundred years."

"It's a portrait?" Aggie twirled her dark gold hair into a bun and stabbed a pencil through it.

"All of Cornelia van der Zee's work is portraiture. This one has far less character than the one at Oxford. A dour merchant couple who haven't missed many meals. They look like they're in a food coma. Restored fairly recently, so the paint quality is fantastic. And the artist signed it, which makes it unusual. She only signed a few of her paintings." Zari put down her pencil and wiped her hands on a paper napkin. "Mrs. Gordon-Fitzhughes did have a newsflash that got my heart pounding a bit. A painting was sold at auction a few weeks ago to a collector in France. It's attributed to Cornelia van der Zee. Apparently it was holed up in a little old lady's house somewhere in the Pyrenees for years, and when the owner died it resurfaced."

"Another merchant couple?"

"A family. Mom, dad, two young girls. Three quarter length, early sixteenth century clothing, dark background."

"Did she sign it?"

"No."

"Will you wrangle a visit to see it, then?"

"I'm going to try. Private collections are tricky, as you know. But from what I can tell, the painting has some of the hallmarks of the Fontbroke College portrait. Plus they're both unsigned. If this new discovery turns out to be a Van der Zee, that might help me prove that Cornelia also painted the one at Oxford."

"Cornelia? You're on a first-name basis with her now," Aggie observed.

"I don't think she minds."

Aggie flipped through the sketchpad. She paused at a drawing of a group of sandpipers picking their way through the foam of a retreating wave. The next drawing was of a grove of redwood trees with ferns clustered at their bases, in the recesses of a shady canyon. She looked up at Zari. Instead of speaking, she balanced a nub of cheese on a walnut, then stacked them on a slice of apple and handed the whole assemblage to Zari.

"How did you know I only eat vertical food?" Zari said in an astonished voice, inserting the whole thing in her mouth. "Mmm."

"Don't think I forgot about my threat to help you decorate your room."

"I think I'll save my pennies for travel."

"In the posh neighborhoods, people put stuff they don't want on the curb in front of their houses. Good stuff. High quality sometimes. Art, furniture. We'll go on a hunt, find you some treasures."

"Treasures like this?" Zari reached across the table and picked up the magnifying glass. She held it up to her face and regarded Aggie through the lens. "Pretty impressive."

"I'll have you know that's a valuable research tool," Aggie said archly. "A gift from my Uncle Liam. You should see what people wove into textiles hundreds of years ago. Drawings, words. The scale of those things is all over the map. Some of it could have been created by ants."

Zari replaced the magnifying glass gently on the stack of folders.

"Anyway, tell me more about these garage sales."

"Not sales. People just leave their stuff at the curb, and then you rummage through it."

"Oh—like dumpster diving?"

"There are no dumpsters involved."

"We both speak English, but sometimes we are completely unintelligible to each other," Zari said.

"I speak English, you speak American."

"Let's call the whole thing off."

"Seriously, Zari. You have to settle in, make your mark on this place. Enjoy your time here."

"I'm a transient."

"Get to know the locals." Aggie waggled her eyebrows.

"Ha. There's no point in starting a relationship with someone who lives 7,000 miles from home." Zari leafed through the pages of her sketchpad.

"You're missing your redwood forests and golden beaches."

"Maybe more than I want to admit."

"Do you think your family will be able to come visit you?"

"My mother and my brother are saving their pennies. I just spoke to Gus. He tried to convince me that it would be a good idea to ship his kids over here for a few weeks. A sanity break for him. He's having a hard time right now." Zari sighed. "If we could scrape together the airfare, I'd do it in a heartbeat. I love those kids more than anything—I miss them the most."

"You've told me loads about your mum and your brother, but you never speak of your dad," Aggie said, selecting an apple slice.

Zari hesitated.

"I'm sorry. Is he—?"

"He's still alive," Zari said drily. "My parents divorced when I was young. He remarried in the blink of an eye and had two more daughters. I barely know them. His wife keeps them all on a tight leash."

"That must hurt."

"I've made my peace with it. My dad—both my parents—were the quintessential hippies back in the seventies. My mother never really stopped being part of that world, because it morphed into New Age living. Crystals, yoga, meditation, hemp clothing. That's her thing now. Not my dad—he got rid of the long hair and got into commercial real estate. He completely reinvented himself, and in the process he shed us."

Aggie leaned her head against the wall. "My parents have been married forty years, but sometimes I wonder how they stay together. They bicker day and night. I'm in no hurry to get married. If I wait a few more decades, my marriage will be in the honeymoon phase until death do us part."

Zari laughed. "The longest relationship I've had lasted less than a year. I'm pretty sure I've just never been in love. In lust, yes, but not in love. Marriage has never been a goal of mine."

"Let me clarify something. If you're not sure, you haven't been in love. Nothing wrong there. You just haven't met the right person yet. Look around you, Zari. You have no shortage of admirers, do you know that? I bet Richard Crone will be flapping past your door on an hourly basis from now on."

"I attract oddballs. It's a knack of mine."

"Seriously." Aggie jabbed the apple slice in Zari's direction. "You're an exotic Californian. You haven't escaped notice, believe me."

"Thank you for the vote of confidence. But for the next year I'll be shuttling around Europe nonstop. A relationship would be too complicated."

"All the more reason to make this flat a home."

"Why fill up my room with stuff if I'm just leaving again this summer? It seems pointless."

"Come on, Zari! Commit."

Zari shook her head, smiling. "I can't help it—I'm a master of keeping my options open."

13

Autumn, 2014
London, England
Zari

ZARI EMERGED IN A driving rain from the Charing Cross
tube stop. She flicked up the hood of her raincoat and
hurried past the stone lions standing guard over the
sloped expanse of Trafalgar Square. This morning she had left
her friends' flat in Islington with plenty of time to spare, but
a line closure forced her to reroute and take a lengthy detour.

In the cavernous lobby, a placard next to an information kiosk
read, *"Winter speaker series. Conservation of Paintings: Secrets
Revealed. Dr. John Drake, Art Conservator."*

"Where is this, please?" Zari asked the clerk at the desk, pointing at the placard.

"You're late." The woman waved at a vast set of double doors,
her polished pink nails gleaming. "That way."

Zari speed-walked into an immense gallery with polished
parquet wood floors, persimmon colored walls, and a vaulted

ceiling. A wash of light filtered in from skylights overhead. She approached a group of people gathered around a bespectacled man wearing a gray suit.

"Ah! Welcome," John said, flicking his eyes in her direction. She nearly blurted out a hearty American-style greeting, then downgraded it to a head bob and a vague approximation of a smile. When in Rome, she reminded herself.

"The conservation of paintings is about the marriage of art and science," he said, gesturing to the group to follow him. "Our eyes can trick us. But with infrared cameras, x-rays and other gifts of technology, we can now see what's invisible to our eyes. That's why my favorite part of the job, when I channel my inner Sherlock Holmes, is going into the lab." He rubbed his hands together like a witch crowing over her bubbling cauldron, eliciting a laugh from the group.

John's theatrical side had not been in evidence when Zari met him the first time. She eyed his gray suit. Was that bespoke? It was a trimmer fit than an American man would wear. And he wore it well.

"Is your job also to verify the history of a painting?" asked an elderly woman with a cloud of white hair.

"Yes. Some of the most intriguing questions involve paintings whose assumed provenance is proven wrong, but whose date of origin is correct. So if a painting is wrongly attributed to Botticelli, but is proven to have been painted in Botticelli's time, the question remains: whose work is it?"

They entered a series of galleries painted in pale neutrals, their floors made of simple hardwood planks. A low barrier that looked like a dark metal pipe ran around the perimeter of each room, mounted at arm's length from the walls. Frosted windows over connecting doorways let natural light filter into the galleries.

John stopped in front of a modestly sized portrait of a man wearing a long brown robe and a hat that resembled a fez.

"This painting was assumed to be the work of Hans Holbein the Younger, one of the German masters in the early Renaissance period. And it has been sold as such to a long string of owners. Eventually it came into the possession of the museum." He held up a large color photograph. "Look closely at this."

"But it's the same man! Wearing a different hat—and with a different background," said the white-haired woman.

"Correct. It is the same man. In fact, it is the same painting. When the museum acquired it, the man wore this black skull-cap and was standing in front of a blue background. It turns out that the painting was actually executed by an unknown German painter, then doctored up a few hundred years after its creation to appear more like a Holbein. The blue paint and the short hat were added sometime in the eighteenth century."

"Why are some paintings analyzed like this while others are ignored?" asked a whip-thin man whose hands were stuffed in the pockets of his dark jeans.

"All the paintings in this museum are cared for, but mostly to prevent any further deterioration. Intensive conservation is simply too costly—both monetarily and in terms of damage to the work. Mind you, our techniques are becoming less invasive, but there are always risks involved when you deal with linen or wood or paint that dates back hundreds of years. It's all very fragile."

Zari spoke up. "NGOs cover the cost of art conservation in some cases. There's a group based in the U.S. that restores the work of women artists."

The thin man swiveled and stared at her. "From this time period? Women just weren't artists in those days."

A few of the women in the group directed icy looks at him. He shoved his hands even further into his pockets and his voice took on a defensive tone. "It's not opinion—it's fact."

"I'm sorry, but that's not true," Zari shot back. "There *were* women artists."

"I'd like to hear what the expert has to say," the man said. His narrow face and small, pointy nose put her in mind of a rodent. And not a chinchilla or a long-eared rabbit. A rat.

"Dr. Durrell *is* an expert," John said firmly. "She knows more about the topic of women artists during this era than I do." He nodded in Zari's direction. "Please continue, Dr. Durrell."

"Take Artemisia Gentileschi," Zari said after a moment, sifting through her mind for the right words. "An Italian painter of the seventeenth century. Her father was an artist and her early teacher. She was the first female student to be admitted to the Academy of Art in Florence, where artists learned the techniques of Renaissance masters. For a long time after her death she was ignored and forgotten, but she's been gaining recognition over the past few decades."

Zari glanced at John. His open expression was all the encouragement she needed to continue.

"In the sixteenth century, a nun in Florence named Suor Plautilla Nelli churned out paintings on commission for churches and private citizens alike," she went on. "Her father was an artist, like Artemisia's. Even with training by an artist father or brother, women faced the obstacle of not being permitted to work with live models. The figurative work of masters like Leonardo da Vinci depended on years of experience drawing and painting the nude human body. Women did not have that privilege. There are many more examples I could share with you, but I'll give you just one: Judith Leyster, a Dutch painter of the seventeenth century whose work was so similar to the master Frans Hals' that many of her paintings were falsely attributed to him after her death."

"What?" said an American voice. It belonged to a round-faced woman wearing white sneakers and a pink raincoat that was partially unzipped, revealing a black fanny pack around her waist.

Zari nodded. "It's true—and it was common. Women's work was not valued in the art marketplace. Female artists' paintings were often unsigned or attributed to men in order to fetch a better price."

The group was silent.

She pointed at the portrait of the somber man in the fez-style hat. "This is a perfect example of what I'm talking about. We don't know who painted him. We know now that Hans Holbein did not. But perhaps some German woman artist was responsible, someone whose work was exquisite but whose gender made her paintings worthless. It's entirely possible." She shrugged. When she spoke again, it was in a low, dramatic whisper. "There are some things we'll never know."

A laugh rippled through the group.

When the lecture was over, Zari and John walked to the room that contained Flemish and Dutch works from the sixteenth century. Some of the paintings were immense, with ornate golden frames. Others were small and framed in plain wood. Most of their subjects were richly dressed merchants whose fortunes had been made during the medieval heydays of Flanders and Amsterdam. Their clothes were elegant but simple, their wealth displayed mostly through the jewels that adorned their fingers, necks and wrists.

They stopped in front of a small painting with a gold frame. It was Cornelia van der Zee's portrait of Saskia Hootje, a middle-aged woman growing stout around the middle. She was dressed in similar fashion to the woman in Fontbroke College's portrait, her black dress topped with a Tudor-style pleated collar. Her hands, their fingers laced together, rested at her waist.

Despite her obvious wealth and comfortable place in the world, Saskia Hootje's well-padded face was entirely somber, her dark eyes revealing nothing. No matter how long Zari stared at the portrait, no matter the angle she approached it from, she was unmoved.

"I don't know, John. When I look into her eyes, I get nothing back."

"Were you expecting her to chat with you?"

"No—it's just that the Fontbroke portrait is different. That woman's eyes *communicate*. They follow you around. Whereas Saskia Hootje's—well, 'dead fish eyes' comes to mind."

"Your descriptive powers are remarkable."

Zari laughed. "Thanks. It's a skill I take great pride in."

"Speaking of the Fontbroke portrait," John said, "Our imaging process is revealing quite a lot."

"Such as?"

"Painters in that era typically began the initial drawing on a cartoon—a piece of paper, essentially—and transferred it onto the panel. Our images showed the underdrawing of the portrait was not transferred from a cartoon. It was done freehand with a metal stylus directly on the panel, and it is extraordinarily detailed. On the drawing, in Latin, are written in charcoal the words 'pray for my mother.' I'll e-mail you photos. There's one detail that I had to share with you today, though."

"What?"

"This." He held out a cream-colored envelope.

Zari opened it and slid out a photocopy of a black and white drawing that showed the word 'Mira' in italic lettering. A drawing of a young nun made up the letter 'a.' Her body was draped languorously over the top of the letter, her habit trailing out to form its long tail. She had wide eyes and dark eyebrows. Zari stared at the tiny image for a moment in silence.

"Is this normal?" she finally asked. "I mean, finding something like this?"

He smiled. "There is no normal when it comes to 500-year-old works of art. I've seen plenty of underdrawings, the odd word or phrase scribbled on the panel. But nothing like this, no."

She traced the outline of the nun's body with a fingertip. "But what does it *mean*?"

"It could mean something profoundly significant. The trouble is, we'll likely never know."

"And what about the background?"

"You were right—the dark background was not original."

Zari drew in a sharp breath. "It wasn't?"

"There appears to be a landscape underneath it."

"That's fantastic!" In the next instant, Zari's elation vanished. "But all of Cornelia van der Zee's other known works are interiors. Every last one."

"This doesn't bode well for Cornelia van der Zee," John admitted. "But the more pressing issue is the fact that the restoration is proving to be quite complex. And complex equals costly. I've given an estimate to the client for the treatment phase of the job, and I have yet to hear back."

"You mean you might not finish the analysis?"

"If the client chooses not to go forward with the treatment phase, we're done."

On the train from London to Scotland, Zari wrapped a wool scarf around her neck. Her throat burned and she had the beginnings of a headache. She leaned her head against her seat-back and stared dully out the window, watching the rain-soaked landscape flash by in a muddle of green. Frayed leaves tore loose from the trees that bordered the fields and streams on either side of the tracks and swirled in a flurry to the sky.

She fished out a packet of cough drops from her bag and unwrapped one. Would her first significant discovery be to debunk the Fontbroke College portrait as the work of Cornelia van der Zee? An imaginary headline unfurled in her mind. *"Naive postdoc discredits the very artist she set out to illuminate."* She envisioned the social media bashing that would follow, a roar of insults echoing across cyberspace. #Postdocdummy. #zariDUHrell. The abusive hashtags would rain from the sky like hot tar from a white tower and detonate in the fields below, wreaking havoc on hapless postdocs while armor-clad tenured professors looked on stonily from the parapets.

The absurdity of the image made her smile, but only for a moment. What she accomplished during this year in Europe would either boost or derail her academic career. Her goal was a tenure-track position at a university in California or the Pacific Northwest. Such jobs were scarce for scholars of art history, and her debt load from student loans was never far from her thoughts. Landing a tenured position was the only way she could earn enough income in academia to live comfortably and pay off her debts.

She had moonlighted her way through graduate school designing and building websites. She liked the work. It was easy and satisfying, and it paid well. There was the added bonus of being able to work at any hour of the day or night, in yoga pants, listening to loud medleys of Broadway show tunes and 1970s funk. The truth was, she could make far more income working in the high-tech industry than she would ever earn as a professor. But the work that fueled her—the work she loved—was the joyful chaos of diving down research rabbit holes and connecting threads of history that had unraveled long ago. And she had only just begun.

Zari closed her eyes. The image of John in his gray suit and wire-rimmed spectacles surfaced in her mind. She pushed it away, rummaged in her messenger bag and pulled out her laptop.

She had tracked down the owner of Cornelia van der Zee's portrait that sold at auction in France: Laurence Ceravet, a scholar of medieval art who lived in a small French city called Pau. The city was in the foothills of the Pyrenees, maybe a bit more than an hour's drive from the Atlantic coast, not far from the border with Spain. Zari began tapping out an e-mail to Laurence Ceravet, conscious of the gentle sway of the train rolling along the slick tracks.

Perhaps the underdrawings were meaningless. Perhaps the landscape hidden under the black background was, too. And even if the Fontbroke portrait wasn't the work of Cornelia van der Zee, perhaps this new find in France was. Zari peered at a thumbnail image of the merchant family's portrait on her laptop screen, hesitated a moment, and resumed typing. *Cornelia van der Zee,* she pleaded silently. *Reveal yourself.*

BOOK 2

Fallaces sunt rerum species. The appearances of things are deceptive.

1

Summer, 1492
Abbey of Belarac, Béarn
Mira

MIRA EMERGED FROM THE tunnel of brambles, breathing hard. She had slithered like a snake through the secret pathways, propelled by the rustlings and murmurings of the other children making their way through the prickly shrubs. Mira always won these games. She was quicker than the others, longer-limbed, and she never gave away her hiding places. Now she shaded her eyes against the glare of the sun and stared at the forested ridges that surrounded the valley. In the distance loomed the high white peaks of the mountains, casting shadows over the endless hills clothed in their mantle of summer green.

The far-off rattle of an iron bell echoed through the air. She saw movement on a steep hillside just past the fields of barley and the tangled vines of hops. There they were—the shepherds of Ronzal, descending the rocky trail with their flocks. Mira counted five shepherds and fifteen dogs, and a dozen or more mules. They were here early this year, come to build the washing and shearing stations for Mother Béatrice.

The children emerged one after another from the brambles. Their chattering ceased when they saw what Mira was staring at.

"Uncle!" a boy shouted.

He ran along the edge of the barley fields, whooping and waving his arms. One of the shepherds stopped and brought his hands to his mouth. His long trilling whistle rose up over the clang of the bells. The other children followed the boy, running at full speed to meet the shepherds. All save Mira. She hung back, knowing Mother Béatrice would punish her if she followed them. These children were Belarac villagers now, but their parents had come from Ronzal, the brothers and sisters of the shepherds who descended the hills with their flocks.

Mira wondered what it would be like to be one of the village children, to know where she came from and who her people were. Even though she was an orphan, she might still have family in the world—the brothers and sisters and aunts and uncles of her dead parents. There could be people in these very mountains who shared her blood. But how would she ever find them?

The chapel bell interrupted her thoughts. Mother Béatrice had been alerted to the approach of the shepherds. If Mira did not turn and run back to the abbey at once, she could count on an afternoon spent scrubbing floors. Mother Béatrice had told her she would be allowed to fetch water with the other children during the construction project, but only if she was good in all things.

Imagining she was the oldest, lamest mule that ever lived, she plodded back past the fields and through the orchards. She stood at the bottom of the ladder for a moment, watching the shifting figures of people and animals at the far end of the valley. Finally, rung by rung, she inched herself up the ladder and over the wall.

Mira straightened up, hoisting the heavy bucket from the stream with difficulty. The water was low this year and the path from the streambed was a steep jumble of loose rocks. But she knew better than to complain. She was lucky to be outside the walls of the abbey. If she had to carry water, so be it. She lugged the bucket to Mother Béatrice, who stood over a battered wooden table strewn with sheets of parchment, deep in conversation with Jorge de Luz. Mother Béatrice dipped a wooden ladle into the bucket and offered it to the shepherd.

"Brother Arros's plans are an exact replica of his own operation," Béatrice said. "But I wonder if it is wise to place them close to the stream. It swells so in the springtime."

Jorge drank his fill. "Ah! That's mountain water," he said, smiling at Mira. "Just yesterday—maybe this morning, who knows—it was snow. That's why it tastes so good and feels like ice on your tongue."

Mira smiled back, pleased to be noticed. She had been hauling water for the shepherds for many days, and until this moment none of them had acknowledged her presence.

She followed Jorge and Mother Béatrice along the banks of the stream to the old chapel that would become the washing station. Next to it the earth had been dug out in a rectangle and large foundation stones placed for the sweating room. She watched their two shadows bob along the ground. Jorge's shadow was taller, but Mother Béatrice's was thinner. Water sloshed over the rim of the bucket, wetting her brown homespun dress.

"Clean water is the key to shearing and washing," Jorge was saying. "If a flood comes, it comes."

Béatrice surveyed the outline of the foundation stones for the sweating room. "This seems small."

"That's the purpose of a sweating room," Jorge explained. "With the sheep packed in tight, the room grows hot, the sheep begin to sweat, and the sweat softens the wool."

"But why not just make them go in the stream to get wet?" Mira asked. She slapped a hand over her mouth. Mother Béatrice would surely punish her for such impertinence.

"Ah! There's a difference between wool softened by sweat and truly wet wool," said Jorge. "If the wool gets wet, it takes days to dry. And before it's dry it can rot. Rotten wool is worthless."

Mother Béatrice's eyes were on Jorge, not Mira, and she had not reprimanded Mira for her question. Mira decided to chance another. Before she could speak, a high whistle resonated through the air. All three of them looked west. Coming along the track from the main road was a string of mules carrying the hooded figures of a dozen monks.

"Ah—Brother Arros is here," Mother Béatrice said, as if it were the most unremarkable sight in the world.

Mira wanted to scream with excitement. Monks from San Juan de la Peña regularly stopped at the abbey, but Brother Arros, the man who figured large in many of Elena's most fascinating stories, was never among them. Now he was here. She set the bucket down with a thump, squinting against the glare of the midday sun. Which one was he?

Mother Béatrice turned back to Jorge. "Come along, Mira," she said over her shoulder. "Your task is not finished."

Reluctantly, Mira obeyed.

2

Summer, 1492
Abbey of Belarac, Béarn
Béatrice

ÉATRICE AND BROTHER ARROS watched Mira kneel by
a toddler who had fallen in the grass. Mira wiped tears
from the sobbing girl's face with the hem of her apron
and helped her stand up.

"What wonders you have worked here, Mother Abbess,"
Brother Arros said. "The Abbey is alive with the spirit of children, the kitchen gardens burst with ripe vegetables, and what
is the greenery I spy twining about those columns?"

"Roses. Not yet in flower."

"I swear I can smell their sweetness already. And lavender
spikes wave their heads at me at every turn."

"Medicinal, both of them."

"Beautiful nonetheless. Beauty has been sorely lacking here
for many years."

Béatrice bent down and pulled a weed from the grass. "It is a start," she said.

Another toddler stumbled and Mira righted him before he fell. He flung his arms around her and she tickled him under the chin, setting him into a spasm of laughter. Béatrice looked the girl up and down, noting the sorry state of her homespun wool dress. Her limbs were lengthening and her face was losing its roundness. The beginnings of a woman's face, its planes and angles, were evident. She favored her mother, mostly in the hair and the eyes and the sharp set of her jaw. Her skin, though, was the color of seasoned oak, like her father's. And she had his way of restlessness, of barely contained energy.

"There is too much life in the girl—it leads her to mischief." Béatrice sighed. "She so often disobeys that I fear the stone pavers in the chapel will be scoured into sand."

"Why?"

"Because that is her punishment, of course—cleaning floors with a bristle-brush."

"Physical labor is sometimes the best thing for that which ails us," Brother Arros said, his eyes on the children. "Although the idea of a nobleborn child on her hands and knees with a bristle-brush is a bit unsettling."

Béatrice stiffened. "I see to it that the girl's mind is never idle. When she is not with the children, she is schooled in Latin, Aragónese, and arithmetic. And I have found a use for her ridiculous wanderings with Elena—I require them to harvest herbs and roots for our infirmary. There is work to be done day and night, now that we receive a steady stream of pilgrims once more who require our aid. She has proved a great help. She shows no fear of blood, nor is she bothered by the moans and screams of the ill."

"A useful addition to the abbey, then. In many ways."

Mira tossed a girl in the air and caught her again, eliciting screams of delight. Béatrice's expression tightened, watching them.

"Her utility comes at a cost."

"Perhaps the wildness you see in her will lead the girl out of these gates, to the benefit of all," Brother Arros said. "She was born bold, you say—let that be a gift, not an impediment."

"I have always admired your imagination, Brother Arros. It would interest me greatly to hear what she is to do with herself once she is out in the wide world. I will eagerly await your counsel on the matter."

Mira broke away from the younger children and approached them. "Brother Arros, will you tell the children a story?" she asked.

"My dear child, you mistake me for a storyteller," he teased.

"But Elena said stories spill out of you all the day long," Mira insisted. "And Elena always tells the truth."

Béatrice regarded Brother Arros with an expectant look.

"The saints above," he said. "Does she indeed? What kinds of stories does Elena say that I tell, then?"

"Stories about pilgrims, mostly."

"Stories about pilgrims," he repeated, rubbing his bald head and eyeing the skies above as if a story might be hovering in the clouds. "Let me think on it for a moment. Yes, there is one that comes to mind. A pilgrim passed through the monastery last autumn who had lived a richer life than most, studying with a master painter in Flanders. Sebastian was his name, I believe. Well, this Sebastian told us how he painted the portraits of the rich until, by the skin of his teeth, he escaped the plague—"

"Brother Arros, forgive me, but your story must wait for another time," Béatrice interrupted. "You and I have matters to discuss. Mira, your place is with the children. It is nearly their suppertime."

In the hottest part of the afternoon, Brother Arros and Béatrice exited the gates of the abbey and passed through the orchards to the wool washing station by the stream. The doorway was framed with new-hewn oak. Inside, half the rafters had been replaced. The faint scent of raw wood hung in the air.

"This place now comes back to life," said Béatrice. "The Ronzal shepherds are rebuilding it. I have found no fault with their craftsmanship."

"The structure is solid," Brother Arros agreed. "But you lack the most important part—the guts of the operation. The copper vats, the rinsing channels."

"The vats will come from Nay later this summer." She patted sweat from her upper lip with her sleeve. "The profit from the washed wool will raise the funds we need for other ventures."

"I'd not count on too much profit from the abbey's flocks."

"Why not? Merino wool fetches a high price."

"But you do not possess merino sheep."

"Not on parchment, no."

A pigeon cooed somewhere in the rafters.

Brother Arros was silent for a moment, staring at her. He mopped at his face and the back of his neck with the square of flax cloth he always kept in a pocket. "If the Ronzal shepherds have sold you merino sheep, their lives could be forfeit."

"What do you mean?" Béatrice scanned the darkness overhead for a nest.

"I've heard that the Queen governs the selling of sheep with iron-clad rules. One of which is that if a man sells a merino sheep outside of the kingdom he will pay with his life."

"That rule applies to sheep breeding in Castilla, not Aragón," Béatrice said, shrugging.

"Queen Isabella may be Castilian, but all of Aragón lies within her realm, including Ronzal. Surely the value of Aragón's merino flocks has not escaped her."

"Even so, Ronzal and Belarac have an ancient agreement. Merino flocks have always wintered here. Nothing has changed."

"To the contrary," Brother Arros said, "it seems to me that much has changed. Allowing merino sheep to overwinter in Béarn is one thing. A Béarnaise abbess profiting from the sale of their wool is quite another."

"The ancient agreements still govern these lands!" Béatrice's voice rose in irritation. "You know the royals and nobles must honor those accords."

He nodded. "And yet royals and nobles do not always display honor in their dealings with the rest of us, do they?"

She did not answer.

Brother Arros tilted his head to one side, studying her face.

"All of your plans hinge on this dangerous scheme," he said quietly. "You have always seemed to me a pragmatic woman, but now I am not so sure."

"There is nothing more pragmatic than seeking new sources of gold," she protested. "From the very first, when Lady Marguerite called upon us to raise the girl, we have been tied to the house of Oto. Relying on one family's fortunes is foolish, but I've had no other choice. The only way for me to change our course is to think less like an abbess and more like a merchant."

"May God watch over you then," said Brother Arros. "I shall pray for you. And for young Mira too."

3

Summer, 1492
Abbey of Belarac, Béarn
Mira

MIRA STOOD IN THE stables watching Brother Arros and the other monks prepare their animals. The mules stamped their hooves, sending up clouds of fine dust from the hay strewn across the stable floor.

"How long is the journey back to San Juan de la Peña?" Mira asked. She picked at a long splinter that protruded from a new wooden post, breathing in the raw scent of the oak.

"A few days and nights," Brother Arros said.

"But when darkness falls, are you not afraid of wolves and bears?"

"I would be a fool not to fear the wild creatures of the woods. At night, though, we are safely indoors."

"What of the smugglers and bandits who lurk along the way?" She pulled the splinter from the post and flicked it onto the floor.

"Mira!" said Béatrice. She stood at the entrance to the stables with Mathilde at her side, a leather-bound book in her arms. "We only just replaced those posts. Have a care."

"I beg your pardon, Mother Abbess."

Béatrice and Mathilde moved down the row of stalls, heads bent together. Mira waited until they were out of earshot.

"Bandits and smugglers," she repeated softly.

"The way is thick with them, I'll not deny it." Brother Arros slid a ceramic container of wheat berries into a basket on the mule's saddle. "We stay on the royal roads, for the smaller tracks used by the smugglers are too steep and narrow for mules and their burdens. And as for the bandits, their fear of God is usually enough to prevent them harassing monks. If we do encounter trouble, there is always this." He lifted his cloak just enough so she could see a quiver of arrows that hung from a strap over his shoulder.

Mira's face brightened. "I did not know monks wield weapons," she whispered.

"Not many do. The advantage of surprise is thus always on our side. As is God." He slipped his cloak back into place. "But come, child. There are other, far more pleasant beings who travel the road to Aragón. The pilgrims, for example."

"Do they all journey to the same place?"

"Indeed. To Compostela, where Santiago's bones lie."

"Have you seen the bones?"

"Of course. That is why I came to Aragón as a young man. I left my monastery in the north and walked for months, all the way to Compostela. I followed the stars—well, truth be told, I followed other pilgrims. It was safer that way. I stopped at San Juan de la Peña for a few nights and assisted in the infirmary there. I knew right away that it would one day be my home."

"Did you not want to stay in Compostela, to be near Santiago?"

He shook his head. "The sea was not to my liking."

"Why?"

"It is a place of crashing waves and strange creatures, where rivers go when they reach the ends of the earth. It swallows ships whole, spits out shells and sand and long tangled ribbons of green, squeezes the life out of fish and casts them up on the shore where crabs feast upon their eyes. It stinks of salt, and rot, and creeping fogs. Not a place for the likes of me."

He rummaged in a deep pocket that was hidden in a fold of his brown robes, drew out a small white object strung on a leather cord, and pressed it into Mira's hand.

She turned it over in her palm. "Is this a stone?"

"No, it is hard like stone, but it comes from the sea. It once housed a creature called a scallop, a slimy morsel of a thing."

"What happened to the scallop?"

"Eaten up by some other creature long ago, I suppose, or perhaps tossed in a stew."

"Have you tried them?"

"Yes, when I went to Compostela, I ate all manner of sea creatures. Fish, mostly. The fish in the sea are not like our trout. Some of them are bigger than ships. Some have horns like unicorns. Some can fly. Some have teeth as fearsome as a bear's." Brother Arros patted her shoulder. "I hope I do not frighten you, dear child. The shell was given me by one who had made the journey to Compostela not once, but three times. God rest his soul, he did not survive the return journey on his third try. I eased his passage out of this world, and he bade me promise to give this shell to a worthy recipient. I have been waiting for just the right person, and I have found her."

Mira's fingers closed around the smooth, time-worn ridges of the shell.

"What happened to the pilgrim Sebastian, the one you began to tell us about?"

Brother Arros buckled a strap on his mule's bridle. "We have no more time for stories, I'm afraid. Next time I visit, I will tell you that tale."

"One day I will follow the pilgrim's trail to Compostela and see the waves crash on the shore myself," Mira vowed, her eyes shining. "I would like to stand at the edge of the earth and watch the rivers pour into the sea."

"Then you have a spirit far more adventurous than most. Run along now, child." He turned back to the mule, leaving Mira wondering if she had said something wrong.

She slipped outside, the necklace clutched in her hand. The great iron gates rose up across the courtyard. One day she would cease climbing over the walls with the village children. She would be a grown woman and those gates would open for her. Something waited for her out in the world, something other than Belarac.

She was certain of it.

4

Spring, 1493
Nay, Béarn
Amadina

IT WAS NEARLY TIME for supper, and her brother Carlo would soon be at the door. Amadina picked up a silver plate and looked at her reflection. It would not do to allow mirrors in a convent, for vanity was a sin. But there was no harm in ensuring that one looked presentable, especially in the privacy of one's own chambers. Her eyes widened in distaste at the sight of the wimple constricting the rosy apples of her cheeks. She scowled.

Her mind drifted back to a memory of herself at six years old, sitting in the rectangle of sunlight that slanted through a tall window. The wooden shutters were flung open to the courtyard and the spring air mingled with the aromas of winter—tallow and smoke, dank sweat and yeasty beer, moldering turnips and withered apples that had sat too long in the cellars. Amadina hummed to herself, tracing with her finger the line that the sunlight made on the red wool carpet. Then she spied a butterfly fluttering from the courtyard through the window.

"Mama! Mama! A butterfly!"

Her hands flew to her mouth. Her mother had warned her so many times that it was burned into her brain: do not speak unless spoken to. Yet Amadina forgot the rule often, and each time her mother would signal to the nurse, who would bring a switch and strike Amadina's hand until it stung.

Carlo, on the other hand, spoke to their mother, father and grandfather whenever the fancy struck him. This was so patently unfair that Amadina had once complained to her father about the injustice of it. Amadina's father had not struck her, had explained that it was not a girl's place to speak. Her job was to listen, to learn, and to follow the example of her mother in everything.

Amadina was allowed to take part in her brother's tutoring, but only to learn reading and simple arithmetic. That was all she would need to run a home, after all. Carlo, seeing how taken she was with his studies of Latin and astrology, sometimes shared with her what he had learned of verbs and constellations. He taught her the mathematics he had learned from a Moorish tutor, he taught her the histories of Aragón he had read and memorized. Considering how rudely she treated him most of the time, his kindness was admirable. But that was Carlo—generous to a fault.

Her brother, she came to understand, was the only member of the household who actually *saw* her. He saw that she did not want a domestic life and was entirely unsuited for it. When the time came, it was he who convinced their parents that rather than marry her off to a merchant, they would be better served to entrust her to God.

And now, thanks to him, Amadina was the abbess of her own convent in the foothills of the Pyrenees, the mistress of her own fate. She owed Carlo everything, and all the world knew it. He saw himself as her protector, yet often it was she who protected him. For instance, the matter of Béatrice of Belarac. The woman's abrupt appearance in their lives had prompted Amadina to don a mantle of vigilance. After all, someone had to guard the family honor and—more importantly—the family fortune.

The new abbess from the run-down convent in the mountains had pegged her brother for a big-hearted fool, that was obvious. Carlo was no fool. But he saw only the good in people. He had no reason to believe otherwise. After all, he was the son, the favorite, the one whom fortune smiled upon. So it had fallen to Amadina to keep abreast of Béatrice's activities. It had been easy enough.

One autumn, the wind had turned especially bitter. More women than usual turned up at Amadina's doorstep in search of a home, yet she did not have room enough for them all. She wrote to Béatrice outlining the predicament and made a delicate plea for help. The response came swiftly. In her letter, Béatrice proposed that the women come to Belarac. She was in need of servants to run her paper-making workshop and spin her wool. It was a splendid arrangement for both parties.

Amadina hand-picked three women to make the journey—they were all widows of middle age, hardworking, quiet, discreet, and loath to abandon their ties in Nay. She promised them safe haven should they ever want to return for visits. In fact, she would see to it that they received a coin or two for making the journey back from time to time. The only condition was that they were to be her eyes and ears in Belarac. No detail, no scrap of gossip was too small. They all three gladly agreed.

She had sent them by oxcart to the Abbey of Belarac, and hadn't she got a fascinating quilt of tidbits since then? It amused her to hear Carlo go on at the supper table about the accomplishments of Béatrice—most of what he told Amadina she already knew, thanks to her informants.

She looked at her reflection once more. Two dark, glinting pools for eyes, a ruddy smear for a nose, a blurred frown for a mouth. This would never do. Amadina rearranged her features into a more pleasing composition, turning her head this way and that, stretching her mouth into a wide, brilliant smile. She nodded in satisfaction.

It was time to go downstairs.

5

Spring, 1493
Abbey of Belarac, Béarn
Mira

MOTHER BÉATRICE WAS NOT cruel, but she expected total obedience. When Mira or the other children misbehaved, a punishment immediately followed. Bristle-brushes and wooden buckets were their constant companions as a result.

Mira alone of the orphans was taught to read and write. This was no benefit. All it meant was that in addition to scrubbing floors, she spent countless hours copying letters, numbers, psalms, and bits of scripture onto scraps of parchment and linen paper. Sitting on a bench hunched over her letters was worse than scrubbing floors, she told the other children. Once she had found a sparrow frozen in its nest after a winter storm, and that was how she felt on the bench—immobilized, the life knocked out of her.

During long hours in the chapel, Mira prayed to God to hurry the days along so that summer would return, and with it, Elena.

When she tired of that, she repeated to herself a prayer that Elena had invented: "I pray for the mothers, the children, the beasts in the fields, for the sun that warms us, for the moon that lights our darkest nights, and for the starry skies that guide us."

Now she repeated that prayer to herself in a whispery sing-song voice while she carried out her latest punishment. She bent over the linen paper, dipped her quill in ink, and constructed a row of neat letters. When that page was filled, she salted and blotted it and set it aside. She listened for footsteps in the corridor and heard nothing. On the next page, instead of copying a long string of letters again, she built a cottage of L's and I's crowned with a roof of M's. She drafted a letter to an imaginary friend, Millicente P., and inquired about her health. At the bottom of the page she saved a space for her name. She wrote it rather plainly except for the 'a,' which she turned into a miniature self-portrait, her arms holding up the round top portion of the letter and her legs curving to the right to form the tail. She blew on the ink, impatient for it to dry.

The door opened. Mira flinched, knocking over the ink pot. A glistening black pool oozed across the page, obliterating the letter to Millicente P.

"Oh!" Mira gasped.

Béatrice came to stand behind her. "Fetch a rag and clean this up at once."

Mira flew across the room to rummage in the rag bag.

"What have you done here?" Béatrice pointed at the 'A.'

Mira reached out to blot the page.

"Leave it." Béatrice put her hand over Mira's. Her touch was gentle. "You made a good likeness."

Mira felt a rush of pride. She rubbed her ink-stained fingertips with the rag.

"That will not do it," Béatrice said absently. "You must soak your fingers in vinegar tonight." She righted the ink pot, still staring at Mira's self-portrait. "You draw on the step of the old well in the courtyard. I have seen the charcoal sticks the kitchen servants save for you."

Was Mother Béatrice going to take away her one pleasure? Mira's shoulders slumped.

"Why not put your talent with a quill to work for the abbey, if you are so bent on drawing? The library is full of books that are old and damaged and need recopying. If you show discipline with the quill, you might one day be permitted to paint the illuminations."

Mira's face must have registered the astonishment she felt, because Béatrice smiled.

"Why am I the only one who learns these things?" Mira blurted.

The smile disappeared from Béatrice's face.

"Forgive me, Mother Abbess. But the other children ask me that question, and I do not know what to tell them."

Béatrice cocked her head to one side. She stayed silent a moment, her blue eyes assessing Mira with a long look. "You've a quick mind and you are helpful to me," she said. "Reading and writing make you useful to the abbey. I encourage your skill in drawing for the same reason. And the discipline required to carry out these tasks is good preparation for your confinement."

"My confinement?"

"When you turn twelve, you will cease your childish pursuits and begin your training as a novice nun. When you are eighteen, you will choose whether to take the veil or to live out your days as a boarder."

Mira felt as if she had been slapped. She willed herself not to cry. Tears never had a good outcome.

"What if I desire neither of those things?" Her voice faltered.

"You are lucky to have a choice at all. Most girls are not so fortunate."

"I might have a family somewhere. Uncles, aunts. I could go live with them!"

The defiant words hung in the air between them. Mira knew she had gone too far.

"Your parents are dead. You have no one else."

"There must be someone."

"No," Béatrice said softly, and her voice held none of the usual irritation at Mira's impertinence. "You have no other family, Miramonde." She hesitated a moment, as if she wanted to say something else. But when she spoke again, her voice held its usual crisp authority. "Now, go to the kitchens. Cook will tell you which floor to scrub. You must keep at it until the bell rings for vespers."

The tears flowed freely down Mira's face as she stalked away. Her life beyond the walls was coming to an end. She would sit on a hard bench and dip a quill into ink and copy Latin words. She would file into the chapel with the other novice nuns and kneel to pray. She would tend to the ill in the infirmary. And each time she caught sight of the abbey gates, she would despair. Her world was closing in.

Caught up in this dreary rendering of the future, her vision muddled by tears, she stumbled on an uneven paver and fell. She lay with her face pressed against the cold stone, convulsed by silent sobs. Soon it would be summer, she told herself. Soon Elena would descend the mountain trails to Belarac and make things right again. Her tears ebbed away. The wild beating of her heart slowed.

Getting to her feet, she wiped her face with her sleeve and set off for the kitchens.

6

Spring, 1493
San Juan de la Peña, Aragón
Elena

ELENA MADE HER WAY to San Juan de la Peña through oak forests and beech woods, casting dark glances at the crows in the treetops, her leather satchel bulging with herbs and ground-up roots. Always her bow was at the ready, and in her leather belt hung a dagger. She knew the safe paths, the caves carved into the limestone cliffs, the hidden spaces behind waterfalls. She had spent her life memorizing the places where one could hide from a bear, a wolf or a man.

When she descended the steep path that led from the broad meadow above the cliffs to the monastery, she watched a griffon vulture circling high above, a dark speck in a sea of blue. The copper-colored soil under her feet was crumbly. She slipped, reaching down to steady herself against a juniper shrub, and her eyes were drawn to the bleached skull of a bird on the edge of the path. For a moment she stood motionless, studying it.

This had been no songbird, but something larger. Most likely it was a crow.

Elena skidded away. Had the gods placed the skull there as a warning to her? The ominous thought chased her down the trail. When she reached the monastery her lungs ached, her legs trembled with fatigue and her mouth was dry as dust.

Exclaiming over the bounty she had brought him, Brother Arros sat down opposite her at the long table and ordered a servant to bring a pitcher of beer. For a long moment he studied her in the candlelight.

"The sun and wind leave their marks upon your face. You live like a wild thing, like a bird in flight."

"Ha! That bird was captured and put inside a cage long ago."

"You traipse all over these mountains alone. You walk the high trails, crossing from one kingdom into the next at the mercy of bandits and beasts. I ask you this each year, and each year you refuse—*why* will you not wait and accompany the monks on the main road?"

"What? Me, shuffling along in a mule train?" She laughed. "Don't fear on my account. I carry a bow and a blade." She patted the hilt of her dagger. It was housed in a leather sheath he had not seen her wear before, carved with tool-work that resembled twining vines.

"That is a handsome thing, your sheath."

"Someone made it for me."

"Have you no more explanation than that? Such a gift merits a good story."

"Not always." Her eyes revealed nothing. "Where's your recipe book, then? I've herbs for you. And honey. Everything you asked for. Though it does seem overmuch for one infirmary."

He sighed. "We have had such a wave of pilgrims this spring— but that is how they always come. Either a trickle or a flood. I think it is because there are two types of pilgrims: those who are afraid to travel alone, and those who hate traveling in groups."

"Which do you like best?"

"The ones who travel alone tend to fare worse," he said. "Safety in numbers, you know. There was one this spring who came not from the pilgrim's way, but from the east—a serf from Oto lands. One eye was burned from the socket, and the fingers of one hand were stumps. He said he'd been that way since he was a boy, when the steward accused him of cheating the baron."

"Was it true?"

"God only knows. He claimed that Ramón de Oto released him from service and let him make the pilgrimage to Compostela. I treated him as best I could, then sent him west. He may lie dead in the forest for all I know."

"A shred of kindness from Ramón de Oto? Until the business with young Mira, I never would have believed that. My whole life long, I swore I'd sooner live in a dragon's den than on that family's lands. Now I dwell within his walls half the year."

"And he has yet to harm you."

"True. But Ramón de Oto shares his father's blood. When he comes for me, my dagger will be ready."

"When will you believe me? You have nothing to fear from him."

"I've seen his wife's face purple with bruises. I've seen servants whipped at his command to the edge of death, and I've nursed them back to life. Don't tell me I have nothing to fear."

"I vow it. You are safe from him. Truly. Before God." Brother Arros sat back, satisfied.

"You protect me with a vow? I thank you, but I'll keep my dagger close just the same."

"Enough of these dark thoughts," he urged. "Let us imagine that all is well in the world."

"But it is not."

"Humor me."

"As you wish." Her voice softened. "For tonight, for you, all is well in the world."

The pitcher of beer sat between them on the rough wooden table. Brother Arros refilled Elena's cup as soon as it was half-empty. He lifted the latch of his great 'herbal,' the leather-bound book whose parchment pages were filled with pressed flowers and recipes, and carefully opened it.

"Ah—one of the first recipes I was taught." Elena put her finger on a drawing of a willow tree bordered by neat Latin script. "Boiled bark of the willow."

He nodded. "It lessens their pain so. We could not do without it."

"That's how I learned to handle a blade, peeling away bark from the tree."

"Remember the year I held up my recipe book and pointed to each dried flower and plant in turn and you recited the names and uses of each one? I was dumbstruck. I thought somehow you had taught yourself to read. You had memorized the entire contents of my book."

"My mother couldn't read a word and had no need of it. What she taught me can't be learned from a book." Elena pulled a handful of dried cherries from her satchel and laid them on the table.

"She knew more than anyone in these mountains about wild plants and ancient remedies. But who taught her?"

"Perhaps she taught herself." Elena shrugged. "She never spoke of her people. She never spoke of mine. She always said I was a gift of the mountains."

"You came from the village by the River Arazas, I thought." He pressed a dried cherry under the bottom of his cup to work the pit loose.

"That's where she found me, yes. When she came across me I was a girl old enough to walk but not old enough to talk, sitting in a cold hearth covered with ash, surrounded by corpses."

Brother Arros crossed himself. "God was watching over you that day." He popped the cherry in his mouth.

"Don't remember a thing about it," Elena said, shrugging. "I can't tell you if He was or not. He did let the plague slither into Arazas, that I know."

"He was watching," Brother Arros said firmly. "He had plans for you. Without you, where would young Mira be?"

"I do what I can for her. There's too little joy in that child's life."

"Mother Béatrice is strict with her, as she should be."

"She wishes the girl to be a nun. The girl's not got the temperament for it, I'll vouch for that."

"I agree, she was not meant for a cloistered life, but what other path can a girl of her circumstances take? The truth is, she is lucky to exist at all."

Elena shook her head fiercely. "No. Existence isn't enough. She deserves to *live*."

7

Summer, 1493
Abbey of Belarac, Béarn
Mira

SQUATTING IN AN OVERGROWN corner of the infirmary garden by the well, Mira rummaged in the willow basket and selected a slender piece of black charcoal. It was still early. She had been up since dawn praying in the chapel and reading scripture with the novice nuns in the library.

Now, while Mother Béatrice and the other sisters were in their chapter meeting, she had her own private ritual. She let her hand decide what to draw on the well's marble step, and each day it chose something new. Today, the scene of a duel took shape under her hand. The two figures locked in combat were no men, but a cricket and a spider. The spider had a natural advantage with its venomous fangs. To even the match she gave the cricket two swords and, upon further reflection, a belt strung with an axe and a dagger.

Satisfied with her sketch, Mira imagined the battle unfolding. The cricket would chirp, as crickets do, and the spider—though she had never heard a spider make a sound—would likely hiss. Their weaponry would clash, making all manner of clatter that would attract hordes of onlookers. Dust would rise, obviously. She drew a cloud of dust and a band of curious ants near the cricket, then caught a movement out of the corner of her eye. A bird was building a nest in the cloister wall. It flitted about the grounds, plucking tiny twigs and errant tufts of uncombed wool from the courtyard. She leaned back on her heels, watching it fly to the stone wall and stuff its treasures into a crack.

"Mira!" The high voice of one of the cooks pierced the silence in the garden. "The apple boy says to come look."

She dropped her charcoal stick and ran to the kitchen door, rubbing her hands vigorously on her apron. The apple boy peered at her from behind the cook's skirts, grinning.

"Go on, the both of you." The cook turned to the boy, glowering at him. "And next time no bruised apples."

The children sprinted out of the courtyard and across the cobblestones to the stone walls that encircled the abbey. Mira clambered up the ladder with the apple boy in close pursuit. At the top she scanned the green fields and orchards that stretched across the valley to the forested ridges beyond.

"I don't see—"

The boy poked her leg. "Hurry."

Mira climbed down the rungs of the ladder on the other side of the wall. The boy let out a whoop, slid halfway down the ladder, then jumped to the ground. He rolled around, clutching his ankle and moaning.

"Why did you jump?" Mira said, annoyed. "It's too high. Of course you're hurt. Serves you right." She knelt and put her hand on his ankle. "Is this where it hurts?"

He covered his face with an arm, sobbing. Suspicious, she pulled his arm away from his grimy face. He jumped up, jammed his apple basket upside down on his head and hooted.

Mira wanted to laugh but turned her mouth down into a scowl instead. "You should never pretend to be hurt."

He stuck out his tongue at her and skipped away. "She's coming down the sheep trail," he called over his shoulder, swinging the basket from hand to hand.

Elena's slender form descended the trail, the hood of her black cloak obscuring her face. Mira ran through the grain fields, feeling the whispery touch of the green wheat shafts on her palms. Racing up the hillside, she was brought up short by Elena herself, who stood in the trail laughing.

"By the sun and stars, girl, you're nearly as tall as me. When did that happen?" Elena's dark hair was pulled back from her face in a single long braid. For the first time, Mira saw that it was streaked with coarse silver strands.

"It has been nearly a year, Elena. Children do grow."

"Oh, do they now? Clever girl, you've grown taller *and* wiser."

"How long will you stay?" Mira looped an arm around Elena's waist. They strolled back through the fields to the orchard.

"I've good news, my love. I'll stay until autumn turns the leaves, for I've many things to teach you."

"Teach me?" Mira stopped walking. All her joy drained away. "Mother Bèatrice says when I turn twelve I will no longer be allowed outside the abbey. I will sit in the library copying manuscripts and reading Latin, memorizing psalms and scripture. Please do not force me to spend the summer studying as well."

Hot tears stung her eyes, blurring the sight of the apple trees laden with fruit that fanned out in neat rows before them. She blotted her face with her apron, angry at herself for crying. Beyond the orchard loomed the high walls of the abbey. The iron gates had never looked so foreboding.

"By the sun and stars," Elena said in astonishment, pulling Mira into the circle of her arms. "Is it not clear to you by now?

Nothing I teach can be learned within those walls."

She pressed her head against Elena's chest and squeezed shut her eyes. The thudding of Elena's heart sounded in one ear; in the other, the whisper of leaves riffling in the breeze. She took a deep, shuddering breath. Elena smelled like everything good in the world—lavender and beeswax and sunshine and wool and wood-smoke.

For the first time, Mira understood that Elena was the closest thing to family she would ever have.

8

Summer, 1493
Abbey of Belarac, Béarn
Elena

THERE WAS NO LONGER parchment but glass in the windows of the abbess's parlor and the new wool rugs were soft under Elena's bare feet. A crucifix was nailed to the whitewashed wall behind the wide desk. Underneath it stood a high oak table, upon which lay a Bible. A long ribbon of brilliant blue that must have been a page marker was clamped inside the book, the end of it hanging off the table like the garish tail feather of a bird.

"So do you believe me, now that you've read the letter?" Elena asked. "What I've told you is true."

Béatrice folded the linen paper into a tiny square and stuffed it in her pocket. She weighed the bag of coins in her palm.

"Marguerite de Oto desires her daughter to journey to the high mountains for the summer meeting of the mountain people. The dangers you will encounter! I cannot say I have ever heard of a more foolish plan." She eyed Elena across the desk.

"Foolish or not, the plan comes with the gold you crave, so it must be done. And here I am to carry out the task." Elena thrust back her shoulders.

"Yes, here you are again, and no less impertinent than ever." Béatrice's voice was cool. "One day soon your summer wanderings will end. When she is twelve, she must submit to enclosure. It is safer for her, and you and her mother both know it."

"I'll not deny her mother's agreed to the plan, but only until a path out of these walls is found for her."

"What path? Marriage to a noble?" Béatrice snorted. "I think not. No one knows her origins. Why would any noble worth his salt take interest in her? I would better see her wed to a mountain man, since her mother is so bent on teaching her their ways." She shook her head. "It is dangerous to let her roam in the woods, to handle a blade and a bow, and it will make her despise this place in the end—if it has not already."

"As I've told you before, I don't make the plans, I'm the messenger."

Béatrice's expression darkened. "For eleven years, I have spent autumn, winter and spring coaxing the wildness out of that girl, and then, come summer, you undo it all."

Elena shrugged. "She was born with a restless nature. Nothing to be done for that—what's in the blood cannot be cured. Besides, I don't see you turning down the herbs and honey she brings back from our wanderings. You yourself brag about the salve Mira makes. The nuns slather it all over the pilgrims in the infirmary. Seems to me you rely on us collecting it for you."

"I know how you spend your time with her—and very little of it is devoted to gathering roots and leaves. The village children gossip about her skill with a bow. One does not learn to shoot an arrow overnight."

"Ha!" Elena shook her head. "Children stretch the truth as often as their parents do. I only wish she could hit a target. We've not spent nearly enough time practicing, but I'll remedy that soon enough."

"I will be gone half the summer in Nay. I am sure you will find ways to tease the discipline out of her while I am away. But when I return I do not want to find her transformed into a filthy heathen. Is that clear?"

"Heathen, she won't be. You've made sure of that. But clean—now, there's a promise I can't make, Abbess."

Béatrice's gaze returned to the bag of coins. "Our disputes are meaningless in the end, for gold dictates the terms of this arrangement."

Elena nodded. "We're in agreement, finally."

"There is enough here to outfit the wool washing station with more copper vats, repair the gates, purchase a new iron bell, and replace the parchment on the chapel windows with panes of glass." Béatrice's voice softened to a low whisper, as if she were talking to herself. "So in truth, if the Baroness of Oto asks that her daughter be sent on the next trade ship to Venice, I will honor her desire. The future of the abbey depends on it."

"I'm pleased to know how you truly feel about the girl." Elena heard the venom in her own voice, but made no effort to tamp it down.

"We are fond of her, you and I," said Béatrice. "But she is nothing more than a pawn in a noblewoman's game, and for that matter, so are the both of us."

Elena gave a short laugh, her hands balled into fists. "Speak for yourself."

"Do not deny that you hate living in the shadow of the family that has wronged you more than any other."

Elena balanced her knuckles on the edge of Béatrice's desk. "Mountain creatures adapt. In wintertime I live in a warm cottage fueled by wood I don't have to gather myself. I tend to the sick and bring babies into the world. Come spring, I am free to leave and do what I love best, collecting herbs and honey high in the mountains. In summer, I make the passage here to Belarac. And this girl, Mira—she has burrowed into my heart, I won't deny it. You may be fond of her. I'm glad to hear it. But I love that girl, and I know her better than you ever will. If there's a place in this world for her, I'll help her find it."

"Belarac is the only safe place for her."

"What about plague, what about fire, what about smugglers and bandits climbing your tall gates? What about war?" Elena felt her composure finally snap. "This place is no safer than any other—and perhaps the girls in it are worse off for not learning the first thing about surviving the world outside these walls! You imagine that you're shoring up this place with gold, with the profits from all your schemes. What you don't understand is how the world can turn dark in an instant, how your dreams can shatter into dust and ash. You don't account for that. But it will happen. It always does."

Béatrice straightened her shoulders. "If I went about my days fearing the end of all things, I would get nothing accomplished. This is a house of God, and we do the work of God. Everything I do to build a future for the abbey is rooted in that faith. Of course I know disaster could strike at any moment—I am no fool. I may be an abbess, but I am a woman, the same as you. I have a heart, though you seem not to believe it. I have worries that keep me awake in the hours before dawn. But for the sake of this place and the people who live within its walls, I must act as if we have a future. It is my God-given duty!"

Elena's gaze flicked from Béatrice's flushed face to the cross hanging on the wall above her head. "Well said, Mother Abbess. The truth suits you." She pulled aside her cloak to reveal a bone-handled dagger in a leather sheath at her waist. "And one more thing. This dagger is a gift for Mira from her mother. A Moorish blade, she said, one of her husband's spoils from the southern wars."

"No resident of Belarac can carry a weapon," Béatrice said flatly.

"I agree, especially a blade this fine. But as you just said, no matter what the Baroness of Oto desires for her daughter, even if it be strange or downright mad, you will honor it." Elena slid the sheath from around her waist and laid it on the desk in front of Béatrice.

"I cannot give it to her." Béatrice eyed the dagger with distaste. "You take it. On your wild wanderings, I have no doubt you will find the perfect moment to offer her this dangerous gift. Now leave my chambers."

9

Summer, 1493
Valley of Belarac, Béarn
Mira

MIRA STRUCK THE FIRE steel against the flint. Nothing happened. A bead of sweat tickled her spine. She ignored the itch, set her jaw and struck the steel against the stone again.

Elena was perched on a boulder nearby, her bare feet dangling into the stream. She sent a pebble careening across the surface of the water. A dragonfly chased the ripples for a moment, then disappeared into the willows.

This time when Mira clapped the steel against the flint, a bright spark shimmered. She stared at the spot where it had flared, wondering if she had imagined it.

"Good," Elena said. "But you have to get a bigger spark. And the spark has to land on your touchwood, and smolder, and then you must tend it until it becomes a flame."

Mira slapped at a fly on her arm. A family of crows settled in a pine tree just upstream and began chattering in raspy voices. Elena picked up a stone and hurled it in their direction. The crows exploded out of the tree, screeching indignantly.

"Be gone!" Elena shouted after them.

"Why do you hate crows so?"

"Crows are death's messengers." Elena sank back down on her stone perch and used her sleeve to wipe the sweat from her brow. "They lurk about, waiting for an advantage."

A tiny plume of smoke curled upward from the touchwood. Mira didn't know why it was called wood, because it was just a slice of dried fungus that Elena had hacked off the trunk of a twisted oak. It made the best tinder, she said.

Elena leaned forward. "Blow on it."

Mira filled her lungs with a great gulp of air. Elena held up a hand.

"Not as a dragon would, girl. More a mouse. A sickly one."

Under Mira's gentle breath, the merest hint of a flame licked upward.

"It's alive, girl, but only just," warned Elena. "Feed the flames. Be attentive to them."

Finally, the fire blazed hot enough to ignite a hunk of worm-eaten oak. Mira rocked back on her heels, staring at the flames in satisfaction. Then Elena took a green stick and drove it into the heart of the fire, spreading the blaze over the pebbly ground until it smoldered into a dark, throbbing mess.

They left their clothes in a heap by the stream. After they had splashed in the shallows for a while, cooling off, Elena slipped under the surface of the water and disappeared. She soon emerged, dripping, from the far side of the stream. The crows settled in a young birch tree nearby, observing in silence. Elena wiped the water out of her eyes, picked up a handful of stones and in one quick motion flung them up at the birds. They flapped away, scolding.

She turned back to Mira and squeezed the water out of her braid. "Now you."

Mira took a deep breath and pushed off with her feet, paddling desperately with her arms while her legs churned the water. When her feet touched the rocky bottom on the other side, she scrambled out of the water and stood in the sunlight, catching her breath.

"I'll not call that graceful. But it'll do."

They lay down in the dappled light under an oak, letting the warm noonday sun wash over their bodies. Mira had left the scallop shell necklace on. The wet leather cord felt heavy around her neck.

"Planning a pilgrim's journey, are you?" Elena asked, her eyes on the shell.

"Brother Arros gave it to me. I wear it always."

Elena smiled at the mention of his name, folding her hands behind her head. "Someday we'll swim where water bubbles up from the earth, steaming with heat," she promised. "Nothing like sliding into a hot pool under a starry winter sky."

"Why are you teaching me these things?" Mira asked after a moment.

Elena closed her eyes. "You may have need of them someday."

When they were dressed again, Elena led Mira to a small meadow. She walked a short distance away and launched into a whirling dance, her bare feet pointing and stepping in neatly executed patterns, her hands tracing circles in the air.

"See how I cross my foot in front of the other, and then leap back to the side?" Elena threw her weight to the left. "I do it first on one side, then the other. And then I whirl again—like this." She finished with her arms thrust high, fingers spread wide, then sank down on the grass. "Your turn."

"I must be a fire-starter, a swimmer, and a dancer?"

"If you can dance with the mountain people, you'll find a place at a table in every valley."

Mira got to her feet. Her dark auburn hair was still wet from the swimming lesson. It fell in a glistening tangle down her shoulders.

"Spread your fingers," Elena ordered. "Point your hands to the treetops."

Mira tried to execute the steps, tripping over her own feet. Elena clapped her hands to the rhythm of an invisible drum. After Mira's fourth attempt, Elena finally nodded her satisfaction.

Mira flopped down on the grass and stared up at the canopy of trees. Feathery leaves were layered like fans against the blue sky. She rolled over and flicked a blade of grass with her finger, trying to dislodge an ant. With a twig, she poked the ant until it fell into the dirt, righted itself, and resumed its forward march.

"Ants always seem to be on a journey." She propped her chin on her hands. "Do they have a purpose? Do they have a plan? Or are they just wandering?"

"All creatures have a purpose," Elena said. "That I believe. Shepherds wander with their flocks—but always in search of food or shelter. Ants aren't much different, I warrant."

"Perhaps they are guided by the sun or the moon." Mira put her face so close to the ground that her nose nearly touched the ant.

"Or the light or the darkness. The wind, maybe?" Elena suggested.

"Mother Béatrice would say they are guided by God."

"She would."

Elena rummaged in the satchel, pulling out a small round of cheese. She bit off a chunk and handed the rest to Mira.

"Eat as we walk," she said, getting to her feet. "Saves time."

"Where are we going?"

Elena pointed ahead at a hillside bristling with dark pines. "I've something to show you up there."

Though it would be light for hours, the sun was slipping lower. As she always did when she looked west, Mira thought about the sea. Was it truly swarming with creatures that flew, and had horns, and wings? Why did long ribbons of green grow in the sea, and what were they made of? What did scallops taste like? Swallowing the last of the cheese, she put one hand to her chest and traced the outline of the scallop shell under her blouse.

"Elena, how long would it take us to reach the sea if we keep walking west?"

"I don't think I could mark it in days, love. I've a friend, a shepherd, who makes the journey from time to time."

"Does he bring his flocks with him?"

Elena shook her head. "He travels alone to visit his family in Basque country. His people live near the sea."

"What does he do with his flocks, then?"

"He has no flocks of his own. He finds flocks that need tending and hires himself out."

They came to a small stream that was running low. Someone had dragged an alder trunk across the streambed to form a bridge. Two blue butterflies chased each other over the water, weaving patterns in the air with their pulsing wings. In the meadow on the other side of the stream, Mira amused herself by counting the crickets that flew up, startled, as they trampled the grass. Soon they entered the cool of the pine grove. She thrust out a hand to touch the rough bark of the trees as they passed. Thick yellow sap oozed like honey down their trunks.

"The sap is stickier than glue," Elena warned from ahead, without a backward glance. Mira sucked in her breath. Did the woman have eyes in the back of her head?

Deep inside the pine grove, Elena stopped. Mira looked up at the sunlight filtering through the branches. She could see slivers of blue sky overhead, but down here the air was still and warm. The dimness felt cloying, as if she were back inside the corridors of the abbey. The tangy scent of pine needles filled her lungs. She couldn't contain an impatient sigh.

"Well?" Elena's voice rang out in the stillness. "Where is it? Where is the thing I brought you here to see?"

Mira's gaze tracked through the trees. A short distance away she saw something crimson pushing up from the earth. She pointed.

"Do you know what that is?" Elena asked.

"A mushroom. Is it for eating?"

"Never. This is a death cap. One of the most deadly growing things there is. It kills silently, and with no trace."

The red skin of the mushroom was smooth and shiny. Mira thought it looked nothing like an agent of death.

"The more beautiful a thing is, the more cautious you should be."

Elena knelt. With a swift stroke of her dagger, she cut the death cap off at the base and wrapped it in a length of flax cloth. Then she scraped the top layer of brittle pine needles away from a patch of earth and wiped her blade several times against the peaty soil.

"But—" Mira began.

"Someone in the mountains always has need of poison."

"You would provide a murderer with his weapon?" Mira asked, incredulous.

"Death at another's hands is not always murder. Sometimes it's merciful. Those that linger at death's door too long—a kind poison can end such misery. I know. I once eased the passage for one I loved."

"That is not the Christian way, Elena!"

"No, 'tis not. But when did I ever claim to be a Christian?" Elena disappeared around the stout trunk of a tree.

Mira stood, shocked into silence, until Elena reemerged from the gloom.

"Time to get back, girl." Elena patted the pouch at her waist. "I've got what I need. Now mind you, I'll need to boil my blade tonight to get all the poison off. Only way to be sure." She passed Mira with a wink.

"Why did you show me this?" Mira hurried along behind her, scuffing the pine needles with her bare feet.

"Same reasons I show you anything—the bark of the willow, the leaves of the butterwort, the snow flower, the boxwood."

"But those are healing plants. These mushrooms bring death. You used them to kill. Are you teaching me to do the same?"

Elena whirled, her brown eyes glittering, and Mira was caught up short an arm's length away from her.

"What you choose to *do* with anything I teach you is your business, not mine."

Elena set off again, slowing her pace. Mira drew alongside her.

"I do not like what you did. How could I? Harvesting poison is wrong. A sin. It is evil!"

"I do what I must. The world is full of evils, Mira, and sometimes we must choose one over another."

"That makes no sense. Evil is evil. A person is bad or good. One is a murderer, or one is not."

Elena laughed bitterly. "I wish it were as simple as that. I do." She glanced sideways at Mira. "It would be best if you keep this lesson to yourself."

Mira felt a wave of anger rise up from her chest. Hunting for death caps was a terrible lesson. How could Elena laugh at this? Why was she baring this ugly side of herself? It felt like everything was changing, and not for the better.

"I will not tell Mother Béatrice. I learned long ago not to talk about you to her, nor talk about her to you. I am no fool."

Mira did not notice the crickets leaping desperately ahead of their shadows as they trampled the meadow grasses, nor did she search the streambed for butterflies when they crossed over the fallen alder tree. She stomped all the way to the abbey walls, consumed with rage at the one person in the world she truly loved.

10

Summer, 1493
Pyrenees Mountains
Mira

MIRA'S BARE TOES SANK into the soft beech leaves that lay rotting on the forest floor. She watched Elena stride up the path just ahead. It had been several days since the strange lesson in the pine grove, and her heart still raced when she remembered the angry words they had exchanged. But this morning when Elena shook her awake and said they were going on another adventure, her warm brown eyes shone at Mira with their customary light. Perhaps the dark mood that had taken hold of her was gone.

"You're not angry anymore," Mira said tentatively.

"I was never angry," Elena tossed back.

"About the death caps?"

"*You* were angry, not me."

"We were both angry," Mira protested.

Elena was silent.

"Does Mother Béatrice know where we are going?"

"She's in Nay. How could she know?"

"When she discovers what we've done, she will have me copy whole chapters of the Bible."

"She knows you're with me. Nothing else matters."

Mira wiped a trickle of sweat from her cheek with the back of her hand and hurried to catch up. Even the shade of the woods seemed to offer little protection from the heat. Dark spots bloomed on Elena's blouse where sweat had soaked through.

Without warning, Elena stopped and put one hand up. She slipped a dagger out of the leather scabbard at her waist. Mira peered ahead. In the bright glare where the woods opened up into a clearing, a gray wolf crouched on a boulder. Its yellow eyes were fixed upon them. A low, rumbling growl rose from its throat. The muscles in its shoulders tensed.

Before it could spring, there was a tremendous crashing in the forest and a pack of golden dogs surged into view. Their hoarse barking filled the air as they raced toward the wolf. It lunged away from them, landed heavily in a patch of brambles, and limped into the forest. The dogs sprinted past Mira and Elena, their spiked iron collars jangling.

"That wolf is doomed," Elena said, watching the animals disappear into the woods. She sheathed her dagger.

"Because it is lame?" Mira felt shaky. She picked up a rock and weighed it in her palm.

"Yes. It was mad with pain."

There was a frenzy of barks and high-pitched whines, then silence.

"A quick death," Elena said approvingly.

Mira held up the rock. "This would not be much help against a wolf. If you take me to the woods again, may I have a dagger of my own?"

"As it happens, you do have a dagger."

"I do?"

"I brought one over the mountains for you. A fine one, too. But it's no use carrying a weapon if you've no clue how to use it."

Mira's eyes grew wide. She imagined herself wielding a blade with the same confidence as Elena.

"May I see it? Do you have it now?"

"Impatient as usual. I'll teach you to handle a blade, never fear. Now let's start off again."

Elena tramped ahead. Mira watched her braid swing and tried to forget about the wolf. When they emerged into the meadow, the sun's heat felt like a hot stone pressing down on her head. Elena plucked a long strand of grass from the soil, put it to her lips and blew as she walked. Mira followed, shading her eyes with a hand. Just ahead were the figures of women and men standing in the tall grasses, children darting among them.

A smiling woman broke away from the group and threw her arms around Elena. Her honey-colored hair was massed in a pile of tiny braids on the back of her head, and the sleeves of her red dress were embroidered with yellow and violet thread.

"Thérèse de Luz, my dear friend," Elena said in the mountain dialect.

Behind them, the dogs appeared at the edge of the woods and loped across the grass in a loose pack. Thérèse's smile faltered when she saw the animals' bloody faces.

"What happened?"

"A wounded wolf," Elena said. "I was ready to kill it, but the dogs did the job for me."

"Thank the sun and stars you were not hurt, either of you." Thérèse looked Mira up and down. "Now wait one moment. Who is this tall girl?"

"I am Mira."

"Ah. Elena speaks of you often," Thérèse said. "She says you have a quick mind and a kind heart."

"Thank you. You are Béarnaise, like me?"

Thérèse nodded. "Béarn is in my blood, yes, but my husband is Aragónese. He made me a woman of Ronzal."

"A good match," Elena said, staring across the meadow at a broad-shouldered man who stood under an oak tree addressing a group of people seated on a circle of boulders. "There's no better man than Jorge de Luz."

"I've no complaints," Thérèse said, her eyes following Elena's gaze. "He's given me three sons, and there's still time for a fourth, with a bit of luck."

The two women exchanged a knowing look and laughed.

Mira said nothing, mesmerized by the delicate embroidery on Thérèse's sleeves. She glanced at her own clothes, uncomfortably aware of how plain and ill-fitting they were.

Thérèse studied Mira a moment. Her eyes were kind, but there was something in them—curiosity, perhaps—that made Mira feel awkward.

"I'm a mountain woman, nothing more," Thérèse said, smiling. "Once a year we put on our finery and try to impress one another. Come." She held out a hand to Mira. "Let's join the feast. You'll not be bored, I promise."

They walked to a clearing where people had hacked down the tall grass with scythes. The buzzing of crickets rang in Mira's ears and her lungs filled with the scents of fresh-chopped wood and crushed grass. In the clearing, long planks balanced atop wooden stumps. On the planks lay more food and drink than Mira had ever seen. Ceramic tankards brimmed with wine. Sausages were coiled like snakes next to enormous yellow cheeses that sweated in the afternoon heat. Round loaves of dark, crusty bread were heaped in piles, and dusty purple plums were stacked in small pyramids.

Nearby a group of musicians had gathered, readying their instruments. One man held a wooden drum, another a tambourine, and a third tuned his guitar. Still another blew through a wooden tube into a strange curved bladder, emitting strangled wails and bleats that sounded like an animal in distress. Thérèse draped an arm around Mira's shoulders.

"After a few cups of wine, his playing will improve," she whispered. "It always does."

When the feast began, Elena handed Mira a hunk of cheese and a handful of plums and led her to a place in the grass near a group of women. The July heat lingered even as the sun sank lower in the sky.

"Ah, there's my first born." Thérèse waved at a lanky boy with wiry black hair. "Arnaud!"

"So tall," said Elena, wiping the dust off a plum with the hem of her skirt.

Thérèse put her arm around Mira again as the boy approached. "Arnaud," she said to her son, "make sure Mira is looked after."

Arnaud took Mira's hand and led her to a group of children who were piling sticks and branches in a heap. Then he disappeared. Several dogs lay panting in the grass, watching the children work. Mira was hunting for sticks when Arnaud returned, carrying a linen cloth filled with sausages, fruit, and cheese. He put the food on the ground and rocked back on his heels.

"Eat," he said.

A small boy with curly brown hair ran up toting an enormous round loaf of bread.

"No one saw me take this!" He dropped the loaf on the cloth.

"Tomás," Arnaud said sternly. The little boy crossed his arms over his chest, refusing to look his older brother in the eye. An even smaller boy clung to Tomás's leg, his great brown eyes round with wonder.

"Tomás!" he squeaked in imitation of his eldest brother.

"Hush, Luis," Tomás said.

The other children regarded his trophy in admiration, then set about tearing it to pieces.

When the square of linen held only the dried heel of a sausage and a burned crust of bread, the children lay back on the grass, watching the sky turn violet and listening to the hum of insects. They jumped up when they spied adults carrying torches from the feast site across the meadow to the great pile of wood they had spent all day constructing.

"Stand back, children," warned a stout woman with a waddling gait. She waved her torch fiercely at the children until they edged away. "To peace, healthy flocks, and safe passage for all," she cried, tossing the torch on top of the pile.

The others followed suit. Flame devoured flame until the blaze burrowed deep into the stack of wood, sending a wave of heat outward, beating back the night sky with an arc of golden light.

The musicians launched into a song and a group began to dance. Arnaud took Mira's hand and pulled her over to watch.

"That's a shepherd, that's a bear, that's a wolf, and there's Basajaun and his brother Tartaro," he shouted over the roar of the fire, pointing at each dancer in turn. "And there is a lord and a lady, and there an abbot and an abbess."

The whirling players cast grotesque shadows on the meadow, lit from behind by the towering flames of the bonfire. A group of children joined in, portraying a flock of sheep. They bleated with such enthusiasm that the crowd burst into applause. As each dance ended, another began.

When the flames could leap no higher, the adults formed a circle, their arms looped together, and the children made their own smaller circle inside. The dancers stepped and swayed to the beat of the drum. Some of the women wore tiny, jangling bells sewn into their skirts.

Mira glanced sideways and saw Arnaud's eyes on her. He was staring at her neck, and she realized the scallop shell had worked its way loose from her blouse. She felt self-conscious, as if he had discovered a secret about her. He smiled. The warmth in his eyes made her relax. Turning back to face the crowd, she lost herself in the dance.

Huddled next to Elena, wrapped tightly in her woolen cloak, Mira stared up at the shimmering stars. All around them were sprawled the mountain folk, sleeping off their great feast. Her own body thrummed with energy. She found Elena's ear in the dark and the questions bubbled out of her. Who were Basajaun and Tartaro? Why did the people journey to this meadow each summer to feast and dance under the full moon?

Elena shushed her.

"Now's not a time for questions, but sleep, for we have a long journey ahead tomorrow. Be silent, girl."

Mira held her tongue and trained her eyes on the sky. A long string of stars cascaded from north to south. She counted them. They pulsed and glimmered, as if they were dancing in the wind. She lost count and began again. The more she focused on them, the more the stars faded under her gaze. As the sky began to lighten, she drifted off. But it seemed her eyes had only just closed when the sound of conversation awoke her.

"When next you see your Basque shepherd, tell him to pass through Ronzal," she heard Jorge de Luz say. She opened one eye.

Elena was sitting a short distance away with the council leader.

"He's not my shepherd," she said.

Jorge pointed to the leather sheath that hung at her waist. "I recognize his tool work."

"Are there no secrets to be had in these mountains?"

"Warn him not to leave offerings to the gods in the old places." Jorge's voice was sober. "Tell him the safe thing is to leave them higher up, where the priests are afraid to tread."

"Priests." Elena spat the word. Her hand went to her arm.

"They're not all bad," he said gently. "Look at Brother Arros. He's the sun and stars to you."

"He's no priest, but a monk."

"Just the same. The one that caused all that trouble when you were a child is dead, anyway. They say he climbed too high for a city man. Slipped on a rock in the spring rains and fell to his death."

Elena stared at Jorge for a long time, searching his face. Her shoulders trembled. He put a steadying hand on her arm. It dawned on Mira that Elena might be crying, though she had never seen her cry before—she had never entertained the thought that Elena *could* cry. Unsettled at the idea, she burrowed under her cloak and shut her eyes tight.

Just after dawn one morning, Elena and Mira retraced their steps back down the mountain into Béarn. A gibbous moon glowed against the pale blue sky in the west. Just ahead on the trail walked a shepherd armed with his iron-tipped staff and two of his dogs. Despite Elena's protestations, Thérèse had insisted someone accompany them.

"Who are Basajaun and Tartaro?" Mira asked, her eyes lingering on every shadow. She imagined a yellow-eyed wolf leaping from its hiding place with snapping jaws.

"Some call them giants, some call them monsters. Others call them gods. The mountain folk believe that if bad fortune strikes, it's because someone has angered them."

"What do you mean?"

"Blizzards, floods, avalanches—none of that's an accident. That's why the mountain people leave out offerings of cheese and honey in the summer, so the gods will be merciful come winter."

"I did not know there were many gods. I thought there was just one," Mira said.

"The church has its God, the one you pray to at the abbey. When we get down from this mountain, that is the only one you must speak of."

"I know." Mira's pace lagged. "God is all around us, yet I do not feel His presence, as much as I try. My mind wanders during prayers. I think about you and the mountain people. I think about the sea. I think about eating."

"Don't fret, my girl. One day you'll choose your own path, I swear it. No one else will do it for you."

"But how do you know?"

"I can't tell you why, but I know it to be true."

They threaded their way through a beech grove that echoed with birdsong. Water sluiced down a narrow stream crowded with boulders. Overhead, blue strips of sky floated far above the trees.

"Why do the people meet in the meadow each summer?"

"To renew their bonds of peace."

"What does that mean?"

"This peace—it's a fragile thing, like a crust of new snow over a bloody battlefield. The mountain people used to sneak across the mountains and strike each other with fire and iron. They fought over waterways and grazing pastures. They stole livestock. They murdered. No sooner was one wrong righted than another began. But the peace accords, the *fueros,* changed all that. Now the people meet in the meadow each year to do the work of the peace, and to celebrate it."

"Oh." Mira chewed her lip for a moment, wondering if she dared ask the question that burned hottest in her chest. Finally, she blurted it out. "Who was the priest you spoke about with Jorge de Luz?"

"He's dead. The less said of him the better." Elena stopped and turned, stooping so her face was level with Mira's. "Understand?"

Mira sighed. "How many times must I say it? I have no one to share secrets with, Elena. Except you."

11

Autumn, 1493
Ronzal, Aragón
Arnaud

O N A DAY IN his eleventh year when the trees refused to
let go of their last ragged leaves and the wind was just
shy of bitter, Arnaud's parents gave him a pair of boots.
He slipped them on right away. His younger brothers Tomás
and Luis stared with solemn eyes at his feet encased in leather.
After a few tentative laps inside the cottage, he emerged into
the crisp autumn air. Other villagers slapped each other on the
back and pointed at him as he passed by, walking stiffly in his
new footwear. The men called out congratulations; the women
smiled and told him how handsome he looked. By the end of the
day his feet were sore and blistered. But he did not care. Boots
made a boy a man in Ronzal.

Each year at this time the men would exchange their sandals—
if they even wore sandals, for many preferred to walk barefoot
all summer—for boots. It signaled a change of seasons just as

surely as the appearance of frost on bronzed summer grasses. It also meant the time had come to move the sheep to the abbey of Belarac before winter struck. Because he now possessed a pair of boots, Arnaud knew he would finally take part in the journey.

Shepherds, mules, dogs, and sheep made a slow parade across fields and meadows. They splashed through streams, clattered across slippery shale slopes, trampled the soft earth in pine forests and birch stands. When the animals balked or strayed, they were coaxed forward by the call of the shepherds and the incessant ringing of bells. The dogs padded alongside, keeping watch.

Arnaud trailed behind the men, fixated on the chafing his feet were undergoing in their new boots. He longed to take them off. But it was not seemly for a newly minted shepherd to break with tradition. As he limped along, an older shepherd named Domingo hung back for a moment, passing Arnaud a few handfuls of dry grass.

"For stuffing," he said.

Arnaud stopped and crammed the grass down into his boots. It did seem to absorb the sweat. Grateful, he watched Domingo stride away.

They reached the stone cabin well before twilight. Arnaud helped unload the gear from the pack mules. Food for themselves and their dogs, cauldrons for cooking, animal skins and wool blankets, a sack of kitchen utensils, a satchel of medicines for the sheep. He hurried through his tasks, unfurling sheepskins for bedding, starting a fire, fetching water from the nearby stream and setting it to boil.

As soon as he was done he rushed outside and prepared the salt for the sheep. He broke it into small pieces with a hammer and walked among the animals, placing the chunks on the flattest rocks he could find. After the sheep consumed the salt, the men herded them into pens built of willow poles and flax ropes. Once the flocks were penned for the night and the dogs had dispersed to their various stations to guard them, the men gathered inside the cabin.

Under his father's eye, Arnaud prepared the meal, a simple casserole cooked over the open fire. He tossed a hunk of lard in the iron pot, waited for it to melt, then added a handful of chopped garlic and the green tops of wild onions. After he stirred in mutton and bread chunks, his father added a generous splash of wine and settled the lid on top.

Arnaud pulled off his boots and examined his feet in the flickering firelight. There were some red spots but no broken skin, he noted with satisfaction. He turned the boots over and dumped the grass out. As he half-listened to the men talk, he threw bits of grass into the fire, watching it flare brightly and vanish into darkness. The men were discussing the troubles that had broken out in a neighboring valley last summer.

"It's in the code, Pedro," his father said. "Ranchers from Jaca and Zaragoza have the right to graze their animals in the mountain pastures. And the mountain people have the right to graze their sheep in the lowlands come winter. That's the way it's always been. My father went to the house of the sheep breeders in Jaca. He saw the parchment and the seal."

Pedro, who had a reputation as the most temperamental of the shepherds, scowled.

"I know that as well as you, Jorge. But those rich bastards from the lowlands don't respect the mountain peoples' ways. That's why the problems start."

"Agreed. But I don't agree with murder as a solution."

"What would you do if your best pastures were mobbed with a stranger's sheep? If he put sick animals in with your healthy ones? If he insulted your wife, your family—day after day? If he stole your animals from under your nose?" Pedro's voice shook with anger. "My cousin was right to do what he did. They should have treated him with respect all along."

Jorge sighed. "And now he's stuck hiding in a cave. How will that help his family?"

Pedro glowered, staring at the beaten earth floor in silence.

"We should just be thankful our wintering agreement's with the Abbey of Belarac," said Jorge. "Things would be much worse for us if we had to grapple each winter with the sheep breeders of the plains. Each year they force the mountain shepherds farther south." He picked up a long stick and looped it through the handle of the cauldron's lid, lifting it slightly to inspect the casserole. "Not quite done."

"What's good about being shackled to Belarac?" Pedro said. "We're tied to the rise and fall of its fortunes, and by all accounts, its fortunes have been falling for generations."

"Things are better now—even you have to admit that." Jorge's voice tightened with irritation. "Too many of our villagers follow the herds south in search of work, drifting here and there, getting caught up in the whims of nobles or slaughtered in some roadside skirmish. But look at your brother. He lives in Belarac now—he's got a home, a family, he works the land and minds the sheep in winter."

"At the cost of his freedom. The Abbey is my brother's master now. I don't call that good fortune—that's little better than the life of an Oto serf."

There was a short, uncomfortable silence. Then Arnaud flipped the lid off the casserole.

"Supper's ready!" he announced, grabbing a large wooden spoon that he had made from an alder branch.

Old Domingo spoke up when Arnaud was ladling a portion into Pedro's bowl.

"Give him a double, son. Might help brighten that dark mood he's in. And plenty of those green tops." He pointed at the wild onions. "Sometimes a bit of roughage does wonders for blockages. Could be what's ailing him." Could be what's ailing him."

Everyone but Pedro laughed.

12

Autumn, 1493
Abbey of Belarac, Béarn
Mira

MIRA STOOD AT THE gates, one hand shading her eyes against the bright sun. She loved the golden light this time of year, the trees crowned with red leaves that flew like flocks of papery birds in the autumn winds. The clatter of bells assailed her ears, marking the descent of shepherds and their flocks from the pine forests into the valley.

"Mira, come here."

Mother Béatrice was standing on the other side of the courtyard, waving at her. Mira sighed. She pretended not to hear. There were four dogs and five shepherds, or were there six? She squinted. Yes, there were six—but one of the shepherds was smaller than the rest.

"Mira," came the voice again, sharper this time.

She turned and ran over the cobblestones.

"Why did you not obey me the first time I called to you?"

Mira bowed her head. "Forgive me, Mother Abbess."

"It is your safety at risk when you disobey. You know the punishment. Go fetch the bucket and the bristle brush from the kitchens. No—wait. You must practice your lettering. Three pages of calligraphy in the library. First letters, then psalms. Bring them to me when you finish."

Mira retreated into the heart of the abbey, the sound of the jangling bells fading away. She hated sitting in the wavering candlelight of the library on a hard wooden bench, hunched over a book with cramps in her hand and a stiff back, listening to moths bat against the parchment that covered the high windows. If only she, too, had wings. She would smash her way out of this place and fly all the way to the sea, to the place where the rivers met the end of the earth. Where terrible sea creatures swallowed up fishes and birds and spat them out again, and the sea-foam piled up on the sand like billows of meringue.

The next day, Mira clambered over the ladder to play with the village children, but they were all on the hillside, gathered by the stone cabins where the shepherds slept all winter. She climbed the short trail to join them. In their midst, a boy was whittling. In one hand he held a piece of birch wood. With his other hand he used a small knife to deftly peel thin shavings of the wood off the stick. Pale strips of wood curled in clumps at his bare feet.

"Why do you do that?" Mira asked.

She squatted down next to him, her back to the sun. A dog sleeping nearby opened one eye to look at her, then closed it again.

The boy glanced up. His skin was nearly as dark as his brown homespun leggings, and his curly black hair was held back by a leather thong.

"Oh!" she said, recognizing him. "You are the boy from the mountain meeting. Arnaud."

He nodded.

"Are you a shepherd now?"

He nodded again.

"What are you making?"

"Don't know yet."

Mira watched the blade of his knife flash in the sunlight as he peeled off layer after layer of the wood. "Might I try?"

He rocked back on his heels. "You've handled a blade?"

"Of course." She almost bragged about her dagger, but thought better of it. "Elena taught me to skin a rabbit."

"Did she? Well, then." He handed her the stick and the knife.

The handle was still warm from his hand. She pushed the blade lightly over the stick where his whittling had exposed the raw wood under the bark. Nothing happened. She looked up.

"Push the blade harder against the wood." He picked up a piece of straw and stuck it between his teeth.

She pushed again, with force. The blade caught in the wood. She jerked it free but lost her grip on it, watching with dismay as it slipped from her grasp and clattered against a rock.

"It looks easy when you do it."

Arnaud chewed on the straw. "Practice a bit each day. That's the best way."

She picked up the blade and scraped it down the wood again.

"Arnaud!" His father's voice floated over the stubble field.

Arnaud jumped up. He held out his hand for the knife. She thrust it out with the blade pointed at him. "Always point the blade down," he said, slipping it into the tooled leather pouch he wore at his waist.

"Can I come with you?"

Arnaud shrugged and bounded across the field toward his father. She followed at a trot, watching a hawk circling high over the valley. When they reached Jorge de Luz, a small crowd of children and shepherds had formed around him. Next to him on the grass lay a sheep bleeding from a deep gash on its shoulder.

"What happened?" Mira asked.

No one answered. Arnaud retrieved a pouch from the ground near his father and pulled out a pair of shears. Two shepherds moved in and took hold of the sheep to keep it still. After Jorge carefully snipped all the wool from the area surrounding the wound, another shepherd aimed a stream of wine at it from the spout of a leather sack. Wine and blood splattered onto the grass.

Reaching into the pouch again, Arnaud pulled out a curved needle made of bone and a length of flax twine. He threaded the twine through the eye of the needle and offered it to his father. With quick movements, Jorge sewed the gaping wound shut and tied off the twine. From a small ceramic pot he extracted a chunk of greasy ointment, which he smeared over the stitches. The sheep struggled to its feet and wandered off.

"Follow that one," Jorge told Arnaud. "Don't let it out of your sight, and pen it apart from the others tonight."

"Excuse me," Mira dared to say. "But what is in that pot?"

He wiped his needle on his leggings and squinted at her in the bright sunlight.

"Leaves of the butterwort," he said. "Keeps the rot from coming."

A few days later, Mira walked to the sheep enclosures, looking for Arnaud. Four golden dogs lay panting in the shade on the north side of the woven willow pens where the flocks were corralled at night. Arnaud was in the storehouse, his arms crossed, staring impassively at the tall stacks of hay that lined the walls. She poked her head inside the door.

"Is the wounded sheep dead?"

"Of course not. He's right as rain."

"What are you doing?"

"Counting sheaves of hay."

"Can I help?"

He nodded. "Let's see if we get the same number. A stack has five sheaves."

Mira began to count stacks on her fingers, whispering out loud. "One, two, three, four, five…"

Before she got to ten, Arnaud said, "Sixty."

"How did you count them so quickly?"

"Easy—count in groups," he said. "Twelve stacks of hay, five sheaves in a stack. Twelve fives is sixty."

She tipped her head to one side, frowning.

"I count by five like this," he explained, holding up a thumb. "Five." He kept the thumb in the air and added his index finger. "Ten." Then his middle finger shot up. "Fifteen." When all ten fingers were in the air, he said, "Fifty."

Then he dipped his head at her. She held up a finger.

"Fifty-five," they said together.

She held up another finger. "Sixty," she said in amazement. "I never thought of counting in groups like that."

"It's a trick of numbers that my grandfather learned from the Moors he used to trade wool with."

"Does it only work with fives?"

"It works with all the numbers, this trick. I'll show you, if you want."

When they tired of counting stacks of hay they climbed the ladder over the wall into the abbey. Mira led Arnaud to the dried-up well. She picked up a slender piece of charcoal from a pile and quickly sketched an animal on the well's cool marble step.

"A sheep," he said, his voice tinged with admiration.

She wiped away the sheep and sketched a wolf.

"What's the trick to it?"

"I think at the beginning, the best thing is to copy other drawings," she said, holding out a piece of charcoal. "Try drawing this wolf just as I've done it."

Arnaud knelt down, holding the charcoal awkwardly in his hand. He stared at her drawing for a moment, then drew a few shaky lines. After working for a time he leaned back on his heels, comparing the two drawings.

"Mine's nothing like a wolf," he finally said. "More a pig, to my eye."

"The important thing is to practice, just as you told me." She looked at the charcoal dust on her hands and felt self-conscious.

He wiped the stone clean with his hand and sketched again. Standing back to inspect his work, he puffed his cheeks full of air and let it out in a rush.

"Again a pig."

"Perhaps I should draw a pig and you can begin by copying that, since your charcoal wants to draw one anyway," Mira said, wiping the marble clean again.

"And if I draw a wolf instead?"

"Then we'll be pleased to know you can draw something other than a pig."

Arnaud laughed.

They lay on their bellies at the edge of the stream, sucking up mouthfuls of water as it rushed by.

"Ah." Mira sat up and wiped her mouth on her sleeve.

"Good," Arnaud said, "but not as good as the water in Ronzal."

They walked together along the banks of the stream to the shearing and washing buildings. A squat stone room, where the fleeces were stored before transport, extended from one of the structures. Come springtime, tall stacks of fleeces were organized here within wood-framed stalls. Each stall had a wooden plaque affixed to it that was stamped with a mark.

"There's your Ronzal mark, the three-pointed peak with stars above," she said. "And the mark of our patron." She pointed at a coat of arms that displayed two ships, two sheep and two castles.

He nodded. "The house of Oto."

She inspected it, running a finger over the image. "From Aragón, like you."

He did not answer.

"Do you ever see them, the baron and baroness?"

"No, I've never seen them, and I don't wish to."

"Why not?"

"The Otos are feared in the mountains. People say they'd rather meet a bear in the woods than one of those lot."

"How can that be? The nobles protect the commoners."

He shook his head. "Nobles can't be trusted. Cruel one day and kind the next, as it suits them."

"Well, I like your mark the best."

"I used to wish ours was different," he said. "Stars were dull, I thought."

"What changed your mind?"

"Stars are a map in the sky. There's a power to that."

"A map?"

"The shepherds follow stars when they herd flocks. And a trail of stars shows the way to Compostela."

"Where the saint's bones lie."

He nodded. "Where the earth meets the sea."

Mira's fingers found the scallop shell at her neck. "A trail of stars. That makes things easier."

He gave her a questioning look.

"For the pilgrims, I mean to say," she added.

That night Mira slipped out of her bed, crossed to the small window and unlatched the shutter. The cool night air flooded in, bringing with it the pulse of a cricket chirping outside. Staring up, she searched the heavens for a map. At first she could discern no patterns at all. The sky was just a vast expanse of black freckled with glowing pinholes. Then she noticed a long swath that looked as if it had been dusted with flour. Layered over this glowing backdrop, she saw, was a string of bright stars that carved a luminous trail from north to south.

She smiled, hugging her arms to her chest. Arnaud had been right. When the day came for her to leave this place, she would only have to look up to chart her route to the sea.

A few mornings later, the sun was hot on her face as Mira climbed the ladder up the stone wall. Her eyes roamed over the valley, the fields of ragged stubble, the sheep enclosures, the hills rising up toward the mountains to the south. A wave of wildness rose in her chest. She ran to the apple orchard and climbed a tree, then crawled out on a thick limb and picked an apple that was half-hidden by leaves.

"Ugh." She took aim at the nearest tree and threw the apple as hard as she could. With a satisfying plonk, it smashed against the trunk.

"Mira?" a voice asked from somewhere below.

She peered through the branches to see Arnaud standing barefoot in the grass, shading his eyes.

"Worms," she explained.

Arnaud leapt into a tree and shimmied along a branch that still held several apples. Mira held her breath. The branch bent dangerously as he reached out to pluck one. Whistling, he released his grip and dropped gracefully to the ground.

Mira climbed down from the tree. "Does nothing frighten you?"

"Not climbing."

She looked up at the peaks in the distance. "Do you climb those?"

"Of course." He pointed at the jagged outline of a limestone cliff. "We chase our sheep when they get stuck on rocks like those."

Mira stared at the cliffs. "Teach me to climb as you do."

"Ha. You up there—now that frightens me." He handed her the apple.

Examining its red-gold skin closely, she took a bite. "Crisp," she said, chewing. She offered it to him. He accepted it and bit off a hunk.

"I could begin on something small. A safe rock."

"As you like."

They walked to the edge of the valley where the grass gave way to forest and descended to a dry streambed that was strewn with boulders. He selected one that was about their height, placed a foot in a minuscule crack and leaped to the top.

He looked down at Mira. "Now you."

"But where did you put your foot?"

"Feel for cracks and ledges with your toes."

The stone was cool under her fingertips. She found a good-sized crack at knee height and wedged her foot in it. Then she pushed off with her other foot. Clinging like an insect to the face of the rock, she scrabbled with her arms, finally losing balance and falling backward to the earth. She looked up at Arnaud framed against the blue sky, waiting for him to laugh. But he did not.

"Think ahead," he said. "Before you take even one step, plan your route."

She stood up and scrutinized the rock for notches and ledges. Inserting one foot in the low crack again, she sprang up and placed the other foot on a narrow ledge. With all her strength, she heaved herself to the top and collapsed, gasping, on the sun-warmed stone. Arnaud lay on his back, his head resting on his clasped hands.

"Do you miss Ronzal when you're here?" she asked, settling beside him.

"A bit."

They watched an enormous brown bird with long, tapered wings circle overhead. Above it coasted a hawk, screeching a warning. The brown bird tilted its wings and rode a current over the cliffs.

"You'll get better at it," he said. "Climbing. It takes practice, like everything else. In a few years, people'll think you're a mountain goat."

"No," she said glumly. "When I turn twelve I will no longer be allowed outside the abbey walls."

He sat up. "Why?"

"Mother Béatrice says I must practice to be a nun." Her expression brightened. "But Elena says I will be able to leave the abbey when I am older."

"How does Elena know that?" Arnaud stared down at her.

"She says it every time she comes to Belarac, though Mother Béatrice does not like to hear it. They quarrel sometimes."

"Mother Béatrice wants you to be a nun and Elena doesn't. What do *you* want, then?"

"This is a secret, so swear not to tell."

"I swear."

"I wish to leave this place and travel to the sea."

"And do what?"

"I do not know." She looked away, feeling a twinge of embarrassment.

"I'd like to see the sea, too," he said seriously. "Ships and waves, whales and dolphins."

"And fish shaped like stars, and mermaid's hair," she said, more confident now. "Long green ribbons of it tangled in the sand."

"And storms." He lay back again. "Storms that twist up from the waves all the way to the sky and back again."

"Brother Arros says there are monsters in the sea." She slipped her hand into his. "Monsters that glide through the depths with beaks and fins and wings, and teeth sharper than a dragon's."

"We'll capture one and keep it for a pet," he said. "Put a rope round its neck, train it."

Mira laughed. "Like you do with your dogs. Fancy a monster like that guarding your flocks. No wolf would ever dare attack."

He turned his head to face her, one eye squeezed shut against the glare of the sun. She tried to memorize the kindness in his face, the broad smile, the warmth in his gaze. The feel of his callused palm against hers.

An ache of happiness took hold of her bones. Even her skin tingled with delight.

Somehow, in these last fleeting months of childhood, she had made a friend.

13

Winter, 2014
Amsterdam, Holland
Zari

WHEELING HER LUGGAGE OFF the plane in Amsterdam, Zari followed the signs down the brightly-lit, sleek airport corridors to the train station. Within half an hour she was at her hotel. Checking in, she apologized to the receptionist for not speaking Dutch.

"Why?" said the woman, looking somewhat annoyed. "No one speaks Dutch."

At a loss for a fitting response, Zari retrieved her keycard and escaped to her small room on the third floor, which looked like it had been entirely furnished by IKEA. Everything in it was either white or gray, except for the puffy orange duvet cover on the bed.

After a restless night, she got up early and wandered the streets of Amsterdam, striding quickly to stay warm. She explored canals and crossed bridges, gazing at the houseboats moored in the water below. The buildings that lined the streets were tall and narrow, their stark brick facades softened by ornate white-painted trim work carved into decorative patterns. When she could no longer feel her toes, she took refuge in a café, ordering a latte and *uitsmijter*, a pair of sunny-side up eggs draped over a slice of white bread and a layer of cheese.

Feeling fully revived and warmed through, Zari decided to walk to the Rijksmuseum rather than take a train. By the time she got there, her face felt like a frozen mask. After checking her coat, she went to the restroom and held her hands under a stream of hot water until they tingled. Finally, she felt warm enough to roam around the museum.

Rembrandt's *Night Watch* and masterpieces by Bruegel and Vermeer were on her list, but she first made a beeline for Cornelia van der Zee's painting of a Flanders paper merchant. Tucked away in a small room of work by lesser-known Dutch and Flemish artists of the fifteenth and sixteenth centuries, the unsigned portrait was about the same size as the painting of Saskia Hootje that hung in the National Gallery in London. The merchant wore a fur hat and long black robes with red sleeves. He sat at a desk, a quill in one hand. The desk was scattered with sealing wax, scales, piles of coins and yellowish sheets of paper.

Zari had corresponded in advance with a curator at the museum who e-mailed her a description of the painting and its provenance. She pulled it up on her mobile and ran through the details once more. Her eye was drawn to a particular sentence: *The back of the panel is stamped with the city seal of Bruges.* She tapped out a reminder to ask Mrs. Gordon-Fitzhughes in Scotland whether her Van der Zee painting had a stamp on the back, and to ask John Drake the same question about the Fontbroke College portrait. To her immense relief, the benefactor funding its restoration had agreed to foot the bill for the treatment phase of the painting, and John Drake had promised Zari a report on his findings later today.

She had asked the museum curator in her e-mail why unsigned paintings that exhibited markedly different characteristics were still attributed to the same artist. Artists' styles evolved over time and sometimes in response to patrons' desires, the curator replied. They were humans, after all, not machines. Why shouldn't there be variation in their work?

The merchant gazed vacantly ahead with placid, bovine eyes. Zari moved as close as she dared to the panel, standing on tiptoe, and took several photos. Keeping the camera trained on the portrait, she slowly backed away, sweeping first to the right, then the left, taking pictures from every angle. Eventually a museum guard took notice and lurked nearby, staring. Zari pocketed her mobile and spent the rest of the afternoon exploring the other galleries.

When museum fatigue set in, Zari retrieved her coat and bundled up for reentry into the harsh winter air, the curator's words on her mind once again. Did artistic license exist in the sixteenth century? In the seventeenth? She knew that Rembrandt's style had undergone a significant shift after he painted *Night Watch*, exhibiting looser brushwork and creative experimentation with light. That was the only example from the era she could recall.

The differences between the Fontbroke College portrait and this one of the paper merchant were subtle. It was possible that Cornelia van der Zee experimented with different styles. But why would an artist inject life into one subject's eyes and not into another's? She might have simply followed orders from the commissioning patron, Zari decided. But that didn't make sense in this instance, because who would say, "My eyes look too full of life. Give me dead fish eyes, damn it!"

That afternoon she sat in an Internet café, sipping red wine and instant messaging with John Drake.

—*What's Amsterdam like at Christmas?* he wrote.

—*Cold and sparkly. Lots of holiday lights. It's beautiful. What are you doing for the holiday?*

—*I'll be in Cornwall,* came the cryptic reply. Before Zari could probe for details, he got down to business.

—*Do you have any idea what kind of wood panels Cornelia van der Zee typically used?*

—*Hold on.* Zari scrolled through her notes. *All I can come up with is that five of them are on Baltic oak.*

—*That's typical for her lifetime,* came the response. *In the sixteenth century the northern Europeans had stripped their own oak forests bare, so they imported wood from Poland and other points east. The Fontbroke College portrait is oak and dates from about 1500, but it's not Baltic oak. It's from the Pyrenees.*

Zari shifted in her seat, reading his words again.

—*Cornelia van der Zee did travel to France a few times,* she typed. *Maybe that's why.*

While John composed his response, Zari took a long pause to stare out the window and sip wine. All of Amsterdam was preparing for Christmas. It was odd to see the swirl and bustle of holiday preparations and feel so removed from them. But instead of being sad that she was all alone in a foreign city over the holidays, she felt exhilarated. The blinking cursor moved and a torrent of words filled her computer screen.

—*On to the paint analysis. The black background paint dates from the eighteenth century. Other areas of the portrait were layered with newer paint as well. The key findings are related to the background and her clothing and jewelry. The subject appears to be standing in front of a window or balcony of some kind. There are snow-covered mountains in the distance, and cliffs with some kind of horned animal climbing on them.*

—*You mean a mythological animal?* Zari typed.

—*No. It could be a deer or a mountain goat.*

Zari watched the blinking cursor, waiting for John's next message to appear.

—*Whoever painted over the landscape got carried away and eliminated many other details of the original painting. The woman's sleeves were originally slashed so that the white blouse showed through, and the blouse had black geometric patterns on it. The dress looks brownish-black now, but it was in fact originally a deep scarlet. She also wore a pair of gold and emerald earrings, a gold ring, and a gold chain with a white pendant in the shape of a shell.*

—*So one rabbit hole leads to the next,* Zari typed, her heart sinking.

—*Exactly.*

—*One more question, John. On the back of the panel is there any mark or stamp? The painting I saw today at the Rijksmuseum has a stamp on the back, the city seal of Bruges.*

—*Yes. There were layers of paint on the back of the panel, which we removed at our usual snail's pace. Underneath is a stamp, but it's not the city seal of Bruges. I'll send you photos.*

After exchanging holiday pleasantries, they signed off.

Zari watched Dutch people hurry by outside burdened with shopping bags, dressed in heavy wool coats and long down jackets. She had read an article on the plane about a French journalist who gave up her hectic life in Paris, moved to a loft in Amsterdam and spent her days writing novels. She imagined herself slipping into a life in Amsterdam, pedaling a sturdy black bicycle through the narrow streets, its basket overflowing with whole grain bread, fruit, gouda cheese, and tulips. She would wear artisan-crafted wool sweaters and hand-cobbled leather boots. Instead of being a novelist, though, she would be a painter. Canvases and panels would line the walls of her high-ceilinged studio overlooking a charming canal. She would wake at dawn, fix herself a flat white, and sip it while watching the sun rise over the brick facades of the tall houses across the canal. Then, invigorated and inspired, she would prepare her paints and brushes, and begin another day of frenzied creativity.

She finished her wine, paid, and set off into the cold night air.

Her breath spooled out ahead of her in white puffs as she strode along the crowded sidewalk. She threaded her way through the busy streets to the Singel, a canal lined with barges that housed Amsterdam's historic flower market. Blue and white holiday lights were strung overhead and on the bare branches of the street trees. Because it was December, the market bristled with Christmas trees of all sizes. She imagined she was that artist, on her way back to her loft to sleep in an ultramodern bed under a skylight, already planning the composition of the next day's painting. Every so often she crossed a canal, pausing on the high arch of each bridge to admire the reflection of holiday lights in the shifting waters, watching the cyclists who pedaled with swift confidence down the dark, narrow streets.

Would she ever make the leap from drawing to painting? Sketching a landscape or a person's gesture with a stick of vine charcoal had always been satisfying, but she disliked representational drawing that was so accurate it could pass for a photograph. If she were to take up painting, it would have to be abstract. She would paint the same way she drew with charcoal: to capture a moment, a feeling, an expression.

She came to a wider street and waited while a tram rolled along from the right. Checking to make sure no cars were coming, she waited until the tram rumbled by, then hurried across the street. As she took a step up onto the sidewalk, something slammed into her and knocked her to the pavement. The thread of the story she had been weaving for herself snapped. She could see it pulling away from her like the string of a helium balloon, floating up into the night sky and skittering among the stars.

14

Winter, 2014
Amsterdam, Holland
Zari

ZARI LAY THERE FOR a moment, collecting herself, making a mental inventory of all her working parts. Her right hand throbbed. She became aware of a male voice speaking Dutch and noted with vague surprise how similar Dutch and English sounded. A gloved hand appeared in front of her face. She raised her own hand, slipped it into the gloved one, and was pulled gently to her feet.

"What happened?" she asked, her words lost under the clatter of another passing tram. "I don't speak Dutch," she added. She felt something wet on her cheek and touched her fingers to her lips, blanching at the metallic taste of blood.

"You were in the bike lane," the tall man in front of her said flatly. His English bore only a trace of an accent.

"I was? I thought this was the sidewalk."

"The bike lane is on the sidewalk."

Another tram rattled by in the opposite direction. Zari pulled off her wool beanie and gingerly ran her fingers over her skull.

"Are you OK?" he asked, peering down at her in the darkness.

"I'm checking for goose eggs."

"For what?"

"Bumps."

"Goose eggs are bumps?"

"Yeah, big ones." She gave a rueful smile, flinching when she touched a tender spot.

"You're smiling." His tone was faintly accusatory.

"People do. I've seen other people smiling here in Amsterdam so I know it's culturally appropriate."

He gathered up his bike and several packages that were scattered over the sidewalk. He looked about her age, maybe a little younger—she would guess thirty. He wore glasses. Blondish curls protruded underneath his wool cap.

He stuffed the packages into the basket on his bike.

"Are any of those fragile?" she asked.

"No. Let's walk to that street lamp so I can look at your face in the light." She followed him to the lamp and turned her wounded cheek his way. "It's not bad," he announced after a moment. "Not serious."

"Well, that's a relief. It sounds like I have nothing to worry about." Her sarcasm seemed to be lost on him.

"How about when you walk?" he said, frowning at her legs. "Does anything hurt?"

Another cyclist whizzed by, a woman this time. Her bicycle was black, she was dressed in black and there was one weak light on the handlebars. Zari watched her speed away.

"No blinkers, no reflectors, no neon. She's nearly invisible."

"People here know where the bike lane is," he said. "They stay out of it. We can't help it if tourists do stupid things."

Zari felt a flash of anger. "So first you run me down and then you insult me? Nice." She set off, sliding her hat back on her head. "See, I'm fine. I can walk. Have a good night."

"Wait. I'm sorry." He caught up to her in a few long strides, pushing his bike alongside. "I should take you to a medical clinic, just to be sure you're OK."

"I have ibuprofen back at the hotel," she said, stopping under another streetlamp.

"You could be in shock. Let me walk you there." Now he actually looked worried.

She gave him an appraising stare. He was a stranger, after all, and he looked at least fifty pounds heavier than her. In a dark alleyway, in her current state of fragility, she would be no match for him. She hesitated for another moment, then decided to trust him.

"OK."

They strolled down the narrow sidewalk. He pushed his bicycle along the side closest to the bike lane. A few straggling snowflakes floated down from the black sky. She struggled to think of something to say, to break the silence, but her brain still felt fuzzy.

"So why do you speak American-sounding English?" she finally asked. "Why not English-accented English? You're a lot closer to England than the U.S."

"I don't know. Do you speak anything but American-sounding English?"

"My Spanish is pretty good."

"Do you speak it with a Spanish or a Mexican accent?"

"Mexican, I guess. I never thought about it before. How many languages do you speak?"

"Six," he said.

"That's impressive."

"Not here."

They came to an intersection and he stuck an arm out in front of her until he decided it was safe for them to cross. She glanced at him sideways. His face, in repose, was stern.

"Now that we've broken the ice, we should probably tell each other our names," she said as they crossed the street.

"Broken the ice?"

"We've gotten over our awkward first moments."

He laughed, a deep, slow, warm chuckle. Startled, Zari looked sideways at him. His laugh didn't go with his face. She wanted to hear it again.

"Wilhemus Bandstra," he said. "Everyone calls me Wil."

"Zari Durrell. Everyone calls me Zari."

"Where are you from, Zari?"

"California. I'm a long way from home."

"How long are you in Amsterdam?"

"Three more days."

They walked in silence across a bridge. Zari looked at the gleaming water below them, spreading like a dark vein into the blackness beyond. Tethered on either side of the canal were rows of houseboats. Above them loomed the high brick facades of homes that had stood for hundreds of years, silent witnesses to the movement of people, boats, and bicycles below.

They stopped in the pool of light that spilled out on the sidewalk from the hotel lobby. Zari took a step toward the doors, then turned back to him. His eyes behind the glasses were blue. Or were they gray? It was hard to tell.

"Are you sure you'll be OK, Zari? I don't feel right leaving you here."

"I'm fine. Seriously. If I were really hurt, I would have said so. I'm sorry about the accident. No more walking in bike lanes for this tourist." She stuck out her hand, the injured one, and he took it gently in his.

"I don't want to hurt you more than I already have," he said, releasing her hand. He waited until she stepped inside the door to walk away.

The next morning, she awoke with a faint headache, a very tender and slightly tattered cheek, and a massive bruise developing on the back of her right hand. The entire right side of her body felt out of whack, probably because it had taken the brunt of the fall to the pavement. She showered, letting the hot water pound her neck and shoulders. When she got dressed to go out, she saw that the message light was glowing on the room phone. Downstairs, the desk clerk handed her an envelope. Inside was a slip of paper on which was written a mobile phone number and the words "I am across the street in the café—Wil."

She stepped out into the frigid air, the slip of paper clutched in her hand. The sun glared down at her. She squinted, searching up and down the row of narrow brick buildings for a café. In a moment Wil emerged from a doorway. He crossed the street, holding up a hand in greeting.

"Last night I wanted to invite you to Christmas dinner at my family's home," he said, "but I had to check with my grandmother first." He smiled. "She's a bit particular."

"I—oh. Really? You don't have a girlfriend? Or a wife?" Zari felt a flush rise from her chest to her neck. "Before we say anything else can I get some coffee? I'm not awake yet."

They went inside the café. He said something in rapid-fire Dutch to the woman behind the counter, and within a few minutes Zari was sipping an enormous latte at a round wooden table across from Wil. On the table sat a laptop and a black notebook.

His eyes rested on her cheek for a moment, then dropped to her hand. "That must hurt," he said. "I guess I was wrong last night—it does look bad."

"It looks worse than it feels." She tugged loose her hair, which was piled at the back of her head, and shook it forward to hide her injured cheek. "Even with my hair as a disguise, it will look worse tomorrow night. Just warning you in advance, in case you want to rethink that invitation."

He laughed. His laugh was like an unfamiliar song on the radio—something she immediately loved but didn't know the name of, and made her feel delighted and lucky every time she heard it. He held up his left hand, which bore no ring.

"I'm not married. I don't have a girlfriend anymore."

She raised an eyebrow. "Trolling around for a new one?"

That got another laugh. She savored it.

"I had a girlfriend, but we broke up."

"Was this a recent break-up?"

His face grew somber again. "Yeah."

"A long-term girlfriend?"

"Seven years."

"I'm guessing she knows your family well, then?"

"Her brother is my best friend," he admitted. "Our families are close."

"So you're inviting a battered-looking American tourist to fill the shoes of your long-term, beloved-by-all girlfriend at Christmas dinner? It's really OK, you don't have to feel guilty about running me down with your bicycle."

"I don't feel guilty. I just want to see you again."

His words hung over the table for a moment. Either the caffeine was kicking in or this man was triggering an electric current in her very core. Both possibilities were equally pleasurable, she decided, settling back in her chair and holding his gaze.

"Christmas dinner with a big Dutch family," he said. "You will have a story to tell your family in California."

Zari took another sip of her latte, watching him over the rim of her cup, stricken by an image of women in evening gowns and tuxedo-clad men sitting around a table the length of a bowling lane.

"I'd love to." She put her cup down. "But is it going to be formal?"

"Dutch people are not dressy," he assured her. "Just wear what makes you comfortable."

15

ARI STOOD AT WIL'S side in a high-ceilinged room dominated by a Christmas tree on one end and an ornately carved stone fireplace on the other. A pair of tall windows overlooked a canal. Outside, trees lined the street, their bare branches strung with tiny white lights.

Clutching a glass of champagne that was delivered by a server dressed all in black, she attempted to commit to memory the names of Wil's siblings, aunts, uncles, cousins and parents. She hoped to get away with calling all of the older adults "Mr. Bandstra" or "Mrs. Bandstra," but they all insisted she call them by their first names. Wil led her to a long sideboard and topped off her glass from a bottle of champagne that sat in a silver tub filled with ice.

With unfamiliar Dutch names coursing through her brain, she attempted to ignore the throb of her swollen cheek. She had tried to hide the worst of her bruises with concealer and bronzer but that only succeeded in making her feel clownish, since she normally wore very little makeup. As the cocktail hour wore on and the champagne infused her with bubbly goodwill, she forgot her apprehension and began to enjoy herself.

When they all trooped into the dining room for dinner, Wil steered Zari to a seat on the far side of the table. It wasn't quite as long as a bowling lane, but it was the biggest dining table she had ever encountered in a private home, made of some exotic hardwood. The woman who had served their drinks now moved between the kitchen and the dining room, placing steaming platters of food on the table and whisking away empty ones. As they ate, Wil filled Zari in on his family's history.

"We were merchants, trading in spices and then in medicinal plants," he explained, spooning up Brussels sprouts from a heavy ceramic platter. She looked at the walls, which were painted white and hung with modern art.

"So where are the portraits?" she asked.

"Portraits?"

"Yes—all the generations of Bandstra merchants. Don't tell me they didn't have their portraits painted. I just thought since this has been the family home for centuries the ancestors would be here in spirit, hanging on the walls."

He gave her a surprised look.

"I'm an art historian," she explained. "The reason I'm in Europe is to study a sixteenth-century portrait artist. You could say I'm a bit obsessed with portraits at this juncture in my life."

He smiled. "You've come to the right house, then. We have portraits going back hundreds of years. But all of that is in the library, upstairs. My parents don't focus on the past—they like modern art, contemporary design."

Zari looked down the table at his parents. They were both tall, silver-haired, dressed in clothes that looked expensive but understated. His mother's hair was curly like Wil's, and she wore long silver earrings that flashed when they caught the light. For a moment Zari imagined the two of them in somber sixteenth-century clothing, standing stiffly side by side, as an artist captured their images in oil paint on a panel of Baltic oak. She kept her gaze on them, transfixed, until Wil held out a platter of meat dressed in brown sauce.

"Rabbit?" he said. When she hesitated, he deposited a spoonful on her plate. "Come on, try something new. That's what you're here for, right?"

"So are you still spice merchants?" She took a tentative bite of the rabbit. It was sweet and tangy and tender.

"No. We got out of that business a few hundred years ago. My mother is a psychologist and my father is an engineer."

His hand grazed hers. A sudden tingle of anticipation swept through her.

"How about you?" she asked, rattled.

"I design and build furniture." He ran his fingertips over the tabletop. "I made this table."

"It's beautiful."

So were his hands, she saw. Long, elegant fingers, square palms. The kind of anatomically perfect hands that Leonardo da Vinci might have sketched. *Zari,* she chastised herself. *Focus!*

"Thank you," he said. "But my real passion used to be expeditions."

"Expeditions?"

"I spent most of the past ten years traveling the world by foot, by kayak, by sailboat, by bike. A group of friends and I would work for six months or a year, saving money, and then set off on a trip. Usually we would be gone for three months or more. We worked with museums and classrooms to share what we were seeing and experiencing with children all over the world."

"That sounds incredible."

"It was." He sipped his wine. "For a while we had sponsors who would help pay for the journeys, but the last one was a real disaster. I'm done with all of that now."

"What happened?"

He put down his glass and stared at his plate for a moment. Before he could answer, his grandmother teetered into the room on the arm of a burly male relative. A burst of animated Dutch broke out as a place was found for her and she sank down into a plush chair.

"She wasn't feeling well but I knew she would appear," Wil said, amused. "She hates to miss a party." Zari felt eyes upon her and mustered a smile. The moment of reckoning had come. Wil's grandmother looked at him and said something in Dutch. Judging from her solemn expression, Zari assumed it was not a compliment. The gathered group burst out laughing, looking at Zari and Wil.

"She said you are not Hana, but you are pretty," he translated.

"It sounded to me like she said more than that. Something much funnier."

"Well," he said, still gazing at his grandmother. "OK. She said it was typical of me to pick the prettiest tourist to run over. But she warned me that since you are American you're probably going to sue us for everything we own."

Zari slid a sideways glance at Wil's grandmother. Her blue eyes were nearly lost in the deep folds and creases that made up her face. On her mouth was a slash of red lipstick, and she had soft puffs of silvery hair through which her pink scalp was visible. She wore large gold earrings in the shape of flowers, and her simple outfit of a white cable knit sweater and a gray wool skirt was dressed up with a necklace of giant fuchsia beads. She caught Zari's eye and stared her down. Zari felt the tips of her ears burn and reminded herself that she would never see these people again.

At the end of the evening Wil walked Zari back to her hotel. Her down coat was zipped up tight, she had wrapped a long wool scarf around her neck, and her brown leather boots were insulated—but still the night air pierced her lungs with cold, and she had to press her jaws together to keep her teeth from chattering.

"I think she liked you," he said, smiling. "My grandmother."

"How could you tell? I got a lot of looks that had no smile attached."

"You talked to all of my relatives but never spoke about your injuries or the fact that I hit you with my bike. That kind of thing impresses Dutch people, especially coming from an American. And I told you what she said—she was afraid you might get your lawyers involved."

"Clearly you've all been watching too many American crime dramas. But—whatever it takes to be on your grandmother's good side. I also know how to tap dance, if that helps. And I can surf."

They stepped to the edge of the street as a group of young people who had been to one too many holiday parties stumbled past, singing and laughing.

When they started walking again, he slipped his hand around Zari's. They strolled in silence, navigating a maze of canals and passing under an endless series of blue and white holiday lights strung in garlands over the quiet streets. In front of her hotel, in the moment of hesitation before she turned away, he pulled her in for a long kiss. He smelled vaguely of eucalyptus, one of her favorite scents.

She wanted to bury her face in his neck and find the source of that intoxicating aroma but instead she heard herself say in a measured voice, "That was lovely, and I want to invite you up, but I'm not built that way."

"You mean, you don't have the equipment?" He sounded genuinely mystified.

She laughed. "I've got all my lady parts. But I don't know you well enough yet."

There was a short silence. The wind bit into her face.

"Do you?" she finally said.

"Do I have all my lady parts?"

"No." She laughed. "Do you sleep with women you've just met?"

"I'm a little out of practice meeting women. You know I just broke up with—"

"Hana. Yes, yes, I do know."

He kissed her again. This time she felt her resolve wavering. She put her hands on his chest and pushed him gently away from her.

"I am going upstairs before I break my own rule. And believe me—I want to break it."

He laughed, and she felt weak in the knees.

"When does your rule say we can have sex?" he asked.

"You Dutch are really blunt, aren't you?"

"It's kind of a national trait."

"Well, every relationship has to be judged on a case-by-case basis," Zari said.

"How about a more—what is the word—quantitative approach?"

A seriously bundled-up man walking a giant dog passed them, his head bent into the wind.

Zari hugged her arms around her chest, shivering.

"What do you mean? Like three dates and you're in?"

He considered this, tipping his head to one side. "That sounds fine."

"How about three dates and then we'll discuss it."

"Discuss it?" He looked crestfallen.

"Besides, you live here and I live in Scotland," she pointed out.

"Details."

He kissed her again, folding his arms around her. She wanted to surrender, to ignore the practical voice in her head that warned her not to jump into physical intimacy with a man she had just met. For all she knew he was a complete nutcase whose family tolerated him at gatherings just to appease him during his lucid phases. Admittedly, given what she had just experienced at the Bandstra home, the likelihood of Wil turning out to be crazy was slim to none. He was solid, yet she sensed an underlying sadness that seeped from him during moments of silence, when that somber look settled over his face like a shade being drawn down to shut out the light.

She took a step back, willing herself to move. Her toes were going numb.

"This was an extraordinary evening, Wil. Thank you."

She leaned in and kissed him one more time as the cold air swirled around them. Waiting for the elevator, she turned to look back at him through the lobby doors, but he was gone.

16

Winter, 2015
St. Andrews, Scotland
Zari

ZARI AND AGGIE SAT in a café on South Street, drinking cappuccinos. Rain spattered the sidewalks. The awning outside the plate glass window flapped dangerously with each gust of wind.

"There must be a big storm coming." Zari wrapped her hands around her cup, willing the heat trapped in the porcelain to pass through her skin and permeate her bones.

"It's dreich, that's all." Aggie sipped her cappuccino, unperturbed.

"What's dreich?"

"Winter in Scotland. Cold, damp, miserable."

"That is the perfect word for it."

"Aren't you glad I forced you to turn your room into a cozy nest?" Aggie asked. "It takes a bit of the winter blues away, having a nice space to go home to."

Zari nodded and raised her cup in a salute.

When the couple who lived in the flat beneath them moved out in January, Zari had filled her room with their castoffs—a small wooden dresser, a set of rattan baskets, a paisley-patterned red and yellow wool rug with a tea stain in one corner. The crowning glory was a framed Matisse print with a hairline crack in the glass that now hung over her bed. And last week Aggie's mother had visited and given Zari a begonia in a sunflower-yellow ceramic pot. The room was starting to feel homey, welcoming even. When the weather improved in the spring she would troll the sidewalks in search of more castoff treasures.

Aggie's voice interrupted her thoughts. "So—any news from your man John Drake?"

"My man? No. He's not."

"I'm just putting two and two together. You told me, after London, that he wore his suit well."

"Maybe too well." Zari swirled the last of her cappuccino, capturing errant bits of foam that clung to the sides of the cup.

"Is that so?" There was an amused glint in Aggie's eyes. "I didn't know a man could wear a suit too well."

Zari had not told anyone, not even Aggie, about Wil Bandstra. She explained away her bruises by concocting a tale about slipping on icy cobblestones. The entire experience had taken on a dreamlike quality. When she scrolled through the memories of her time in Amsterdam, a gentle fluttery buzz took hold of her body.

"Anyway, there's plenty of news from John," Zari went on, ignoring Aggie's comment. "The back of the portrait is stamped with three inverted V's that have the initials 'ADL' inside them. I checked with the National Gallery, and their portrait of Saskia Hootje is stamped with the seal of the city of Bruges. So is Van der Zee's portrait of the paper merchant at the Rijksmuseum."

"Do any of her other portraits have the 'ADL' stamp?"

"I've contacted every owner of a Van der Zee asking that question—at this point, the Fontbroke painting is the only one."

"So Cornelia van der Zee might not be the artist, then."

"I don't want to go there yet." Zari's fingers tightened around her cup. "It takes a long time to excavate what lies beneath the surface because each layer of the painting has to be tested for age and origin, and then a solvent is mixed up to remove that layer alone."

"Sounds complicated."

"It takes cotton swabs and a lot of patience. We're just lucky it's being done at all."

"Why?"

"This has turned out to be a really costly project. At one point, John thought Moneybags was getting cold feet—"

"Who is Moneybags?" Aggie interrupted.

"The anonymous benefactor. I think John knows, but he's not saying. Dotie Butterfield-Swinton believes it's a descendent of Cornelia van der Zee or Marie de Béart."

"Imagine throwing all that money at a restoration and then discovering your ancestor had nothing to do with it."

"That's what I worry about in the middle of the night. I try not to think about it during the day."

Aggie winced. "Sorry I mentioned it."

"Here's how you can make it up to me." Zari found an image on her mobile. "You're the textile maven of Scotland. Maybe you can tell me if there's any significance in the geometric designs on her blouse."

"Ah." Aggie tapped the screen with her fingertip, nodding. "Those interlacing lines, repeated again and again in a pattern? Classic Hispano-Moorish technique. The Iberian Peninsula— today's Spain—was strongly influenced by the Moors at that time. So I'd bet this Lady Muck was from Spain, not France."

"The Pyrenees are in Spain," Zari said slowly. A map of the mountain chain materialized in her imagination.

"You know your geography. Well done."

"I mean, the painting's wooden panel originated in the Pyrenees. That book the woman's holding, with the 'B' on it—if she's Spanish, maybe it's from a place in the Spanish part of the Pyrenees." Zari's thoughts swerved to Wil Bandstra again. That was the name beginning with 'B' that she couldn't get out of her head.

"Och—the letter 'B'. There's a juicy clue." Aggie used a spoon to scrape the foam from the bottom of her cup.

"I don't even know where to begin with that one. It could be the initial of her family's name, or the religious house where it originated. I wish I knew a scholar specializing in Renaissance-era book spines." Zari stuffed her mobile back into her bag, frowning.

"Where's that American optimism I love to mock?" Aggie feigned a look of astonishment.

"I don't know." Zari sighed. "Everything I've learned about that painting is tantalizing, but it all raises more questions than it answers. It's like unwinding a spool of thread. Just when you think you've about reached the end, you realize there's way more to unwind."

Aggie was tapping out something on her mobile.

"I'm sending you a contact," she said. "My uncle, Liam. Absolutely nutters, and obsessed with genealogy. If anyone's your man, he is."

Outside, a brutal rain began to fall.

Liam MacLean lived north of Inverness in a tiny former fishing village called Ardersier. He was retired and spent his days surfing the Internet in search of genealogical tidbits, walking his English sheepdog mix, and visiting with friends in the pub.

"It's a bit daft to think you can find anything useful when all you're going on is the letter 'B'," he spluttered when Zari phoned him, his Scottish brogue nearly unintelligible to her.

"It's like saying you're looking for a black-and-white cow in a field of black-and-white cows."

"Agreed. But it's not just any 'B'. It's either French or Spanish," she pointed out. "It could be the initial of a noble family or a religious house. The time period is the end of the fifteenth century and the beginning of the sixteenth. Our best guess is to search in the Pyrenees."

"Och, that *significantly* narrows it down," he snorted. "Do you have any idea of the complexity of the Pyrenees? Sure, now it's simply a matter of France and Spain with a convenient border running down the spine of the mountains. In those days, it was a hodgepodge of kingdoms. And politically, it was explosive!" His tone had swelled to an indignant roar.

Zari pulled the mobile a few inches away from her ear.

"On the southern side," he continued, "you had the end of the Arab Empire and the expulsion of the Jews by Isabella and Ferdinand. You had feudal warfare in Aragón and Catalonia, you had Castilla trying to swallow up Navarra and Galicia. In the north, hanging on for dear life, were the last independent holdouts in what's now France. You had Béarn, you had Comminges, you had Foix. The list goes on." He paused to take a breath, then slurped noisily from whatever beverage was fueling his fire.

"You're very knowledgeable about the history of the region," Zari said, trying to fill the silence with something encouraging. She put the mobile on the tabletop, flicked open her sketchpad and picked up a pencil.

"Aye, for good reason. Independent communities in pre-industrial Europe were the topic of my graduate dissertation. And the Pyrenees figured large in my research."

"Why?"

"That was the place where freedom reigned. Nomadic shepherds wandered those mountains, not beholden to any lord or king." He unleashed a barrage of coughing.

She waited, doodling on the sketchpad, until he got himself back under control. A vague approximation of a sheepdog began to appear beneath her pencil. When his coughing fit had passed and all she could hear was a gentle wheezing, she deemed it safe to speak again.

"How did they manage that?"

"They had a whole system of peace agreements engineered by the common people," he said. "It was done in the interest of sharing resources, of course. They all needed the grazing pastures, the water, the rights-of-way. The only way to survive was to share."

"And the nobility let them get away with that? Why?"

"Geography, mostly. Those mountains were feared. Crawling with man-eating beasts, haunted by floods and avalanches. So the high-mountain folk were left alone. There were very few people in those days who were the masters of their own destinies. But they did exist. Once you've known freedom and have it taken from you, well—you can become obsessed with the topic. We Scots know. You Yanks don't. Your day will come, though." He let loose a devilish chuckle, as if he couldn't wait for the come-uppance of America.

"Wait a minute. Our history has its share of people whose freedom was taken from them," she said, feeling defensive. "Let's not forget slavery—or smallpox-infected blankets."

"What kind of blankets, now?" he asked, baffled.

"The kind that the Yanks handed out to Native Americans in order to expedite their disappearance."

"Be that as it may," he said, his tone implying that she had taken the wind out of his sails. "But I'm guessing *you* aren't descended from any of those repressed peoples."

"True," Zari admitted.

"Now then, young lady, you are clearly unaware that French and Spanish history is bloated with 'B's. Bergerac, Burgundy,

Bellagio—or is that Italian?" The enthusiasm returned to his voice. "Nobles practically grew on trees in those days, especially in what's now called France. Trouble was, gold just slipped through their fingers. And then all they had left were their names. That's when they hit upon the idea of selling their names to the highest bidder. 'Here's 500 acres and a run-down monastery. I now pronounce you Lord Muck.' That sort of thing."

He let out an exaggerated sigh. Zari drew a kilt on the dog.

"You're asking me to get blood from a stone, do you realize that?" he finally said. "Blood from a bloody stone. I'll look into it, but only because Aggie asked me to. That's a good girl, is Aggie. Well, I'm off to walk the dog. It's the daily interruption in his twenty-three-hour regimen of sleeping. He hates me for it. Until we get on the beach and then I'll hate him. Because he'll be making a beeline to the nearest dead thing and have a good long roll in it. Getting the smell of a moldering gull out of his hair is no small task, I assure you."

With that, he rang off.

17

Winter, 2015
St. Andrews, Scotland
Zari

A T THE END OF January, Aggie went to a conference in Leeds and Zari took advantage of the time alone to map out two papers to submit to academic journals. She prepared for presentations at conferences in Germany, Luxembourg and Bruges, where she would also visit Van der Zee portraits in museums and private collections and conduct research in city archives. She was particularly hopeful about what she would find in Bruges, because Cornelia van der Zee had grown up in the city, where she was trained as a painter by her artist father. He was a wealthy citizen, so the likelihood of finding solid information in the city archives about the family was strong.

She woke early on the last day of Aggie's absence, went for a run in the rain-slicked streets, took a shower, and put her pajamas back on. Wrapping a long cardigan over herself, she sat at the rickety kitchen table with a cup of tea, a plate of buttered toast and her laptop.

Her inbox showed a new e-mail from Laurence Ceravet.

> To: zdurrell80@inep.edu
> From: lceravet@institutpyr.edu
> Dear Zari,
> Thank you for your interest in my painting by Cornelia van der Zee. I will send it to an art restoration group in Paris this spring. I do not know how long the conservation treatment will last, but I imagine the painting will be returned to me this summer. It will be my pleasure to welcome you if you wish to visit the painting then.
> Cordially,
> Laurence Ceravet
> <Attachment>

Zari clicked on the attachment. It contained a portrait of a merchant family. The middle-aged parents both had dark eyes and round faces, and were garbed in luxurious fur-trimmed sixteenth-century clothing. Seated in front of them were two adorable little girls wearing miniature replicas of their mother's red dress.

She printed it, then pinned it next to the photo of the Fontbroke College painting on her kitchen wall. Staring at the two portraits, she did some stretches and repeated her mother's chant of daily positive affirmations, a habit from childhood that was both deeply comforting and a frequent target of her own ridicule. When they were growing up, she and her brother did the chant in zany accents and sent each other into spasms of crazed laughter. They often did this in full view of their mother, who, rather than get offended, usually joined in. She could never be accused of taking herself too seriously. Also, she believed a deep belly laugh each day was necessary for optimal wellness.

Zari heated a bowl of tomato soup, sliced an apple, and unwrapped a hunk of cheddar cheese. She fired up the kettle again for another round of black tea. She had discovered a passion for Irish Breakfast and a severe aversion to Earl Grey.

She spent the afternoon happily tunneling through a wild maze of Internet research on the social and political history of the Pyrenees and poring over maps of the mountain range. When she searched for 'small horned deer Pyrenees,' the results showed the Pyrenean ibex, a horned wild goat that once roamed the mountain range but was now extinct.

The last drops of her tea were cold and a crust of bread lay hardening on her plate. Her back ached from sitting in one position too long. Before she got up, she composed an e-mail.

> To: lceravet@institutpyr.edu
> From: zdurrell80@inep.edu
> Dear Laurence,
>
> Thank you for your response. Does your painting have a stamp on the back that could help identify its origins? Some of Cornelia van der Zee's known works are stamped with the seal of Bruges. However, the Fontbroke College portrait has a stamp of three upside-down 'V's (two small ones with a larger one in the middle). Within each peak is a letter: 'A-D-L.'
>
> Will your restoration include x-ray photography and carbon dating of the panel? I attach an image of what we found under the paint on the Fontbroke College portrait. The identity of 'Mira' in the drawing is a mystery, but both the presence of her name and the words 'pray for my mother' must have some significance. The panel was made of Pyrenean oak and

dates from about 1500.

I would very much like to meet you and see your painting. Thank you for your kind invitation. If your schedule permits perhaps I can make the trip this summer before I go back to the States.

Sincerely,

Zari Durrell

<Attachment>

She leaned back in her chair, staring out the windows at the rooftop across the street, its outline barely visible in the faint glow thrown out by the lights in the flats around her. A filmy darkness descended over the city. Somehow Friday's entire allotment of daylight was nearly gone, and she had not spoken a word all day.

"Well, that's a fine how-do-you-do," she said aloud, just to break the silence.

The only sound in the kitchen was the ticking of the wall clock that hung over the doorway. It was probably time to get out of her pajamas and go out, even if it was just for a walk to the corner pub. She was eager to see Aggie again—this had been just enough time alone. Loneliness hovered at the edge of her consciousness, but it didn't have a foothold. Not yet.

Her thoughts slipped to Wil Bandstra. They had been texting regularly since Christmas. She had invited him to join her in Bruges, and he had accepted. It was still weeks away, though— and part of her feared it would be an awkward reunion. Maybe the intimacy that their accident had spawned in Amsterdam would be impossible to recreate. Maybe they would have nothing to say to each other.

She forced herself to shut down that line of useless drivel and was about to get up when her inbox chimed again.

To: zdurrell80@inep.edu
From:lceravet@institutpyr.edu
Dear Zari,

Our paintings do have something in common. Mine also has the stamp on the back with the three peaks and the letters 'A-D-L.' A furniture maker named Arnaud de Luz who lived in Bayonne during the sixteenth century put this stamp on his work.

The painting will be examined using all the techniques that are available at the conservation laboratory in Paris. The treatment may include x-rays and dendrochronology, but we are not yet certain of all the details.

Cordially,
Laurence Ceravet

Zari opened her browser history and clicked on the link to a map of the Pyrenees again. She zoomed in on the southwestern section of France. The city of Bayonne was located close to the border with Spain, probably about an hour's drive from Pau. Propping her chin on her hands, she traced the undulating line of the French coast with her eyes.

As things stood now, the 'ADL' stamp pushed a deeper wedge between Cornelia van der Zee and the Fontbroke portrait. But it was possible that the artist had traveled more extensively throughout France than anyone knew. If Zari could just connect her with the Pyrenees or Bayonne, the stamp would make sense.

Her gaze returned to the windows. The strident whine of an emergency vehicle rose and fell, fading with the light until there was nothing to see or hear but her own reflection and the hollow tick of the clock.

18

Winter, 2015
St. Andrews, Scotland
Zari

EVERY SUNDAY SHE WAS in town, Zari had a video call date with her mother. Tonight was a particularly nasty winter evening in St. Andrews. A bitter wind slapped freezing rain on the windows of the flat, the muffled clatter interspersed with haunting silence. She pulled her gray fleece blanket tighter around her shoulders and sank back on the saggy beige couch, her laptop balanced on her knees. A glass of red wine sat on the squat coffee table next to her.

"Did you get my care package?" her mother asked.

The connection wasn't great, so her mother's face would sporadically freeze while her voice continued to talk. Portia was curled up on an upholstered armchair with a knitted afghan over her legs and a cup of steaming tea in her hands. Sun streamed in through the double-hung window next to her.

She lived in a tiny cottage on the grounds of a Victorian mansion in Sausalito, just north of San Francisco. One side of it was a porch that had been fitted with windows at some point. A curtain and a folding screen served as the barrier between the bed and the rest of the space. The mansion's owner was only in residence a few months each year. In exchange for serving as the property's caretaker, Portia lived in the cottage rent-free.

"Yes. I love it. Thank you."

Zari glanced at the small cracked ceramic vase she had found hunting for treasures with Aggie one day. In it she had arranged the eucalyptus and bay leaves her mother had sent. Next to her bed sat a green beaded velvet bag filled with bell-shaped eucalyptus seed pods. The scent took her back to California as she drifted off to sleep. And, she had to admit, to lustful thoughts of Wil Bandstra.

Portia beamed. Her torrent of silver-streaked black hair was gathered in a messy bun on the back of her head. As usual, she had not a trace of makeup on.

"I'm going to the beach later. I'll collect other things that remind you of home for your next package. Birds, maybe. I know how much you love those sandpipers."

"My neighbors would adore that," Zari said, laughing. "Maybe have them stuffed first."

"I would send you more jewelry, but I'm low on inventory."

"How is that possible? You're the bead queen."

"I've entered the world of online retailing," explained Portia. "I had an overabundance of beads in my life. I just decided to send them back out into the universe. Who knew so many people would like my stuff?"

Her mother held up a necklace. It was a long silver chain hung with a cluster of white crystals in various sizes, each wrapped in bands of thin silver wire.

"A few of the women I housesit for started wearing my stuff and one of them blogged about it. She's got one of those mommy blogs that's sort of a combination of advice column and fashion commentary. Then I sold some work in that bead shop in town, Gus set me up online, and—I'll just say it, honey—the universe was ready to receive what I'm giving. Now I've got beading workshops lined up in three stores. Which is no coincidence. Because—"

Zari said the words along with her. "There are no coincidences."

Portia beamed. "You know what I'm about to say, don't you?"

"Do what you love and the money will follow."

"That's right. It really works, because—brace yourself—I made $2,000 last month."

"Get out of town!"

"Yep," Portia said. "I'm more excited about the workshops, though, because I like teaching. My working title is 'The Zen of Beading.' There are a lot of people who swear by knitting for mindfulness practice. Well, beading has the same benefits as knitting, and more power because of the energetic properties of the crystal beads. I think my second series will be called 'Letting the Heart Speak: Beading is Healing.'"

"You know what this means?" Zari said. "You might be able to cut back on the pet-sitting. Starting with that coddled little pain in the ass Taffy."

"Done," said her mother. "I quit last week."

"Yes!" Zari raised her wine glass and Portia saluted her with the mug of tea.

In other news, her nephew Jasper had lost both his front teeth and was tormenting his sister Eva at every turn by squirting streams of water at her through the gap in his mouth. Eva, meanwhile, had received a head-to-toe fairy makeover on Christmas morning and had refused to take off her wings or her fairy princess crown since then. Every time Zari's brother Gus brought up the idea of a bath, she ran away from him screaming "Nooooo! My wings!"

Through her laughter, Zari felt a stab of homesickness.

"How are Gus and Jenny?" she asked.

"Jenny's traveling even more than usual. And when she's in town, she's gone twelve hours a day at least. The kids miss her, but Gus has it all handled on the home front. He's training again. The hamstring is better."

"Maybe he should substitute the elliptical machine for running a few times a week so he doesn't injure it again." Zari sipped her wine. "I'll tell him that."

"Zari, relax. His injury healed."

"I know, but everything hinges on exercise now. He traded one addiction for another."

"And it's been what, nine years now? Those days are behind him."

"I want to believe that."

"Then believe it, Zari. You know how grounded he is now."

Zari got up and pivoted the laptop with the camera facing out so her mother could see the flat. She walked down the dark hallway to her room.

"Oh, my word!" Portia's horrified voice floated up from the speaker. "Your place desperately needs some feng shui. What is that on the wall?"

"Decor." Zari trained the laptop camera on a purple and white fringed rectangle of cloth that covered part of a plaster wall, and then on her begonia, its leaves straining toward the weak winter light coming from the west-facing window. "To be honest, I think way more about Cornelia van der Zee than about decorating."

"That reminds me, honey," Portia said. "I was looking at the photo you sent of the painting. The gold belt the woman is wearing, with the big pendant? I wonder if the circle and the cross could have another meaning."

"Such as?" Zari padded to the kitchen doorway.

"Could they be letters? O is a circle, and T is a cross. Just another way to look at it."

"O-T. Someone's initials, maybe?"

"Maybe. But it could be interpreted as O-T-O, as well. Because there's that little circle under the cross too. That could also be an 'O.'"

"O-T-O." Zari glanced at the images of the paintings thumbtacked to the wall. From here, the woman's gold belt was barely visible. "I never would have thought of that, Mom."

Portia smiled and her face froze on the screen again. For a moment Zari wished she were there, getting ready to drive over the mountain to Stinson Beach in her mother's rattling truck for a day of wandering the beach, scanning the waves for harbor seals and watching sandpipers race over the sand on their matchstick legs.

"How's your love life?" her mother asked. "Any hot Scottish men sweeping you off your feet?" Instantly, Zari's mind flashed to Wil Bandstra.

"Nothing to report in that area," she said. "What about you? I'm sure you'll have a fresh crop of emotionally available men nipping at your heels once those bead workshops get going."

"Emotional availability is overrated. I'm kind of exclusive these days with Obsidian. I'm not looking for anyone new."

"Is it serious?"

"As serious as it gets with a guy ten years younger than me."

"*Mom*."

"What? Men can be with younger women. Why not the other way around?"

"Just don't date anyone younger than me, OK?"

"I won't make a promise about something that's never going to happen."

"Fine. One last thing—do you need help with paperwork for the beading business? Taxes and all that boring stuff?"

"Gus has it covered. He's filling in for you as my paperwork guru. I don't know how he finds the time, between dad duties and training for an Ironman. But you know how he is. Always has to stay busy."

They said their goodbyes and Zari watched the image of her mother's face disappear from the screen. The fact that Portia had a new, promising source of income slowly sank in, as did the realization that for the time being, she was truly exempt from overseeing her mother's scattered approach to details like insurance payments and tax statements. She sank down on the couch, freed from a weight she hadn't even known was there, and let out an exultant whoop.

19

Spring, 2015
Bruges, Belgium
Zari

ZARI THOUGHT SHE WAS accustomed to historic sights after living in Scotland for months, but nothing could have prepared her for Bruges. She felt like an extra walking around on the movie set of some medieval epic. The city was perfectly preserved, an architectural jewel, though the illusion was marred by the presence of thousands of modern humans wearing skinny jeans and puffy down jackets, with mobile phones pressed to their ears.

The rental apartment Wil had recommended was situated close to the city center in a restored building that looked ancient on the outside and was full of brightly lit contemporary spaces inside. Zari's little studio on the top floor had two skylights through which she could see the spires of the church on the main square, whose bells were pealing thunderously. In one corner was a tiny, well-outfitted kitchen with all-white cabinetry and concrete countertops, and in the other, a bathroom with a heated tile floor and a deep tub.

Before allowing herself a soak in the tub, she set up her laptop and placed a video call to Aggie's uncle Liam MacLean. He had just gotten back from his afternoon walk on the beach with his dog.

"Immediate gratification you're wanting, is it? Do you know how many 'B's I've come up with?" he huffed, still winded. "Boggles the mind, it does. Boggles the mind. Now I'll send what I've found to you, lassie, but just be prepared. I hope you have loads of time on your hands."

"In a few weeks I'll be Aggie's sidekick on a trip to York. I'll have plenty of time to look over what you've found."

"Oh, bless her heart, she's giving that talk about medieval embroidery. She practiced with me over the Christmas holiday. Tell her to keep it slow and steady, will you? She talks a silver streak when she's nervous."

"I will. Mr. MacLean, I wonder if you wouldn't mind looking into another mystery. It's an actual name this time, not just a letter. O-T-O."

"How's that, now? Do you think I exist to serve you, Miss Zari Durrell? I'm a busy man."

"I'm so sorry, Mr. MacLean. I can't thank you enough for all you've done. It just seems that O-T-O, Oto, could be a name. I didn't understand that until recently."

"Very interesting indeed, but I'm afraid you've used up your favor—Aggie's favor—with the 'B's. Too bad it hadn't been 'Q's or 'Y's in the first place. Then I might have conserved some energy for a fresh lot of looking. But 'B's! Ridiculous."

The line went dead. Zari stared at the mobile in her hand for a moment, shaking her head. Flipping open her laptop, she scrolled through her e-mails, convulsing with the occasional spasm of laughter at the recollection of Liam MacLean's wee fit of rage. A new e-mail from Laurence Ceravet caught her eye. She clicked on it.

> To: zdurrell80@inep.edu
> From: lceravet@institutpyr.edu
> Dear Zari,
> Just today I received a report from the laboratory in Paris. The panel of my painting is oak and it comes from the Pyrenees, and is dated to about 1500. This is not a surprise, because we know that Arnaud de Luz, who made the panel, lived in Bayonne at that time.
> I attach a photograph of the underdrawings for you. The original background is a landscape, but it has not been completely restored yet. And there is the complication of the words written on the panel's underdrawings (see attachment).
> The underdrawings give us much new information, but in my opinion these drawings only create more questions about who painted the portrait.
> Cordially,
> Laurence Ceravet
> <Attachment>

Zari clicked the attachment. The black and white underdrawing showed the same technique as that of the Fontbroke College painting. The artist had employed a metal tool to create a detailed freehand etching of the merchant family, using long, sweeping lines to delineate their clothing and careful cross-hatching for the shadows. The same whimsical drawing of the word 'Mira' with the portrait of the nun in the letter 'A' appeared on the lower right-hand corner. Within the prongs of the 'M' was a decorative repeated pattern. In the upper left corner, a charcoal pencil had been used to scrawl the word 'Bermejo' on the panel.

She stared at the image, turning over the word 'Bermejo' in her mind. There had been a Spanish artist named Bartolomé Bermejo whose work dated from the early Renaissance. Perhaps this was some reference to him? She resolved to look into his work. She knew relatively little about Spanish painters.

The cathedral bells began chiming furiously again. It was time to prepare her talk for tomorrow's presentation. But first she would take a walk and savor the last hour of daylight in these exquisite medieval streets. Just before she stood up, she forwarded Laurence's e-mail to John Drake and Dotie Butterfield-Swinton.

As Vanessa had predicted, Dotie's interest in the Fontbroke College portrait seemed to have dropped off precipitously since their conversation in August. John Drake had mentioned meeting with him a few times but had offered no details, and she had not pressed for any. Just to be collegial, Zari had copied him on her first e-mail to John regarding Laurence Ceravet's painting, and Dotie had expressed a keen interest in it. So now she felt obligated to continue informing him of related news. However annoying he could be, Dotie was a power player in the European art history scene. It would be stupid for her, a junior academic trying to establish a foothold in that world, to alienate him.

The next several days she split her time between the conference and the city archives. She also spent a few hours in the Groeninge Museum, where two signed Cornelia van der Zee portraits hung in a gallery devoted to the school of 'Flemish primitives.'

The two portraits were sandwiched between a colorful triptych that once hung over a church altar and a towering group portrait of a Flemish merchant family. Both were slightly smaller than the Fontbroke College painting and showed their subjects from the hips up. One was of a broody-looking young woman in a pale blue dress with pearl-encrusted sleeves, standing against a neutral green-gold background; the other portrayed a more modestly dressed woman of similar age, with a hardened face that already showed the burdens of life's responsibilities. That one, too, was on a neutral background, though it was darker, a mottled greenish-brown. Zari spent two hours examining the paintings, comparing them to the others in the gallery and writing notes. She had contacted a curator ahead of her visit to inquire about the backs of the panels, and learned that they both bore the city seal of Bruges.

A school group trooped in at one point, and a few tourists straggled through, but for the most part she had the gallery to herself. When her mobile buzzed in her pocket, disturbing the silence of the high-ceilinged space, she jumped. It was a text from Wil asking her to meet him at a church a short walk away. She pulled on her coat.

Outside, the sky was leaden and a wintery chill clung to the streets. She passed a museum devoted to chocolate, a hair salon, and a series of tall, narrow buildings painted in somber tones. Soon she found herself in the Grand Square, an immense cobblestoned space lined with brick Gothic buildings. The square was dominated by a soaring cathedral with what sounded like the hardest-working belfry in western Europe. Every fifteen minutes, an arsenal of bells unleashed ear-splitting chimes.

Small groups of tourists gathered outside the church, gawking at the two round clock faces on its main tower and posing for pictures. Behind them was a phalanx of shiny black carriages hitched to draft horses. Past the square, Zari walked down a shopping street that was filled with high-end chocolate shops, clothing boutiques, and homeware stores.

She entered the church through a pair of double doors and stood silently, taking in the hushed splendor of the place. Piped-in monastic chanting floated down from the arched stone ceilings. She walked along the center aisle to the main altar, which was topped with five silver candlesticks that held tall wax tapers. Above the altar, towering pink marble columns bookended an enormous painting. Its subject was Jesus rising from the dead, his simple white linen wrap fluttering around him, while two burly Roman soldiers looked on.

"I can't decide if the Romans are surprised or terrified," a voice said.

She turned. The sight of Wil's smiling face launched a flood of unabashed joy within her. On impulse, Zari leaned in and kissed him.

"Maybe that's inappropriate in here," she said, casting a guilty look around. No one was visible, but they could hear footsteps in the outer corridors. They retreated back down the main aisle of the church. Above the rows of dark wooden benches on either side of them were painted coats-of-arms.

"That seems odd, having family crests in a cathedral." She used what she imagined to be a church voice, just a shade louder than a whisper.

"Patrons," said Wil. "They had the best seats in the house. The family crests showed their generosity. Think of them as corporate logos."

"Is the Bandstra family crest displayed in a church back in Amsterdam?"

"If it is, I don't know about it."

"Your family doesn't go to church?"

"No."

They stopped at the far end of the aisle. Zari looked up at Wil.

"Not even your grandmother?"

"Especially not her."

"Really? I would have thought the older generation—"

Wil stepped forward, put a gentle hand on her cheek and silenced her with a kiss.

20

Spring, 2015
Bruges, Belgium
Zari

IN A RESTAURANT ACROSS the small square, they hung up their coats on hooks by the door and sat down at a table overlooking a narrow alleyway that was closed to vehicles. Wil ordered them both the three-course dinner, which consisted of a salad, fried chicken cutlets, and chocolate torte for dessert.

"A friend recommended this place because the tourists don't know about it," he said over the first course, taking a sip of beer. "Simple food, but good."

She picked up her wine glass, looking around at the low-ceilinged dining room with its polished wooden bar running along the interior wall. There were perhaps ten tables in the place, and it had the relaxed air of a local hangout.

"How are you liking Bruges?" Wil asked.

"It's so beautiful. I could wander the streets for weeks. But I've been working a lot."

"What did you find at the city archives?"

"Quite a bit, luckily. The Van der Zees were a prominent family here. Cornelia is in the birth register, born 1486. There's also a betrothal register that city residents were obligated to use, to declare their intention to get married. She's in that as well—she married a musician from Antwerp in 1505, and the two of them moved to southeastern France with the household of a noble family. Various sources confirm that she died there, probably about 1530."

"That's a short life."

Zari nodded. "I was hoping to find proof that she'd traveled to the Pyrenees as well. But I found nothing about that."

"What did you think of her paintings at the museum?" he asked.

"They look like her work." She put down her glass and stared out the window for a moment. "In fact, there's something that connects all the Cornelia van der Zee paintings I've seen—with the exception of the Fontbroke College portrait."

"What is it?"

"The difference is in the eyes. The Fontbroke College woman—Marie de Béart, or whoever she is—has eyes that burn into you. You get a prickly feeling on the back of your neck, looking at those eyes. The other works by Van der Zee don't have that quality. They have bland eyes. They're looking off at an angle, or if they're looking directly at the viewer, their gaze is muted. There's no life in them."

Zari found John Drake's latest photo of the portrait on her mobile and showed it to Wil.

"See what I mean?"

Wil stared at the photo for a moment. He tapped on the screen, zooming in on the image.

"Her jewelry is strange," he remarked.

"Why do you say that?"

"I didn't get a chance to show you all of our family portraits at Christmas. But we have some from this era. Her necklace seems out of place. A wealthy woman usually wore pearls, rubies, those kinds of jewels, around her throat. That white shell on her necklace. It doesn't fit."

Zari tugged a small sketchbook from her bag, opening it to a drawing she had made of the woman's golden belt. "Look at this. My mother pointed out that this could spell O-T-O. Which, thanks to the Internet, I learned could signify either a village in the Pyrenees, a religious cult that originated in the 1800s, or a Native American tribe. I'm going with the village."

"I've been there—or near there," Wil said, nodding.

"Seriously?"

"It's near a national park in Spain."

"Wil! This is huge. What's Oto like?"

"There's not much to it. Maybe 20 houses on a hill, with a medieval tower."

"Wait—do you mean a castle?"

"No, a defensive tower. With arrow slits. The area is beautiful. Deep valleys, cliffs, rivers. Good climbing."

"I'm going to see it for myself." Zari was startled by the conviction in her own voice.

"Are you? When?"

"This summer I'm going to Pau. Oto can't be too far from there. I have to see it."

Their main course arrived. The chicken cutlets were so large they hung over the edges of the heavy white china plates.

"When they said cutlet I think they meant manhole cover," Zari said, picking up her knife and fork and giving her chicken a tentative prod.

"What's that?"

"The round thing on top of sewer holes in the pavement."

"Round thing?"

"Never mind," Zari said. "This looks like a giant, deep-fried pancake."

"Pancake?" A sly grin crept across his face.

"Come on, you know what pancake means. I bet your word for it is similar—'*pankooke*' or something."

"Close. '*Pannenkoek*.'"

She looked around at the other diners. "People aren't fat here. But there are chocolate shops on every corner and this is the portion size in a restaurant. I don't get it."

Wil shrugged. "People here walk a lot and they don't eat all day long the way you Americans do."

"That's true." She considered her forkful of chicken. "We do tend to stuff our faces at all hours of the day and night."

After Zari embarrassed herself by asking if she could take the uneaten portion of her meal home and was politely informed that it was not possible, the chocolate torte was served. The first bite melted on her tongue—rich, crumbly, earthy-sweet. The flavors of cocoa, vanilla, butter and sea salt all converged on her taste buds at once.

"This could be the best thing I've ever eaten." She savored another bite. "Yes. It is."

Wil looked amused.

"We are in Bruges. If they can do one thing right here, it's chocolate. They have no excuse."

"Is that so?"

"If you're known for something you need to live up to the expectation. In the U.S., what are you known for that you do well?"

"The U.S. is so huge that I can't generalize. No, that's not true. We are amazing at drive-through food. You can eat and drink everything you want, morning, noon and night, in the comfort of your car."

"And that's a good thing?"

"You asked what we do well. In the areas of convenience, imme-diate gratification, and 'the customer's always right,' we're number one."

The server brought two tiny glasses of strong liquor.

"To our second date," Wil said, holding his glass aloft.

"Oh, you're keeping track?" she teased. "For the quantitative approach we discussed."

"Exactly." His eyes lingered on hers. They were definitely blue. But maybe it was just his navy shirt playing tricks on her, pull-ing out the flecks of indigo in his irises. Her own golden brown irises contained so many scattered pinpoints of green that the colors she wore sometimes created the illusion of green eyes. She put down her glass.

"Tell me about Hana."

There was a short silence.

"OK, don't—not if it makes you uncomfortable. I'm just curious, after spending time with your family and knowing how close she was—is?—to them. I just want to know the backstory."

He shifted in his chair, staring out the window. She followed his gaze. The slim branches of the street trees outside trembled in the wind.

"We were together for so long," he finally said. "Everyone thought we would get married. After university her brother Filip and I started doing these adventure trips I told you about. We did a skiing trip to the North Pole last year. It was a com-plete disaster." He ran a hand through his hair, then removed his glasses and rubbed his eyes. "Filip was more of a daredevil than any of us. He always pushed us to go a little farther, a little faster. Which was good. Until it wasn't." He fell silent.

Zari waited.

"The weather was much worse than we expected. We got to within a day's journey of the pole and two of us got sick. We were depleted. We could not keep up with the others. Filip was so set on reaching the pole. I told him not to go, that it was too dangerous. But he didn't listen." He put his glasses back on and looked at her.

"Filip fell into a crevasse and broke his back. Getting him out of there was hell. He survived, but he's paralyzed from the waist down and he lost all of his toes to frostbite. Hana blamed me. Blames me. She thinks I should have talked him out of going. She thinks I didn't do enough to stop him."

"Does Filip blame you too?" She reached across the table and took his hand.

"No. He blames himself. He has been depressed since it happened. I don't know if he will ever recover mentally."

"Do you blame yourself?"

Wil gripped her hand in both of his. "Sometimes. Usually at night when I can't sleep. I replay the argument we had that morning in the tent again and again. Then the sun rises and I forgive myself. Usually."

"Wil, it's not your fault. Those middle of the night self-hate sessions are the worst. I'm so sorry. What a devastating experience."

He smiled and shook his head. "Thank you for not saying 'at least.' So many people hear this story and say 'At least Filip didn't die,' or 'At least you all came back alive,' or something of that nature."

"Trying to force you to see the silver lining," she said.

"What is that?"

"The good that comes out of something bad."

"Ah—exactly. I don't see a silver lining for Filip. For me, my best friend is disabled for life, and my girlfriend left me. That's not a silver lining." There was a vein of bitterness in his voice she had never heard.

"It's still early days, Wil," she said softly. "Give yourself time— give Filip time."

He dropped his gaze to their entwined hands for a moment.

"Let's stop talking about it, OK? I've been looking forward to this time with you for so long. Let's just be together and keep our histories out of it." His eyes on hers were pleading.

Zari stared back at him for a moment, then disentangled their hands and signaled the server for the check.

"What are you doing?" Wil asked, watching as she pulled out her wallet.

"Paying. And then taking you back to my place."

"But it's only the second date."

"Case by case basis, remember?"

His expression softened.

"Are all American women this….what is the word…"

"Bossy?" she offered.

He held out her coat. "Here, bossy."

They walked out into the dark night. He put his arm around her and pulled her close.

"Zari Durrell," he said low into her ear. "I feel as if I have known you for a long time."

She wrapped her arm around his broad back. They strolled through the quiet streets, past the church where they had reunited that afternoon, following the sound of chiming that echoed somewhere ahead of them. When they reached the Grand Square, it was empty of tourists and all the horse-drawn carriages were gone, but the church bells pealed incessantly, masking the sound of their steps on the uneven cobblestones.

BOOK 3

Empta dolore docet experientia. Experience teaches when bought with pain.

1

Spring, 1496
Castle Oto, Aragón
Marguerite

MARGUERITE STOOD ON THE dusty road, a baby in her arms. Heat shimmered on the hard-packed dirt. Pine trees towered overhead. A low thudding noise rose up in the east, a swelling roar that rushed along the road, flooding her ears with a great relentless wave of sound. In its wake appeared a pack of horsemen clad in mail and red leather vests, their faces obscured by silver helmets. The horses' black hooves pounded the road so fiercely that the earth shook beneath her feet. Yet she could not run, could not take even a step. She watched in horror, helpless. Just as the horses were upon her, she screamed, "My son!"

Trembling, she sprang out of bed and flung open the balcony shutters. It was rare that a nightmare intruded upon her sleep. Never before had such fear jolted her awake. Dawn crept across the sky, illuminating the chalk-colored cliffs beyond the castle.

Some far-off wolf howled and set off a chorus of tangled echoes. Her feeling of uneasiness grew.

Ramón was due home any day from his raid in the northern territory of Cerdagna. She dreaded the violence he would inflict upon her in the night. It was always worse when he returned from battle. If his fatigue was great, she received only a shadowy bruise on her cheek or the purplish imprints of fingertips encircling an arm. But when his energy was high he fell upon her with such force she feared he would split her in two. She thought of the life growing within her and she felt both dread and hope. Dread that the child would not survive his assaults, and hope that its small unfurling life would be extinguished quietly, without her husband ever knowing it existed. That way the question of whether it was a boy or a girl would cease to exist as well.

On the day of his return, she watched her husband embrace Pelegrín in the great hall.

"Thank God you are home uninjured," she said, descending the stairs. A bitter film coated her tongue. Each time she swallowed nausea rippled through her gut.

"The journey was not wasted." Ramón heaved the dusty helmet off his head and thrust it at a page. "I lost no men."

His eyes settled on her for a moment, roaming up and down the length of her body, then flickered to his son. Pelegrín shifted his weight impatiently, watching the servants unbuckle the leather straps that held the various pieces of his father's armor together.

"Father, how many Frenchmen did you kill?"

A page slipped off Ramón's mud-spattered chest plate. "We honored our ancestors, I can assure you."

"And our castle, father? What about—"

A dark look from Ramón made Pelegrín hesitate.

"Pelegrín, we have time for battle stories later. Women cannot suffer the details of war. Wife, see to it that my bath is ready soon. And send Beltrán to the armory." Ramón took a step closer to Marguerite and examined her face. "You do not look well. Have you been ill?"

"I—no. Your bath will be drawn at once."

She bowed her head to him and hurried out of the room. Soon her husband would school their son in the ways of a raid. Pelegrín would ride north at his father's side, would learn to stab and torch and smash alongside the rest of the men. There was nothing she could do to protect her son from his fate.

In the kitchens, she instructed two maids to haul hot water to the bedchamber of the baron. Then she climbed the stairs to the upper hallway, her feet feeling more leaden with each step. Her mind veered to the one homecoming that had deviated from this numbing routine. The day she had believed—foolish woman —that everything would change.

When word of his parents' death had reached Ramón in the south all those years ago, he returned immediately to Castle Oto with a wounded knight in his entourage whom Marguerite had never seen before. As soon as her husband entered the castle, his armor covered in spatters of mud, his dusty face streaked with sweat, Marguerite showed him the testimony of the serfs who had taken up arms against his father. They had all claimed the same thing—that the steward's men stole their grain, their pigs, their wool, and sold them down the River Ebro. But the steward, clever man, had blamed them for his own thievery, and the baron had believed him.

She recorded the serfs' words herself in a squalid corner of the dungeon under the light of a torch, witnessed by two guards. Then she gave the order to behead them. Next she dispatched three horsemen to the river. When they returned, they said the bargemen who poled goods east to Tortosa confirmed the story.

Then she showed Ramón what she had discovered in the steward's chambers: gold and trinkets that he had stolen from the Oto family and stored in a great wooden chest with a false bottom. Ramón read the testimony and listened to her tale in silence.

That night, the weight of him pinning her to the wool-stuffed mattress made her eyes burn with tears. But afterward, instead of striding wordlessly from the room as was his custom, he stayed.

"The steward skimmed the cream off the house of Oto, and my father was murdered for it." He studied her face. "You did well, Marguerite. And you are a baroness now. Perhaps you will be better at it than my mother was. God rest her soul."

She lay there astonished, replaying his words in her mind. He had never complimented her before, nor addressed her by name. After he had fallen asleep, she watched his chest rise and fall. His skin had darkened to a rich brown during his time in the southern sun, and his face had grown leaner. Asleep, he looked like a kind man, a man with a heart. Nothing like the man she had wed. She stared at him until her own eyelids grew heavy. For the first time in their married life, the new Baron and Baroness of Oto slept together.

There had been a shift after that night. Ramón allowed her to keep the keys. She wore them hooked into a tooled leather belt around her waist. The wounded man he had brought back from the south, Beltrán Fivalas, had lost an eye defending her husband from the lance of a Moor. His reward was the position of steward at Castle Oto. He ingratiated himself toward Ramón and treated the servants brutally. Whenever she caught him looking her way, his eyes roamed from the swell of her breasts to the jangling mass of iron keys at her waist. She was glad in a way that he made his desires so obvious. The last steward had woven a web of deceit and betrayal, and her father-in-law had paid for that with his life. This man, with his wandering eye and his covetous habit of licking his thin lips with a darting red tongue, would be easier to manage.

For a while Ramón had treated her with more deference, had slept at her side in the night. But as years slipped away with no more babies, his manner toward her grew brusque. She reached the landing and put a hand out to the wall to steady herself. The one thing that would rekindle a blaze of warmth in him toward her had finally happened. Would she allow the pregnancy to play out and risk bearing another girl? Or would she consume the potion that Elena had left in a ceramic jar in her chamber and hope it extinguished the tiny pulse of life within her? There was not much time left to make a choice.

Ramón's foray into Cerdagna had ignited in him a lust that would not be sated. Each morning Marguerite inspected her sheets for blood, ran her hands over her growing breasts and thickening waist, wondered if her husband's roughness had ended the life within her. But her belly continued to swell.

When Marguerite told Ramón she was with child, the boundaries of her world shrank to the four walls of a room. On her husband's orders, she rarely left her chamber and sat in a leather-backed chair by the balcony working her embroidery or reading prayer books to pass the time. She watched hawks gliding on invisible currents of air. She heard the sounds of the castle drifting upward, the creak and shudder of the great gates opening and closing, voices raised in argument, the sudden booming cascade of a man's laugh.

She waited each evening at dusk for a glimpse of the ibex on the pale cliffs and was sometimes rewarded with the sight of their spiked horns silhouetted against the darkening sky. Elena was out there somewhere. As soon as the winter snows began to melt, Marguerite had sent her away, had encouraged her to journey to the valley in the west where she took refuge from time to time, a place full of strange pools that bubbled with steaming water.

She could send word, summon Elena in time to execute a secret plan once more. But the days ticked by and she took no action. She was strangely serene. Her mind returned constantly to the dream of the horsemen and the baby boy. She made provisions for the birth, gathered supplies, assembled what she needed. Through it all, she clung to a hope that her dream foretold the truth, that she carried another son.

Perhaps God had taken pity on her after all.

2

Summer, 1496
Ronzal, Aragón
Arnaud

THE BLACKSMITH WAS ALWAYS in need of wooden handles, and Arnaud was always in need of tools. As a result, an easy bartering relationship had developed between them. On this day, Arnaud carried a pile of beech handles in a willow basket to the blacksmith's workshop.

"Are you there?" he called through the open doorway.

He saw no one, but there were squares of cow's leather piled on the floor, tied with a thong. Arnaud dropped the basket and raced to the town water fountain, which served as a communal meeting area. A pack mule was tied to the iron railing at the foot of the fountain and the blacksmith stood chatting with the muleteer and several other village men.

"The news from Jaca is bad as usual," the muleteer was saying. With his long brown face, sad eyes and floppy hair, the muleteer resembled his pack animal. His leggings were so thickly plastered with mule hair they appeared to be made of fur. "There's been a war on across the ocean. Something to do with the Kingdom of Naples, whatever that is. And the blasphemers and the heretics burn in the south, though that's not news."

He rubbed his eyes and stretched, letting out a long yawn.

"What does that mean for us?" Arnaud's father asked.

The muleteer snorted. "You? Safe on your mountaintop? Nothing. Life goes on as usual, as long as the plague doesn't strike."

More murmuring. Arnaud felt a knot of anxiety form in his stomach. The plague. No one knew what caused it, let alone how to cure it. Just thinking about it might bring it on, he had heard, although he was fairly certain that was nonsense.

"What other news do you bring?" he called out boldly.

Some of the men turned to look at him, the audacious boy who would speak up in front of his elders. But he didn't care. He knew his father would be proud.

The muleteer took a long look at him, then sauntered over to the fountain and immersed his head in it. He scrubbed at his hair with his hands and flung his head back. With water streaming down his face, he let out a loud sigh.

"Well, let's see. I told you about Naples and the heretics. Mmm, what else?" Everyone stared at him expectantly. "There was one more thing, I'm sure of it," he began. "But my mind is distracted. Must be the growling in my belly."

In a flurry, several people rushed to their houses. Soon the muleteer was sitting on a stool in the shade of a giant pine tree, surveying a table laid with bread, sausage, cheese, cherries, and a cup of beer.

"Ah, this will help sharpen my memory!"

He tore off a hunk of bread. As he plowed through his meal he took no notice of the group of villagers standing in a semi-circle around him, watching. Some of the women had gathered behind the men, and children played just beyond them. The muleteer gulped from his cup.

"Now it's starting to come to me," he remarked, droplets of beer glistening in his beard. He sat contemplating his surroundings for a few moments, the wreckage of his meal spread out on the table before him. "I declare, these mountains are pretty," he said. "Fine views you have here, fine views."

He fell silent again. The villagers waited.

Finally he spoke. "Well, the stars and sun above. It all comes back to me. Yes, indeed."

Arnaud felt like exploding. He hopped from one foot to the other.

"'Tis not good news, I should warn you. There's not a speck of joy in what I have to say. Are you sure you want to hear it?"

"Yes!" the entire town roared. The muleteer flinched, his eyes wide. Several dogs trotted away from the crowd, confused by the noise.

"By the sun and stars, people, simmer down. Now you all know who old Baron de Oto was, right? Not the one we have now, Ramón, but his father, who died many years ago."

Another communal affirmation rose up from the crowd.

"A guard at the wool merchants' guild in Jaca told me this story. Mind you, he could be lying. But then again, why would he lie? This man, his own father worked for the old baron. He lived in the keep and stood guard outside the baron's chamber at night. One night, the baroness gave birth to a girl. And what did her husband do? He handed that baby to the guard, wrapped in a blanket, and ordered him to take her into the woods and leave her there."

Everyone gasped. A few women cried out in horror. Arnaud was skeptical. Babies were precious. They were hard to keep alive. What harm would one little girl do? He glanced up to see his mother, Thérèse, join the other women who stood at the fringes of the crowd. He followed her gaze and saw that she was looking at his father.

"And so the guard, with his faithful mastiff, took that baby girl with him into the woods and he stood with her in his arms, listening to the bitter wind blow in the trees," the muleteer continued. "He imagined her tiny helpless body being torn apart by a wolf. And he knew he couldn't do it. But he also knew he wouldn't survive his master's wrath if he did not. So he walked north through a long valley, 'til he came to the mouth of the great canyon where the River Arazas flows. And he made his mastiff lie down under an old oak tree and he dug a little hollow in the leaves next to it for the baby. And then he walked to a village deep in the canyon on the banks of the river. He knocked on the door of a small stone house where he heard a baby squalling."

The muleteer paused and picked up his beer cup. He peered inside it and turned it upside down. A few drops splashed onto his breeches.

"All this yammering is making me mighty parched. A throat as dry as mine can't be expected to spout this many words."

At this, one of the women rushed forward with a tankard and filled his cup again.

He grinned at her broadly. "That's more like it," he said, slurping with enthusiasm.

"Now where was I?"

Arnaud shouted, "He knocked on the door!"

The muleteer's gaze swiveled to Arnaud. His bushy eyebrows merged into one, like a giant black caterpillar marching across his forehead.

"Right you are, son, right you are. Now, the guard had a plan, you see. He bade the man of the house come with him, and the two of 'em went back to the place where he'd left the dog and the baby. This time he bade the other man to pick up the girl, and they set off for the village. About halfway there they heard a wolf-song begin."

At this several of the women gasped.

"The guard had his sword and his mastiff, but is that any comfort against a pack of wolves?"

Several of the men muttered, "No."

"Just as they entered the clearing at the outskirts of the village, they heard the pack closing in behind them. The wolves were getting ready for a good feed, snarling and barking like crazy."

Arnaud's heart raced. After an excruciating pause, the muleteer continued.

"Now you all know the practice of a night watchman." The villagers assented. "Well, that night, in that village, the watchman did his duty. He checked on the flocks as usual, making his rounds. He heard those wolves from a long way off. He pounded on doors, yelling 'Wolf! Wolf!' Quick as lightning the villagers sprang into action. Some of them grabbed bows and arrows, others lit torches."

There were more gasps.

"They split up. Half went to protect the flocks and half went to help the travelers. The night guard, as soon as he saw the first wolf enter the clearing right on the heels of those men, he sent up a long arrow of fire. Didn't hit the wolf but scared it good!"

A few of the men cheered.

"With their arrows and torches, the villagers held off that wolf pack long enough for the guard and the man carrying the babe to get to safety."

The muleteer crossed one leg over the other, resting his ankle on his knee. He examined his bare foot, the sole of which was spangled with yellow calluses. Seemingly oblivious to the tension vibrating throughout his rapt audience, he picked at a toenail for a moment.

"Well, I'd best be going," he said finally. "All this talk of wolves reminds me of the long road ahead and the darkness that awaits."

Indignant chatter began. Arnaud felt cheated.

"But please!" he cried. "What happened to the baby?"

"Yes, yes!" chorused a few other voices.

The muleteer scowled. "If you're hoping for a happy ending, you'll be disappointed. The guard told his lord the truth: he walked many miles and left the baby out in the woods under an oak tree. The only other detail he included was that he heard a wolf pack—a mighty large one, too—on the hunt that night. The baron was free to conclude whatever he wished."

Arnaud grinned. Claps and cheers rose up.

"Before you get too excited, let me finish," interjected the muleteer. "That baby went to the wrong village. Hit hard by the plague, it was. Not a soul survived. The girl was doomed after all."

Though it was just past noon on a summer day and he was hot from standing in the sun, Arnaud began to shiver.

Late that night he woke to the sound of his parents talking in low voices by the dying fire. He lay still, straining to hear over the moan of the wind.

"Does she know?" asked his mother. "Has she heard this tale?"

"There might be nothing to it," his father replied.

"I've always wondered if that woman was out of her head with madness, sending her baby over the mountains in the dead of night. The danger of it! Now I understand. I'd have done the same."

"Aye, but you've just heard the tale of a muleteer. Untrustworthy, the lot of them. You think his story contains even a kernel of truth?"

"Arazas—the whole village perished of the plague, that was true. And barons are a bloodthirsty lot. There's two kernels of truth."

"Agreed. But nothing else in his story is accounted for."

There was the sound of embers being poked with a stick, the sudden flare of a last lick of flame. Arnaud watched shadows dance on the walls.

"The girl is safe over the mountains," his father concluded. "The only thing her mother didn't reckon for is her face."

"What do you mean?"

"She favors her mother, Elena says. It's in the eyes, mostly. Those strange pale eyes. Nothing to be done about that."

"She's a kingdom away from her mother, and nobody knows who she is."

"We know. Elena knows. Could be others too. There's danger to be had in any secret," his father said. "No telling what might come of it."

The wind picked up again, muting his parents' conversation.

His brothers Tomás and Luis asleep beside him on the alder bedframe he had crafted himself, Arnaud mulled over what he had just heard. The questions crowding his mind kept him awake until dawn, more distracting than the rise and fall of the wind. He kept coming back to the truth: his playmate, the odd copper-haired girl with gray-green eyes, was the daughter of barons.

Now one more soul knew Mira's secret.

3

Autumn, 1496
Castle Oto, Aragón
Ramón

ETURNING FROM THE HUNT, Ramón took the steps from the great hall two at a time. Pelegrín trailed behind him. The mountain woman stood outside the door of his wife's chamber, one ear pressed against it.

"Why in God's name are you out here?" he shouted, pushing Elena aside.

The muffled sounds of Marguerite's moaning drifted under the threshold.

Ramón turned on Elena, his blood pounding in his veins. "You should be in there making sure my son lives!"

He raised his arm as if to strike her. Elena took a step back and Pelegrín slipped between them.

"My lord, I returned to the castle this morning myself," she said. "I've been in the mountains all summer. I didn't know the baroness was with child." Her usual defiance was missing.

Instead, she sounded shaken.

"What good are you, then? Absent when you're most needed." He turned his back on her and gave the door a mighty shove. When it did not open, he rattled the latch, then commenced pounding on it with both fists. "Where is the key? Where in God's name is the key?" he roared.

Beltrán rounded the corner, the iron keyring clanking on his hip.

"My lord. At your service." He seemed to have memorized the set of keys, for he held up a middling-sized one immediately. "Allow me."

He inserted it in the lock, but it struck iron.

Ramón ripped the key out of Beltrán's hand and forced it into the lock. Again, the key jammed. He glared at the steward.

"Enter through the servant's entrance," he ordered.

Beltrán disappeared down the corridor. There was frantic banging and rattling, followed by silence. Beltrán reappeared.

"That door is locked as well, my lord. Something is wedged in the keyhole."

"Then fetch me an axe!" Ramón was still in full hunting gear, his chest plate and leggings splattered with mud. The only thing he had taken time to remove was his helmet, which he now flung after the retreating form of Beltrán.

At that moment they heard a faint squalling.

"Great Christ above," Ramón groaned, his voice breaking. Pelegrín and Elena stood motionless, waiting.

Beltrán reappeared, gasping for breath, an axe clutched in his hand. Ramón jerked it away from him and began cleaving his wife's door down the middle. Each blow was accompanied by a deep grunt. There was a splintering noise and a raw gash appeared in the wide center plank. With renewed vigor, Ramón smashed the plank to pieces and pushed his way in.

Sinking to his knees at Marguerite's side, his face taut with tension, he said, "Is it—"

"A boy," she interrupted flatly, her sweat-streaked face plastered with long strands of loose hair. "Another Oto warrior in your image, my lord."

The baby lay on her chest, still attached to his mother by the birth cord. With gentle hands, Ramón pulled a dagger out of his belt and carefully cut the cord. Then he sliced a thin leather thong from the tassel that decorated the top of his boot and tied off the cord with it.

He buried his face in his hands. "Another boy. Thank God, thank God. Now my line is assured."

His shoulders heaved. He stayed motionless on his knees for several moments, overcome by relief. Then he looked up at his wife, his eyes shining with pride.

"You have done well, Marguerite," he said. "We will call him Alejandro."

She smiled weakly. "As you wish."

4

Autumn, 1496
Castle Oto, Aragón
Elena

ELENA WATCHED RAMÓN POUND down the corridor and hastened to the bedside to tend Marguerite and the baby. Pelegrín stood at the doorway, pulling down the splintered bits of wood that remained.

"What are you staring at?" she heard him snap at Beltrán. "We need a new door. Fetch a carpenter."

Elena swaddled the boy and settled him at his mother's breast. She put the afterbirth in a ceramic pot and pulled the drapes around the bed. In the process of changing the sheets, she slipped a hand under Marguerite's pillow and her fingertips struck metal. Carefully, she slid out a dagger.

"What is the meaning of this, my lady?"

"You know what it means." Marguerite's eyes were half-shut, her voice pitched low. "If this baby had been a girl, my husband would have buried a daughter and a wife today. If you had been in the room, you would have tried to stop me. And if you failed in that, my husband would have blamed you for my death."

Elena sank to her knees. "So the locks—"

"I made provisions. In the end, all went as I hoped. As I dreamed."

Tears pricked Elena's eyes. She said nothing, just put her hand on Marguerite's cheek. Then she tucked the dagger away in a wooden box and dragged a chair closer to the bed. She sat facing the doorway, her arms folded across her chest, keeping guard over the baroness and her new son.

How could she have missed it? She often guessed women were pregnant weeks before they themselves knew. She did not possess the skill to read words on a page, but she read the signs of pregnancy with ease—it was evident in a woman's body, in her actions, in her habits. Even her scent.

A rush of shame overtook her. In her haste to flee the castle at the first sign of spring and escape into her mountain valley, she had ignored the signs.

No, not ignored—she had chosen not to see.

5

Autumn, 1496
Castle of Oto, Aragón
Ramón

BATHED AND BOOTLESS, RAMÓN sat in his chair in front of the fire, savoring the moment. He had two sons now. Two fine, healthy sons. Leaning back against the thick wolf pelt that draped his chair, he closed his eyes and luxuriated in the silvery burn of wine traveling through his gut.

Beltrán's voice broke the silence. "My lord."

"What is it?"

"May I have a word?"

Ramón reluctantly opened his eyes. The steward's hands were clasped at his chest and he leaned forward in a supplicating manner.

"Sit, then. Have your word." He sipped his wine.

"First, my congratulations to you, my lord, on the birth of your new son. What a fine, strapping—"

"What else would you speak of? Get on with it."

"Of course, my lord. Speaking of matters close to home—you are so frequently away, my lord. And the—ah—difficulty with the keys today during the birth of the baby. I wonder if it would be wise to allow me the keys to the castle during your absences—my own set of keys, to keep with me at all times. I know of many noble houses that entrust the keys to the steward. For the safety of all."

There was a long silence. A knot of pine pitch in one of the logs in the fireplace burst with a resounding crack. Ramón set his eyes upon Beltrán.

"My wife alone wears the keys. The only time I will require you to take possession of them is in the event that she is ill. Or, of course, if we are both called away. That is how it will always be."

Beltrán stood and bowed. A lock of hair fell into his face, obscuring it from view.

"You conceal your disfigurement," Ramón said. "You should be proud of your war wound. Show it to all the world without apology."

Beltrán smoothed the lock of hair behind his ear. "Yes, my lord."

"Now send my son to join me."

The steward bowed and strode from the room, his displeasure evident.

Ramón stared after him with narrowed eyes. The man could not hide his feelings a whit. Whatever emotion took hold of Beltrán washed across his face like wind ruffling a field of barley. Even if he did manage to mask his face with that forelock of hair, his voice betrayed him. Ramón knew full well that Beltrán abused his power when his master was away, made the servant girls his playthings, coveted his wife. None of these things mattered. What mattered was the man's loyalty.

After Beltrán had come to his aid on a southern battlefield, Ramón had allowed him to convalesce in his own tent. During the days that followed, Beltrán confided in Ramón the financial troubles of his father, a minor figure in the Barcelona court of King Ferdinand. Ramón had no source of information in the court himself, so he devised a plan that killed two birds with one stone. He offered to make Beltrán his steward. In return, he would pay Beltrán enough gold to keep his father solvent. He would also expect frequent updates on news of the court.

The plan had proved sound. When Ramón traveled to war, he needed a captain to defend his home and his lands, someone who did not flinch from brutality, whose threats were backed with the gleam of a sword. Beltrán had proved he was that man. And true to his word, he shared his gold with his father in Barcelona, who repaid the debt with long letters to Ramón detailing the minutiae of King Ferdinand and Queen Isabella's court. As long as Beltrán never mastered the art of deceit, never resorted to the conniving two-faced plots of his predecessor, he would keep his post.

Ramón's thoughts turned to his own father. He shifted in his seat, scowling. His father had displayed an alarming breach of judgement by accepting the whispered lies and schemes of a mere steward as truth, and he had paid dearly for that.

It was a mistake that would not happen again in the house of Oto.

6

Winter, 1497
Castle Oto, Aragón
Pelegrín

PELEGRÍN STOOD AT THE door, staring at the wolf pelt that was draped over his father's chair. When he was small, he had been frightened of the puckered eye slits. It was a wolf his father had shot himself, a reminder of his skill with a bow and arrow. The castle was full of such reminders. There were bear rugs and ibex rugs, chandeliers made of deer antlers and pillows stuffed with the downy feathers of waterfowl and falcons.

These prizes were simply the backdrop to the real treasure that the family had accrued over the generations: gold coins in iron chests, jewelry embedded with rubies and emeralds, silver plate that gleamed, hammered copper bowls decorated with Moorish designs. Ever since he could remember, his father had come home from war bearing gifts from the south, possessions of the Moors whom he had killed in battle.

"Come, sit," his father said, waving an arm in Pelegrín's direction.

"Yes, father."

He settled in the chair next to Ramón, glancing sideways at his father's waxed beard. For a time they sat this way, in front of the fire, in companionable silence. His father drained a cup of wine and poured himself another. Pelegrín stared at the flames and felt himself drift into a kind of dreamy torpor. The sharp scent of burning pitch filled his nostrils and he watched a plume of smoke curling up from a knot of pine.

His eyelids grew heavy. Sleep was coming for him. Drowsily, he imagined the fun he would have with his brother once the boy was old enough to ride a horse and wield a wooden sword. He himself had started riding at three. His mother used to come outside to the courtyard so she could watch his lessons. One day he sat astride an old mare while a page walked the horse around in circles. When he turned to wave to his mother, he lost his balance and slipped out of the saddle. She rushed to his side, gathered him in her arms and rocked him.

"Nothing is wrong," she whispered in his ear. "You are safe."

Then his father's voice rang out. "Get up, boy."

Over his mother's shoulder, Pelegrín saw his father turn to the page who held the reins and strike him across the face.

"Make sure he does not lose his seat again, or you'll regret it."

Pelegrín was settled in the leather saddle again. His mother's long green dress had sleeves that hung almost to the ground, and her dark auburn hair was covered with a veil. His father took her arm in his hand and squeezed so hard that a gasp of pain escaped her lips. He leaned down so his nose nearly touched hers, and his voice crackled with anger.

"Go inside and rest. Grow me another son."

A kernel of fear lodged in Pelegrín's chest that day. From then on, when his father spoke, he adjusted his behavior in the manner that would be least likely to provoke an outburst. When he saw bruises on his mother's face, he grew impatient with her. Why could she not grow a son? As soon as one took root in her womb, his father could stop being angry.

Now, finally, his mother had done it. She had grown her husband another son. Pelegrín had just visited baby Alejandro, snuggled next to his mother on the great oak bed, the drapes drawn around them to create a cozy, private den.

The sound of his father's voice interrupted Pelegrín's dream-state.

"Pelegrín, listen closely." Ramón sipped his wine. "This is a story I have not told you before."

Pelegrín sat up straight in his chair.

"Long ago, a Baron of Oto saved the kingdom of Aragón from ruin," his father went on. "That is no lie. We—our family—are responsible for the existence of this realm. Never forget that, son."

Pelegrín nodded gravely.

"It was during the time of the plague. The Baroness of Oto was visiting the family of a squire nearby, helping to bring a new baby into the world. But while she was there, the plague crept into the household and cut the whole family down one by one. The baron rode out to save his wife, but he was too late. He found her dead in a bed made of yew, and for that reason you will never see any furniture made of yew in this castle."

Pelegrín privately resolved to ask the steward to show him a yew tree the next time they rode into the woods.

As if his father knew his thoughts, he added, "Nor will you ever see a yew tree growing on our lands. In his grief, the baron had all the yews in these mountains lopped off at the base."

Pelegrín gripped the armrests of his chair with all his strength.

"The plague seeped like a deadly fog across the land," Ramón continued. "Thievery and murdering became commonplace.

Any fine house that was shuttered during those dark days would soon be looted. Street urchins paraded around in stolen finery."

There was a hard glitter in his father's eyes. He set down his cup and laid a hand on Pelegrín's arm.

"With most of the serfs dead, the sheep and other livestock had run off or succumbed to predators and poachers. The crop fields lay fallow. The baron began to rise at dawn and ride his horse around the countryside, armed with a sword, shield and dagger. His task now was guarding the fortunes of our neighbors. For years, he patrolled their lands, checking on widows, finding homes for orphaned children. If the entire family had perished, he would bury the bodies, dismiss any remaining servants and collect all the valuables he could find. For safekeeping."

Ramón shot a meaningful look at his son and his hand tightened around Pelegrín's arm.

"Ah!" Pelegrín blurted, as if his father had squeezed the word out of him. "To protect it."

"Precisely. To make matters worse, the king's treasury was empty. He had to rebuild the kingdom, but he had no way to pay for it. To raise money, the king was forced to sell vast tracts of land in the north. The baron stepped in and offered to buy the land so that it would stay in the possession of a family of Aragón."

Pelegrín nodded doubtfully. Something was not quite right. "Is that when our family got the castle in Cerdagna?"

"Yes. The castle that was stolen by the French when I was a boy. But do not fear, Pelegrín, we will win back our castle and all our northern lands one day. And you will be by my side when that day comes."

Pelegrín thought of something. "The gold he used to buy the lands, father—was it the gold he had saved from those dead families?"

"Without any heirs to claim it, the wealth belonged to no one." His father's voice held an undercurrent of menace that made the back of Pelegrín's neck prickle. "Your ancestor, the baron, risked his life to save that gold, and he used it to make the kingdom of Aragón great again. All the same, he never spoke of his deeds to anyone but his sons. And neither will you."

"Yes, father."

"I'm pleased that you understand." Ramón relinquished Pelegrín's arm and leaned back against the wolf pelt. His voice, when it came again, was a low purr in Pelegrín's ears.

"Never forget, my son—the stories I tell you of our family are lessons. Listen closely, and remember. If you do not heed them, our future will crumble into dust."

7

Autumn, 1498
Abbey of Belarac, Béarn
Béatrice

THE INSISTENT CHIME OF the gate bell rang out, disturbing the stillness of dusk. The door of the refectory was open for whatever trace of cool air might make its way inside. Though it was early autumn, the heat of summer lingered. A trickle of sweat ran down Béatrice's back, somehow finding a path to trace despite the sticky wool habit plastered to her skin. Giving no indication of her discomfort, she flicked her gaze from face to face, watching as the nuns consumed their nightly bowls of barley stew in silence. The bell continued ringing in a steady rhythm. Several of the nuns glanced at Béatrice. She ignored them, dipping her spoon into her own bowl until it was empty.

Béatrice pushed back her chair and stood.

"You are dismissed," she announced, sweeping out of the room.

A great scraping of benches commenced, and she heard the creaking doors of the cabinet that held the lutes and guitars.

Every evening after supper, she allowed the nuns to play and sing, to write skits and perform them for one another. Such activities would be forbidden in Amadina Sacazar's convent, she mused as she hurried to the gates. But the women in that convent were likely too exhausted from working spindles and looms day and night to muster even a whistle.

In the warming room a man lay on a pallet by the door, clad in a black pilgrim's cloak, a bloody rag over his face. Gingerly she reached down and peeled back a corner of the rag. The fabric tugged at the flesh where blood had dried and bonded it to the wound. The man moaned.

"God save this man. What befell him?"

The villager who had delivered the pilgrim by oxcart explained that he had found the man lying unconscious under an oak tree, where the valley track merged with the main road through the mountains.

"He was traveling alone, Mother Abbess. Pilgrims are foolish that way. Some forest creature made short work of him, poor fellow. From the looks of him, 'twas a bear."

She slipped a coin to the villager, who ducked his head in thanks and let himself out.

The pilgrim moaned again. Béatrice had no idea how to manage a wound such as this. But it was just as well. He would not survive the night.

8

Autumn, 1498
Abbey of Belarac, Béarn
Mira

"THEY TOLD ME TO come quickly," Mira said, slipping through the door of the infirmary with her pouch of herbs and ointments. She heard the moans of the pilgrim, whose pallet had been arranged in a corner. Béatrice led her past a high-backed bench that screened him from the other patients.

"We can do little for him other than ease his pain." Béatrice lifted the corner of the rag that lay over his face.

Mira drew in a breath and held it, leaning in to get a closer look. It was an ugly, ragged wound. Flaps of skin peeled back from his flesh, and his skin was nearly black in places where the blood had clotted and dried.

"If we clean it off we can better see what must be fixed."

"Fixed? This man is dying. We can only ease his passage."

"The shepherds can sew him back together," Mira said. "I saw

Arnaud's father sew up the wound of a sheep. The shepherds are in the valley now. Let a villager fetch them."

Mother Béatrice laid the cloth over the man's face again and stood.

"That is absurd. A man is not a sheep."

Mira rose and faced her. "No, but flesh is flesh. If we do nothing, he will surely die."

"Whether he dies or lives is up to God."

"If we do not do everything in our power to help the suffering, we will fail in our Christian duty. That is what Brother Arros says."

Béatrice studied Mira's pleading face a moment. "Very well. Clean his wound. I will send word to the shepherds."

When Béatrice left the infirmary Mira lugged an iron pot filled with hot water to the man's bedside. She wet a length of linen and patted it gently on his bandages until they came loose from the wounds. His moans turned to ragged cries. She rummaged in her pouch for a pot of willow bark syrup. Supporting his head, she held it to his lips and whispered words of encouragement until he swallowed.

Arnaud de Luz came around the side of the screen. Mira caught her breath at the sight of him. He looked scarcely different, if perhaps a bit taller and lankier, his cheekbones more prominent. His brown eyes held the same warm, open expression they always did.

"Where is your father?" she asked after a moment, collecting herself.

"He stayed in Ronzal. But I can sew up a wound as well as he." Arnaud knelt by the pilgrim and pulled a wine sack, a curved bone needle and a length of flax twine from his satchel. "This looks like the work of a bear. It'll be no tidy repair job, but I'll do my best."

He squirted wine on the pilgrim's face, prompting a moan.

"There's more pain in store for him." Arnaud hesitated, holding up the needle in the candlelight. His eyes met Mira's.

"I fed him willow bark syrup," she said. "It will ease his pain. And I have butterwort salve to stop the rot from coming, after."

He nodded in approval. She felt self-conscious under his gaze. She did not know why. She was still the same girl who had climbed trees and boulders with him, who had danced under the stars at the mountain meeting by his side, who had told him of her secret wish to visit the sea. And he, about to plunge a curving needle into the bloodied cheek of a pilgrim, was still the same boy.

Arnaud bent over the man and set about sewing his face back together.

For two days and nights, the pilgrim drifted in and out of consciousness. At intervals, Mira fed him willow bark syrup and smeared his wound with salve. He moaned and thrashed his limbs under the coverlet. If the man survived, his face would be an ugly latticework of furrows and ridges. But at least he would be alive.

On the third morning, he opened his eyes.

"Here I am," he rasped. A dry cough rumbled up from his chest.

Mira turned to a servant. "Quickly—bring him a cup of ale."

The woman scurried from the room.

The pilgrim's good eye darted around. The makeshift screen was gone, so he had full view of the other patients stretched out on their pallets and the women who tended them.

"Nuns," he observed. "So—a convent."

"This is the Abbey of Belarac," Mira said. When the servant returned with the cup of ale, she held it to his mouth while he drank. "Some creature attacked you and mauled your face. Perhaps a bear. A villager found you near the road and brought you to us, and a shepherd sewed up your face again. But it will never be the same."

He put a tentative hand to his cheek.

"Stop," she said. "I know it itches, but you must not scratch it. Not until it heals." She cast about for a distracting thread of conversation. "You are a pilgrim. Did you go to Compostela?"

"Yes. Twice now I have walked all the way from Flanders to Compostela, and I saw the bones of the saint. I saw the sea. I saw the very ends of the earth." His voice faltered and he was wracked with another bout of coughing.

Mira held the cup to his lips again and he drained it dry.

"Santiago protected you," she said.

"True enough. If these wounds are indeed the work of a bear, by rights I should be dead. But here I am in this convent. Perhaps I will heal enough one day to make the journey back to Flanders."

"I suppose that is up to God." She smeared a glob of ointment onto his wounds.

He groaned. "If this mixture is as powerful as it smells, I should be right as rain in no time at all."

She laughed. "It does have a strong scent." She was so used to the earthy, acrid smell that she did not notice it anymore. "I'll have your cup refilled, with wine this time, and it will put you to sleep. That is the best thing for healing—sleep."

"What is your name, so that I may thank you properly for caring for me?"

"Mira."

"And I, Mira, am Sebastian de Scolna."

Her eyes widened. "I know that name."

"How?"

"A friend told me your name long ago. Brother Arros of San Juan de la Peña."

"Now that is a comfort indeed—to know he is your friend as well as mine."

With difficulty, he patted his chest until he found an object there, then pulled forth a necklace from beneath his shirt.

"Brother Arros gave me this the first time I passed through San Juan de la Peña. He told me the saints would watch over me as long as I wore it. And blessed man, he was right."

Sebastian's eyes closed.

Mira grasped the cord around her own neck. But she said nothing. Her scallop shell was a private thing, something she only shared with those she trusted.

Her mind turned back to Arnaud.

9

S EBASTIAN SAT ON A bench in the chapel wrapped in two cloaks, his shoulders slumped, his head bowed. His wounds had left him so weak his bones seemed barely able to support his weight. His lungs squeaked and his ribs ached every time he took a gasping breath. The worst was the pain in his face, which throbbed and ached day and night. And the itching! He longed to rake his cheeks with his fingernails, to relieve that confounded itch.

This was his first visit to the chapel since his undignified arrival at Belarac. With the aid of a servant, he had dragged himself here to thank God for sparing his life. He was too weak to kneel, as much as he desired to, so here he sat, quivering on the bench, his lips moving in prayer, eyes closed.

The chapel door opened and closed behind him and soft footsteps padded around the perimeter of the room. He heard the quiet flare of a wick catching fire and opened his eyes. A figure moved through the space, lighting tallow candles. In the flickering light he saw the faded, soot-blackened images of two angels on the wall behind the altar. One of the angels seemed to move, swaying her body as she reached up to heaven. He watched the faint lines of her robes shimmer, transfixed, until tears blurred his eyes and the servant's footsteps faded away behind him.

The next day, he asked Béatrice to accompany him to the chapel. They walked slowly around the perimeter of the building, inspecting the remains of the frescoes that once ornamented the walls.

"Abbess, you have housed me, fed me, and healed me. More than anything, I wish to repay your kindness. I am trained as a painter. Will you let me repair these frescoes?"

Béatrice hesitated.

"You are not well enough for such work."

"I am far too weak to travel. I must convalesce here until spring." He swept his hand over the soot-stained wall. "The act of painting nourishes me. If anything, it will speed my healing."

"I am touched that you wish to attempt it, but—"

"Please, let me explain."

Béatrice turned toward him and folded her arms across her chest, waiting.

"As a third son of a squire, I was not destined to inherit either home or wealth," he began. "The only course left to me was the religious life. Before I began my life of service to God, one night I had a dream in which God told me to celebrate His glory by creating beauty. My oldest brother gave me a small allowance to apprentice with an artist in Flanders."

"There were many of us from the south in his workshop. I lodged with the other apprentices in his home. I learned as much from them as I did from the master. Especially a fellow from Aragón by the name of Bermejo."

"When our master was struck down by smallpox, the debt collectors came after the apprentices, and we all fled. Bermejo and I made our way south again, first in an oxcart, then, when we ran out of money, on foot. We found refuge in a monastery and offered the brothers our skills as artists. There were walls in their chapel that had been so faded and blackened over the years that we had no idea there had ever been a lick of paint on them. But we cleaned each wall and brought each fresco back to life. Then Bermejo and I followed the pilgrim's road to Compostela. After we saw the saint's bones, he returned to Aragón. I went back to Flanders and found steady work as a portrait artist for merchants. As the years passed, a longing to return to Compostela tugged at me. I decided to make the journey once more before I die. And so I have."

He turned to the faded angels on the wall, tracing their outlines in the air with his fingertips.

"Can you not see that God himself sent me to you? This work is what I was meant to do."

"We sorely need the help of an artist like yourself," Béatrice said. "And I admit your tale is moving, though I fear you lack the strength to carry out the task."

There was a warmth in her voice he had never heard before. Encouraged, he attempted a smile. The pain of it made him wince.

"Very well." She nodded, looking him up and down. "You may proceed."

10

A BITTER WIND COURSED down the hills and swept through the abbey. The gusts leaked in through chinks in the walls and tore slate shingles from the rooftops, sending them clattering down on the cobblestones. Inside the chapel a constant draft circulated. The stuttering candlelight threw shadows everywhere.

Sebastian stood with one arm outstretched, dabbing paint on the chapel wall. Mira could make out an angel's pale shimmery wing and a long robe of luminous blue. After weeks of work, this was all he had accomplished.

"There is supper for you in the warming room," she said, approaching him.

He did not turn his head. "Ah. My thanks. A bit of soup might give me the strength to finish this angel."

"What will you do next?"

"I'll mix some blue pigment with egg yolk and a drop or two of water." He pointed at a row of ceramic jars laid out on an oak table. "And then I'll finish those robes. It is a tedious process, filling in the robes."

"How do you make the folds and drapes look real?"

"A trick of the eye. All in the shading. Use a slightly lighter shade and an object appears farther away; a slightly darker shade and it appears closer."

Mira bent down and picked up his walking stick. "I will walk you to the warming house."

He smiled. "A fine nurse you'll make. A fine nurse you *are*, I should say." He braced an arm on the back of the bench and heaved himself up. "A nap will do me wonders, after my soup. A nap and some more of that salve for my face. What do you say, young Mira?"

She handed him the stick. "It is a good plan."

Later she crept back into the chapel and stood in front of the half-finished angel. How difficult would it be to do it herself? She could draw, she was a fine copyist, and she mixed paint to illuminate manuscripts. She glanced around. She knew no one would enter the chapel until the bell rang for vespers. The jars of pigment and a ceramic cup full of brushes were laid out on the table. Three eggs sat in a small dish next to them, and beside that a slab of stone on which Sebastian mixed his paints. She took a tentative step forward and reached for an egg.

The next day a servant girl found her in the infirmary and told her Sebastian needed assistance in the chapel. On the walk there, her feet were leaden, her chest tight with dread. Would he scold her? Had he told Mother Béatrice? He would likely have to undo everything she had done.

When she entered the chapel Sebastian was applying the finishing touches to the angel's hands. His brush flew from the dish of paint to the wall and back again, dabbing and swiping.

"Approach, young Mira."

He wiped a blob of paint off the wall with a rag.

She scuffed down the narrow side alley of the chapel, her head bowed.

"Look what I have done," he said in satisfaction. "I finally got to the hands."

She nodded, waiting for his tone to shift, anticipating an angry reprimand.

"And it is all thanks to you!" He beamed at her. "Your shading was admirable. I did adjust it here and there, but truly, you did the same work of any apprentice in my workshop. Why did you not tell me you had talent with a brush? We would be nearly finished by now if you had only helped me from the beginning." He wiped the excess paint off his brush with his rag.

Mira's mouth worked but no words came out.

"Does the abbess know of your skill?"

"Yes." She stared at the floor. "But I did not ask permission."

"I see. I shall ask her if I can use your services as my assistant, to speed my job along."

"Truly?"

"Truly. And I shall ask her if I may teach you a few lessons about painting, so you become more useful to me."

Relief flooded her and she relaxed into a smile. Sebastian grinned back, then stiffened.

"This confounded face of mine," he grumbled. "Dare I ask how it looks?"

"It looks as if you survived a great duel."

She was so used to his tattered face that the sight of it never disturbed her, but it did not look wholly human.

His expression brightened. "A duel," he mused, picking up his brush again. "I like the sound of that."

11

Winter, 1498
Abbey of Belarac, Béarn
Arnaud

WINTER'S GRIP SETTLED OVER the valley. The fields were white with snow, the apple trees waved their bare limbs at the pale sky. A skim of ice formed over the stream and it thickened until the village children dared to slide across its slick, milky surface.

Just outside the abbey walls was a stable where the shepherds housed their mules during the winter. One end of the building had been walled off and was devoted to a workshop for the men to build whatever was needed to keep the flocks safe and warm in their winter enclosures. A stack of willow branches lay in a corner and piles of oak and beech timber were stacked along the walls. A fire burned from dawn until well after nightfall and the men often gathered there, repairing tools, telling stories and drinking wine from leather sacks. Someone usually produced a flute and a tambourine, because a winter evening around the fire was not complete without song.

This year a new object crowded the space: a wooden loom that had been a gift to the abbey from the merchant Carlo Sacazar. Arnaud had been tasked the job by Mother Béatrice of creating another loom exactly like it. The skeleton of his loom was beginning to take shape, but it was exacting work. Though he was a skilled carpenter, he had never built anything like it. So while the men laughed and sang and drank in front of the fire, he carved and sanded and planed by candlelight, determined to finish before winter's end. His father was in Ronzal this winter, because Thérèse was expecting again. Jorge's parting instructions still rang in his ears.

"Build as many looms as possible," he had said. "When the abbey begins selling finished merino fabrics in the north, the Ronzal villagers will share in the proceeds."

A boisterous laugh rippled through the room. Addled by the noise, Arnaud's dog padded over to him and nosed a pile of fragrant wood shavings. His great bulk blocked the candlelight. All of the other dogs were at their posts, guarding the flocks. But his own was recovering from a wound.

"Go lie down," Arnaud ordered, rocking back on his heels.

The dog shook his massive head, setting the spiked iron collar around his neck jangling, then limped to the corner, circled a few times, and slowly lowered himself. He was a good dog, a veteran of a few tangles with wolves and, just days ago, a nasty encounter with a lynx. The claws of the lynx had sliced neat gashes, so the repair job had not been difficult.

His dog had yet to confront a bear, and if he did, his life would likely end with one swipe of a massive paw. The damage a bear inflicted was unmatched by any other forest creature. Sewing up the deep, ragged wounds of the pilgrim

Sebastian had been nearly impossible. Somehow, the man had incited the wrath of a bear and survived.

Arnaud's thoughts turned to Mira. In her novice's habit, she looked nothing like the barefoot little girl who once followed him around. She moved through the infirmary with quiet confidence, dispensing her salves and herbs to the ill, murmuring instructions to the servants. He had caught himself staring at her a few times when they tended to the pilgrim Sebastian.

She had always treated him like an equal. But that was likely because she did not know she had noble blood. What good did it do to wonder if she knew her secret or not? She had this life now, the convent life, and perhaps it suited her after all.

It was better than being cast into the woods to die.

12

Spring, 1498
Abbey of Belarac, Béarn
Béatrice

SEBASTIAN ACCOMPANIED BÉATRICE TO the weaving work-shop. A fire blazed in the hearth to keep the workers' fingers supple as they toiled, and tall iron candelabras bearing stout tallow candles lit the space. Near the hearth sat a semi-circle of nuns spinning wool from piles of clean, dyed fleece. Behind them were two looms, the one Béatrice had been gifted by Carlo Sacazar, and the copy of it made by Arnaud. God willing, the boy would complete a third loom by summer. The hands and feet of the women working the looms flew, depressing pedals and flicking shuttles back and forth.

Béatrice drew out a length of black cloth from a cabinet.

"Our finest sample yet." She handed it to Sebastian. "Merino, of course."

Sebastian stroked the fabric with a finger.

"Excellent quality, Abbess."

"I travel north this summer to find a market for our fabric."
She folded the cloth and replaced it on the cabinet shelf.

"Why not sell it in Nay?"

"I know better than to compete with Amadina Sacazar." She
kept her voice low. It was never prudent to speak of sensitive
matters in front of the other women, no matter how trustworthy
they seemed. "No, I must establish a foothold elsewhere, in
another market town. Fabric this fine merits a high price. I
must find a merchant who can pay it."

"I know another source of income for this place," Sebastian
said.

His hood slipped off his head and he quickly pulled it
back into place. The bear attack had left his face permanently
deformed, with one eye obscured by a flap of scar tissue that had
healed badly. He covered his ruined face, she knew, to protect
the nuns from the shock of seeing it.

"The chapel walls are fully restored and more than half the job
was done by Mira," he went on. "You know the girl has a talent.
Why not put it to use for the abbey? She could earn money for
you if her skill is nurtured."

"How so?"

"She could do what I did in Flanders—paint portraits of the
wealthy. Nay is a merchant town. Send her there."

"Mira is a novice nun. The artist's life is impossible for her."

"A novice nun—or a nurse? How many novice nuns spend
their days tending to the ill?"

"The infirmary is where she is most needed at present," Béatrice
said.

"Because of her skill at healing?"

"Yes."

"By the same logic, you should allow her to paint. I know
of nuns who paint. There was one in Flanders. She received a
number of commissions from merchants."

Béatrice did not bother to conceal her irritation. "What is logical about putting the girl in danger? Life outside these gates would not be suitable for her, or safe."

"You saw she had a talent to heal, and you nurtured it. Why is this talent any different? God gave her skill with a paintbrush, and now it must be nurtured."

She bristled. Of course he would bring God into it. He was a sly man, for all his soft-spoken dreaminess, and he knew exactly the words that would needle her.

"Twice now you have told me you know what God sees fit to do," she snapped. "Yet you are no man of the cloth."

"Please forgive me. But surely you see the benefit of bringing more gold into Belarac."

Naturally, the notion did interest Béatrice. But if anything befell Mira, the stream of gold that Elena delivered annually from the Baroness of Oto would dry up. Still, she supposed there was no harm in allowing Mira to train alongside Sebastian. And truth be told, the baroness had implored her many times to nurture Mira's talent with a quill. She had ignored that plea too long.

"I will allow her to paint within these walls," she said, "and I will see to it that she has what she needs to carry out the task. But that is all. Mira will not leave the abbey. Her place is here at Belarac."

13

Summer, 1498
Abbey of Belarac, Béarn
Mira

"Now!" Sebastian directed his gaze at Mira. "You must be a master of color if you are to paint. You can draw quite well, but as you learned when you helped me in the chapel, painting is another thing entirely. You will mix your paints and then you will copy that."

He pointed at a small painting of the Virgin Mary, which Béatrice had removed from the wall in her own bedchamber that morning.

"Who is she?" he asked.

"The mother of Christ, of course," Mira said in surprise.

"The artist wanted us to think she is, but truly, the woman who sat for the portrait was just a common person off the streets."

"Sat?"

"When you paint a portrait you must have a sitter—a model—who stays still so you can copy what you see onto your board.

Or you can copy from another painting. As you will do with this one."

Mira crouched down and regarded the painting. The Virgin's rosy flesh glowed, her eyes looked wet and full of life, the folds of her red gown and blue robes seemed to emerge from the painting in glowing ripples. She could not see how she would be able to replicate it, but she held her tongue.

"There is no time to waste," Sebastian said. "Begin mixing your pigments. You'll then do an underdrawing and build up layers of color. And every day, you must draw with charcoal on slate, stone, parchment—any material you can find."

She was lucky to steal a few moments a day at the marble step of the old well. Her basket of charcoal was always at the ready, kept full by a kitchen servant whom she was teaching to read.

But Sebastian seemed to be able to read her thoughts. "I will see to it that you are relieved of your nursing duties each afternoon so that you have ample time for it. Draw people, animals, plants, mountains, fields, rivers. Everything you see, Mira. And when you are tired of drawing, draw some more."

He pressed a hand to his chest, overcome by a fit of coughing. Mira dragged a chair to him and he sank into it, casting a grateful glance her way.

The sun slanted in through the narrow window, forming a long rectangle of golden light on the stone floor. The faint sound of birdsong echoed in the courtyard. Mira sighed. She pulled a brown leather smock out of her satchel and tugged it over her head, wishing she were outside. Instead, she dutifully took her place next to Sebastian and stared at her painting. She hated it. The colors were all wrong, the face had a demented expression and the proportions made no sense.

Sebastian laughed. "Do not despair. This is how all painters begin. Painting is difficult, Mira. You draw well, but that skill does not transfer seamlessly to a palette and a paintbrush, I assure you. It is simply a matter of practice."

"I hope you are planning to stay here for many years, because that is how long it will take me to succeed," Mira said.

She plunged her brushes in the jar of spirits, splattering the front of her apron.

"Gently, gently," he said.

"How long did it take you to learn?"

"In the beginning, I feared I would never succeed. At the master's atelier we all had different tasks. The least experienced among us—for a long time, that was me—would paint the skies. See those castles and mountains in the distance?" He pointed at the background of the painting Mira had copied. "Bermejo was skilled at painting those. I copied him as best I could, because his work was exquisite."

He hefted a rectangular wooden panel in the air, examined it and laid it on the table, tracing his fingers over the line where the two thin slabs of oak were glued together.

"That Arnaud boy, the shepherd, is a fine woodworker."

"Yes," said Mira, brightening at the thought of him. "There is nothing he cannot build or carve. Or climb."

Sebastian's good eye rested on her for a moment. Then he picked up a small ceramic jar that was marked with a dab of white paint.

"Eggshells can be ground up to make a fine white pigment. There's white lead, of course, which many of us prefer. But it is deadly poison. Old bones work—hens and other fowl are best—if you burn them and grind them down to dust. That's not the best white, because it's rather runny and thin, but it will do in a pinch."

She scribbled notes on a piece of linen paper with a stub of vine charcoal.

He pointed to the charcoal in her hand. "That works for black, ground down."

He went on describing the sources and methods for creating every color in the palette, and she wrote out his instructions, distracted by the throaty coo of a dove nesting outside the window.

Her mind wandered to Sebastian's descriptions of his time in Compostela, where the earth came to an end and all the rivers poured into a great, writhing sea. Brother Arros's stories of the sea still played over and over in her mind, and now she had even more fodder for her imagination. She saw foam-capped waves on glittering waters that stretched on forever, heard the keening of gulls overhead, smelled the stench of fish and seabirds that had washed up dead on shore.

Someday, she promised herself, she would witness the spectacle with her own eyes.

One afternoon near the end of the summer, while Mira toiled at her easel, she was distracted by the clang of the gate bell.

"Arnaud!" she whispered, cramming her brush in a pot and rushing from Sebastian's classroom without excusing herself.

She appeared at the gates, winded, the paint-speckled leather apron still tied over her clothes. They had always been about the same height but now he was taller than her. His dark hair was pulled back in a cord, just like his father's, and his feet were bare. The golden dog sat at Arnaud's heels, his eyes on Mira.

"I knew it was you," she said after she caught her breath.

He smiled and pulled two satchels off the mule's back, then passed them to her through the bars of the gate.

"These are full to bursting," she said. "What have you gathered for me this time?"

He pointed at one satchel. "Wooden panels, a pot of glue, two more of linseed oil and boiled pine pitch." He gestured at the other one. "Red ochre, lilies, berries, leaves and bark. Whittled some handles and gathered fur for brushes, too."

Her eyes shone. "My thanks, Arnaud. Such a generous bounty."

He shrugged, pleased. "'Tis a start, anyway."

"How are the high meadows?"

"As usual. Stragglers to find come evening, a few sick animals to tend to. Cheese to make. I'm glad for the chance to make my rounds, searching for your supplies. Adds a bit of variety to my days."

"I wish I could go with you." As soon as the words left her mouth a flush rose from her chest to her neck. "I miss summertime, is what I meant. I miss the world outside these gates."

"It misses you." His eyes held hers for a moment. Then he swung back up into his saddle. "I'll be back once more before fall."

He rode away, the dog padding along behind. The noontime sun pounded down from the sky. Mira shaded her eyes, watching the mule pick its way along the path back to the mountain meadows and the flocks.

She carried the satchels to Sebastian, who did not scold her for her rude exit, nor for her lack of care with her paintbrush. Instead, he cleared off a place on the oak table and bade her set them there. Mira fished out a leather pouch filled with brushes.

"Ah!" he said approvingly. "A good observer, our helper. Handles are sanded smooth, weighted correctly. What a splendid variety. Squirrel, which will be for every day, and a few mink, which will be reserved for your finest work. And this—" he held up a large brush tipped with long, coarse, brown hairs. "I do not recognize."

"I do," a voice said from behind them. Mother Béatrice had slipped in the open door unnoticed. "It is the fur of the bear."

She walked around the table and surveyed the objects spread out on its surface.

"Saints above," said Sebastian with a note of admiration in his voice. He touched the brush to his palm and gave it a few flicks. "My worthy opponent. Reduced to a few hairs on a stick."

Mira held up a flax bag full of tubers, roots, and fresh flowers, and a small pouch filled with red earth.

"Ah!" Sebastian put down the bear brush. "Your pigments. We will set to work grinding these at once."

Mira felt inside the satchel once more, and her fingers encountered a sheet of parchment. She pulled it out. It was the page she had filled with her list of items for Arnaud to find. He had crossed off each item in ink. Mira looked at the other side. It was filled with math riddles. She took in a sharp breath, her eyes scanning the page.

"You had best begin on those riddles this evening, if you want to complete them before his next appearance," Mother Béatrice said dryly.

"Yes. I have heard that your talent with a paintbrush does not extend to the world of mathematics," Sebastian said, shuffling around the table to fetch the grinding stone. His shoulders shook as he laughed at his own joke.

Mira barely heard them. She was already puzzling out the first riddle in her mind.

"Mira!" Mother Béatrice said. "Give me the parchment. It will await you in your chamber this evening."

Reluctantly, Mira handed over the parchment and got to work. These lessons with Sebastian were not what she had imagined they would be. Drawing had always been a pleasure for her. But painting was different. When she attempted to draw with her paintbrush, her brushstrokes were childlike and ugly. Her back ached and her arm was stiff from so much time in front of the easel.

She picked up a brush and dipped it in a pot of rust-red paint, thinking of the parchment sheet with its riddles, of the lanky dark-haired boy at the gate. If she could just find a way to escape these walls, to luxuriate in the freedom of summer the way she had as a child.

Raising her brush to the panel, her mind caught on the image of Arnaud again. She pressed the paintbrush too hard against the wood. A red drip torqued down the panel.

"Mira," Sebastian said sharply. "Mind yourself."

The paintbrush clattered onto the floor, spattering paint everywhere. She fetched a rag and wiped the paint from the stone pavers. Sebastian waited in silence, his hands clasped over his belly.

"I am not a talented painter," she blurted, on the edge of tears. "I can draw, I can copy, I can mix colors. But I cannot bring a painting to life the way you want me to."

He shook his head. "You are impatient because you are young. But you are wrong. God has seen to it that you have talent."

She bowed her head, still crouched on the floor. "Why do I not see it?" she whispered.

"Talent is nothing without work," he said. "What matters is practice. The master I apprenticed with in Flanders was called master because he devoted his life to practicing the art of painting. His *life*, Mira. You have practiced for a winter, a spring, and part of a summer. What makes you think you can master something in a few seasons?"

He rummaged in a box of tools. "Come, child, I have something for you."

She stood. He held out a slender metal tool with a sharp edge.

"You are a fine illustrator, it is true. I believe your painting would benefit from detailed underdrawings. It is one thing to draw the broad outlines with charcoal, but quite another to fill in the details with a lead stylus. Put some extra detail into the underdrawing, and I believe the painting will bloom under your fingertips."

Mira grasped the tool in her hand and nodded her thanks. "I am sorry to be so outspoken. You have taught me so much—"

"I forgive you," he interrupted. "For you are young, and you have much to learn. Now, clean your brush and begin again. And this time, quiet your mind."

14

Fall, 1499
Castle Oto, Aragón
Marguerite

MARGUERITE STOOD AT THE top of the staircase and watched servants peel off Ramón's armor. Once again, Beltrán had neglected to mention that her husband was returning until his entourage clattered through the castle gates.

"Welcome home, my husband," she murmured, descending the steps and curtsying in Ramón's direction. "I thank God you are safe. I only wish I had been informed of your return sooner." She threw a hard glance at Beltrán, who kept his gaze trained on her husband. "Please, sit in front of the fire. I will have the maid bring hot wine for you."

"No," Ramón said, running his eyes over her body. Her dark red silk gown, with its low, square neckline, was having its usual effect on him. "I want you to sit with me. And where are my sons?"

"Alejandro is asleep. Pelegrín is with his tutor."

"Have him come to me as soon as he completes his studies."

"As you wish," she said, withdrawing in the direction of the kitchens. When she returned, Ramón was seated in his high-backed oak chair and Beltrán stood before him, outlined by the glow of the fire.

Marguerite poured the wine. When she gave Ramón his cup, his fingertips brushed her own. She had always admired the beauty of his hands. Long, square-tipped fingers, skin the color of oak. When those hands wielded a weapon no enemy was safe. They could be gentle, as when he cradled his sons. For her, his hands were tools of grim efficiency, attendant to his goal of impregnating her. Tonight he would set those hands upon her like a pair of vises while he filled her to bursting with his seed.

She settled into the chair on her husband's right side, ignoring Beltrán. If he awaited an invitation to sit, he would turn to stone before it came from her. Since the arrival of Alejandro, she had often usurped Beltrán from this chair, much to his chagrin. Who knew when Ramón's benevolence toward her would fade, but until then she would enjoy its every advantage.

Ramón drew a scroll from the pouch at his waist and handed it to Beltrán. Upon it was the seal of the king.

"Finally, the royals heed our call for aid in the north. With the weight of their army behind us, we will prevail." Her husband's voice rang with satisfaction.

"Ah!" Beltrán unrolled the parchment and squinted at the words with his good eye.

"It will be as I desired," Ramón went on. "Regular sieges into French-occupied territory. Stealing cattle, murdering, ravishing, setting homes ablaze—we shall rain misery upon them."

He turned to Beltrán. "Tomorrow, send word over the mountains to Béarn that we seek knights-for-hire. Traveling knights will put us at an advantage, and Béarn crawls with them."

Like my father, Marguerite thought. The impoverished noblemen of my birthplace, reduced to mercenary soldiers.

"And General Fernández de Córdoba, will he come?" Beltrán asked.

"The Great Captain, you mean," Ramón said. "Give credit where credit is due."

"Yes, the Great Captain."

"No, he luxuriates on an estate in the south. One of the many rewards bestowed upon him by the queen after the battle for Naples."

"I've heard he hands out gifts to his favored men after a battle as well," Beltrán said. "Lands, titles, estates, jewels—all without permission of the queen."

"Yet her favorite he remains." Ramón let out a grunt. "And as for me, I've received nothing for the loss of the ship I lent to the royals for the war in Naples. It rots on the bottom of the sea."

"But the King—surely he would find you recompense for such a loss."

Ramón flicked Beltrán an irritated look. "Everyone knows the royal coffers are under the Castilian queen's lock and key. There is nothing to be done now, except to learn from it."

"That a woman now rules the kingdom of Aragón!" Beltrán exclaimed.

"Complaining will get you nowhere, and it might cost you your head if you do not have a care. I like it as little as you, but I adapt. If loyalty to her buys back my lands in Cerdagna, so be it."

Pelegrín appeared in the doorway and came to stand next to Beltrán. He bowed to Ramón.

"Father, what news?"

Ramón rose and put his hands on his son's shoulders. "We have been called to war. At long last we will win back our family holdings in Cerdagna. You are very nearly a man. It is time you came along."

Pelegrín's eyes shone. Marguerite felt as if a great bellows had sucked the air out of her lungs. She set her cup down on the table.

"My lord, he is so young."

"His sixteenth winter approaches. He is of age to marry. Why can he not go to battle?" Ramón gripped Pelegrín by the shoulders and swung him around toward Marguerite. "Look at our son. My knights have been training him with the sword for years. Beltrán instructs him in the hunt, with the bow. You have seen him on a horse. There is no better rider in Aragón."

"But what of armor for a boy? Surely we have nothing suitable for him," Marguerite said in desperation. The light in her son's eyes dimmed at the sound of her anxious voice.

"What does a woman know of armor?" Ramón said irritably. "Beltrán, take my son to the armory. Find him a full set—mail, leathers, breastplate, helmet. I'll choose his sword myself. That will calm my wife's nerves."

Beltrán led Pelegrín away. Ramón watched his son leave the room, then turned back to Marguerite.

"Concern yourself with Alejandro, woman. He will be hiding behind your skirts for a few years yet."

Marguerite frantically combed through her mind for some excuse, some obstacle that would delay Pelegrín's transition to manhood. She fumbled for the right thought, tried to string a sentence together. It was no use. The words would not come. Their son might die so his father could settle an old grudge and she was powerless to stop it.

"It is time for Pelegrín to take up the banner of Aragón beside me," Ramón said.

She did not respond.

"Do you not agree?" In his cool voice lurked the promise of violence.

"Yes, I agree, my lord," she lied. "He must go with you. I will pray every moment of his absence for his safe return."

"I knew we would be of the same mind on this," he said with a satisfied smile, drumming his fingertips on the armrest of his chair.

We are of *your* mind, she corrected silently. Anger pulsed through her. She took up her cup again and a few drops sloshed over the rim.

"Ah!" her husband said. "Your hands betray your fear. There is nothing to be done for it. A woman is always ruled by her heart."

On the day of their departure, pounding at the doors to the great hall woke Marguerite before dawn. She lit a candle and slipped through the servants' corridors to her son's chamber. Rain pattered against the window and a fierce wind shrieked through cracks in the stone. Stumbling in his excitement, Pelegrín shoved his feet into boots.

Marguerite put a hand on his arm. He frowned.

"Listen, my son. You must stay near your father and do as he says. Promise me."

She tightened her grip on his arm. Sighing in exasperation, Pelegrín nodded. He twisted out of her grasp and flew down the steps to join his father in the great hall, hacking at the air with an imaginary sword, cutting down a thicket of foes. Marguerite shadowed him, her heart racing.

Before the massive fireplace, a page slid a heavy chainmail shirt over Pelegrín's head, scraping his cheek with a sharp point of metal. Blood beaded on the spot.

Ramón glanced up. "Your blood is too precious to waste, my son—servants will be careless unless they are taught to fear." He gestured to the steward, who strode to the page and struck him. The boy fell to the stone floor and lay motionless.

Ramón spied his wife on the landing.

"You know our son is safe with me. The steward will serve as your captain in my absence. We will send word when we can."

"God be with you both. I shall pray for your safe return."

She pulled her wool wrap tight around her shoulders and watched her son walk away from her, out through the great double doors to the waiting warhorses.

The doors clanged shut. Beltrán turned and looked at her, silent.

"You may go to the kitchens," she called down to the page. "Cook will tend to you."

"The boy does not need to be coddled for his error," Beltrán called out. In his wide-legged stance and presumptive tone, there was a challenge.

"In my household the servants are treated for their injuries," she retorted. "Their work suffers otherwise." The boy remained motionless.

"Go, boy!" Her voice was sharp.

He crept away to the kitchen stairwell. Beltrán stared at her a moment longer, then turned away.

She climbed the Tower of Blood and unlocked the door to the small wind-lashed chamber at the top. Crossing to the arrow slit that faced west, she watched the men ride away on their horses. In their armor, weighed down with weaponry and banners, they looked like grotesque giants out of a winter's tale.

She stared unblinking at the distant figures, one hand on the shell pendant at her throat, watching until her son was swallowed up by the forest. Then she turned toward the door, contemplating its massive iron lock, its well-oiled hinges, and looked around her. This chamber was as bleak now as the first time she laid eyes upon it.

Early in her marriage, the family hosted a banquet to introduce young Ramón's bride to their vassals. During the meal, a knight had asked her about the leading families of Béarn. Ramón answered for her with a blast of misinformation. The knight pressed Marguerite to respond, and not wanting to appear rude, she told him what she knew. Her words contradicted those of her husband. Under the table, Ramón reached over and gripped her thigh so tightly she feared the bone would snap.

When the guests left, he marched her to this room in the Tower of Blood. From sundown to sunrise she lay on the thin straw pallet in complete darkness, aching with cold. Each day, a tray of bread and a cup of wine was placed on the floor, and she passed the time by charting the progress of a narrow strip of sunlight that pierced the arrow slits and moved across the floor. When he released her four days later, Ramón pointed at the floor until she sank to her knees before him, shivering in her linen nightdress.

"It is because you are young and stupid that I have punished you so lightly." His voice was cold with fury. "Never contradict me in front of anyone again."

Now love had tugged her up the stairs to her former prison, had compelled her to press her face against the cold stone, seeking one last glimpse of her son. To keep from sobbing, she began reciting a poem in Béarnaise. She got halfway through it, then faltered. How did it go? Her fatigue was endless lately. A wave of dizziness pushed her to the floor. Curled up in a ball, she let out a sound that began as a laugh and ended as a sob. She had been reduced to a quavering heap, felled by the one thing that could still strike terror into her heart.

"Here, drink." Elena handed Marguerite the ceramic cup.

She held it to her face and inhaled. It smelled like wet earth. She downed it in a few long gulps, her face twisting at the bitter taste.

"That was as horrible as you said it would be."

"I do not lie to you, my lady."

Elena wiped out the cup with a flax cloth. Marguerite felt the liquid burn a hot path to her stomach.

There was a thump at the door. Elena rose.

"Who is there?"

"The steward." Beltrán's voice was muffled by the thick oak.

"And?"

"I wish to speak with the baroness."

"She is resting. When she is ready to speak with you, she will."

Silence. The sound of heavy footsteps striding away.

Elena returned to Marguerite's bedside.

"That man pesters you like a hen-pecking wife when your husband is away."

"He wants nothing more than these," Marguerite said, one hand toying with the iron key ring at her waist. "Once my husband told him he could only have the keys if I am ill. Now his undying wish is for me to be struck with a fever. So whatever this concoction does to me, I am *not* ill. Even if I do not emerge from the room for weeks, he cannot know why."

"Don't trouble yourself with thoughts of the steward, my lady." Elena said. "He'll soon be too busy to come knocking at your door."

Marguerite looked up, surprised. "What do you mean?"

"A steward has much to do and little time to do it, my lady. Knights to oversee, an armory and kitchens to run, dogs and guardsmen and flocks and—oh, 'tis enough to give you a stitch in your side, thinking on all that work."

"He is accustomed to that."

"Sometimes, my lady, it's an odd thing—all goes wrong at once. Something breaks, something is lost, something catches fire. There's no accounting for it. And I've a feeling that now is one of those times." Elena clucked her tongue. "Poor man."

Marguerite's forehead creased with the effort of holding back a moan and she reached for Elena's hand. The sound of a dozen hounds barking rose up from the keep.

"Ah." Elena nodded. "Just as I suspected."

They fell into silence again, Marguerite wrestling with her pain. After a long while, a violent gust of wind rattled the balcony shutters. Moments later, the gentle plink of hail on wood swelled into a hammering clatter.

A faint smile crossed Marguerite's face. "I suppose you had something to do with this."

"A ruckus in the keep—maybe I had a hand in that," Elena allowed. "But wind and hail—those are a god's tools, not mine."

15

St. Andrews, Scotland
Spring, 2015
Zari

I N THE SPRING, AGGIE and Zari were both slated to speak at
a conference on Renaissance arts at the University of York.
"It could be warm, so be prepared for that," Aggie called
from her room while she was packing. "But it could also be
raining buckets. Spring in Northern England is a bit schizo-
phrenic, weather-wise."

Across the hall, Zari rolled up a long-sleeved shirt and slid
it into her suitcase. She threw her raincoat on top of that. Her
laptop sat open on her dresser, and a chime indicated she had
a new e-mail. She paused to check it.

> To: zdurrell80@inep.edu
> From: lceravet@institutpyr.edu
> Dear Zari,
> I was contacted by a scholar from Oxford, Hero-

dotus Butterfield-Swinton, who wants to visit my
painting with a group of art historians. I wonder if
he is your colleague? Will you be part of the group?
　　Cordially,
　　Laurence

Zari filtered through her e-mails to see if she had missed a
related newsflash from John Drake, but found nothing. He had
sent her the most recent image of the Fontbroke College painting; it was pinned to the kitchen wall. The edges of the paper
were curling in from repeated exposure to steam rising from
the countertop tea kettle. The portrait's black background was
now gone. In its place was an intricately detailed landscape that
showed snow-covered peaks, gray cliffs, mountain goats, and
stands of conifers and oaks.

As promised, she had sent the image to Dotie Butterfield-Swinton. "*Looks less and less like a Van der Zee, I'm afraid,*" he'd
written in response. "*The most damning evidence, of course, is
the fact that not a single landscape exists in the entire body of Van
der Zee's work. Moreover, as a minor portraitist of the era, she
would never have been capable of that level of mastery.*"

Zari snatched up her mobile and dialed John Drake.

He picked up on the first ring. "Hello, Zari."

"John, did Dotie Butterfield-Swinton come see you recently?"

"Yes. He wanted to see the painting."

"What did he say about it?" She chewed on a fingernail.

"He had a colleague with him, a scholar of late medieval Spanish art, I believe. I was busy with another project, so I left them
alone."

"Did they say anything to you about Bartolomé Bermejo?"

"They had very little to say to me. And nothing about him."

"Thanks to me, they know about Laurence Ceravet's painting too—about the underdrawing with the word 'Bermejo.' I'm

guessing they've concocted a theory that Bermejo was responsible for both portraits."

"I'm looking at images of Bermejo's work now," John said after a short silence. "And I can see why the parallel would be drawn."

"That's the thing, he was known for detailed background landscapes. He painted like a Flemish master. But most of his work was religious, commissioned for churches. Big pieces behind altars, that sort of thing—not portraits."

"His work is much more highly valued than Cornelia van der Zee's," John said pointedly. "Discovering a few long-lost Bermejos would be quite a career boost for an academic."

Zari felt a slow burn begin on her neck and rise to her hairline. Of course. Whatever secrets these paintings had to tell, they would not be revealed just for the sake of truth. There were other, more compelling rewards.

"Don't worry, Zari," John said, as if he knew her thoughts. "This Bermejo theory is not evidence-based. It's pure conjecture. We still have no idea who painted these portraits."

He rang off.

Zari rummaged through her toiletries and tossed a toothbrush, toothpaste, and a large tube of sunscreen into a zip-locked plastic bag. Like her mother, she had olive skin that turned a lovely brown in the sun. But after a lifetime of sun worship, her mother had developed several early-stage skin cancers in the past few years. As a result, Zari was now a committed slatherer—whether it was effective or not.

"Dotie Butterfield-Swinton is planning and scheming behind my back," she called across the hall to Aggie.

"Of course he is, my sweet naive Yank," Aggie's voice floated back.

"What do you mean?"

"It's the game we play in academia."

"That's not what I signed on for when I got my doctorate."

"None of us did." Aggie poked her head around the doorframe and fixed Zari with a serious look. "Newsflash: no job is perfect."

"Och."

"Och is right. Fight fire with fire, Zari. It just takes a wee bit of practice."

Aggie was out running an errand when Zari's mobile buzzed. It was Wil. At the sound of his voice, Zari sank down on her bed. She closed her eyes and allowed herself to teleport back to Bruges.

"Are you still planning to go to Oto this summer?" he asked.

"Yes—first Pau, then Oto."

"How are you going to get around?"

"By bus, I guess." She had booked a flight to Biarritz and a train reservation from there to Pau, but that was the extent of her planning so far.

"You should walk part of 'the Way,'" Wil said. "The pilgrimage route of Santiago de Compostela. It goes through southern France and crosses over the Pyrenees."

"I've heard of that. But I thought the Way was farther west."

"There are a couple of different routes. The Arles-Aragón route passes closer to Oto. I looked it up."

"Really?"

"Yeah. It's supposed to be beautiful. I've always wanted to do it."

"Then do it this summer," she said impulsively. "With me. It'll be romantic."

"If you call walking 20 kilometers a day and staying in hostels at night romantic."

"Think it over if you like. But I'm in." Zari flipped open her laptop and navigated to a map of southwestern France.

"You'll need to get in good shape. It's not easy, that journey."

"There's a lot you don't know about me, Wil. Including the fact that I'm a triathlete."

"When did you start doing triathlons?"

"My brother got into them about ten years ago and needed a partner. We used to do at least one a year together, but he's way out of my league now. He's training for an Ironman."

"So maybe I would have trouble keeping up with *you*."

"I promise to go at your pace. As long as on one of the nights we can ditch the group accommodations and find a romantic retreat."

"Let me think about this and get back to you," he said in a fake-formal voice.

"You're in a teasing mood today. I like it."

"I just got a commission to build a teak table and chairs. And I sourced some wood that was sitting at the bottom of a river in Indonesia for decades. Now it's going to get a new life. The client is letting me do what I want with the design, so I'm happy."

"How are your nights?"

"Since Bruges, much better. I give you credit for that, Zari." His voice was serious again.

"Thank you. I don't know if I deserve it, but I'll take it. How's Filip?"

"I visit him once a week whether he wants me or not. He's about the same. In a dark place."

"You're a good friend, Wil."

"I'm trying to be. I don't know." His voice trailed off.

"I'm looking at maps," she said to fill the silence. She zoomed in on a satellite image of the western Pyrenees. "Pau isn't actually that far as the crow flies from Oto."

"As the crow flies?"

"Quickest way from point A to point B is through the air. I wish I could speak Dutch so that *you* could be the one to explain sayings to me."

"Don't bother," he said.

"You don't want me to learn your language?" she asked, feeling hurt.

"No, I mean there's no value in you learning Dutch. Improve your Spanish if you want, but Dutch isn't going to get you anywhere."

"Not even with you?"

"You don't need to do anything to impress me, Zari." His tone softened. "I'm already impressed. If I wanted to speak Dutch with my girlfriend, I would have a Dutch girlfriend."

"Your girlfriend," she repeated, speed-worrying about possible complications, setbacks, pitfalls, and disappointments related to having a long-distance relationship with a Dutch man.

In the background she heard the rattle and whoosh of a tram.

"Are you talking and riding your bike at the same time?"

"Yeah."

"Don't hit any more tourists, or if you do, make sure they're built like oak trees." She took a deep breath. "Wil, what are we doing? I can't help but feel the shadow of you and Hana looming over us. It doesn't seem completely finished to me."

"It is. She broke up with me, remember?"

"I know. That means you didn't choose to end it. She did."

"Zari, all I know is I want more time with you. We haven't even gotten to the third date yet." His voice grew lower, more intimate. "But the second one was…"

"Epic?"

He laughed. "Yeah. I would say epic."

"I don't think it can be categorized as a date."

"What should we call it, then?"

"Let's just call it Bruges." She smiled, remembering. "And when we say Bruges, we'll know exactly what we mean."

16

Yorkshire, England
Spring, 2015
Zari

I T WAS ZARI'S FIRST time in a car since she moved to Scotland. Aggie was a calm, careful driver. Traffic was rolling along smoothly on the A92 and it was a dry, overcast day. Yet Zari had never been so uncomfortable in a moving vehicle.

"This feels like a bad dream," she said. "Why am I sitting in the driver's seat with no steering wheel? And look at all those cars whizzing down the wrong side of the road. It's terrifying."

"Ha! Americans always assume that your way is the right way. Well, guess what? It's you Yanks who drive on the wrong side of the road, not to mention the wrong side of the car."

"But we invented cars."

"That doesn't mean you can tell everyone else how to drive them. Besides, I thought the Germans invented gas-powered cars."

"Well, we brought cars to the masses. Remember the model T?"

"Just because you create something doesn't mean you can tell people how to use it."

"But most of the world does it our way, not yours."

"Most of the world is deluded."

"I'm going to humor you." Zari patted Aggie on the arm. "After all, I'm a guest in your country. Your way *is* better than our way. You can't deny that our gift of cars for all came packaged with extra bonuses, though—like oil addiction and melting glaciers. In America, we're all about value. Bang for the buck."

"Thanks for that," said Aggie. "So many unsolicited gifts come from across the pond."

"It's our pleasure."

That night they dined on ramen and rice bowls in downtown York with Lucy Karem Wixton, a friend of Aggie's who had traveled from London for the conference.

Zari twirled a forkful of noodles in spicy peanut sauce. "You said you were on the science side of textiles rather than the art side," she said to Lucy. "How does that work?"

"I use isotope analysis to track the origin of wool that's recovered in archaeological digs." Lucy's accent was difficult to place. She sounded British, but a few of her words were spoken with a melodic inflection that indicated some other heritage, as did her dark gold skin, almond-shaped eyes and glossy black hair.

"So you're an archaeologist?"

"Archaeozoologist, to be exact." Lucy grinned. "Try saying that five times fast."

"Hold on," Aggie said. "I'm guessing Zari didn't have to memorize facts about the English wool economy as a schoolgirl."

"That's true," Zari said. "Compared to Europeans, we aren't required to learn much history outside of our own. And a lot of us know far too little about that."

Lucy put down her glass. "The story is, English wool was in high demand from the Middle Ages right up to the Renaissance. The best wools came from Yorkshire—they were coveted all over Europe. A lot of the wool went to Italy, but there was a massive market in Northern Europe as well—Bruges, Amsterdam, some German cities."

"What went wrong?" Zari asked.

"The market suffered during the Hundred Years' War between France and England. This is an island, mind you. Getting the wool past French warships was dodgy at best. When that happened, the Spanish stepped in with merino wool. Eventually it displaced English wool for high-end fabrics."

"My shirt is merino wool." Zari's black long-sleeved shirt was actually an undershirt, but its soft sheen helped it pass for something a little classier.

Lucy reached out and took a pinch of the fabric between her thumb and forefinger. "Yeah—this is the stuff. It was so valuable that at one time, Spanish law decreed that anyone who took a merino sheep out of the country would be executed."

"Seriously?" Zari put down her fork.

"It's true. It's hard to imagine a sheep being that valuable, but those animals were like gold. The entire economy rode on them."

"What would be the equivalent today?" Aggie asked.

"Oil is probably closest. Fine wool became such an overvalued commodity that the big players grew unbelievably wealthy and powerful. The death penalty was a symbol of their power." Lucy leaned back in her chair. "And that, in a circuitous fashion, is why my talk tomorrow will attract hordes of fans. Yorkshire was the epicenter of the English wool trade. Underneath us lies an enormous treasure trove of long-dead sheep, and all around us are people with careers devoted to teasing out the secrets trapped in their remains."

Before returning to the flat they had rented for the weekend, they strolled the path along the medieval stone wall that ringed the city center. The spires of York Cathedral towered over everything. Its colossal scale was all the more impressive, Zari thought, considering when it was built. The laborers of the Middle Ages had no forklifts, no steel beams, no cranes, no power tools, no hard hats. Whatever tools they used they made themselves out of wood and iron. The cathedral builders were stretching the limits of physics and art and imagination, going big in an age when the scale of human building was small, creating structures so massive that the common people assumed God's hand must have been in it. How easy it would be, in a time of one-room huts, to arrive at that conclusion.

She turned to Lucy. "I wanted to ask you at dinner—what is your heritage?"

Lucy smiled. "My mysterious accent, right?"

Zari nodded.

"My mother is Lebanese and my father's English. They're both academics. We lived all over the world when I was growing up."

"You must speak several languages, then."

"Eight, I think. No, nine."

Lucy laughed at Zari's stunned expression.

"I know it sounds glamorous, but it has its disadvantages."

"Like what?"

"Well, you're American and California is home, right? And Scotland is home for Aggie. But I don't have a home."

"You're a global citizen," Aggie pointed out. "You can be at home anywhere, communicate with anyone."

"It's true, I'm adaptable. I can move between worlds. But I've always wished for the feeling that comes from being rooted somewhere." She shrugged and returned her gaze to the spires of the cathedral. "I'll never have that."

The last flare of sunlight set the stonework on the cathedral's spires aglow. Zari's eyes followed a line from the bell tower down to the foundation, and in her mind she saw the line plunge beneath the cobblestones to the artifacts that lay underneath, trapped in soundless layers of sediment.

She imagined every passing generation having its turn at life, then taking its place in the dust and ash that shrouded the stories of the people who came before. Traces of them lingered, secrets waiting to be unearthed: a wool dress rotting in the soil; a child's leather boot shot through with decay; the dark tarnish on a silver spoon that once stirred countless cups of tea. All buried below the quiet streets of York.

Though it was a warm night, she felt a shiver run down the knobs of her spine.

17

Spring, 2015
Yorkshire, England
Zari

O N THE TRIP NORTH after the conference, Aggie exited the
highway and followed a road deep into lush countryside. Blue seams opened up in the gloom overhead. The
road passed between the shadows of forested hills and snaked
through fields along the banks of a stream.

"Are you taking the long way back to Scotland?"

Nausea began to curdle in Zari's belly, triggering childhood
memories of miserable carsickness. She lowered the window
halfway and stared out. The sun slipped between the clouds,
long bars of light descending to the green fields below.

Aggie shook her head. "Surprise detour. We're in the valley
of Rye."

They pulled into a gravel parking lot and eased into a space
in front of a small stone building with a black slate roof. Tidy
rows of yellow tulips bordered the path that led to the building.

Zari heaved herself out of the car and stretched, raising her arms over her head and gulping in air. Deep healing breaths, as her mother would say. Aggie gave her a quizzical look.

"Channeling Richard Crone, are you?"

"Ha. Carsickness."

"When you're ready, walk around the back of the building. I'll buy our entrance tickets and meet you there."

Behind the building was a lush green lawn dominated by a single oak tree. Zari stood under its shade, transfixed. A gently sloping grassy hillside angled away from her, strewn with the half-ruined structures of some ancient stone complex. The skeleton of a cathedral loomed in the center of it all. Beyond the crumbling buildings a forest of oaks swept up the hill to the ridgeline.

"Well? What do you think?" Aggie asked from behind her.

"It's magical. What is this place?"

"Rievaulx Abbey. One of the first Cistercian monasteries in England. Its heyday was nearly a thousand years ago. During Henry the Eighth's reign, in the sixteenth century, it was pillaged. It's been falling into ruin ever since."

Inside the decaying cathedral, Zari paced around an enormous hewn stone slab. Grass crowded around it, softening its hard edges.

"The altar base," Aggie said.

Sun slanted through the Gothic arches of three perfectly preserved windows in the cathedral's east end. The piers and vaults of its upper reaches were carved with thin, graceful lines that recalled the repeating patterns on a seashell.

"I've never seen anything so beautiful and desolate at the same time," Zari said.

"It's one of my favorite places. A bit out of the way, but well worth it." Stepping across a still-intact threshold, Aggie pointed at a row of foundation stones. "This was the refectory, where the monks ate."

"I don't know much about the monastic world. But a life spent in silent prayer sounds pretty grim."

"They probably cherished prayer time as an opportunity to rest. This monastery was self-sufficient. It relied on the labor of the monks for income. They raised sheep, tanned leather, made beer, grew crops."

Closing her eyes, Zari conjured up an image of the complex bustling with life. The men in their brown robes at work in the fields, at prayer in the cathedral. Centuries of their labor had built this place. And now it sank into the earth millimeter by millimeter, being reclaimed by the soil. Keeping all its secrets. Shapeshifting.

"So much time and energy," she said with a sigh. "And this is all that's left."

"That's what they'll say about us in a few hundred years."

Zari imagined a big-box store with a caved-in roof, a strip mall with blown out windows, its neon-spangled signs obscured by climbing vines. Whoever had built this place could never be accused of inflicting ugliness on the world.

"The ruins of modern civilization won't hold a candle to this," she said.

Aggie began climbing up the hill toward the oaks. Zari wandered through the cloisters, running her hands over the smooth stone of the columns that stood around its perimeter, imagining the monks moving silently through the shaded corridors on their way to morning prayers.

In the shop adjacent to the monastery, she leafed through a book about illuminated manuscripts and paused at a page that showed a monk crouched inside the space formed by a gilded letter 'U.' An angel cupped her hands over his head, blessing him.

Zari bent closer and traced the illustration with her fingertip, pulled into the quiet world of the artist who drew these figures. She smelled the scent of beeswax, saw the flicker of candlelight on his desk, heard his quill scraping over parchment.

The buzz of her mobile in her pocket startled her.

It was Wil.

She stepped outside. The patchy clouds had closed their seams again and the sky was gray.

"Hey, you," she said. "Did you get my itinerary for the Way?"

"Yeah."

"Do you think it's realistic, or did I—"

"Zari," he cut in. "I need to tell you something."

A van rumbled by, gravel crunching under its wheels. Zari retreated under the canopy of an oak tree on the south side of the parking lot. A crow perched in a branch cocked its head at her.

"Okay. What's up?"

"Hana wants to try again."

Zari felt as if something inside her had been punctured by a needle. She took a shaky breath, her eyes on the crow.

"And what do you want, Wil?"

"I want to know you better, Zari. I want to spend more time with you. But I feel I need to try with Hana again. Not just for her, but for Filip. He wants this, too."

The guilt card. There was no arguing with that.

"I'm not going to say I'm happy for you, Wil. But I understand why you feel that way. I really do." Her eyes pricked with tears.

"I'm sorry." He was silent a moment. "There's so much history with Hana and me, and Filip, and our families."

"I get it, Wil. I knew you and Hana weren't done yet."

"I wish—" he began.

Aggie appeared around the side of the building.

"Sorry, Wil," Zari said softly. "I've got to go."

"Wait, Zari—"

She ended the call.

"Ready for the road?" Aggie called, fishing her car keys out of her bag. "What's wrong?"

The words reached Zari slowly, as if they had traveled through a thick fog. She swiped tears from her cheeks with the back of a hand.

"I made a plan. With a man. And..." She took a ragged breath and laughed in spite of herself. "Sounds like the beginning of a bad song, doesn't it?"

"Which man?"

"Wil. He's Dutch. He knocked me over with his bicycle in Amsterdam."

"That's why you were black and blue!"

"Yeah."

"Bastard." Aggie's eyes narrowed.

"No, no, he's a good guy. A great guy. I was going to walk the Way of St. James with him this summer. I thought he was calling me to confirm our plan." She struggled to maintain control of her voice. "But he was calling to say he's getting back together with his girlfriend."

"Bastard again," Aggie said, jangling her keys for emphasis.

"It's not like that. There's a whole complicated history—"

"You're too kind, Zari. Where's your anger? Own it."

"I know too much, is all. I can't be angry at him. I'm just sad. Mostly because I was so excited about walking the Way with him."

"You can still do it on your own."

"No." Zari shook her head. "I can't."

Aggie put an arm around Zari's shoulders and steered her through the parking lot. A lone yellow tulip lay flattened on the gravel near the car, its fragile petals splayed in all directions. At the sight of the flower Zari hesitated, her eyes welling up again. She blotted her eyes with a sleeve.

"What is it?" Aggie asked.

"My mother would say the universe is offering me a sign."

"Would she? Well, I say that I've always hated tulips." Aggie kicked the flower under the car and opened the passenger door for Zari.

"Let's get you back to Scotland."

18

Spring, 2015
St. Andrews, Scotland
Zari

ZARI GREW OBSESSED WITH the vanished societies that were entombed under every sidewalk, every building, every country village. She spent her spare moments researching religious houses in the Pyrenees. Most of them were just stories now; only rarely a ruin as gorgeous as Rievaulx Abbey still existed. Usually all that remained was a foundation, or a reconstructed church.

One place tugged at her imagination: a convent called the Abbey of Belarac that had been a stop along the Way of St. James on the French side of the mountains, back when the region was called Béarn. It was created by a Béarnais count and his Aragónese wife in the twelfth century and had been destroyed some five hundred years later.

Those slivers of information were all she had found. With the help of a librarian, she had hunted through French search engines and trolled the online archives of French history journals, but so far the Abbey of Belarac was another dead end.

A giant brown bear dug in a meadow. Zari watched it tear up the sod, flinging clumps of grass in all directions. It snuffled and grunted, its whole body vibrating with energy. Rising up on its massive hind legs, the bear spotted her and let out a furious roar. A desire to flee overtook her, but she was frozen, rooted to the spot. The bear pounded toward her through the tall grass. She opened her mouth to scream.

The sound of her own muffled cry woke her. Groping for the lamp switch, she sat up in bed, pressing the velvet bag of eucalyptus seedpods to her face, breathing deeply until her heart rate slowed. *It was just a dream, Zari.* Throwing back the sheets, she padded into the kitchen for a glass of water and sank into a chair at the kitchen table.

She pushed aside a stack of notes from her Oto research. The word Belarac caught her eye. It was nothing but a scar in the earth, she thought, feeling a rush of despair. She was chasing ghosts, and Belarac was one of them. She raised her head, her eyes drifting to the thumbtacked images of the two paintings on the wall. She had pinned two more images there when they got back from Rievaulx Abbey: the underdrawings of the paintings, showing the words 'Mira,' 'pray for my mother' and 'Bermejo.' She drew closer to them. The one difference between the two depictions of the word 'Mira' was that in Laurence Ceravet's painting, there were those repetitive patterns drawn into the prongs of the 'M.'

Aggie shuffled into the kitchen, yawning.

"What are you doing up?" she asked, pushing her hair out of her eyes.

"Can't sleep," Zari said. "Do you have a headlamp? And can I borrow your magnifying glass?"

Aggie rubbed her eyes. "Headlamp, no. Torch, yes."

She went back to her room and returned with a flashlight and the magnifying glass.

Zari flicked on the flashlight and shone it on the underdrawing of the merchant family's portrait. She peered through the magnifying glass at the 'M' in 'Mira.'

"These are words," she said excitedly. "Inside the letter 'M.' There are four—no, five—Latin words." She stepped back. "What do they say?"

Aggie peered through the magnifying glass. "The first word is 'Mira.'"

"Um, yeah, I can read that from here."

"No, the first *tiny* word is 'Mira' as well, just like the big one. Then we've got 'pinxit.'" She spelled it aloud and Zari scribbled it down on a notepad. "Next is 'et,' then 'Dei.' Shine the light closer." Aggie squinted, leaning in. "The last word is ridiculously small. It starts with an 'a.'" Her lips moved silently as she attempted to decipher the word. "I've got it. 'Adiutrix.'"

Aggie straightened up and regarded Zari. "Would you be so kind as to explain why you had me perform this wee task for you in the middle of the night?"

"Sorry. I thought that was a decorative design. I didn't realize they were words until just now."

"'Et' is 'and,' and 'Dei' is God," Aggie said. "So we know three of them: Mira and God. That's a start."

Zari went to her laptop and typed the words into a search engine. A moment later she laughed.

"If we're to believe this translation, it means: 'Wonderful painted and the cooperation.' No mention of God."

"I promise you 'Dei' means God in Latin."

Zari located a Latin-English translation site.

"OK, this is more like it. 'Mira' does translate to 'wonderful.' Also 'strange,' 'remarkable,' and 'amazing.' And 'pinxit' translates to 'paint.' Also 'draw,' 'depict,' 'embroider' and so on. 'Adiutrix' is 'female helper' or 'assistant' or 'accomplice.'"

"So what have we got, then?" Aggie yawned again.

"Wonderful Mira paints and is God's assistant?"

"Strange Mira embroiders and is God's accomplice," Aggie suggested.

"Or it could be 'amazing Mira draws and is God's female helper.'"

Aggie turned toward the doorway. "I'm going to sleep on it."

"Wait." Zari put her hand on Aggie's arm. "Would it be crazy for me to walk the Way of St. James alone?"

"Are you afraid?"

"No. Yes—a little," she admitted. "But why should that stop me?"

"Then go."

"I'll never get this chance again."

Aggie grinned.

"That's the spirit. And from what I've heard, you're never truly alone on the Way."

Aggie went back to bed. Zari resumed her post at the kitchen table, feeling a rush of energy. Raindrops pelted the window with silvery pings. She stared past her reflection in the glass to the darkness beyond, imagining a river of needles pouring from the sky. Forcing her attention back to the computer, she trolled through various social media sites. Her eyes caught on an image of Dotie Butterfield-Swinton's prim face. Next to it were two photographs of the Fontbroke painting, shown before and after the restoration. In all of his posts, he had used the hashtag #Bermejo.

Zari pulled on a sweater and clicked through her web browser's bookmarks for Bartolomé Bermejo, selecting an image of one of his paintings. The background of the painting—a multi-panel piece that had once hung in a church behind an altar—was extraordinarily detailed, with an illusion of three-dimensionality not many Spanish painters of the era had mastered. Her heart sank. Dotie's theory was plausible—the original background of the Fontbroke College portrait did look like Bermejo's work.

She waited until 8 a.m. to phone Vanessa Conlon.

"Did you get the images I sent you of the Fontbroke College portrait and the one of the merchant family? And the underdrawings?"

"Indeed I have," Vanessa said. "And a good morning to you, too."

"Sorry—I've got a bee in my bonnet. Have you seen this '#Bermejo' campaign of Dotie's?"

Vanessa laughed. "It's been hard to miss."

"We can't have one of the few examples of a woman artist's work simply erased from the record and attributed to a man because it makes a good story in the art world."

"Stranger things have happened, I'm afraid."

"How's this for strange: Why doesn't anyone float the theory that a young nun named Mira painted these portraits?"

"If you're going to make that claim, don't criticize what Dotie's doing. You're going down the same path of conjecture."

Zari gripped the edge of the table with one hand, pressing her thumb fiercely into the wood.

"Am I? What about silenced stories, Vanessa? Maybe this is one of them. We have evidence that an artist named Mira wrote her name on the portraits she painted, deep underneath the layers because she knew her work would be devalued or even rejected if her gender was known. If that name was a man's and that drawing was of a monk, I'm sure there would be all sorts of theorizing about a long-lost artist monk."

Vanessa was silent a moment.

"What does John Drake think?" she finally asked.

"He thinks there's a strong possibility that whoever painted the Fontbroke College portrait also painted the portrait of the merchant family."

"But he doesn't believe they were painted by Cornelia van der Zee?"

"No—for several reasons. All of her works are painted on Baltic oak, and her backgrounds are interiors rather than landscapes." She paused a moment, gathering her thoughts.

"Go on," prodded Vanessa.

"These two portraits are on Pyrenean oak, their backgrounds show landscapes, and they both have detailed underdrawings made with a metal stylus. There are plenty of examples of artists being identified through their underdrawings. I think the underdrawings are the key to figuring out who painted them. If we can just get x-rays done of a few known Van der Zee and Bermejo paintings, we'll know if the drawings underneath have the same characteristics. If not, we'll know neither of those artists were responsible for these two paintings. The National Gallery owns a Bermejo as well as a Cornelia van der Zee. We can start there."

"That sounds expensive."

"Yes—and that's why I called you, Vanessa." Zari cleared her throat. Her mouth was suddenly dry. "The real story here is the artist Mira. I want to keep tracing her path. I've already researched the possibilities. There's a chance I can qualify for a fellowship at the Mendenfield Trust in Oxford. But the only way I can get in the door is with the support of someone influential—someone like you."

She waited, her pulse pounding in her ears.

"I like boldness," Vanessa said. "It got me to Oxford, and it kept me here. And yes, I love to dig at those dark places where silenced stories live. The tricky part with your particular story is it doesn't have enough meat on its bones. This idea of Mira is tantalizing, and it's worth pursuing. But all you've got is a ghost. That's not enough to throw my weight behind. Not yet. You need more evidence of her existence and her work. You need to find solid documentation about her, you need a better paper trail—then I'll support your project."

Zari took a deep breath and slowly let it out.

"When I'm in the Pyrenees this summer I'll make stronger connections and build evidence. My hunch is that Mira lived in those mountains. Whatever else can be learned about her is there—I know it."

"Good luck, Zari."

"In the meantime, I'm going to start my own social media campaign. If Dotie can, why can't I?"

Vanessa laughed. "Won't he be surprised?"

Zari's eyes burned with fatigue. She staggered down the hall and fell into bed, pulling a pillow over her head to shut out the morning light. A year ago she had seen herself as a champion of Cornelia van der Zee, helping illuminate the life and work of one of the few women artists of the early Renaissance. When she had realized the importance of the Fontbroke College portrait to the women who worked and studied there, she became emotionally attached to it—never a good idea for an academic researcher. Then the news came of Laurence Ceravet's painting in Pau, and she had seen it as a bonus coup for her research. *The truth is*, she thought, burrowing under the blankets, *I wanted professional glory. I wanted to confirm the existence of one Van der Zee portrait and herald the discovery of another to the world.*

She groaned. Neither of those things would happen now. A wave of self-pity engulfed her. It was clearly time for some Portia-style deep breathing. After a few moments, she felt her anxiety dissipate. What was important now was teasing out this ghost Mira. Zari would try to set the art world on fire about her, this shadow who had spent five centuries slipping through the cracks of history. With that reassuring thought in mind, she fell asleep.

Four hours later, showered, dressed and caffeinated, Zari opened her laptop again. She took a long slug of Irish Breakfast and began to type.

"You might be a stickler for facts, Dotie," she said in her best Oxford accent, firing off one post after the next to various social media platforms and art history bloggers. "But I'm a stickler for keywords and search engine optimization. And I believe that gives me a bit of an advantage when it comes to a battle of hashtags."

BOOK 4

Caveat viator. Let the traveler beware.

1

Spring, 1500
Zaragoza, Aragón
Marguerite

RAMÓN WROTE TO MARGUERITE from the family's castle in the northern territory of Cerdagna. Her fingertips traced over the words *vengeance is ours,* so finely drawn they could have been inscribed by the careful hands of a monk. It was another of her husband's inconsistencies. He was a ruthless slaughterer of men, yet his long, elegant fingers wielded a quill with delicate precision.

Ramón and Pelegrín and their men had finally wrested the castle away from the French and now awaited a troop of knights-for-hire who traveled through the foothills of the Pyrenees from Béarn. In the meantime, Ramón was dispatching her, Marguerite, to represent the family at the annual council meeting of sheep breeders in Zaragoza. She could kill two birds with one stone, he wrote, by combing the ranks of Zaragoza's elite for young, titled girls with large dowries. For it was time they found Pelegrín a bride. To ensure she carried out her tasks efficiently, he forbade her from bringing Alejandro along.

Marguerite stood in the entryway of the family's Zaragoza home, staring at the likenesses of the former owners carved in stone above the doorway to the sitting room. The echoing footsteps of the servants chased away the silence that had accumulated in the house for the past year. There was a series of sharp thumps as a servant flung open the heavy wooden shutters to the interior courtyard.

She mentally ran through the list of noble families who kept homes in Zaragoza, discarding more than half of them based on her husband's political affiliations and known enemies. Then she sent servants to call on each family in turn and request a visit. There was no time to waste; she wanted to leave Zaragoza as soon as the council meeting was over. Every moment Alejandro was left under the care of Beltrán was a moment too long.

During the meeting, Marguerite had difficulty following the minutiae of the council members' grievances and agenda items. Most of the talking was done by two members of the group: the wool merchant Carlo Sacazar and the royal representative of King Ferdinand and Queen Isabella. Carlo was determined to secure funding for road maintenance and security between Zaragoza and the mountain pass into Béarn. He brought up the topic relentlessly, even when the other men were deep into discussions about disputes involving the mountain folk. She amused herself counting the annoyed sighs and grimaces of the other men whenever the merchant interjected another comment about royal road funding. Just before the meeting's end, the royal agent brought out a parchment roll embossed with the seal of the queen.

"The Queen desires that each of you sign this decree," he said. "It states that any man who willfully takes merino sheep outside the borders of the kingdom, or sells any such sheep to a foreigner, will receive a penalty of death."

Marguerite sat up straighter in her chair. One of the council members stood.

"Since when does the Castilian queen run the affairs of sheep breeders in Aragón?" he asked. Two spots of color burned on his cheeks.

"The queen may not share her husband's Aragónese blood, but I assure you they rule as one," the royal agent snapped. "Do you question her majesty's authority?"

The man quickly sat, his eyes fixed on the table before him, a muscle twitching in his jaw. Marguerite knew the royal agent would report any treasonous reactions to Queen Isabella.

Carlo cleared his throat. "What about the peace agreements between the valleys in the high mountains? The animals pass back and forth across boundaries in those places with the blessing of kings and nobles alike."

The royal agent scoffed. "We care not about the comings and goings of simpletons and their paltry flocks. This decree is about fine merino wool, about the biggest and best breeding operations in the land. In short, it is about you!" He pointed at each man around the table, ignoring Marguerite.

The council members fell to grumbling amongst themselves. Marguerite glanced at Carlo. A trace of anxiety was visible on his round face. When he saw her looking at him, he pulled up the corners of his mouth into a placid smile.

One of the men spoke. "Can we no longer sell the flesh or the wool of sheep across the mountains?"

The royal agent jabbed a finger at the parchment. "Read it for yourselves. This is about keeping live animals out of foreign lands. No foreigner may profit from breeding merino sheep. It is as simple as that."

After the meeting, Carlo approached Marguerite. He bowed deeply.

"My lady, I am honored to be in your presence," he said. "I have had the honor of dining with your husband on a number of occasions, and we have made some very fortuitous business arrangements between us. I take it you are here in the baron's place. May I ask why he was not able to attend?"

"He is at war in the north with our eldest son."

"May they both see victory and return to you as soon as God wills it," Carlo said. "Please know that I am at your service while you visit Zaragoza. Anything you require—anything at all—it would be my pleasure to provide. In fact, my wife is here visiting with old friends and family while I conduct business. If I do not extend our hospitality to you, she will have my hide."

Marguerite smiled. "That would be quite unpleasant, I imagine."

He followed her out into the sun.

"The Abbey of Belarac raises merino sheep, does it not?" Marguerite pulled her hood down to shade her eyes. Two of her guards walked behind them, their long swords protruding under the hems of their cloaks. Carlo's own men ranged a few paces in front of them.

"Ah! You know the workings of their arrangement?"

"Our family are patrons of the abbey."

"Of course, of course. But I confess I am surprised." He glanced at her sideways. "Women rarely share their husbands' interest in these details."

"My husband is often away. He counsels me to stay apprised of our affairs in his absence. It is not wise to leave those matters in the hands of a steward."

Carlo tilted his head toward her with a conspiratorial air. "As the royal agent said, the queen does not concern herself with the ancient agreements. Belarac, in the grand scheme of things, means nothing to her. In my opinion—" he leaned in closer still, his voice barely audible, "—this so-called law is all bluster."

"How can you be sure?"

They entered a square that faced a small church, its stone façade blackened with age. Two teams of mules pulled wooden carts loaded with casks and woven baskets across the square.

"The affairs of the royals are not that much different from the affairs of merchants. On a much grander scale, of course," he said. "War is costly. There is always the difficulty of finding funds for the next battle. Now the problem, as I see it, is this: they have banished the Moors and Jews from the kingdom, and squeezed what riches they could from them."

"You refer to the confessions?"

"Yes, yes. They rid the land of heretics and replenished the royal coffers at the same time, killing two birds with one stone, as it were."

"How men love that phrase."

He laughed. "Do you find it tiresome? Or perhaps too violent. What would you suggest instead?"

They left the square and entered the lane where the Oto home stood.

"Perhaps one could better say, 'Pluck two apples with one grasp.'"

"I will remember that. Now, the royals—and rightly so, I might add—want to keep their gold in the kingdom. The merino sheep become more valuable with each passing year. And the numbers grow beyond comprehension. During the transhumance from north to south, you would swear an inland ocean crowned with foam roils across the land. But of course it is not water but sheep spreading out as far as the eye can see."

"If these sheep are so valuable, why are you confident Belarac's flock is immune to the royal decree?"

"Ah—it all circles back to the gold I mentioned. Belarac has done nicely for itself with a small flock of sheep. That is true. But what is a drop of water when you have an entire sea at your feet?"

They had reached her doorway.

"I am much relieved. Now I will take my leave of you, sir." She half-turned toward the door.

"Baroness, where are my manners? You must come for supper. I will never hear the end of it from my wife if you do not."

"I leave again for Castle Oto in a few days."

"Then tomorrow! Let it be tomorrow. Please, you would honor us so."

She hesitated.

"You are too kind," she said. "It would be my pleasure."

As soon as Marguerite entered the Sacazar home and was relieved of her cloak, Flora Sacazar led her to the fireplace that dominated the sitting room off the cavernous entry hall.

"Please warm yourself."

She clapped her hands. A servant disappeared and reentered a moment later leading two small girls. The girls, dressed in diminutive versions of their mother's wine-red velvet gown and puffed white sleeves, bowed their heads.

"How sweet they are," Marguerite said. "How lovely."

She smiled at the girls, who regarded her from under their dark lashes. They curtsied as one.

Carlo Sacazar entered the room, beaming. "Oh, our girls are a treasure. A treasure!" he boomed.

The girls broke into broad grins at the sight of their father. One was a bit taller than the other, but their faces were nearly identical.

"Yes, yes, they are the sun and the moon to us, are they not, dear? Do you have any daughters, Baroness?" Flora waved a hand at the servant, dismissing the children. The girls followed the servant out of the room, holding hands.

Marguerite shook her head. "Two sons. One is at war in the north with my husband. The other is still young, at home with his nurse."

"Ah! How old is he?" asked Flora.

"He has seen four winters," she said.

"The age of my youngest!" Flora sucked in her breath as if it were a shocking coincidence. "Perhaps one day they will wed." She fixed her husband with a meaningful gaze.

"By the grace of God, the house of Sacazar is now titled two times over and our girls may marry into the ranks of the noble-born," Carlo explained. "So it is not outside the realm of possibility."

Flora clasped her hands together against her bosom, setting her triple string of pearls into a riot of gentle clacking. "Imagine if our daughters wed your sons. The glorious children they would make together. The strapping boys, the beautiful girls."

Marguerite tipped her head back and stared at Flora. "You had best set your sights on another family if you desire granddaughters," she said coolly. "In the house of Oto, warriors beget warriors."

2

Spring, 1500
Béarn
Béatrice

JUST AFTER THE SPRING shearing, Béatrice left the abbey, her oxcart ensconced within a great mule train that made its way from the monastery of San Juan de la Peña over the mountains into the rolling plains of Béarn. The journey was slowed by the shambling pace of the mules and the monks' frequent rest breaks.

When her cart passed through the modest port doors of Rébénacq, the anxiety that had thrummed in her veins on the rutted roads lifted. Though she and her driver Gaston had traveled in relative safety amongst the monks, she was haunted by fear of the bandits who plied the roads and the bears and wolves that lurked in the shadowy forests.

Rébénacq was much smaller than Nay, and she entertained no hopes of finding a wealthy wool merchant here. But it was a start—the first of the market towns that studded the way north into France. The dull clop of the mules' hooves echoed through the narrow lane. The modest houses were built of whitewashed cob and timbers, and the thatched roofs put her in mind of so many bristle-brushes. She squinted at each doorway they passed, searching the walls. Finally, she spied it. Embedded above a double oak door, a scallop shell carved in stone.

"We've arrived, Gaston," she said.

Under a cloudy sky she made her way to the Place de la Bielle, where merchants hawked their wares. Spindly-legged goats and wet-eyed sheep milled about in willow holding pens. An iron forger piled stakes and nails on a low table. Nearby a tanner laid out cured rectangles of leather and piles of parchment, and next to him stood a stout woman whose table was heaped with balls of coarse wool.

"Quite an assortment you have here, Madame," Béatrice said. She picked up a roll of nubby gray yarn and turned it over in her hands. "Well spun."

"My thanks, Abbess." The woman's wide blue eyes were on Béatrice's signet ring. "We usually see but one abbess at this market. She comes every year without fail. Always in search of better wool, and always disappointed. Wants to know if anyone in these parts sells the fine wool, the merino." She chuckled, shaking her head. "I don't believe a soul in this town would recognize a ball of merino wool if it struck 'em between the eyeballs."

"Which abbess was that?" Béatrice asked.

"A foreigner. Aragónese, I think. Though her servants all speak the local tongue."

"Ah, I believe I know the lady. Has she come this year?"

The woman shook her head. "Haven't caught a glimpse of her yet. And she's hard to miss, if you don't mind me saying. Which convent do you come from, if I might ask?"

"Belarac, in the mountains." Béatrice replaced the ball of coarse yarn in its basket. "Do you sell your wool to merchants?"

"Wouldn't that be a fine thing! Wool merchants don't have much use for Rébénacq."

The tanner, a compact man with bulging brown eyes and a red knob of a nose, stepped closer. "If you're wanting a wool merchant, Abbess, you've just missed him. There was one rented a room from the notary not a week ago. From Toulouse, he was. He'd traveled all the way to Jaca searching for the finest woolens, was what he told the notary."

"Toulouse to Jaca? That is quite a distance to travel."

"He made his fortune in pastel, that was the gossip. There's plenty like him in the north, wanting the finest fabrics for their blue dye."

"My homespun wasn't good enough for him," the stout woman said. "Didn't even warrant a sniff."

"Where did he go when he left Rébénacq?" Béatrice asked.

A housewife in a long brown cloak with a woven basket over one arm approached the tanner's table.

"The wool market in Pau," he said, turning away to help the woman.

Béatrice stood over the great bulk of Gaston in the stable, calling his name. She prodded him in the shoulder with her foot.

"Gaston! Arise!"

His eyelids flapped open. "What's wrong?"

"Nothing is wrong. We must ride north without delay. Ready the mules."

He sat up and ran a hand through his wiry yellow hair. "Did we not just arrive here?"

"Yes, but there is nothing of interest to me in this town." She crossed her arms. "Time is wasting."

He heaved himself up without another word.

3

Spring, 1500
Béarn
Béatrice

THE RIDE FROM RÉBÉNACQ to Pau through undulating
fields and along a narrow, snaking stream was unevent-
ful. Bèatrice reasoned to herself that they were safe here
in the broad plains because there was no place for a bandit to
hide. A stray dog followed them for a while, but Gaston's shouts
frightened it away.

When they rolled across the stone bridge that straddled the
river in Pau, the sun glowed behind a bank of wispy clouds
in the west. This place was a far cry from the modest market
towns of the south. The towers of a great castle loomed on the
cliffs overlooking the river. The counts of Béarn ruled these
lands from that castle, Béatrice knew. Perhaps a member of the
ruling family looked down upon them even now, marking their
progress over the bridge. Béatrice drew a deep breath. She must
not let fear get the best of her. She had only to fix her mind on

one task—finding the wool merchant from Toulouse.

In the morning Béatrice went from her lodging in a convent's guesthouse straight to the livestock market and made her inquiries at the sheep stalls. The oily scent of lanolin was nearly overwhelming, the cobblestones littered with dung and mud-spattered clumps of fleece. The merchant of Toulouse was well known by the livestock breeders, especially those who traded in sheep. He visited twice a year, she was told, and stayed at the residence of a notary who lived nearby at the Place des Marchands.

The square was quiet when she passed through it to the notary's house later that day, though the aroma of lanolin still clung to the air. In the notary's small parlor sat a man wearing a long blue robe fastened with a golden clasp at his throat. Laid before him on a writing table lit by beeswax candles was a leather-bound parchment book. It was opened to a page crammed with rows of numbers.

"Esteven de Vernier at your service, Abbess," he said, standing.

She nodded. "Merchant of Toulouse?"

"Yes. What is your business with me, Abbess?"

"I was told you seek fine woolens." She fumbled with the satchel around her shoulder and pulled out a square of finished but undyed merino fabric.

The merchant took the square of fabric and ran his hands over it, turning it this way and that in the candlelight.

"This equals anything I saw in Nay—and the best fabrics of Béarn come from there. Where did you procure it?"

"My own nuns washed the wool, spun the yarn and wove the fabric. I wish to find a buyer in the north."

"I'm afraid I require a quantity greater than your nuns can produce."

The angles of his face were sharp, his eyes half-hidden under puffy lids, and his mouth was a thin red gash.

"Tell me how much you require and we will provide what you need. We source our merino wool from the highlands of Aragón, and there is no better fleece than that. We have many looms and more hands," she said in as confident a voice she could muster. "And as you would be my first buyer, I will give you a lower price than you now pay anyone else. If the quality of our fabric is not to your standards, you are free to break any contract we make."

He tossed the square of fabric on the table. "Aragón, eh? I will entertain the idea. In the morning I shall have a good look at this fabric in the daylight. Only then will I know if it truly merits my interest."

He nodded to her and she knew the interview was over.

The next morning Béatrice had her answer. A folded-up rectangle of linen paper in her pocket outlined the arrangement. She stared at the swirl of letters and numbers. What on earth had she been thinking, promising so much to the merchant of Toulouse? She crossed to the shutter and flung it open. Drizzle was falling from a dull gray sky, and the open window did little to illuminate her cramped room.

Across the lane a housewife emptied a chamber pot into the gutter, barking commands over her shoulder at an unseen servant. Three children burst into view, chasing an orange cat down the lane. It slipped through the housewife's open door, igniting a flurry of loud whispers from the children. They gathered in a fidgety clump just beyond the threshold of the door, bobbing and ducking their heads in an effort to catch sight of the cat. One of them spotted Béatrice. His eyes widened in fear at the sight of her. She repressed a laugh, forcing the corners of her mouth down, wagging a finger back and forth at the children. They spun on their heels and sprinted away across the rain-slicked cobblestones.

The worst of it was, none of the problems that assaulted her mind could be solved now. She did not dare return on the mountain roads to Belarac alone—they must find a mule train or a caravan of oxcarts to join. She drummed her fingers on the windowsill. The orange face of the cat appeared in the doorway across the lane. It took a cautious step forward and froze, its eyes caught by the movement of Béatrice's hand. She stilled her fingers and the cat relaxed, sauntering off down the lane as if it hadn't a care in the world.

The road through the plains that connected each market town had been safe enough, she reasoned. If she and Gaston returned on that road to the town of Arudy, they stood a better chance of finding a mule train or some other group of travelers because three roads converged there. Gaston would protest, he would cite the dangers of the open road, but she would counter with the argument that the roadway between Pau and Arudy was the safest portion of the journey.

The sky darkened and its mantle of gray clouds unleashed a shower, sending a spray of rain through the window. She swung the shutters closed. Whether Gaston liked it or not, they would leave in the morning.

The rain was fierce as Béatrice and Gaston exited the port door of Pau and rattled along the track to the main road. Overhead billowed storm clouds the color of granite. Ominous booms of thunder drifted in from the south. No other carts or riders were visible in the pelting rain, and though Gaston had ceased his muttering, Béatrice knew he simmered with resentment at having to undertake the journey in such conditions. The wheels sank into the muck, wracking and jolting the cart with irritating regularity. The going was slow but they would still make Arudy well before nightfall. Their cart carried no load, the mules were well fed and rested.

The emptiness of the road was eerie. The farm laborers who would normally be readying the fields for planting were waiting out the rain; the livestock were huddled under oak and walnut trees. She saw not a single rabbit skittering across the road nor a bird in the sky. It was as if she and Gaston drove a ghost cart pulled by invisible beasts, their passage unseen and unmarked. No creature with any wits went abroad in such weather, she reminded herself.

"I suppose that makes me witless," she said aloud.

"Abbess?"

"Never mind, Gaston."

In Arudy they rolled across the bridge that spanned the River d'Ossau. The water ran high and the mountains that stood sentinel over the valley were shrouded by storm clouds. When they clattered to a halt outside the abbey, Gaston dismounted and rang the bell, raindrops cascading off the broad rim of his felt hat. Beatrice's sodden wool cloak felt as if it was weighted with iron, and she set her jaw to keep her teeth from chattering. However long they had to wait in this town, she told herself, no danger had befallen them on the roadway. The risk had been worth it.

But the next morning their luck changed. The rains had only worsened in the night. Now the river had burst its banks and the road to Belarac was washed out. They were trapped in Arudy, at the mercy of the rain.

There was nothing Béatrice could do but wait.

4

Spring, 1500
Nay, Béarn
Amadina

MARKET DAY WAS ALWAYS crammed with so much activity Amadina fell into bed exhausted at the end of it. Today was no exception. In fact, it was worse than usual. The events of the day had so consumed her that she almost forgot about the letter she had stuffed in her pocket that morning, unread. Sitting at her desk in the weak evening light, Amadina pored over the lines of dark script. Esteven de Vernier, the merchant from Toulouse who had faithfully purchased her wool fabrics for the past decade, had found another supplier in the region who provided him with equally high-quality merino fabrics, at a cheaper price. He was terminating their contract.

She dropped the letter on her desk and stood, her hands balling into fists. Picking up a fine Venetian glass cup, she weighed it in her palm, then flung it with all her force at the fireplace. It shattered into the flames.

Her wimple felt like a vise around her face, squeezing her cheeks with excruciating force. She tore at it, ripping the fabric in her haste to get it off, and threw it into the fire. The wool smoked, giving off a nauseating odor. She shook out her long black hair with trembling fingers, her eyes fixed on the smoldering fabric. The Toulouse merchant had never breathed a word of discontent to her. Now this letter had appeared with no warning.

Where else in Béarn could anyone produce a finished merino fabric as fine as hers? There were merchant towns running all the way down the river Pau, but no Béarnais sheep breeder owned merinos. Then there was Bayonne, the port city in the west. The Basque shepherds of the coastal mountains, if they had any brains, certainly plied their goods there. Whether they raised merino sheep, she did not know. She scratched her scalp fiercely, relieving the constant itch of the lice that prowled the roots of her hair.

Plucking another Venetian cup from her desk, she lobbed it at the fire. The sound of the glass shattering against the stone hearth was profoundly satisfying. The searing rage in her chest began to dwindle. It leaked out through her lungs in short exhalations and the pulse in her temple slowed.

Anger had always been her weakness. Now was the time to wait and think things through, instead of acting in haste. She mopped her face and throat with a square of linen, then buried her face in it, breathing in the scent of the ambergris oil she dabbed on her neck each morning.

For now, she would tamp down the current of impulsivity that led her around, jerking her this way and that like a donkey on a tether. She wrinkled her brow, the linen square balled in one hand, and set about devising a plan. First, she would make up the lost income by selling her wool fabric in other market towns around the region. A few words to the right people, greased with a gold coin or two, and her product would be shipped down the River Pau all the way to the sea if necessary.

As for this new rival—naturally, her mind had turned at first to Béatrice of Belarac. Her spies had told her when last they visited Nay that Béatrice had a shepherd boy building looms for her. But no coarse shepherd could fashion a loom capable of producing fabric fine enough for a merchant of Toulouse. What was more, no one at Belarac could work a loom with the requisite skill. Béatrice would have to be watched, yes, but she was not a danger yet.

Instead, Amadina would send servants at once to Rébénacq and Pau, have them make inquiries about this new rival. Gossip flowed like wine along the market road of Béarn. Any new-comer—any deviance from the usual order of things—would be a topic of great interest, snipped apart and stitched back together for weeks by the flapping tongues of housewives and artisans. If those efforts turned up nothing, she would personally take up the matter and travel all the way to Toulouse, to the home of Esteven de Vernier himself. She would know soon enough who had stolen her best contract.

Straightening her shoulders, she tossed the balled-up linen on the charred wreckage of her wimple. This would be more complicated than simply asking for Carlo's help, but there was something delicious about devising a solution on her own. Just as that heady thought passed through her mind, the linen square caught fire.

Amadina's eyes gleamed. She watched the flames blaze, reducing all evidence of her rage into hot black dust, and was overcome with a sense of deep peace.

5

URING BÉATRICE'S ABSENCE, MIRA and Sister Agathe supervised the washing and dyeing operations. Nuns heaved the matted wool into copper cauldrons full of hot water and stirred it with long wooden sticks, then rinsed it in water up to their knees until they were numb with cold. Finally they lugged the wet fibers outside and spread them on willow drying racks, standing guard to keep birds from stealing bits of the wool for their nests as it steamed in the sun.

The dyeing process was less physically demanding, but it was filthy work. Village children patrolled walnut trees in the valley each fall, collecting nuts and saving the shells. The crushed shells were tossed in iron vats of hot water and simmered with the wool until the fibers turned black.

Busying herself with pigments and oils in the chapel, Mira examined her dye-stained hands. The black marks had faded to the color of a walnut shell—the same color as Elena's skin. She imagined Elena's reaction to the cherubs, angels, and saints that glowed with life on the stone walls. Even if God meant nothing to her, surely she would be impressed by this show of devotion to Him.

Mira had saved the Virgin Mary for last. The pilgrim Sebastian had advised her to do so. With each day of practice, he said, her skills grew stronger. Therefore, she should wait until the end of the project to execute the most complicated part.

She missed him and his stories. Her fantasies about leaving Belarac and striking out for Compostela and the sea had begun to radiate in new directions, like the petals of a buttercup opening to the dawn light. She still longed to visit the sea, but now there were other attractions tugging at her imagination: the compact, winding streets of Flanders, the spires of great cathedrals on the long road north. As she mixed her pigments, measured out linseed oil, and stirred her paints, she spun a dream world in which she followed the stars north, then east, then south again, winding her way between the ateliers of the great masters who taught their apprentices all they knew.

A few weeks after Béatrice's departure the valley of Belarac was pummeled by heavy rain and hail. The gentle plink of spring rain showers was expected, but the ferocious clatter made by sheets of icy rain was unsettling. After several days of this, every resident of the abbey was on edge. Outside the gates, the villagers watched the skies and worried. The normal spring routines of tilling and sowing were delayed.

One morning, Mira awoke to an eerie silence. The rain had stopped. A sunbeam played on the floor near her bed. Quickly she dressed and padded through the cool corridors of the dormitory, past the cloisters, across the courtyard to the abbey gates.

To get a better view she hauled out the ladder that she had used to scale the walls as a child. From the high stone wall, she saw partially submerged fields forming a long, glistening pool of mud. The stream had burst its banks.

Clambering down the ladder, she pounded on the door of the warming house and woke the elderly gatekeeper.

"I only open the gate for the abbess, and when she's not here, for Sister Agathe," the woman said, her voice blurred by sleep.

"If the tools in the washing station rust because you would not let me fetch them," Mira said crisply, "the abbess will make sure you see the sharp end of a switch."

The gatekeeper fumbled for the keys.

The early morning sun was just beginning to illuminate the flooded valley. Mira slogged to the doorway of the washing station, her skirts in her hands. Her feet ached with cold in their boiled wool shoes.

The great copper cauldrons were half-submerged and the tool chest was on its side in a corner. Sodden sticks and brambles bobbed in the dark water. She pushed through the mess.

"Careful now," a deep voice said.

She turned. A man stood in the doorway, wearing the distinctive felted wool vest and hat of the Aragónese shepherds. He pushed his hat back on his head, revealing the angles of his face.

"Arnaud?"

He was much taller than her now, his jaws edged with a short beard. Where was her childhood friend? His flesh had been transformed into that of a man.

She wiped her muddy hands on her cloak. "You are so tall! And your voice. What happened to it?"

He laughed.

She pointed at the chest. "The tools will rust."

"I know." He waded to her and held out a sack. "Hold this."

With a mighty shove, he righted the chest. Then he unlatched the front door and pushed it open, revealing the mud-covered tools. "We'll clean these off, give them a lick of oil. They'll be fine," he said.

"What about the sheep?"

He fished out a set of shearing blades and stuffed them into the sack. "We moved them to higher ground last night."

"And your cabin?"

"Flooded. We'll camp near the sheep with our dogs."

"What about wolves and bears?"

"We've got our dogs, our staffs and daggers, and I carry a bow and arrows. Fire frightens the wild beasts too. We'll keep it burning all night."

Slowly they made their way back across the soggy fields. Mira stumbled and sank into the muck. Jerking up a leg to free herself, she lost her balance and fell.

"Blast!" she cursed.

Arnaud extended an arm to pull her up. She watched his brown fingers close over her own. The feel of his skin on hers set off a strange tingle in her belly.

She took one step and fell again.

They looked at one another in silence for a moment, then both burst out laughing.

He pulled her up again and they walked hand in hand to the gates. Vapor rose from the stone walls in the heat of the morning sun.

"It's hard to imagine you living out your days behind those gates," Arnaud said.

Mira withdrew her hand from his. "Where else would I go?"

"You dream of the sea. Of journeying west."

She was shocked into silence for a moment.

"Do you mock me?" she finally said. "We were children when I said those things. You shared the same dreams, and yet I do not see you abandoning Ronzal and tramping over the mountains to the sea. One day you will assume your place on the council of households and your days of roaming the mountains will be over."

"Maybe so," he said amiably. "But Mira, you have a choice. You can refuse the veil." His voice grew sober. "Once you take the vows you'll be trapped in there for good."

"How dare you say such things to me?" Her astonishment was now eclipsed by anger. "You know nothing of my life. You are one of the mountain folk. What can possibly make you believe you have any right to advise me on my future?" The harsh words tumbled out in a rush.

"What I say is true." His eyes never left hers. "You're not bound to this place. Not yet."

A crow perched on the roof of the warming house rasped. There was a rush of wings as the bird took flight and wheeled across the blue sky. Mira longed to follow it, to glide across the mountains west to the sea.

"Mira...?" Sister Agathe's voice floated across the courtyard.

It was time to take her punishment, although Sister Agathe was much too soft-hearted to wield the kind of discipline that Mother Béatrice displayed. Besides, Mira needed a task, any task, no matter how menial or dull—anything to take her mind off Arnaud's words.

Just past dawn the next day, Mira heard the frantic clanging of the gate bell. She followed Sister Agathe to the courtyard. As soon as she saw who was at the gates she broke into a run.

"Arnaud!"

He was supporting the sagging figure of a man. The gatekeeper let them in and two servants emerged from the kitchens.

"Fetch blankets, hot water and wine. And clean linen. Hurry!" Mira ordered.

They laid the man out on a straw pallet in the infirmary. His face was pale, his eyes shut. His arm was smeared with blood and dirt.

She plunged a linen rag into the kettle of hot water, then opened a small leather bag and placed a pinch of dried herbs on the man's tongue.

"Boxwood tips, for fever," she explained. "I have no butterwort, though. Can you fetch some from the cliffs for him today?"

Arnaud nodded, pressing a jug of wine to the man's lips.

"How did it happen?" She unrolled a length of linen and wound it around the man's arm, tied it off and tucked the ends in.

"Wolves. They got into a pen, attacked the sheep and killed his dog." He tipped his head at the man. "He got in the middle of it. Seems stupid, but our dogs mean everything to us."

"How did you fight them off?"

"Arrows, torches. We harassed them 'til dawn. They only attack under cover of darkness."

"Now that the flood waters have receded, will you bring the sheep back down to the valley?" asked Agathe.

"And stand in muck up to their knees? Their hooves'll rot. We've no choice but to keep them on higher ground."

"Will you send some of the village men to help stand guard tonight?" Mira asked Agathe. There was a long silence. "Mother Béatrice would not want more sheep to be killed," Mira added. "It would be a blow to the abbey's income, the loss of good wool."

"Yes," Agathe said reluctantly. "The villagers will help."

"We're grateful," Arnaud said. He bowed to both women and left the room.

Mira followed, ignoring Sister Agathe's disapproving stare.

"Wait for me at the gates!" she called after him.

She flew down the corridors to her chamber, scribbled some lines in Latin on a sheet of linen paper, then salted the ink and blotted it. She sped across the courtyard, waving the paper in the air.

"Dry, dry!" she said.

He had already been let out by the gatekeeper, and she slid

the paper through the iron bars to him. Behind him, the flooded fields shimmered under the sunlight.

"You speak to paper now, is that it?" Arnaud asked.

"Yes. Paper listens and never judges."

"Ah." A smile creased his face and the old familiar warmth lit up his eyes.

She smiled back at him, relieved.

"I am sorry for yesterday." She wanted to say more but the words tangled in her throat.

He gave her a searching look, then shrugged. "As am I."

She handed him the paper. "A riddle. I had the idea in my head last night. It is my turn, you know."

He read the words aloud.

"I am as delicate as a leaf
and more powerful than a bear.
I am a giver of life
and a bringer of death.
I can kiss a baby's cheek in the evening
and bend iron the next morning.
I travel by land, by sea, by air.
I am at once visible and invisible.
What am I?"

"It's a tricky one, this. Your trickiest riddle yet, I warrant."

"Do you know the answer?"

"Nothing comes to mind." He rubbed his chin. "I'll have to think on it a while."

"Are you just being kind?"

"No. This riddle confounds me. It truly does."

She took hold of the iron bars. "When you are ready with your answer, come find me."

"If I survive this night, I will. With the wolves and such."

"You are not afraid of wolves, Arnaud de Luz. You are not afraid of anything, as far as I can tell."

"Oh, you're wrong there, Mira. I do fear something."

"What?"

"This creature you speak of in your riddle." He chuckled.

"What is so amusing?"

"You," he said.

He turned and walked away, the paper rolled up in his hand. Over the hiss of the stream she heard him whistling.

Mira watched him scale the hillside until he vanished into a dense stand of pines. She clasped her hands and prayed, asking that her friend Arnaud be spared in the event of another wolf attack this night. Then she returned to the infirmary to administer more herbs to the wounded shepherd, trying not to think about the approach of twilight or the snapping jaws of wolves.

6

Spring, 1500
Abbey of Belarac, Béarn
Mira

IT WAS THE HOUR of vespers. The nuns were on their knees in the chapel, their joined voices murmuring prayer after prayer. Their wavering voices rose and fell, mingling with the distant tolling of the gate bell. Beyond the carved wooden candlesticks on the altar, the luminous colors of the frescoes on the chapel walls gleamed.

Mira willed herself to pay attention to the prayers, but the insistent ringing of the bell conjured up images of wounded shepherds and snarling wolves in her mind. The frothing waters of the valley stream had receded since the days of the flood, but some of the fields were still awash in mud and the soil was so unstable on the hillsides that the Ronzal shepherds had not yet taken the flocks to the high pastures. Perhaps another wounded shepherd stood outside, bleeding. Why did the gatekeeper not attend to the visitor? She threw an apologetic glance at Agathe, slipped out of the chapel and ran to the abbey gates.

Before her stood the gatekeeper, key in hand. The gates were flung wide and an oxcart stood just outside them. Standing in front of the cart were two monks. Gaston had hold of the leather thong that rang the iron bell outside the gates, and it was he who jangled it.

"Gaston!" Mira shouted. "Stop that at once. The gates are open. Drive the cart inside."

He stilled his hand, but kept it wrapped around the cord.

One of the monks approached her and bowed. "With the grace of God, we come bearing sorrowful news." He gestured at the cart. "There rests your abbess."

Mira's hands flew to her mouth.

"God took her at the abbey in Arudy, in the night. We made the journey in haste to bring her back to you."

Mira rushed to the cart and stared inside. A rough wooden box lay the length of the cart bed, its top fastened with iron latches.

A stream of curious nuns and servants drifted toward the gate. Agathe's voice rose up.

"What is this commotion about?"

Mira could not speak. Her mind was fogged by disbelief. She half-listened to Agathe's measured voice dispensing directions to the monks and cajoling Gaston into releasing the bell cord. She followed Gaston to the stable, watched him unhitch the mules from their harnesses and slip the bridles off their heads. He picked up a handful of straw and wiped sweat from the flank of one of the mules.

"What happened, Gaston?" She put a steadying hand on the oak post where he had hung the bridles.

He threw the straw on the floor and grabbed a fresh handful.

"I told her we shouldn't go. I know about roads, I know about rain. An abbess doesn't know what's best to do out in the world. But did she listen?" He moved to the second mule and wiped a foamy streak of sweat off its swayed back.

"Why were you at Arudy?"

"She didn't want to wait for a mule train in Pau. Thought we'd have better luck finding an escort in Arudy. The rains swelled the river there until it burst its banks. We were trapped for a fortnight. Then the rain stopped. Another group of travelers came along the market road to lodge at the guesthouse, and we were set to leave with them. The next morning the abbess was dead. Died in her sleep, they said. Peaceable."

Gaston poured grain into a trough for the mules.

"Peaceable," she repeated. "Was she ill?"

He shook his head. "More grumbly than usual, she was. In a hurry to get back here, that was the thing. Some business about a merchant from Toulouse."

Mira returned to the courtyard, where Agathe was conversing with the monks. In Agathe's hands was a small leather bag. Agathe loosened the cord on the bag and examined the contents.

"A letter and a few coins. Very few." She frowned.

"What about her ring?" Mira said.

One of the monks held up his hands in a gesture of non-culpability. "We know nothing of a ring."

"Perhaps it is yet on her hand," Mira said hopefully.

"No," he said. "I helped lay the body in that box, and I saw no gold on her fingers."

When the monks had been ensconced in the warming house for the evening, Agathe and Mira walked to the catacombs in the cellars, where the body lay awaiting burial. On the way they passed through the kitchens, where Mira lit two torches and ordered a servant to bring lavender water and linens to the cellars. She dispatched another servant to fetch a fresh habit and wimple from Béatrice's chambers. Agathe raised an eyebrow.

"Mother Béatrice would be horrified if we buried her without removing the sweat and dust of her journey first." Mira held out a length of flax cloth. "Wrap this around your mouth and nose before we open the box."

"You may spend more time in the infirmary, but I too have handled the dead," Agathe said tartly.

In the cellars, the torches cast pools of golden light on the curved lines of the stone arches overhead. Mira stooped to right an overturned keg of beer and a rat scurried behind a stack of barrels. Dread inhabited every fiber of her being at the task that lay ahead, but she straightened up and moved forward.

Later, in Béatrice's chambers, Mira built a small fire and lit two tapers from the flames. She unfolded the letter that had been in the bag the monks carried, written to Béatrice from the merchant Estevan de Vernier of Toulouse. It outlined a contract for the sale of merino wool fabric from the abbey to the merchant. After reading the letter she decided to search for other correspondence from the man.

One by one, she slid open the drawers of Béatrice's desk. They were loaded with paper, parchment, quills, ink pots, salt and blotting cloths. She found small keepsakes from the abbey's various endeavors—squares of finished wool fabric, linen paper in decorative wooden boxes, dried lavender, dried hops. The last drawer she opened contained a stack of letters. On top of the pile lay a folded square of linen paper with a broken seal. She recognized on it the herald of the Sacazar family.

She smoothed the letter open on Mother Béatrice's desk, the flame of her candle casting a pale wash of light upon it. Carlo Sacazar's bold black script covered the page. She scanned the words once, twice, then quickly tucked it into her pocket.

The next morning Mira ordered the gatekeeper to let her out. A dense, swirling fog had taken hold of the valley in the night, but the glowing disc of the sun was visible through the mist. A jay shrilled at her as she tramped along the short path to the stream. She pushed open the door of the washing station. Inside, she stood motionless, remembering Béatrice's stories of what it once was—empty, with gaping holes where the windows once were, pigeons nesting in the rafters and glimpses of blue sky visible through the rotting roof. And now it had become the beating heart of the abbey. She would do what she could to keep the washing station and the wool business thriving, but Béatrice's knack for all things in the world of commerce was something she did not possess.

She walked to the door and turned back for a final glance at the copper vats and rinsing channels, her vision blurred by tears. She could do one more thing for Bèatrice. She would go back to her chamber and create a mortuary roll on a sheet of fine parchment. She would use the best pigments, the rarest colors—the scarlet realgar and white lead and blue lapis powder. She would have the roll carried to all the religious houses in Béarn and over the mountains to Aragón, so that every man and woman who had known or heard of Mother Béatrice could pay their respects with a signature, a psalm, a poem.

Mira opened the door and was confronted by a blaze of sunlight. The fog was burning off; it promised to be a fine day. Squinting, she made out the figure of a man striding across the stubble fields from the hills. She shaded her eyes with her hand.

"By the sun and stars, Mira! What brings you out here again?"

The sound of Arnaud's voice filled her with relief and a strange kind of longing. She fought back tears.

"Mother Béatrice is dead."

"What?" In a moment Arnaud was at her side.

"She went north visiting market towns, searching for a buyer for our fabric. She died on the way back, in the abbey at Arudy." Mira covered her face with her hands, fighting to maintain her composure. "Tomorrow we bury her."

"Did she fall ill?"

Mira shook her head. "The monks said she died peaceably in her sleep. But her ring was not on her finger when they brought her here, and the monks swore they never saw it."

"Not all monks are honest, nor drivers."

"I have known Gaston since he was a boy. He is no thief."

"All the same, liars and thieves walk among us."

"What will become of this place without her?" Mira whispered.

Arnaud leaned close and pressed his forehead against hers. She felt his hands on her back, tracing the sweep of her spine. Just for a moment, with her body fitted against his, the swarm of anxious thoughts in her mind evaporated.

The sound of voices approaching made them draw apart. Two other shepherds entered the washing station. She heard herself repeating the news of Béatrice's death to the men, and a suffocating haze of disbelief descended on her once more.

Arnaud walked her back to the gates. The mist was rising all around them, burning under the harsh gaze of the sun, revealing pink buds on the apple trees and green shoots pushing out of the earth underfoot. But the dank smell of fog lingered, masking the scent of spring. Mira remembered the letter and pulled it out of her pocket.

"I found this letter in Mother Béatrice's chambers. Carlo Sacazar invites me to Nay to paint portraits of his family. He wishes to pay me."

"Can you carry out such work?"

"I am ready."

"Then go. Go before another abbess takes Mother Béatrice's place."

She hesitated.

"Why did Mother Béatrice not tell me of his letter? There must have been a reason."

He shrugged. "The dead cannot speak."

When she did not answer, he moved closer and took her hand.

"What is the thing you always longed for?" There was a trace of exasperation in his voice. "Escape from these walls. Now is your chance. You won't get another."

"How do you know?"

"Because death brings change. Take advantage of that."

She stared at him in silence, shocked.

"Mira, you can do more for Belarac out in the world than you ever will within these gates. If you wait too long, your chance will slip away."

The gatekeeper approached. Mira reluctantly slid her fingers out from Arnaud's grasp, tucked the letter back in her pocket.

The gates clanged shut behind her.

Mira hunched over her desk, the flame on her nubby candle casting an arc of light on the linen paper before her. Wind crept through the cracks around the small window. She implored her trembling fingers to be still. She had to write in the hand of Mother Béatrice, to copy the script of the woman who patiently taught her how to put quill to paper all those years ago when she was a willful child.

It was not difficult to do. She was a fine copyist of words, of images, of faces, of the fold of a robe or the expression of a pair of eyes. There was nothing she could not replicate. So it was not fear of failure that set her hands to shaking. No, it was the knowledge that she was embarking on a lie. In truth, it was far more than just a lie—it was a calculated falsehood of spectacular proportions.

She shook off the thought, dipped her quill in the ink pot, and began to write. Halfway through, she thought she heard murmuring voices in the corridor. She froze, panicked, ready to blow out the candle and stuff the paper up her sleeve. But it was simply the whine of the shifting wind that she heard, not whisperings outside her door. So she breathed, calmed her racing heart, stilled her hands again. She wrote fluidly now, the quill making a soft scratching sound as it glided over the cream-colored paper.

And then she did the worst thing of all. Dipping the quill into the ink one last time, she forged Béatrice's name.

7

Summer, 1500
Oto, Aragón
Pelegrín

I T WAS A HUNTING lesson like any other. Pelegrín and Beltrán
rode their horses through the beech groves and past the
jumble of boulders where Pelegrín used to play as a young
boy. They passed beneath an ancient oak with twisted, moss-cov-
ered limbs. A crow scolded them from a high branch. Under
the horses' hooves, brittle leaves shattered into tiny fragments.

"Let's stop here," Beltrán called out, pulling on his horse's reins
at the edge of a stand of pines.

The rattling blows of a woodpecker sounded somewhere up
high. It was the kind of day Pelegrín loved best: sunny and
warm, not too hot, when summer cloaked the mountains with
shimmery green and the snow on the highest peaks melted into
icy streams that fed the valleys below.

"There are meadows beyond the pines where quail nest,"
Beltrán said. "That will be your challenge for today—can you

surprise a quail, I wonder? Nock your arrow and shoot it before it flies to safety?"

Pelegrín halted his horse, grinning. "I can and I will."

"Oh—the confidence of youth," Beltrán said, swinging a leg over his horse's back and jumping heavily to the ground. He tied the reins to a tree. "I tell you what. You go that way and I'll go this way." He pointed each arm at a different angle through the woods. "The first to come out with a quail in hand wins!"

"Be prepared to come out empty handed," Pelegrín replied, dismounting and tying up his horse. He fished an arrow from the quiver over his shoulder, readied his bow. "See you at the top."

Pelegrín moved through the pine forest, cursing the sound of the pine needles crunching underfoot. He stopped to take off his boots and returned them to the horse. Now he moved silently, but his feet stung from the prick of the pine needles. He comforted himself with the thought that once they reached the meadow, the grass would be soft and springy, carpeted with those delicate white flowers his mother loved so much. What were they called? Asters. Star asters. He would pick some for her.

He reached the edge of the meadow and crouched down, listening for quail. Squinting into the sun, he saw a figure move across the grass—a girl with a woven basket on her back. Of course. Every year at this time his mother sent servants to the meadow to gather star asters. The girl moved quickly, pinching off the stems of the flowers and tossing them into the basket strapped onto her back. Another movement caught his eye. It was Beltrán, approaching the servant girl with loping strides. When he reached her, the steward pushed her viciously to the ground and batted aside her skirts. She screamed in terror.

Pelegrín leapt into the grass, his heart pounding in his chest. He saw another girl approach Beltrán from behind, holding something aloft. When Pelegrín realized what it was, he bellowed a warning. It was too late. The girl slammed a rock into Beltrán's head. He slumped to the ground.

In a moment Pelegrín was upon them. The girl who had hit Beltrán with the rock turned in surprise. When she recognized him, the color drained from her face and she sank to her knees, her hands over her eyes.

"My lord," she whispered.

The other girl stayed prone, weeping quietly. Star asters lay piled around her like snowdrifts.

"Is he dead?" Pelegrín asked, rolling Beltrán over on his back. The man's chest still rose and fell. "You are lucky you did not kill him."

"My lord, he attacked her." The girl kept her eyes trained on Pelegrín's feet. "He meant to—"

"I know," Pelegrín cut in. "I saw. Can she get up?"

The other girl slowly got to her feet. Her face was smeared with dirt and tears. When she saw Pelegrín, she shrank back.

"I will not hurt you," he said. "Fill your baskets with the flowers that have fallen. Then return to the castle as quickly as you can and go to my mother. She will take care of you. Do not speak of this to anyone."

The girls scooped up the flowers with shaking hands, then disappeared into the pine forest. Pelegrín knelt by Beltrán, examining him. There was blood on the back of his head.

Pelegrín gathered a handful of white blossoms and weighed them in his palm. He had heard servants whispering about Beltrán's appetites. It was one thing for a man to do that in a raid—it was part of war, everyone knew that. His own father bragged of such exploits. But to attack a woman on their own lands, a servant from his father's own household—that was not only savage but it was wrong.

Beltrán's eyelids fluttered.

Pelegrín let the flowers sift through his fingers to the ground.

When his father returned to the castle from Zaragoza a few days later, Pelegrín waited until he was settled in front of the fire to approach.

"Father! Welcome home."

Ramón stood and embraced his son, then bade him sit down in the chair to his right.

"I heard your steps and thought it was Beltrán," he said. "Where is the man? I called for him the moment I arrived."

"There has been some trouble." Pelegrín hesitated, searching for suitable words.

"Yes?" Ramón stared at his son with narrowed eyes.

The servants appeared lugging a copper tub of steaming water. Pelegrín waited until it had been deposited in front of his father, who lowered his feet into the water, grimacing.

"Go on." His father let out a long sigh.

"Beltrán attacked a servant girl in the high meadow. I saw it. He meant to ravish her."

"One of our servants?" His father drew out the last 's' like the hiss of a snake, wincing as the heat took hold of his feet.

"Yes."

"And?"

"And I stopped him."

"Well, where is he? Why has he not come? I summoned him ages ago."

"He is locked up, Father. I had him put in a cell in the dungeons while we awaited your return."

Ramón looked at his son, incredulous. After a moment, he laughed. He leaned forward, stuck his hands in the hot water, and brought them dripping to his face.

"Towel," he said.

Pelegrín picked up the linen cloth that hung over the edge of the copper tub and handed it to his father.

"That is a grave punishment, to lock the steward in the dungeon."

"It was a grave crime, in my opinion," Pelegrín said. "To attack a woman of your household in such a way, Father. It is not right."

Ramón rubbed the towel briskly over his face, then balled it up and threw it on the floor. His eyes settled on his son.

"What would you have said if it were I, and not Beltrán, who was ravishing the wench on the meadow? Would you have me locked up, as well?"

Pelegrín was silent a moment.

"I would have thought the lord of the land can do as he wants. But Beltrán is not the lord of the land. He is your servant. Why should he take what belongs to you, from a woman doing work for the benefit of our family?"

Ramón mulled over this, watching the flames of the fire dance through a mist of steam.

"Beltrán has a habit of taking our servant girls when and where he wishes, it is true. I find the matter tiresome. What would you do in my stead, to punish the man?"

"Keep him locked up for a fortnight. Make it clear that his behavior must change. And if it does not—pay him nothing until he learns to do as he is bidden."

Ramón nodded. "A wise course. A fair course. I will think on it, son. Now take your leave so I can rest."

A few weeks later, Pelegrín went to the armory for a bout of swordplay. Affixed to one wall was a wooden frame that held a dozen lances and in a tall oak cabinet next to them was a collection of practice swords. In two great wooden chests were stacked leather breast plates and leg armor. Chain mail shirts hung from hooks on a wall. Hanging from the arched ceiling was a dragon constructed of iron with leather wings that stretched nearly the length of the room. When he was small, Pelegrín had been terrified by it. Now he barely noticed the thing. He selected a sword from the cabinet.

"My lord." Beltrán's voice was low.

Pelegrín wheeled around. From fingertips to elbow, Beltrán's arm was wrapped in layers of linen.

"What is that?" Pelegrín gestured at the bandage.

Beltrán stared at him, his good eye boring into Pelegrín the way a crow's does, unblinking and shiny. "You did not hear?"

"Hear what?"

"Your father visited me in the dungeon. And he made his displeasure clear."

"What do you mean?" Pelegrín felt sick.

"He removed my finger. With a dull little blade. It took a lot of sawing—I think. I do not remember much, except for his warning that the next time, it would not be a finger he would cut off."

"Perhaps you should not engage in sword training with that injury," Pelegrín said, slipping a battered helmet over his head.

"Your father ordered it. He said I am to be your training partner from this day forward."

Pelegrín turned away and busied himself fastening the straps of his leather armor.

All afternoon, no matter how diligently he forced his gaze elsewhere, his eyes slid back to Beltrán's bandaged hand, to the red flower of blood that bloomed on the linen.

8

Autumn, 1500
Béarn
Mira

MIRA ADJUSTED HER CLOAK again, trying to keep out the chill of dawn. Gaston wore an extra tunic and thick wool gloves, but his nose and the tips of his ears were pink. Fog obscured the road ahead. Somewhere behind them was another cart driven by Arnaud de Luz. Both of the carts were loaded with sacks of washed wool.

"This mist brings ill tidings, it does," Gaston grumbled.

The mules balked. He cracked the whip over their backs and they plodded forward again.

"The week that Mother Béatrice passed away, God rest her soul, a thick fog came on," he added.

"The fog comes when it wants," Mira said. "The sun will burn a hole through it soon enough and then we will wish for a wisp of fog to cool us. Besides, we have no choice. If we want to join the mule train, we must make haste. The villagers said it already passed through Accous."

While they rolled through the valley, she inventoried in her mind the supplies that filled the baskets under the bench they sat on. She had several oak panels made by Arnaud, pots of pigment, a supply bag filled with brushes, pencils, linseed oil and rags. And in the satchel around her neck, the mortuary roll and the letter.

They were not long on the main road north when a gruff voice spoke up from the gloom. "Halt! Stop this cart at once."

Two men appeared on either side of the mules. One held a dagger in his clenched fist.

"Give us your coins and be quick about it," said the man with the dagger.

He was slight, with a sharp nose and ashy skin. His companion had a thick, doughy body and a shock of tangled yellow hair. Mira waited for Gaston to reply, but he said nothing. Glancing at him, she saw his face was twisted in fear.

"We have no coins," she ventured.

The man with the dagger took a step forward.

"We're no fools," he shouted. "Give us your coins, and be quick about it."

"We go to Nay to sell our wool," she said firmly, jerking a thumb back at the cart they pulled. "We will have no coins until we sell it."

The yellow-haired man edged closer to Mira. "You're a bold one for a nun." He fingered the edge of her cloak.

"Get back, in the name of God!" She ripped the cloak out of his grasp.

He faltered, his face uncertain. Then he sidled forward again while the other man walked around the cart, thrusting his arms between the heavy sacks of wool in search of other goods.

"You've truly got nothing but wool here."

"As we said. Now let us go." Mira willed her voice to be steady. Where was Arnaud?

The slight man held up his dagger and pretended to clean his nails with it. "We must have something for our troubles," he said.

"That's right," replied the yellow-haired man. "A little reward."

He reached out a hand and put it on Mira's skirt, then gave her thigh a violent pinch.

"Get off!" she shouted.

Gaston finally moved. He let out an unintelligible bleat, raised the mule whip and cracked it in the air.

"A feisty one is always better, I warrant," said the man with the dagger.

Both men hauled Mira off the bench.

Standing up, Gaston found his voice. "Put her down! Give her back! Stop!" he roared. The black tip of the whip flicked the head of the man holding the dagger.

"Putting up a fight, are you?" taunted the man. "Come down here and show me your skills, then." He waved the blade at Gaston.

The other man picked up Mira as if she were a bag of millet and lugged her toward the edge of the woods. She kicked at him and tore at his hair, screaming.

"You will go straight to hell if you abuse me, do you hear? You will burn in hell forever! For all eternity!"

She heard the crack of the whip behind them.

"Enough talk out of you." He dumped her on the ground. His eyes went to the satchel at her waist.

"What's in your bag of goods?" he asked, his lips pulled back to reveal a set of mossy-looking teeth. She struggled to her feet. He raised his arm to slap her and she kicked with all her strength at his knee. He bellowed in pain.

Mira slipped her hand under her skirt and found the smooth bone handle of her dagger. Before he could strike her again, she thrust the blade in the fleshy part of his thigh. At the same moment, an arrow lodged in his shoulder. He cried out and fell to the ground. She scrambled away from him.

"Mira!"

Arnaud was striding toward her.

"Thank God," she whispered.

Arnaud walked past her and pulled the dagger out of the man's thigh, prompting new roars of pain. He wiped it in the grass and handed it to Mira, then dragged the wounded man back to the edge of the road. With Gaston's help, he bound the bandits together back to back.

"Too bad there's no room for you fellows in our cart," Arnaud said. "Since we've no room to spare, you'll wait for the bailiff here. Take comfort from each other 'til then."

The wounded man moaned. "My shoulder! Have mercy. Remove that arrow, for God's sake."

Arnaud walked a slow circle around them. "The thing is," he said, "the arrow keeps your blood in. If I pull it out now, blood'll spurt everywhere. Once a hole opens up like that, it gets worse. Could be there's a crack in one of your bones; could be your very marrow might ooze out and mix with your blood. Quite a steaming soup that'd be." He let out a long, low whistle. "No, we'll let the arrow stay where it is, doing a great service for you."

"You devil." The man let out an anguished groan.

"The devil is at work here, no doubt," said Arnaud. "But he's not riding on *my* shoulder."

Gaston collected himself. "Robbing good folk on their way to the market before they even have a coin in their purses, it takes a special brand of idiots to do that," he declared. He held out a hand to Mira.

"Thank you, Gaston." She climbed back into the wagon, trying to ignore the wild thudding of her heart.

The wounded man peered up at her from the dusty roadside. "What kind of an accursed nun stabs a man?"

"What kind of a monster attacks a nun?" she retorted.

She had an urge to climb back down and stab him again, this time through the heart. The savage thought startled her. She tore her gaze away from him, staring resolutely ahead as the cart began moving again.

For the rest of the journey, the memory of her attacker's horrible grin taunted her. She sat motionless on the bench, her arms clasped tightly around the satchel, consumed by the miserable awareness that she wanted more than anything to murder him.

By the time they entered the gates of Nay, a throbbing ache coursed through her skull. The carts rolled over the cobblestones, threading through the narrow streets until they came to the Sacazars' home on the edge of the main square.

"Did they truly do no harm to you?" Arnaud asked, springing to the ground.

"I am unhurt." Mira climbed down from her perch in the cart.

He crossed his arms over his chest, unconvinced.

"I do not lie. Elena taught me well." She heaved the straps of the satchels over her shoulder.

"Before you go inside, I've something else to tell you. I know the answer to your riddle," Arnaud said. "I puzzled over it since the flood. But it came to me on the road, just now."

"What is the answer, then?"

"Water."

Her eyes lit up in a smile. The smile he gave her in return was so kind and familiar that she wanted to hurtle into his arms. Instead, she bowed her head to him and walked to the great oak doors without another word.

Mira stood motionless, her hand poised over the iron knocker, wanting more than anything to watch Arnaud ride away. But if she turned back for one last glimpse of him the veneer of courage she had plastered over her fear would crumble into dust.

Listening to his cart rattle over the cobblestones, she took a deep breath, squared her shoulders and rapped the knocker hard against the door.

9

Autumn, 1500
Nay, Béarn
Mira

T HE SACAZAR RESIDENCE LOOKED nothing like the other plaster-and-timber buildings that lined the main square. It was made of sand-colored stone, its tall windows fitted with diamond-shaped panes of sparkling glass. Inside the wide iron-studded oak doors was a soaring central courtyard. The courtyard floor was composed of silver-grey river rocks laid on their edges in circular patterns. Looking up, Mira saw three stories of long, open-air corridors, their vaulted arches freshly plastered and painted white.

Waiting in the reception hall, she admired the bright dyes of the woolen tapestries that adorned the walls. When Carlo Sacazar entered the room with his wife, Mira recognized their faces from the stone likenesses that were carved into the entryway.

"Your stonemasons are men of talent, sir," she said.

"You must address my husband by his proper title: Lord Sacazar," his wife objected.

"I beg your pardon, Lady Sacazar," said Mira. She folded her hands together to stop them from shaking. The bruise on her thigh throbbed. "Please forgive me."

"You are forgiven," Carlo said, a broad grin on his face. "We import our stonemasons from Florence," he explained, waving her into another room. The walls were hung with Flemish tapestries, beeswax candles burned in tall silver candlesticks, and gleaming silver plateware was displayed on a carved wooden chest. They settled in low, leather-backed chairs arranged in a semi-circle before the fire.

"It has taken seven years to construct our home," he said, watching Mira's eyes track around the room.

"And in truth it is not yet complete," his wife said, gesturing to a servant to pour wine. "Although my husband has turned his attention to other matters."

"Yes, my dear, there is always more to do." If his wife's critical tone bothered him, he did not let on.

He wore a fine black wool tunic with velvet sleeves and his wife wore a crimson dress with sleeves of some shiny embroidered material Mira had never seen before. Around her neck was an enormous cross of gold and a triple strand of pearls. Her dark hair was parted in the middle and smoothed low over her ears, but the back was swept into an ornately beaded cloth that looked as delicate as a spider's web.

Mira took a sip of wine. The time for her story had come. Reaching into her satchel, she withdrew the mortuary roll.

"What's this?" Carlo's eyebrows met in the middle when he frowned. He unfurled the roll of parchment, holding the polished wooden handles aloft.

"Béatrice of Belarac is dead?" Flora drew in a breath, leaning over her husband's shoulder to examine the document.

Mira nodded, crossing herself. "Death came for her at the abbey of Arudy. She died in the night, in her sleep, they said. It was—it is—a shock. Mother Béatrice thought so highly of you both. She would have wanted your names on her mortuary roll."

"Of course, we would be honored," said Carlo soberly. "What a shock indeed. I admired your Mother Béatrice. I do not envy her superiors the task of finding an adequate replacement for her."

"She—Mother Béatrice—left a letter in her desk. It was addressed to you, Lord Sacazar. She died before she could seal and send it." The lie slid off Mira's tongue easily enough. "I felt it was my duty to bring it to you and ask for your counsel."

He unfolded the paper and walked to the window, holding it up to the light.

"I see," he said when he finished reading. "Sebastian de Scolna visited me after he left Belarac and advised me to engage you as a portrait artist. I wrote to the abbess inquiring about the possibility. I thought her long silence was an answer in itself, but it appears I was wrong." He turned back to Mira. "Truth be told, I would very much like you to carry out the work. But surely there will be a new abbess, with new expectations for you."

"A selection has not yet been made. In the interim, I was given permission to make the journey here to oversee the wool sales at the market. To be frank, there are no sisters at the abbey who are as well acquainted as I with the world outside its walls. I have the necessary—temperament." An image of the roadside attackers rose in her mind. She swallowed, pushing it away. "Since the mortuary roll had to be delivered to you, Lord and Lady Sacazar, and your sister, Abbess Amadina, I took it upon myself to bring Mother Béatrice's letter to you as well."

"Indeed, indeed," Carlo Sacazar said, his eyes flicking back and forth between Mira and the letter in his hand.

"This is fine work," said Flora, holding up the mortuary roll.

On the first section of the parchment, Mira had painted Mother Béatrice laid to rest in her four-poster bed, surrounded by nuns and thickly-fleeced sheep.

"The colors are as vivid as the jewels in my rings, and the faces are delicately rendered," Flora went on.

Carlo went to his wife's side. "Yes," he agreed. "Beautifully done. Who is the artist?"

"I am," Mira said.

He nodded, then launched into a series of questions about her life at the abbey and her training as a painter. She answered as best she could, explaining her work in the chapel and her time under the tutelage of the pilgrim Sebastian.

"I have seen with my own eyes that no mansion in Florence would be complete without portraits of its owners," Carlo said. "Our home is in need of such paintings as well."

"I do wonder where we will find the time for sittings," Flora said, a tight smile on her face. "My husband has so many ideas. He has the will and enthusiasm of twenty men, and an unmatched mind. His cleverness never fails to astound me. But he is so busy, you see." Her voice sounded aggrieved and indulgent at the same time.

Carlo held his hands up in a gesture of culpability. "My wife knows me too well. I serve as abbot of two monasteries in Béarn, so in addition to overseeing my business here in Nay, I am often away."

"And then there is our property in Aragón," Flora said. "The lands, the flocks. Our house in Zaragoza. The list goes on."

"But we digress," Carlo said, a note of irritation in his voice. "This autumn finds me here in Nay, not abroad. We might begin with a portrait of the whole family, do you not agree, my dear?" He looked over at his wife, who was picking at a silver thread on her sleeve.

"A fine idea," she said.

"And if we are happy with that portrait, we will commission you to paint more," he said. "Of course, you will lodge here with us."

"Thank you, Lord Sacazar," Mira said. "When shall we begin?"

"I think tomorrow. Why delay a moment longer?" said Carlo.

"Indeed," said Flora, smoothing her skirts with ring-laden fingers. Her eyes came to rest on Mira. "The work will keep your mind free of dark thoughts. When one is in mourning, there is no better cure than staying busy."

The next afternoon, Mira lined up her pots of pigment on a side table in the Sacazars' sitting room. Carlo settled himself into a high-backed, ornately carved oak chair. This would be a painting of the entire family, but he had insisted that she begin with him alone, so he could get accustomed to the sensation of sitting for a portrait.

"See there," he said, his gaze settling on the portrait of his parents that hung over a collection of beaten gold plates on a long sideboard. "I advise you to study the painting made by Master Bermejo with care. It is my dearest wish to be depicted in the same manner, with the same background, as my parents were. I want to be reminded of Zaragoza and the land of my birth every time I look at our portrait."

Mira nodded, slipping a thin calves-leather apron over her clothing. "Yes, Lord Sacazar, I have made a close study of the painting." She set her paintbrushes side by side on a linen cloth. "I will tell you something that is sure to please you. My teacher worked alongside Master Bermejo in Flanders when he was a young man."

"He told me as much himself," Carlo said, nodding. "That is why I was so eager to retain you for this work." He fiddled with a sleeve. "Perhaps I should not have chosen cream and black. Something more colorful might do better."

"Today I will not be painting the colors of your sleeves, or any other colors, Lord Sacazar. I will simply be making the under-drawings that no one will ever see."

"Ah," he said, relaxing. "In that case, I await your instructions."

She took up a piece of charcoal and wrote *Bermejo* in the space she had blocked out for the background.

"It is the fashion in Florence these days for masters to sign their work," he said.

"My work is done in the name of God." She wiped her hands on a square of linen. "Not my own."

"But why should we in Béarn not rival the fashions of Florence?" For the first time since she met him, Carlo looked unhappy.

"I am no master," she said. "My name means nothing."

He stood, a slight frown on his face, and walked around the panel to her side.

"Ah! You have written 'Bermejo' here." He pointed at the word. "Will it not show through the paint?"

She shook her head. "The layers hide whatever I draw on the panel."

"Then sign your name alongside Bermejo's," he said, his face brightening. "You and I will both know it is there, even if the world does not."

She nodded. "An excellent plan."

A few days later both Carlo and Flora Sacazar sat for the portrait. Before she began, Mira showed them her mark on the underdrawing. In the style of an illuminated manuscript, she had written her name and turned the 'A' into a tiny self-portrait. Written in tiny script within the prongs of the 'M' were the words '*Mira pinxit et Dei adiutrix.*'

"Just as you desired, Lord Sacazar."

"How clever," Flora said. "It is a good likeness too."

"But even a 'painter and a servant of God' has a family name," Carlo said.

Mira shook her head. "I do not know who my people were."

A cork stopper rolled off the table and Mira knelt to retrieve it. When she stood, her veil snagged on a rough splinter that jutted out from the table leg. It slid off, revealing the coiled mass of her dark coppery hair.

She hastened to reposition the veil, aware of the Sacazars' eyes upon her, and reached for her paintbrush.

10

Autumn, 1500
Nay, Béarn
Amadina

A MADINA MARCHED TO HER brother's home in the afternoon sun. It was the kind of day that began shrouded in a veil of fog and ended gloriously bright. She waited in the sitting room for her brother to appear, scowling at the cherubs and angels that gazed down at her from the carved stone mantel. Next to the mantel was a wooden easel upon which rested a panel draped in linen. She stared at it, a frown creasing her brow.

When Carlo entered the room, looking uncharacteristically disheveled in a wrinkled flax blouse that hung untucked around his wool breeches, she crossed to the door and slammed it in the servant's face. Her brother gave her a wary look.

"I suppose I need not ask how your journey north went. What is the matter, Amadina?"

"I warned you from the very beginning. I told you, do not respond to that Béatrice of Belarac. Nothing good would come of it, I said." She stalked back and forth, her cloak swishing around her ankles. "And now you will have to admit that I am right."

"Explain." He sank down on an oak chair in front of the hearth.

"Even you, the unflappable Carlo Sacazar, will feel the prick of rage when you hear. My Toulouse distributor, my good associate for these ten years, terminated our contract. And do you know why? Because he found a new supplier—the Abbey of Belarac. And it is your fault—yours alone—that this has happened. You showered that Béatrice with kindness after kindness, and look what she's done to me!" Amadina hurled the words at her brother as if each one were a curse.

Carlo eyed her with distaste. "Your hatred is misplaced. Béatrice of Belarac is dead, Amadina. I signed her mortuary roll just weeks ago, not long after you left for Toulouse. Surely you of all people, as the leader of a religious house, know better than to speak ill of the dead."

Amadina did not meet his gaze. She crossed herself. "Perhaps her death was no accident," she said, smoothing the fabric of her wimple with plump hands. "She snaked her way around the law—that you cannot deny. By rights she should not have been in possession of merino sheep at all. Nor profiting from their wool."

He sighed. "The merino flocks that overwinter at the abbey belong to the shepherds of Ronzal. If anyone was to be punished for the arrangement, it would be them, not a foreign abbess."

"Where is your loyalty?" she spat. "To your family? To your queen?"

"I have been loyal to you your whole life long. I bought you an abbey. I bought you a title. I bought you your *life*." Carlo's voice dropped dangerously low. "My loyalty to the queen is known throughout Aragón. The gifts I have bestowed upon her are worth enough to finance a small war—in fact, come to think of it, they likely have. What is it you want from me, Amadina? Tell me and be done with it. I have much to do."

THE GIRL FROM OTO

"I have not sat idle since I heard this news. I have found new distributors in market towns west on the River Pau."

"Then why are you lambasting Béatrice of Belarac in this way?"

"If you have any loyalty left for me, you will send your most skilled artisans to my convent. The ones you have recruited from Florence, from Flanders, from Toulouse. The quality of my fabric will eclipse anything Belarac can produce, and I will get my distributor in Toulouse back."

"You want me to go out of business so that you can have your revenge? Without my income, the convent would die a slow death. You've never cared much for numbers, Amadina, but your fabric finishing business does not begin to cover the costs of your convent."

Amadina folded her arms across her chest, fuming. Her mouth was turned down at the corners, the skin between her eyebrows furrowed into a deep V. His mind flashed to a memory of his sister raging at him as a child. The look on her face hadn't changed in forty years.

"For too long I have lived in your shadow. You always assumed that I could never navigate my way through the world without you." She emitted a hollow laugh. "Perhaps you are wrong. Perhaps I am the powerful one. And it is you who need my protection."

"What do you mean?" He seized hold of her arm, just above the elbow. With a savage jerk, she twisted away, strode to the door and flung it open. A tall, slender young woman dressed in the habit of a novice nun stood before her, a paint-spattered apron over her clothes, her arms loaded with satchels. Amadina looked her up and down, nostrils flaring.

"Who in the name of God is this?" she snapped.

Her brother's mild voice floated into the hallway. "Amadina, meet Mira of Belarac. She is the artist I engaged to paint my portrait. Mother Béatrice's last letter gave her blessing to the arrangement."

Amadina stood motionless for a moment, her black-clad bulk blocking Mira's entry into the room. She turned back to Carlo.

"Where is your artist staying?"

"Here with us," he said, unruffled. "She paints by day and teaches our girls their sums and letters in the evenings. Apparently Mother Béatrice saw to it that Mira received a fine education."

Mira dipped her head in thanks. "It is my honor to meet you, Mother Amadina," she said.

"When I see your finished work, if I find it impressive, perhaps I shall commission you to paint my own portrait." Amadina tempered her voice into a syrupy coo.

"You must be prepared to wait. We will keep young Mira busy through the winter, I imagine," Carlo said. "Plans are afoot for portraits of the girls, individual studies of Flora and myself, and miniatures of every one of us—including young Mira herself."

"I beg your pardon?" Mira said.

Carlo held up a hand. "How else can I advertise your talents to the world? I will make it my personal mission to find you employment everywhere I go."

Amadina sniffed. "Advertising the services of a novice nun. There is much to fault in your plan, brother."

"On the contrary, I cannot think of a better way to celebrate the spirit of Abbess Béatrice—and augment the income of her abbey. She had the girl tutored in the arts for this very reason, I am certain of it."

"Are you indeed?" Amadina said. "I wonder."

She swept past Mira and clomped down the corridor. The girl had not been cowed a whit by her authoritarian demeanor. To the contrary, she stood with her shoulders thrust back and her head high, those unnerving pale eyes boring into her own with calm intensity.

A novice nun in Amadina's own convent would never get away with such insolence.

11

Winter, 1500
Nay, Béarn
Mira

MIRA HAD STUDIED CARLO Sacazar's portrait of his parents with care. For her painting of the Sacazar family, she copied as exactly as she could Bermejo's lavishly detailed background showing a terrace blooming with lush flowers and in the distance, the high peaks of the Pyrenees.

"We are so fortunate," Carlo said, turning his attention back to the painting. "Your talent is extraordinary. It rivals anything I saw in Florence."

"Truly?"

"I do not exaggerate. You captured the beauty of my wife and you managed to take a few lines off my face. Our clothing is masterfully rendered. The wool of my vest looks soft enough to touch, the silk of my wife's dress glows. The girls—I marvel at how you managed to reproduce the exquisite innocence in their eyes. And I am most pleased with the background. You copied exactly the style of Master Bermejo, as I desired. There is nothing I would change about the portrait. My dear?" He turned to his wife.

Flora nodded. "I am very pleased, very pleased indeed. There *is* one tiny detail…"

"Yes?" asked Mira.

"I wore my pearls during our sittings. But since then, my dear husband has made a new gift to me that is more fitting a symbol of my status." She patted the heavy gold and ruby necklace that ornamented her throat. "What a woman wears around her neck tells the world who she is."

"That is simple to correct, Lady Sacazar. I can paint over the pearl necklace and add the ruby one. It would be my pleasure."

Flora's expression softened. "Excellent. Then I shall be perfectly content with the painting."

Carlo clapped his hands together. "Now that you have resolved the issue of the necklace, we can discuss the next phase of work. A portrait of me, and one of my wife. And then miniatures of all of us. And one of you as well."

He saw the uncertainty on Mira's face and clucked his tongue.

"I shall not allow you to protest, young Mira! I will take it upon myself to sing your praises to all the merchants I encounter. You will soon have more work than you can possibly undertake." He grinned.

"Lord Sacazar, you are too generous." Mira bowed her head, her eyes inexplicably stinging with tears. She blinked them back, struggling to regain her self-composure.

"Nonsense. I am simply doing what Mother Béatrice would have wanted, and as she is no longer with us, I am more than happy to help you continue along the path that she forged for you."

Mira smiled back at him. She had never felt more duplicitous. Her presence here had nothing to do with Mother Béatrice. It was her own doing, and it was based on a falsehood. Why Carlo Sacazar had simply accepted the letter she presented, though it bore no seal, she still did not understand. But his warm gaze held no suspicion.

All was well, she told herself. The scheme had worked.

12

THE MONK CAME ON the back of a mule in the last weeks of autumn, bearing a mortuary roll on the finest parchment painted with an exquisite image of Béatrice laid to rest in her four-poster bed surrounded by nuns and sad-eyed sheep. The document was crafted, the monk said, by a novice nun who had since left the abbey, under contract to paint portraits for wealthy merchants in the north. He had spent the better part of a year traveling through Béarn and now Aragón, gathering signatures.

He kept his plump fingers wrapped around the roll's wooden handle while Marguerite's eyes traveled down the rows of inscriptions and names. She spotted her daughter's signature, Mira of Belarac, near the top. Not far below that lay the signatures of Lord and Lady Sacazar, emblazoned in bold, swirling script. With cool eyes and a steady hand, she added her signature and a few words of remembrance to the parchment, feigning interest in the monk's chatter about the terrors of the mountain roads. But she heard nothing he said. Her heart raced, her mind blazed with worries. Numbly, she inventoried the dangers that lurked outside a convent's walls.

The monk moaned that his fatigue was great, that he lacked the strength to carry the mortuary roll all the way to San Juan de la Peña. Marguerite allowed him to stay a fortnight. He consumed an eye-popping amount of wine, mumbled an endless stream of platitudes about the generous benevolence of the Oto family, and finally, when she shut him up with a handful of silver coins, mounted his mule and clattered through the castle gates.

No one knew where Elena had gone, though the servants passed around a rumor involving Basque country and a nomadic shepherd, which Marguerite dismissed as idle gossip. But the fact was, the hearth in Elena's cottage had been cold since springtime. And now winter was nearly upon them.

All these years, she had been driven by the knowledge that she could direct Mira's fate. She built a life for her daughter from afar, had fancied herself the master of Mira's destiny. Now, with the girl's future out of her hands, she felt unmoored. The illusion of control that she had harbored since Mira's birth was stripped away. It was fitting, she supposed, that a scroll from Béatrice would end this. After all, a scroll from Béatrice had begun it.

She went to her wooden letter box, fitted the iron key into the lock, and nodded in satisfaction at the sound of a well-oiled click as the mechanism released. Pulling out the roll of parchment, she spread it open on her desk.

The letter was crammed with detail. Marguerite found the section about the infirmary, the long-winded description of the Abbey of Belarac as a refuge for children who had no other hope in the world. The plea for a renewal of the Oto family's ancient pledge.

It had arrived during the early days of her marriage to Ramón, when his parents were still alive. Neither of them had shown any interest in its contents or in rekindling the generosity that the house of Oto once showered upon the Abbey of Belarac. Marguerite had read the letter more out of nostalgia for Béarn than anything else. This Abbess Béatrice's words were overly dramatic, she remembered thinking. Ramón had ordered her to write a letter of refusal, but she had tossed the scroll into the box unanswered. Small acts of defiance had bolstered her spirit in those early years.

For two seasons, the letter lay forgotten. She ignored it while the winds of autumn gave way to swiftly falling snow and then to the spring rains. While every evening her husband came to her bed and forced himself on her without affection. Afterward, he would heave himself up, rearrange his clothing, and return to his chamber in the Tower of Blood. She would lie in the dark and catalog her wounds and listen to the wind hiss through chinks in the stone walls.

And then one day that letter became the most important item in her possession.

It was the morning of a great storm, when she crept into the cellars to see the litter of kittens one of the kitchen cats had produced. She watched the tiny creatures suckle and listened to the mother's rhythmic purring. The sound of voices startled her and she slipped behind a pyramid of stacked wooden beer kegs. She recognized the voices of two kitchen maids.

"Is this a boy kitten or a girl?" she heard one say.

"Look—there, see? Between his legs? That means he's a boy."

"Are they all boys?"

"No. There's always boys *and* girls in a litter."

"Always? How do you know?"

"That's the way for dogs, too. And people."

"Cook says our masters bear no girls. A family of warriors, this is."

The other girl emitted a dismissive grunt and dropped her voice. "There's only one way to make sure you raise up no girls. And if you can't figure it out on your own, you're even stupider than I thought."

Huddled there behind the beer kegs, Marguerite felt as if she had been kicked in the gut. On her wedding night, her mother-in-law had whispered in her ear that Oto women raised boys, and boys alone. It had always been so, she said. Marguerite believed her. Now she understood what that truly meant. A baby girl would come—and then be extinguished like the stuttering flame of a candle.

She felt a wave of shame for judging her mother-in-law, the woman she had come to think of as a walking wound. And then, panic. How did the barons rid themselves of girls? Smother them? Toss them into the fire? Marguerite hugged her knees to her chest, reeling from the images that crowded her mind until the kitchen maids' chattering voices faded from the room and she was left alone with the cats and her racing thoughts.

Looking back, Marguerite felt pity for her young self. Pity and admiration both. For somehow, despite her terror on that dismal stormy day, she had mustered the wits to trudge upstairs and fish the letter out of the wooden box. Finally, Béatrice of Belarac got an answer—and with it an audacious request. How Marguerite's pride had swelled when her secret plan played out just as she hoped. No matter how bleak her existence in Castle Oto became, she was held aloft by the knowledge that Mira thrived across the mountains under Béatrice's care.

But now Béatrice of Belarac was dead. And Mira had entered the wider world, out of reach of her mother's control.

There was nothing more Marguerite could do for the girl. Mira was lost to her now.

13

Summer, 2015
Pau, France
Zari

ZARI STOOD ON THE train platform in Pau, getting her bearings. It was a warm afternoon. Pigeons cooed in the stale air under the vast metal and glass ceiling. She slipped her arms through the straps of her backpack and trudged toward the main part of the station. Somewhere in the crowd was Laurence Ceravet, whom she had only recently learned was a woman. She had assumed Laurence was a man; since they only communicated by e-mail until recently, she had no reason to challenge that assumption. But when she searched online for images of Laurence in preparation for their meeting, she realized her error. When Zari confessed, Laurence informed her that every French person named 'Laurence' was a woman. The male equivalent of the English 'Lawrence' was 'Laurent.'

Zari spied a delicately-built woman standing at the end of the platform, her long brown hair pulled back in a loose bun. From a distance, Laurence appeared to be about Zari's age. She was dressed in dark jeans, a crisp white blouse and a tailored navy jacket, and she wore high platform sandals. Zari felt self-conscious in her sensible walking shoes, but Laurence instantly commented on their utility, saying she had a similar pair for hiking herself. Close up, Zari saw the lines etched around Laurence's eyes, the shadowy hollows beneath them. She was probably nearing fifty, Zari realized.

After dropping the backpack at Zari's rented studio apartment overlooking the Place Royale, they walked to a café for lunch. Despite the fact that she managed to inflect her limited French vocabulary with both American and Spanish accents, Zari successfully ordered a Salade Niçoise and a Perrier. Laurence ordered a quiche and a glass of white wine. All of the servers wore the same uniform: black pants, black shoes, white shirts, and long black aprons tied around the waist. Along with most of the other patrons, Zari and Laurence were crammed outside in the narrow strip of sidewalk delegated to the café. Inside, few of the tables were occupied. When they sat down, Laurence immediately lit a cigarette. Most of the other people around them were also smoking.

"Our no-smoking laws," Laurence explained. "One can still smoke outside, so of course everyone wants to sit outside. Even in winter." She took a puff, then blew it away from Zari. It was a nice gesture, but they were getting full blow-back from smokers at surrounding tables. "People will not change their habits just because of a law." She smiled.

"It's so different in California. It's hard to find a smoker there." Zari's eyes began to water.

When their food arrived, Laurence stubbed out her cigarette.

"Will we be able to see your painting this afternoon?" Zari asked. She picked up her fork and contemplated the potatoes, tuna, tomatoes, and green beans on her plate. The salad was topped with a cluster of tiny, glistening olives.

"My painting is still in Paris. There are so many layers of paint to remove. It is taking longer than we expected. I hoped it would be here by your visit, but—" Laurence saw the disappointment in Zari's eyes. "I am sorry."

Zari dropped her gaze and busied herself eating each olive on her plate in quick succession.

"There was nothing you could do," she said after a moment, regaining her equilibrium. "Your painting is such a big piece of this puzzle, though. I was looking forward to seeing the eyes."

"The eyes?"

"I've seen photos of your painting, but I need to see it in person to truly know the answer. Do the subjects' eyes have life in them? Do they have expression?"

Laurence took a sip of wine. "Yes. Their eyes look alive, as you say."

"Have you seen that quality in Cornelia van der Zee's other works?"

"No, but I never looked for it."

"Do you believe Bermejo painted your portrait?"

Laurence shook her head. "There is no evidence to support that theory. I believe that my portrait and the one at Oxford were painted by the same person. And I believe that person was connected to Arnaud de Luz, the man who made the panels."

"Have you learned anything else about him?"

"Just that he lived in Bayonne." Laurence picked up her fork and knife.

"There's something else I wanted to ask you," Zari said. "Do you know anything about a convent called Belarac?"

"Yes."

Zari noticed that for every three bites of salad she ate, Laurence took one minuscule forkful of quiche. She was beginning to understand why French women were so thin. Smoking and not eating were a fast road to weight loss, if not to health.

"I think there's a connection between the Fontbroke College portrait and the Abbey of Belarac." She told Laurence about the 'B' on the spine of the book in the portrait.

"Some artifacts from Belarac are here in Pau, at the university's archival library."

"Really?" Zari mopped up the last drops of vinaigrette on her plate with a piece of bread.

"There are several documents. Books and manuscripts dating from the fifteenth and sixteenth centuries—they were owned by a merchant family and donated to the university. I can show you tomorrow if you like."

"I would love that, Laurence." Zari felt a twinge of embarrassment. "I still can't believe I thought you were a man."

"Were you disappointed?"

"No." Zari smiled. "I was just thinking about the assumptions we make based on names."

"You have a very unusual name, Zari." Laurence forked another sliver of quiche into her mouth.

"My mother's people were Basque originally, from northwest Spain. They were called the Mendietas, which means 'men of the mountains.' And my father's people were mostly French, although I don't know much about them. It's actually a long, boring story."

"It is not boring to me," said Laurence, as she gestured to the server to remove their plates, even though her quiche was only half-eaten. She lit another cigarette.

"Okay, but stop me anytime." Zari leaned back in her chair, mouth-breathing. The scent of the unfiltered cigarette smoke nauseated her. "My birth name is Izar and my brother's is Eguzki. They're Basque names."

"Yes, *izar* means star and *eguzki* means sun." Laurence exhaled over her left shoulder and flicked her cigarette against the black plastic ashtray on the table.

Zari stared at her in surprise. "How did you know?"

"We can see Basque country from here, Zari. And my husband's people are Basque."

"Ah. Well, my mother was a hippie—do you know what that is?"

Laurence nodded, her eyes creasing in amusement.

"Her birth name was Patricia, but she changed it to Portia. Naturally, when she had kids, she wanted them to have groovy names too. So she picked sun and star. My dad was just enough of a hippie to like the concept, but too much of a snob to want his children answering to the same names as all the other hippie kids. So the compromise was Eguzki and Izar. My brother ended up being called Gus because no one could pronounce Eguzki, and when I was a baby Gus couldn't say 'Izar' and started calling me Zari."

"There are Mendietas all around this area, Zari. Perhaps you will find some of your family." Laurence ordered two coffees from the server and stabbed the tip of her cigarette into the ashtray. She exhaled at the same moment as a woman next to her.

Zari watched the two streams of smoke collide and form one intertwining column that seeped lazily upward, squeezing between the umbrellas that shaded the tables and vanishing into the blue sky.

"Maybe someday," she said. "All I have time for right now is the mystery of Mira."

Laurence's dark eyes settled on her. "Even in the best situations, very little can be discovered about a person who lived so long ago. And we do not have one of those situations."

"If your painting is attributed to Bermejo, its value will rise a lot."

Laurence raised an eyebrow. "And?"

"Does that matter to you?"

"What matters to me is the truth," Laurence said.

"Me too."

The server brought two tiny ceramic cups of fragrant black coffee. Zari followed Laurence's lead and dumped two packets of sugar in hers. She stirred it vigorously, then downed the brew in one gulp. It burned a hot, bittersweet path down her throat. She pushed aside the cup and leaned forward in her chair.

"What if we could prove that Mira painted these portraits, not Bermejo?"

"That is an ambitious goal." Laurence sipped her coffee, regarding Zari with an assessing gaze. "Why is this Mira so important to you?"

"She's a ghost. A ghost we caught a glimpse of. I can't let her disappear again. She lived in the margins of history, but she left us a trail of clues." Zari's throat tightened. She steadied her breath, willing her voice smooth again. "Laurence, I know this sounds strange. But I believe Mira wanted to be found."

14

Summer, 2015
Pau, France
Zari

THE DOCUMENTS FROM BELARAC were kept in a cli-
mate-controlled, windowless room in the basement of
one of the library buildings at the University of Pau. At a
stainless steel sink in the corner of the room, Laurence washed
and dried her hands, then gestured to Zari to follow suit.

"I cannot allow you to touch the documents," she said. "But
you are required to wash your hands all the same."

From a bank of metal shelves, she pulled out several card-
board boxes and laid them on a rectangular metal table. Slipping
the lid off one of the larger boxes, she removed a leather-bound
manuscript. Carefully she eased open the cover, exposing the
first pages of parchment. The italic lettering on the parchment
was all in Latin.

"Oh—I thought it would be in French," Zari said. "Or
Béarnaise."

"These large books are all like this," Laurence said. "In Latin. Every word. They show records of holdings and transactions that took place at the Abbey. They are like the computer spreadsheets of medieval times. We have quite an archive of these from various convents and monasteries." She slid a finger under the parchment and turned the page.

"You don't have to wear gloves to handle them?" Zari asked.

"Parchment and linen paper are durable. The oils on our hands are good for them."

Laurence removed a smaller book from another box. The leather cover of the book was a faded dark scarlet, its spine inscribed with a 'B' and a gold cross. Zari's pulse ticked up a notch.

"The 'B' on the spine is exactly like the one in the Fontbroke painting," she said.

"This is a prayer book. It has not been restored yet, but it is in good condition."

With precise movements, Laurence turned the linen pages one by one. The faint hum of the fluorescent lights overhead was the only sound in the room.

Zari held up a hand when Laurence came to a page decorated with an ornate 'D' that began the word '*dominus*.' Inside the 'D' was the small image of a nun. Four tiny words appeared in a semi-circle around her. Zari leaned closer, willing her hands to stop shaking.

"There's something written here."

Laurence produced headgear much like John Drake's and slipped it on. She flicked on the light and bent over the page.

"'*Mira pinxit hunc librum*,'" she read aloud. "Mira illustrated this book."

A thrill ran through Zari. "If Mira painted these illuminations, she was capable of painting those portraits."

"It is possible," Laurence allowed. She turned off the light on her headgear, removed it, and handed it to Zari. Despite her professional tone, her eyes were glowing with excitement. "It might be true. There is a difference between illustrating a manuscript and painting a portrait, however."

Zari settled the headlamp in place and switched it on. In the circle of light, the young woman's image shimmered. Her face was narrow, with oversized and slanting eyes. Her dark eyebrows had high arches, her mouth was wide. The jewel tones of the original paint had faded over time, but her skin had an unmistakable wheat-colored cast to it, and her eyes were green.

She turned to Laurence. "On the underdrawing of your painting, she wrote '*Mira pinxit et Dei adiutrix*.' I'm not sure of the exact translation, but—"

"Mira, painter and servant of God," Laurence said softly.

Zari nodded. "I've dug into this, and I know there are other examples of self-portraits just like this on medieval illuminations. That was how artists left their mark."

Laurence closed the book and returned it to its box. From a third box she removed an object which looked like a fat rolling pin made of parchment. Two decorative carved wooden handles jutted out from either end.

"When an abbess or abbot died," she said, "a roll of parchment was sent to other religious houses to tell people of the death and ask them to pray. Then they signed the mortuary roll with their names. Sometimes they wrote memories or prayers on the roll."

Laurence peeled up a leather flap and smoothed open the roll about ten inches, revealing an image of the deceased abbess on her deathbed, surrounded by grieving nuns. Two sheep clothed in extravagant fleeces lay on the floor in front of the bed. The Virgin Mary and two saints gazed down at the mourners from above. Underneath the scene was a string of Latin words.

"This describes the abbess." Laurence switched her headlamp back on and squinted at the words. "It says she glorified God by giving life back to Belarac. She ran a merino wool operation at the abbey, grazing and shearing the sheep, washing and finishing the wool. The abbey was known for making fine paper out of linen, a practice she started. The infirmary served pilgrims on the Way of St. Jacques. Women were never turned away from the gates of the abbey while she was the abbess." Laurence placed her gloved fingertips underneath a line of script. "See here—this is her name. Béatrice de Belarac. And the date of her death: 1500."

Zari stared at the neatly drawn Latin, the black ink still crisp against the yellowed parchment. Laurence gently unrolled the document a few more inches, allowing the uppermost portion to curl in upon itself again.

"Below this are other signatures," she went on. "Only the most highly ranked women would sign this document."

Zari leaned in close to read the names. Agnès d'Alouet, Agathe de Fournier, Mira de Belarac.

"Mira de Belarac." The words came out in a whisper.

"There is an inscription in Béarnaise under Mira's name," said Laurence. "'*The Abbess gave us refuge when we did not have homes, food when we went hungry, skills when we had none. She was a mother in deed as well as name. Death visited her too soon.*'"

Farther down the roll, there were uneven creases where new sections of parchment had been sewn onto the old, making room for more names. Laurence pointed at a line of script.

"Lord Carlo Sacazar and his wife, Lady Flora. The Sacazars were a wealthy merchant family who had ties in both Aragón and Béarn. Their home in Nay is now a museum."

Zari's eyes swept down the rows of lettering. Under a stain the color of rust was the signature 'Marguerite de Oto.'

She drew in a sharp breath.

"What is wrong?" asked Laurence.

"Nothing. It's just—Oto is more than a village in the mountains. I think it may be a family, too."

The last section of parchment held the most beautifully drawn Latin script of all. It began with a prayer and was followed by a series of male names.

"Ah—San Juan de la Peña," said Laurence, nodding. "That is a monastery over the mountains in Aragón. I have been there. The friar's signature is here—" She pointed at a name. "Johan Arros. Below his name is written this: '*Where there was ruin, now there is wealth. Béatrice of Belarac was a true servant of God and a friend to many.*'"

Zari photographed every inch of the mortuary roll. At the very least, she had more evidence that Mira of Belarac existed, and was an artist. And now she had teased out a new thread. The woman in Fontbroke College's portrait wore a gold belt with a symbol bearing the letters O-T-O. Now this mortuary roll showed the signature of a woman with the family name of Oto. There had to be a connection between Mira of Belarac and Oto, she was sure of it. Her task was clear: to grasp that fragile thread and pull.

Back in her apartment, Zari opened the windows and flopped down in the chair at the small desk opposite the bed. Since the spring, she had harbored an annoying hope that there would be an e-mail from Wil. She opened her laptop. As usual, there was nothing from him. Out of habit, she mentally chastised herself for hoping.

"Life is too short," she announced to the room.

A pigeon cooed somewhere outside. There were no screens on the windows here. Did pigeons ever scuttle over the sills and make themselves at home in peoples' apartments? Mosquitoes definitely did. She had the bites to prove it.

Sighing, she clicked on a new e-mail from John Drake.

To: zdurrell80@inep.edu
From: jdrake@dorringtonmooreinstitute.com

Zari – Our restoration of the Fontbroke portrait is complete. The background (see attached) does bear great resemblance to the work of Bermejo. The last finding of note is in regards to a section of the panel that had been damaged at some point. Something sharp penetrated it, making a significant gouge. The gouge was filled in with a wool plug, then plastered over with gesso and repainted. We removed the wool and filled the gouge with a synthetic substitute.

—John

<Attachment>

The restored painting barely resembled the portrait she had looked at with Vanessa all those months ago in the basement of Fontbroke College. The plain background was gone. In its place was a lavishly detailed scene of a stone balcony, tall cliffs populated with ibex, and snow-dusted mountains in the distance. The woman's embroidered sleeves, scarlet dress, and emerald jewels softened her severe expression. The stiff collar around her neck was gone, her throat encircled by a chain of gold strung with a white pendant in the shape of a shell. The gold belt that hung at her waist glinted with reflected light; the cover of the prayer book in her hands gleamed red.

Zari forwarded John's e-mail to Lucy Karem Wixton, along with a question. She attached a photo of the mortuary roll section that depicted Abbess Béatrice of Belarac flanked by the two bouffant sheep. She was preparing for bed when Lucy phoned her, less than an hour later.

"The sheep in the mortuary roll painting look like merinos to me," Lucy said. "Loose rolls of skin covered by massive amounts of wool—it's the trademark of that species. As far as the plug of wool is concerned, yes, the technology exists to reveal its origin using DNA analysis. By origin I mean the general geographical locale where the sheep grazed."

"So we could confirm that the sheep was merino and it grazed in the Pyrenees?"

"In theory, yes. The problem is that the selection process in sheep breeding today was not in practice five hundred years ago. Genetically, sheep from that time would have shown a lot more diversity than today's animals. So it would be difficult to pinpoint a specific breed unless you had a huge databank of DNA from lots of other samples of wool. And since this is a very new science, that databank doesn't exist yet."

"In other words, going down that rabbit hole would lead us to a dead end."

"I'm afraid so."

Zari stood at the window, watching the sky turn lilac. The pigeon's throaty murmur started up again, interrupted by the harsh stutter of a passing moped.

"Didn't you tell me there was a penalty of death for anyone who removed merino sheep from Spain?" she asked. "If these nuns raised merinos across the mountains in Béarn, they were pretty badass."

"I'm looking at a map of the medieval Pyrenees online, with the GPS coordinates you gave me for Belarac. The abbey was just over the mountains from Aragón," said Lucy. "That law originated with the Castilian sheep breeders, further west. If the abbess got her sheep from Aragónese breeders, which was likely, she may have circumvented the law."

"But I thought at the time of her death, Spain had been united by Isabella and Ferdinand for decades."

"That's true—but imagine enforcing a law in a world where people communicated via parchment scrolls carried by knights on horseback through the Pyrenees. It's still a wilderness in places today. Back then, it must have been nearly impenetrable."

Zari thanked Lucy and rang off. She posted photos of the mortuary roll and the prayer book page with Mira's self-portrait on several social media sites and wrote guest posts on a few art history blogs, using every trick she knew to catapult her findings to the top of the search engines. Then she e-mailed Vanessa Conlon the photos she had taken in the archival library and a brief outline of her findings.

She flicked off the bedside lamp and climbed under the sheets, listening to evening sounds drift in from the darkness. Thoughts of Wil chafed at her. Something in her had unfurled in his presence, something raw and vital and vulnerable. That feeling was lodged in her heart now, a thudding reminder of him that rode the rhythms of her pulse. It would just seep away over time, she told herself. It would ease up. Drift off. Evaporate.

Tears stung her eyes. She counted backward from one hundred, then started again. A car alarm blared and was silenced. When sleep finally came, it was restless, a fragile mask over her worries punctured by the swell of far-off laughter and the distant thrum of dance music at a summer party.

BOOK 5

Alis volat propriis. She flies with her own wings.

1

Spring, 1502
Zaragoza, Aragón
Ramón

RAMÓN LEANED BACK IN his chair, golden wine goblet in hand, contemplating the man across the table. Carlo Sacazar was surrounded by platters of food: a whole game bird, salted anchovies, olives stuffed with cured ham, a quivering mound of apple jelly studded with bits of meat. He waved away the servants every time they approached, ladling his own sauce, scooping up spoonfuls of this and that.

"Truly, you have the appetite of a warrior," Ramón remarked.

Carlo nodded, his cheeks bulging. "Yes, yes. Eating well is one of my joys." Flecks of cheese sprayed out when he said this, sprinkling the table with snowy granules.

Ramón had always assumed that Carlo's idea of selling Oto wool over the mountains in Béarn was in some way self-serving. It had taken a few years to pinpoint Carlo's true motivation: he wanted a powerful ally in his endless

quest for better road conditions and security for the journey across the mountains. With the house of Oto backing
him, Carlo had made considerable headway toward his goal.
Rather than mistrust the man for using him to achieve his
own ambitions, Ramón regarded him with a new measure
of respect.

"We are not so different, we two," his host said. "I do not possess
an illustrious pedigree like your own, but I am an abbot twice
over, no longer simply a merchant."

Ramón stared, his feeling of warm regard evaporating. Carlo
made a conciliatory gesture with his hands.

"Yes, I may have purchased my titles, but it was not for pride.
I did it for my children, of course. Unfortunately, most of the
bluebloods in Béarn are as poor as peasants. I now turn my
sights on the noble sons of Aragón."

"Is that so?"

"An alliance of wealth with wealth is always preferable."

"When my sons marry, they will be matched with the daughters of Castilian dukes. Or perhaps the daughters of the Great
Captain himself. I soon cross the sea to fight alongside him in
the kingdom of Naples. An alliance may develop between our
two houses."

"Ah. You are wise to set your sights so high. Power begets power,
I like to say." Carlo popped a walnut into a silver nutcracker and
squeezed it shut with a resounding thump.

"Though you've never spent a day on a battlefield, you and
the Great Captain have something in common," Ramón said,
putting down his goblet and taking up his knife. "You both
share the problem of marrying off your girls. In our family, of
course, we have no such problem. No daughters." He stabbed a
piece of beef with the tip of his blade.

Carlo fixed him with a quizzical look. "How unfortunate. Girls
are such a joy," he said, fitting another walnut into the nutcracker.

"I cannot imagine doting upon a boy the way I do with our two girls." He pressed the handles of the nutcracker together. There was another sharp crack.

"I would not know—nor do I care to," said Ramón, finishing off his wine. He put his cup down on the table with a thump. "Girls are useless in a family of warriors. But then you would not understand. When has a Sacazar ever been called to war?"

"Too true, too true," Carlo said, his tone amiable. "But that does leave me time for other pursuits. My house in Nay is finally complete. You must come see it. I imported all the artisans from Florence and their work is faultless. We commissioned an artist to paint our portraits, as you would see in a Florentine mansion." He chewed reflectively. "A woman artist, at that. Though to look at her work, one would swear the paintings were done by a master."

"What kind of woman paints like a master?" Ramón took a gulp of wine. Carlo always served excellent wine.

"She comes from a convent in Béarn," Carlo said, stabbing at a pile of roasted garlic and onions with his knife. At Ramón's surprised expression, he pumped his head up and down. "Oh yes—nuns paint." He shoveled onions between his teeth.

"Whatever for?"

"Some of them have fathers and brothers who are artists themselves. The family trade, as it were."

"Does this woman have an artist for a father, then?"

"I don't know who her father is, nor does she. I warrant she's the bastard of some noble, for she is educated and intelligent, with a high-born face."

"Oh? What does she look like?" Ramón asked, feeling a faint prick of curiosity.

Carlo jumped up and walked to the sideboard, where he yanked open a drawer and pulled out a small object. "Here. Have a look."

The painting was tiny, no higher than his finger. It showed a woman from the shoulders up. She wore the garb of a novice nun and her hair was covered with a veil. Her pale eyes curved up at the corners, her eyebrows were slanted and dark.

"I have seen this woman before, I am certain of it," Ramón said.

"Oh?"

"I cannot think where." He pushed the tiny painting away and turned back to his meal. "So what did she paint, then?"

"Portraits of us all, of course. Myself, my wife, our two daughters. The other merchant families in Nay are lining up for their portraits now. I suppose between the lot of us we shall keep her employed for years."

"Indeed. I have often mulled the idea myself. As a legacy for my sons and grandsons, you see."

"Exactly! There once hung in this house a glorious portrait of my dear parents crafted by the master Bermejo. I spend so much time in Nay these days that I had the painting brought to my home there. Now I can gaze upon my parents' likenesses whenever I wish."

Ramón nodded, his fingers joined at the tips, elbows on the armrests of his chair.

"I wonder if this artist nun would travel to Aragón?" He imagined a portrait of himself hanging in a gold frame just opposite the entry doors in the great hall, where every visitor would be confronted with his authoritative gaze the moment they stepped across the threshold.

"If the price is right, she likely would travel. I can have my wife arrange it with yours, if you wish. It will amuse her." Carlo smiled and saluted Ramón with his goblet, then drained his wine.

"Very well," said Ramón. "Let it be done."

"Excellent, my lord!" Carlo said, beaming. He clapped his hands together. "You will not regret it."

2

Summer, 1502
Castle Oto, Aragón
Marguerite

ARGUERITE STARED AT THE letter in her hand. Lady Flora Sacazar, whose noble title was purchased with gold, wrote of a masterfully trained artist, an orphan raised in the Abbey of Belarac who now found steady employment with the merchant class of Nay. Her husband Carlo had it on the best authority that Baron Ramón de Oto might be interested in commissioning the young woman to paint portraits of his own family. Was that truly the case, Flora wondered?

A thread of heat took hold of Marguerite's chest and rippled upward into her skull. She flung open the balcony shutters and stepped out under a gray sky. So the death of Béatrice had catapulted Mira into the homes of wealthy merchants who desired immortal records of their overfed faces. She bit her lip. Could Ramón truly know of Mira's existence? The sheet of linen paper slipped from her trembling fingers. She stooped to pluck it from the stone pavers before the wind could claim it.

Stepping back inside, Marguerite closed the shutters, leaning her head against the latch. Within the safe confines of her own mind, she allowed a reunion with Mira to play out. She saw herself with arms outstretched in the great hall, saw Mira rushing across the threshold of the doorway for a long embrace. She heard their laughter, felt the warmth of their tears mingling on her cheeks.

What would it have been like to have Mira by her side all these years? Marguerite had walked in her own mother's footsteps through the dim corridors of their house, into the cavernous, smoky kitchens, out to the courtyard where the chickens pecked underfoot and the laundry hung from flax lines, drying in the sun. She followed the sound of iron keys clacking at her mother's waist, peering around her wide skirts whenever the jangling stopped. She learned that running a household was like the orderly shifting of shadows on a sundial. Every hour brought a new chore, a new round of orders and inspections, of punishments and payments rendered.

Perhaps it was not too late to have Mira's companionship on her own daily rounds through the castle. Ramón had made preparations all summer for his next journey. This time he would take their son and sail across the sea to the kingdom of Naples, joining the Great Captain in a battle against the French. It would be his longest absence yet, and fraught with perils—not least of which were the treacherous voyages through stormy seas. She imagined a wooden ship scudding across great waves, sails snapping and billowing, mast creaking with the force of the wind, and Pelegrín trapped in its dripping bowels.

A sound from the corridor startled her. She walked swiftly to the hearth and threw the letter into the flames. Blinking back tears, she stood motionless until the charred bits of paper vanished into the red heart of the fire.

3

Summer, 1502
Castle Oto, Aragón
Pelegrín

PELEGRÍN WATCHED SHADOWS CAST by the firelight dance on the stone floor. He settled back in his chair, waiting. It was a ritual he enjoyed, these evenings before the fire with his father, listening to tales of his ancestors and their exploits. One of his favorite stories concerned a long-ago Baron of Oto. The baron happened upon a group of nobles who had been ambushed by bandits in a fog-shrouded valley. A pregnant woman lay among the dead with a lance in her throat. The baron had slit her bulging belly and pulled out a baby, who let out a lusty cry as soon as the cold air touched his skin.

Tonight his father had promised him a new story, one he had never heard before. It was a special night, because tomorrow they departed for the kingdom of Naples. He was impatient to take up arms against the French, to board a ship and sail across the open sea.

"Ah! Just as I desired," Ramón said, lowering himself into his carved oak chair. He eyed the silver pitcher and goblets on the table between them. "My son awaits me, a great fire burns in the hearth, and my cup is full."

He picked up his cup and drank, then let out a satisfied sigh.

"Now, Pelegrín, it is time you heard the story of the seven sons."

Before he could continue the steward interrupted from the doorway.

"My lord, forgive me, but the preparations in the armory are complete. Everything is in order for your departure."

"Excellent, excellent," Ramón said agreeably. "Bring a chair close to the fire, Beltrán. Have some wine with us."

Pelegrín stiffened in his seat. Things had never been the same between himself and Beltrán since that incident with the girl in the meadow. They engaged in sword practice each day because his father ordered it. But the forays into the woods, Beltrán's lessons on hunting, and his stories about Catalonian intrigues and his childhood in Barcelona had all become remnants of a distant past. In their place had emerged a frosty wariness on both their parts. Sometimes Pelegrín felt they were competing to see who could convey necessary information to the other with the fewest words.

Beltrán gestured to the servant to drag a chair next to Pelegrín, but that was only because Ramón would not tolerate being approached from the left. Pelegrín kept his eyes fixed on the fire as Beltrán settled in his chair. When the steward reached for his cup, Pelegrín's gaze was drawn to the red, puckered stump of his severed finger.

"It was in my great-grandfather's day when the seven sons of Oto made their mark on the world," Ramón began. "For the first time a Baron of Oto was wed to a lady of Béarn. She traveled over the great mountains, across the ancient roads, to become a baroness. And she bore my great-grandfather twelve sons, one after the next. Five of them died, as babies do, but seven grew up to be strapping men and brought glory to their king. They made their mark for Aragón, raiding the Moors and ransacking their palaces. They earned the favor of the king in ways that no men of the house of Oto had since the days of the plague."

Ramón glanced meaningfully at Pelegrín, who nodded in understanding.

"I could speak all night of their deeds, but I will limit my story to this. The king of Aragón had learned of a plot against his life by his brother. The seven sons of Oto rode through the night at his behest to his brother's castle. They wrangled their way inside. As soon as the gates shut behind them, they struck down the king's brother and all of his men, thereby saving the kingdom from certain ruin."

Ramón set his cup down on the table with a thump.

"How did they talk their way in so easily?" Pelegrín asked. His own wine cup was untouched. He preferred ale, but his father abhorred it. "The king's brother had worthless men in his keep, allowing a band of armed strangers inside so quickly. You would never allow such a thing, Father."

Ramón turned his eyes upon his son, pleased. "I was waiting for you to ask me that question. They had come across a pair of bandits in the woods and slain them, then covered themselves in the poor fools' blood. They approached the castle feigning injury, their swords well hidden. It was a masterful ploy."

"Deception is one of the great tools of battle," Beltrán said.

"Only if it is well executed. Courage and cunning can go hand in hand, but at great risk."

The servant refilled the cups with wine. Pelegrín forced down a few sips.

"As I said," Ramón went on, "the seven sons brought glory to our house once more. The king gifted my great-grandfather lands in the north, three hundred mounted soldiers, thirty strands

394

of pearls as fat as chickpeas, and chests of silver that would fill this room." He waved his arms about for emphasis. "My great-grandfather thought long and hard about how best to continue the legacy of his seven sons. He decided to marry off his heir to a Béarnaise woman, just like his own wife, because she had borne him so many fine boys. Soon more sons arrived for the house of Oto: my father and four more sons. When my father wed his own Béarnaise bride, the line of sons continued: myself, and two younger brothers after me, though one died as an infant and the other at twelve, God rest their souls. Then I, too, wed a woman of Béarn. And more sons came to me—two fine sons." He smiled at Pelegrín.

"Your ancestor's idea was sound," Beltrán said. "The house of Oto bears only sons. Though fewer with each passing generation."

The muscles in Ramón's jaw twitched.

"What do you imply?"

Pelegrín caught a trace of menace in his father's voice. He flung a dark look in Beltrán's direction. Did the fool want to lose another finger?

"Nothing, my lord. Many sons are no guarantee of good fortune," Beltrán said.

Ramón stroked his beard, staring at the steward with narrowed eyes.

"I speak from experience." Beltrán's voice was conciliatory now. "I am the fourth of five brothers. You know the state of my father's fortune—and of course he had three daughters to marry off. It was difficult. The dowries, you see."

"Yes, the problem of daughters. A problem no longer known in this house. The Aragón-Béarn alliance has proven its value."

"But girls are inevitable, I suppose—" Beltrán began.

"No," Ramón cut in. "Not for us."

Beltrán's gaze lingered on Ramón for a moment, then slid back to the fire.

Pelegrín shifted in his seat. His father's anger sprang up as quickly as an autumn wind, and Beltrán knew it better than anyone. It was typical of the man to incite his master's ire over a topic as dull as sons and daughters. He cast about for some other subject to discuss, and seized upon the thought that was never far from his mind: the long voyage over the sea, to war. But before he could open his mouth, his father spoke again.

"Our journey begins tomorrow. Go to bed, Pelegrín. I have much to discuss with the steward before we take our leave."

When Pelegrín passed by Beltrán, he saw in the man's face a strange expression. He looked amused and smug and superior all at once, as if he knew something Pelegrín did not. More than ever, the weight of the steward's shiny dark eye upon him made Pelegrín want to ball up his fist and unleash a blow with the force of an axe. But he kept his face neutral, his hands loose at his sides, and simply said goodnight.

4

Summer, 1503
Nay, Béarn
Carlo

THE SACAZARS AND AMADINA were in Nay's central market square just after dawn on a cool summer morning. All along the covered arcades that wrapped around the square, merchants were readying their wares. The Sacazars examined the canvas sacks of wool that had come in the previous day from Belarac. Their own sacks, branded with a leaping dolphin, were piled next to those of the Ronzal shepherds, whose motif was a three-pointed peak topped with a sprinkling of stars. The sacks containing the Oto wool were set a bit apart, emblazoned with the family crest: two ships, two sheep, two castles.

A group of servants from another merchant's house passed by, followed by their mistress, Madame Souchet, who was known throughout Nay as the second-richest woman after Flora Sacazar, and by far the stoutest.

"Ah!" She paused in her rounds. Her servants stopped nearby, waiting. "Good morning to you, one and all."

The three Sacazars made the customary greetings, commenting on the good fortune of what promised to be a mild, sunny market day.

"So much wool." Madame Souchet waddled from sack to sack, her plump pink hand trailing delicately over the rough canvas. "And washed! Time was, one could smell the stink of the wool from a hundred paces. Now—well, I would not call it sweet, but I find it much more tolerable, to be sure." She paused. "Saints above. The herald of the house of Oto. It gives me shivers to see that, it does." She pulled her cloak around herself.

"Why?" asked Carlo. His head itched under his velvet cap. He longed to scratch it, but his wife believed it was vulgar to acknowledge the existence of lice in public. He furrowed his brow repeatedly in an attempt to defuse the itch.

"Have you not heard?" Madame Souchet fished a handkerchief from between her breasts. Carlo wondered what else she had stored in there. "The muleteers like to spread tales, we all know that. Well, the one that's making the rounds these days is enough to break your heart, it is." She paused to blow her nose vigorously, then examined the contents of her handkerchief.

"And which tall tale would that be?" he asked.

Flora and Amadina fixed Madame Souchet with their attention, eager for a story.

She looked cautiously around, then spoke in a low voice. "A warring family, they are. A family of *warriors*. And 'tis no accident. The Otos have a habit of leaving girl babies in the woods to die."

Carlo frowned. "I am well acquainted with the Oto family and it pains me to hear gossip that has been bandied about by peasants and muleteers. I give no credence to it."

Madame Souchet sucked in her breath, offended. "I will be off, then. Good day to you." She stuffed her handkerchief back into her bosom and swept away, her entourage following a few paces behind.

Flora's eyes were fixed on Madame Souchet's retreating form.

"Do you know," she said slowly. "I wonder if there is some truth to that?"

"Flora!" Carlo snapped. "That was the worst kind of gossip."

"No, hear her out." Amadina set her gaze on her sister-in-law. "What it is you wish to say, Flora?"

"Remember, my dear, when we met the Baroness of Oto in Zaragoza?" Under her cloak, Flora worried her long string of pearls. Carlo could hear them clacking together.

"Yes, yes." He shaded his eyes against the sun, watching another wool seller unload his sacks nearby.

"I distinctly remember that she said the house of Oto begets only sons. I recall it clearly because it was quite an odd thing to say."

"Not so very odd as that," Carlo muttered, immersed in counting the sacks. "There are many such houses."

"My brother and I are not of the same mind," Amadina said in a warm, coddling tone. "I find it a strange thing to say, quite strange indeed."

"What fixes in my mind now—it just struck me as Madame Souchet told us her story—is the likeness between the Baroness of Oto and young Mira," Flora continued.

Carlo turned to look at her, astonished. Amadina tilted her head to one side, letting her gaze slide from her sister-in-law to her brother.

"My dear Carlo, you have remarked on it as well," Flora said. "You told me how much young Mira resembles her. I recall you saying once that you could count on the fingers of one hand the number of people you had met with eyes like theirs. And their hair. We both remarked on it. I wonder if it is not mere coincidence—"

Carlo cut off his wife in midsentence. "Idle speculation!"

But she was not finished. "Last autumn we got a letter from the Baroness of Oto telling us she did not want the girl to paint their portraits. She had no interest in the idea. Perhaps there was another reason for her refusal." She dropped her voice. "Perhaps it was because young Mira is the very girl she cast out into the woods to die."

"The hour grows late," Carlo growled, glaring at his wife. "I have no more time to listen to the inventions of your imagination. We have much work to do. Flora, return to our children and see that they have begun their lessons. Amadina and I will finish here."

Flora pressed her lips into a thin line. She whirled and crossed the square, followed by a servant girl who, Carlo grimly noted, had heard every word.

He leaned back on his heels, his eyebrows drawn together, unraveling a memory. The weight of his sister's gaze broke his concentration.

"Will the loose tongues of gossipers ever cease their wagging?" she asked, clucking her tongue against the roof of her mouth. She pulled a bit of wool from one of the Oto sacks and held it up to the sunlight, twirling it in her fingers.

"My wife invents stories. You are well acquainted with her imagination." Carlo stood, frowning down at her. "If you spread this gossip, I will know."

"As you wish, brother," Amadina said carelessly, stuffing the wool back into the sack. "I, too, despise gossip. I am only interested in the truth."

5

Summer, 1503
Nay, Béarn
Mira

MIRA STOOD AT HER window, watching the Sacazar family's oxcarts rattle over the cobblestones of Nay's central square. Carlo, Flora and the children would be at one of their estates in Aragón for the rest of the summer. Fourteen mounted guards followed the carts out of the square. Among the possessions the entourage carried was the family portrait she had made. Carlo planned to hang it in his home in Zaragoza.

Her feet felt leaden, weighed down by dread. For as soon as her employers were beyond the walls of the town, she would gather her supplies and knock on the great oak doors of the convent. She had been commissioned to put her talents to work for another Sacazar.

Mira dipped the squirrel brush in the paint, then tapped it on the side of the pot. A few glistening, amber-colored drops oozed off the brush. She peered around the edge of the oak panel at Amadina Sacazar, who was seated in an ornately carved oak chair next to a table that bore an immense silver urn filled with flowers.

The July heat made the room stifling. The diamond-shaped window panes formed a thick barrier between them and any breeze that might happen by. Mira wished that the Sacazars were not quite so rich and the windows were equipped with wooden shutters that opened rather than glass.

"Have these flowers gone off?" Amadina reached out to pat a blossom. "They seem a bit droopy."

"I believe they appear very much alive, Mother Abbess. Please look directly at me again. We are very nearly done with your face."

Amadina swiveled her head, sitting up stiffly in her chair. "It is so hot I fear I do not look my best. Is this angle flattering?"

"Yes." Mira dabbed paint on the panel.

"Splendid." Amadina fell silent for a scant moment. "I hope you do not find me too forward, but I must confess I have wrestled with a secret that I carry. I do not wish to spread gossip, but on the other hand, it concerns you."

Mira put down her paint brush. "Me?"

"Yes," Amadina said. "I know I want to be told if I am the subject of idle whispers. How can one defend oneself otherwise? That is how I see it."

"What is the gossip, then?" Mira came out from behind the panel, wiping her hands on a rag.

"A muleteer says that the Oto family leaves its girl babies in the woods to die."

Mira rubbed at a spot of paint on her palm. "I have heard that rumor. What has it to do with me?"

"The servants always have an ear out, it seems." Amadina leaned forward. "The gossips are saying that you are one of those girl babies. They say you look for all the world like the

Baroness of Oto, she who only births sons. They say—forgive me, my dear—they say you were cast out by your family to die."

Mira stepped back. The rag fell to the floor. She reached down with a trembling hand and picked it up.

"Oh, my dear, it was the idle talk of servants in the kitchen." Amadina waved an arm dismissively. "Who knows where they heard it? I felt it was my duty to tell you."

Mira picked apart the woman's words in her mind. "But that makes no sense at all. If they leave girl babies in the woods to die, why would I be alive, if I were one of them? Would I not have been torn apart by wolves?"

Amadina shrugged. "The gossips say that once an Oto baby was taken to a village, because the guard would not let her die in the woods. Perhaps your fate was the same. Perhaps such a person took pity on you and spirited you away to the abbey."

"That tale is nothing but lies. Lies upon lies." Mira's face burned. "My parents died when I was small. I am an orphan. That is the truth."

"I am simply the messenger." There was an edge to Amadina's voice now, the crackle of authority. "As I said, the gossips speculate. Nothing to be done about it. Now let us continue, shall we?"

Mira retreated behind the panel. But every time she took up the brush, her hand shook so she could not dip it in the pot, let alone entrust it with the job of painting Amadina's glistening pink face.

Amadina snapped her fingers at a servant. "Fetch a fan. No, two. This heat makes me faint." The woman scurried off.

"Mother Amadina, I implore you to rest," Mira said. "There is no need to continue this afternoon. Tomorrow is bound to be cooler."

Amadina hesitated, mopping her cheeks with a square of linen.

"This air is so heavy and humid, a thunderhead must build in the sky," Mira went on. "When it bursts, we will all be so much cooler. Sitting for your portrait will be more enjoyable." Although she wanted to fling her squirrel brush at Amadina's face, Mira forced a smile.

"Very well, let us pause. We will begin again tomorrow."

Amadina took hold of a servant's arm and heaved herself up. "But I am not nearly ready to let you out of my sight. You must join us in the chapel for vespers and stay for supper. I will not accept your apologies. Consider the meal part of your contract of employment."

Mira's throat constricted with foreboding. "As you wish, Mother Amadina."

Kneeling with the nuns in the chapel, Mira ruminated over Amadina Sacazar's strange claims. The woman was so odd, her face often twisted with anger. It was nearly impossible to believe that she and Carlo originated in the same womb. But Mira could not deny that they shared the same round face, almond-shaped eyes and fleshy lips. She imagined what Elena would say: *Blood does tell.*

At supper, the heavy oak table was set with silver. Mira counted six platters of meat, fruits and cheeses. She watched Amadina down two cups of wine in quick succession and tear the skin off a roasted pigeon with her teeth. As the evening wore on, it became clear that Amadina's dour nature brightened considerably after a copious helping of wine.

"A new abbess has been selected for Belarac, I hear," she said, picking up a red plum from a silver tray and squeezing it. She dropped it and selected another.

Mira nodded. "Sister Agathe has done a fine job managing things in the meantime."

"A passable job, anyway." Amadina weighed the plum in her palm. "The new abbess comes all the way from Gascony. I hope she has been ordered to impose piety upon the place again. Béatrice—God rest her soul—was too little concerned with piety and too much with commerce."

Mira bristled. "With all respect, Mother Amadina, there would be no Belarac without Mother Béatrice. She only did what she had to do to bring the abbey back to life."

"Is that what she told you?" Amadina bit into the plum and a trickle of red juice ran down her hand.

"It is what I observed. I lived there all my life."

"Such is the fate of orphans, I suppose. Poor girl." Amadina took a long pull of her wine. "Sometimes orphans are high born, so do not simply assume you are inferior."

"I have never done so."

"Ah! You deduced that privileges do not simply fall from the sky."

"I beg your pardon?"

"Someone bought your education." Amadina sucked on the stone of the plum. "That is the way of a convent."

Mira shifted uncomfortably in her seat. It was true—not all the orphans at Belarac slept in private chambers and were taught to read and write. Her days were quite different from those of the girls who slept in dormitories and spent their afternoons working in the gardens, the kitchens, and at the paper workshop. And she alone of the novices played a role in the outside world.

She cast around for another topic. "Tell me, would you like me to paint a background for your portrait in the style of Bartolomé Bermejo, as I have done for your brother? So you can enjoy the memories of your youth in Zaragoza, as he does."

Amadina choked on her cream tart. She coughed, then downed her wine. When she spoke again her voice was loose and slurred, and Mira knew her good mood had vanished.

"I am not surprised that my brother wishes to be reminded of his childhood. But I am not so fortunate. I have no fond memories of my youth. In fact, I wish my portrait to be as different from my brother's as you can accomplish. I do not care how you achieve it, but you must."

"Of course, Mother Amadina. What do you desire the background to show?"

"The room I sit in, its furnishings, its ornaments."

"As you wish."

"And—most important, this point—you must sign the portrait." A servant crept to her side and refilled her cup. Amadina waved a hand at the woman. "Leave us!" she muttered.

The servant slipped out of the room and pulled the door shut behind her. Amadina leaned forward, her eyes glittering.

"You will sign your full name: Mira de Oto. For that is who you are. The daughter of a baron. Cast away for the crime of being a girl. I wonder how it all played out? Perhaps some kind-hearted guard spirited you away to a mountain village, just as the muleteer's tale goes. But I think not, because of the gold. Béatrice would not have showered you with privileges unless she was paid to do it. Yes—someone paid for your life in gold coins. I wonder who it was? There is no shame in it, girl. You've a benefactor. And that is something to be proud of."

Mira sat dumbly for a moment, feeling as if she had been struck in the face.

"This tale you tell is fascinating," she said, fighting to keep her voice even.

"I can understand how loath you are to accept it, young Mira, but I am doing you a kindness. Do you not agree it is better to hear this from me than from the flapping tongue of a market gossip?"

"It is most kind of you to take it upon yourself to inform me of this gossip, yes."

Amadina laughed. "To the contrary, you believe me anything but kind. Blast this heat. Nothing slakes my thirst." Slumping back in her chair, she pulled at her veil.

Mira wanted to run from the room, burst out the great oak doors and flee to her chamber in the Sacazars' stately home. Instead, she folded her hands at her waist and gazed steadily across the table at her host, who had lapsed into silence.

"I know what your thoughts are," Amadina finally said. "I see the judgement in your eyes."

Amadina waved a hand, knocking her wine cup over. It rolled onto the red Moorish carpet with a soft thump.

"Your precious Mother Béatrice sat in that very spot with the same look in her eyes. Deemed me inferior, thought of me only as my brother's puppet, bobbing on a string. Poor thing, there was so much she did not know." Amadina snorted. "For a saintly woman, she had enemies enough."

"What enemies?"

"How do you think she met her end? Surely you do not believe it was a natural death. I know the story. It smacks to me of poison."

"That is a strange thing to say." Mira leaned forward in her chair, her pulse quickening.

"Her ring was taken, that is the tale I heard."

"What has that to do with poison?"

"It is commonly known that a murderer must bear away a token to prove to his employer that he truly did the deed. Anyone with a brain can deduce the sequence of events: a healthy woman dies in the night, relieved of her one jewel? It is a story as old as time, my dear. Someone was hired to murder her."

Amadina fell silent. Mira watched her eyelids droop. A moment passed, then another.

"Mother Amadina?"

Amadina's head lolled back on her chair, her eyelids fluttering shut. Her mouth fell open and a gentle snoring commenced.

It took four servants to carry Amadina upstairs to bed. While they were fussing over their inebriated mistress, Mira fetched her cloak and slipped away. Wrenching a torch from the wall sconce outside the convent's doors, she made her way back through the cloying heat to Carlo Sacazar's residence.

Should she tell Lord Sacazar about his sister's allegations? A thought struck her. Perhaps he already knew. Perhaps, as Amadina said, it was obvious that Mother Béatrice had been murdered.

At the Sacazars' home, she hammered the iron knocker against the door until a servant let her in. She climbed the winding stairs to her chamber on the third floor, the torch casting grotesque shadows on the walls.

All that night she lay sleepless, staring into the dark, consumed with worry over Amadina's words.

6

Summer, 1503
Nay, Béarn
Mira

I<small>T WAS A</small> T<small>UESDAY</small> in July, well on its way to being the hottest market day in any living townsperson's memory. The sun beat down upon the market square with the intensity of an open flame. Making her way through the crowd to the wool stalls, Mira felt sweat trickle down her spine. A young mother slapped her child's hand in frustration and the girl started to wail. Two old women argued over a basket of carrots. Mira sidestepped a heap of mule dung and edged around a temporary pen where livestock bleated and groaned in the relentless heat.

She was conscious of eyes upon her. She had always been a subject of curiosity, the artist clothed in the habit of a novice nun who earned money painting portraits of the rich. But now there was a sordid edge to the idea of people discussing her.

She reached the wool stalls just as Arnaud de Luz did. A roar of excitement rose up by the livestock pen. Two of the goats had begun butting heads, causing a crowd to form. Arnaud and Mira ducked behind a pile of wool sacks that were stacked a little distance from the stone wall of the covered arcade. Arnaud's smile faded when he saw her anxious face.

"Have you heard the gossip?" She moved close, keeping her voice low. "Tongues are wagging about the Oto family."

"And what do these idle tongues say?"

"That they leave their girl babies in the woods to die."

The high, thin bleat of a goat rang out, followed by a woman's shriek. Laughter rippled through the crowd in response to some antic in the livestock pen.

"Who told you that?" Arnaud's forehead creased in a frown. "The servants, the merchant wives? Such tales twine among them like grapevines. Most of them lies."

"Even the one about me? The one I heard from the lips of Amadina Sacazar?"

He hesitated a moment too long, avoiding her eyes.

"You know of it, then." Her heart pounded in her chest. The acrid smell of mule dung mixed with the scent of raw wool in her nostrils.

A young woman whom she recognized as a servant from the Sacazar household walked by and gave them a long, curious stare.

"This isn't the place to speak of such things," Arnaud warned.

Perhaps it was the heat; perhaps it was the fact that Mira had slept very little since the night of Amadina's bizarre accusations. Whatever the source, a feeling of recklessness took hold of her. She made no effort to be discreet, but stepped even closer to him.

"The full moon approaches," she said. "That is when they meet, the mountain folk—in high summer at the full moon. Elena will be there. Will you come with me?"

"That'll set tongues wagging fiercer than ever."

"Let them wag." Mira blotted the sweat from her face with the edge of her veil. "Amadina Sacazar rides north in a few days. The moment she leaves, so do I. If you do not wish to accompany me, I will procure a mule and ride up the mountain myself."

"What's got hold of you, Mira?" He frowned. "Head full of bold plans, but still clothed in the habit of a novice nun. A girl about to take her vows has no business tramping through the mountains."

Mira stayed silent a moment. Under all her layers of wool, her knees began to shake.

"Will you take your vows or not?" he asked, exasperated.

"No." Her heart pounded in her ears. "I choose a life outside those gates. I choose the artist's life."

Arnaud's expression softened into a look of relief, as if some weight had been lifted from him. He touched his fingertips to hers. "We'll go together, then. I'll take you to Elena."

The crowd at the livestock pen dispersed and people trickled toward the wool stalls. Arnaud went back to his sacks of wool and Mira turned away, slipping into the shadows of a narrow lane.

She held a hand up to her face, watched the trembling of her fingers. If indeed she was a daughter of the house of Oto and her own parents had cast her out to die, she would have the truth from Elena.

7

Summer, 2015
Oloron Sainte-Marie to Sarrance, France
Zari

Z ARI'S MOBILE BUZZED. IT was Laurence, downstairs. When Zari descended the broad stone staircase, lugging her backpack, Laurence thrust out a pair of battered hiking poles. They were cornflower blue, streaked with silver scratch marks.

"Laurence—*merci*! I don't want to take your poles, though. What if I lose them?"

"It is my pleasure to give them to you." Laurence's long gold earrings swung gently back and forth, catching the light. "I have another pair. These were my husband's. They have been useless to me since he died."

Zari put a hand on Laurence's arm. "I'm so sorry. I had no idea."

"Stéphane walked the Way many times with them. It was something we did together. A different section every year. I lost the desire to do it when he died." Her voice faltered and her shoulders slumped almost imperceptibly in her white linen blouse. She pressed the poles into Zari's hands.

"I will take very good care of them," Zari promised.

"Pilgrims have been walking the Way for a thousand years. It was always dangerous. Now it is safer, but you must be very careful, Zari. Accidents happen when you get tired. So when you are tired, stop!"

"I will be careful," Zari said solemnly. There was no time left to wonder if this was the right moment. She had to ask.

"Laurence, I'm pursuing another fellowship, this time devoted to studying Mira. At Oxford. Would you consider being a reference for me? It's a long shot, and I'm not sure if—"

"*Absolument*." Laurence's face lit up. "It would be my pleasure to help you. I can get you access to any library or museum in France, and most private collections too." Her smile faded. "There are still many people who want my painting to be the work of Bermejo, Zari. And the Oxford painting too. They will not make your research easy."

"I know. Some of those people work at Oxford. I'm sure I'll have plenty of critics. But I'll put on my big girl pants and get the work done."

"Big girl pants? Is that an American fashion?"

Zari shook her head, laughing. "No. It means I'll be brave."

"Ah. Courage. I will tell you something, Zari. If you can walk over these mountains by yourself, you have enough courage to face your colleagues."

Laurence walked ahead of her out the doors into the sunshine, striding quickly over the cobblestones in her cork platform sandals. Lugging her backpack to Laurence's car, Zari marveled at the way French women made fashion work for them. They were never at its mercy, it seemed—or perhaps they were simply masters of illusion.

When Laurence dropped Zari off in Oloron Sainte-Marie, a chill clung to the air. The oppressive heat predicted for the day was still hours away. Laurence pressed a small blue box into Zari's hands and air-kissed her cheeks.

"*Buen camino* and *bonne chance*, Zari."

She climbed back into her Renault. Zari felt a rush of misgiving, watching her drive away. Laurence was her only connection in this part of the world. She was truly on her own now.

At a café across the street from a cathedral, she ordered coffee and a croissant. Seated at a small outdoor table, she leaned her pack against a chair and opened the blue box. Inside were small laminated color photocopies of the restored Fontbroke College portrait and Laurence's painting of the merchant family. Beneath them lay a tiny silver scallop shell on a delicate chain. She hooked the clasp around her neck, then pulled her hair off her shoulders and wound it into a loose bun.

A group of pilgrims emerged from the cathedral and crossed the square to a stone marker, where they snapped photographs of each other posing next to it. One of them was a slight, leathery man wearing a broad-brimmed felt hat. His overstuffed backpack with its aluminum frame reminded Zari of the ones her parents used to wear on long hikes. His companions were two solidly-built women wearing sleek internal frame backpacks. One had short blond hair, the other had long dark hair drawn back in a ponytail. The sight of them was reassuring. Aggie had been right. Zari would not really be alone on the Way. If she needed help, she would find it.

The sun inched higher. Zari savored her coffee, watching the pilgrims disappear up a curving road. She paid for her breakfast and approached the stone marker. The stone bore the carved words '*Voie d'Arles. Saint-Jacques de Compostelle*,' and then, '*948 km.*' Below that was the image of a scallop shell.

She tightened the straps of her backpack, slipped her fingers through the handles of her trekking poles, and set off.

Zari made good time at first, passing through long stretches of shade. Occasionally dogs materialized alongside her, kept pace for a while, then lost interest and wandered away. After several hours spent shambling up a gentle incline, she found herself creeping along a steep drop-off that fell away to a narrow river far below. Zari realized the value of Stéphane's trekking poles as she edged around the washed-out parts. There were dark gouges in the soil below the trail where people had slipped. She willed herself not to look down, suddenly wishing for a companion.

When she arrived at the small hillside town of Sarrance, she sank down on the steps that surrounded an ancient water fountain, a dull ache radiating up from her feet. She had walked a bit more than thirteen miles—half a marathon. She drained her water bottle before hauling herself upright again. The monastery where she would spend the night was just a few steps away.

If the monks who lived in the modest structure possessed long brown robes, they were not in evidence. Zari was greeted by a smiling man in a blue plaid button-down shirt, who checked her in and assigned her a bed in a dormitory. After she took a hot shower, she washed out her socks and underwear and hung them to dry in a furnace room.

The travelers gathered at a long table for a communal supper of roasted potatoes, beef stew and salad. Zari recognized the man and the two women she had watched cross the square in Oloron Sainte-Marie and introduced herself. Mike was a middle-aged man from San Diego who had been downsized from his job and decided to sell his house and all his possessions and travel the world; his companions were a pair of German women who had walked a section of the Way together every summer for the past six years. Across from Zari sat an alarmingly chipper British couple who were in their mid-sixties, and a French couple with their three children. Everyone except the French family spoke English, so the group mostly conversed in English. There was a fair amount of translating done by Mike, the San Diegan, who—completely against type—spoke excellent French.

Mike turned to her. "The French family are unschooling their children," he said, spearing a chunk of beef with his fork.

"Unschooling?" Zari shook her head. "Never heard of it."

"Apparently it's like homeschooling but with no curriculum. You just let the kids decide what they want to do."

"Wow. If I had that choice as a kid, I never would have learned math," Zari said.

"Apparently these kids don't like math either, so they don't do it."

"We have four children," the female half of the British couple chimed in. She had the bright, darting eyes of a bird. "They're all grown now. I would have rather chewed off my own arm than homeschooled them." She launched into a story about her early years as a mother.

One of Portia's sayings came back to Zari: Authentic listening is an act of respect. Portia always brought that up when Zari and her brother weren't paying enough attention. Authentic listening, her mother said, took self-control. Nodding and smiling while your thoughts were a million miles away did not. Zari kept her eyes on the chattering woman next to her, but her thoughts wandered repeatedly north, to Amsterdam and a certain tall, bespectacled Dutchman. *Damn you, Wil Bandstra,* she thought.

Finally the woman wrapped up her story with a cascade of laughter, then glanced at her husband. "But to each his own! Isn't that right, my love?"

He smiled. "The Camino connects us with so many people," he said, nodding. "This is our fourth time as pilgrims, and we've learned over the years not to judge. Just listen and learn, that's what we do. Listen and learn."

Zari felt a stab of sadness, wondering if her own parents ever looked at each other that way even in their early days together. If they did, she had no memory of it. The conflict-laden years that led up to their divorce took center stage in her mind.

"I've heard so many terms for this journey," she said. "The Camino of Santiago, the Way of St. James, the Route of Arles, Via Tolosana…"

"They're all correct," Mike said.

"They all lead to the same place—Compostela," said the blond German woman. "It was once necessary to reach Compostela and see the saint's bones to get one of those." She dipped her head, her eyes on the silver shell at Zari's throat.

"Oh, lovely necklace," said the British woman.

"I don't feel as if I've earned it," said Zari haltingly, "and I guess I'm not officially a pilgrim, because I'm only walking the Way for a few days. But a friend gave it to me today, so I wore it."

"You don't have to earn it," said Mike. "The shell's a symbol of the Way—not proof of your journey. Anyone can wear one."

The German woman shook her head. "I don't agree," she said. "It should be earned. The first time I walked the Way, I only wore mine after completing the journey. And I got a stamp in my *credencial* every night."

Mike leaned closer to Zari. "That's a sort of passport of the Way."

The other German woman laughed. "Once there was no one at the inn to stamp it. We had to stay another night to get a stamp!"

The blond woman looked annoyed. "If you have no proof, nobody knows you did it."

"I know what I have done," said her friend, shrugging. "I don't care if anyone else does."

8

Summer, 2015
Sarrance to Belarac, France
Zari

ASTER BREAKFAST THE NEXT morning, while the travelers made preparations to get back on the trail, the monk appeared carrying a rubber stamp and a pad of ink. Everyone clustered around him to get their books stamped.

When the knot of people dispersed, Zari approached him. Behind small wire-rimmed glasses, his brown eyes were kind. She held out a laminated map with an X on it to mark the location of the Abbey of Belarac.

"I know this is a bit off the trail," she said. "Do you know of it?"

He regarded the map, brow furrowed.

"Belarac," she said. "*Où est* Belarac?"

He frowned and unleashed a torrent of French. Zari caught the words "*attention*" and "*dangereux*."

Mike walked up, backpack cinched in place, battered felt hat on his head.

418

"There's been flooding near there," he translated. "He says it's not too far off the main trail, maybe a couple of hours' walk, but all the streams in the area are flowing high because of summer rains. And more storms are forecast."

"Okay," Zari said. "I'll be careful."

The monk handed Zari her map but kept talking.

"He doesn't think you should go alone," Mike said.

"How do you say 'strong' in French?"

"*Forte,*" Mike said.

"*Je suis forte,*" she said.

"*Oh la la la la la.*" The monk looked beseechingly skyward as if to say, "See, God. This is what I have to deal with."

Outside, Zari sank down on the fountain steps to lace up her boots. A stream of water flowed from a tarnished metal spout behind her. Mike stood nearby, adjusting the straps of his pack.

"I'll walk to Accous with you," he said after a moment. "That's where the split-off for Belarac is."

She smiled in gratitude.

"I'd like that."

The path followed the curves of a river, so narrow and steep in places that Zari concentrated hard on keeping the weight of her pack balanced. She saw villages clinging to the hillsides, the dark slate roofs and stone walls of the houses a stark contrast to the cool greens of the grass and trees all around. In a small meadow, shimmery movements ahead startled her. A cloud of blue butterflies was drifting across the trail, sunlight glittering on their delicate wings.

"Mike—look!"

Mike stopped at her side, leaning forward on his poles. They watched, mesmerized, until the butterflies pulsated out of sight, riding a current of air into the glare of the sun.

The day wore on. In the village of Accous they bought sandwiches, fruit and water. The sun was rapidly being smothered by a bank of silvery clouds and a light rain began to sift down. In the shelter of a hawthorn tree at the turnoff for Zari's route to Belarac, they pulled rain gear from their packs. Properly suited up, they unwrapped their sandwiches, soft baguettes stuffed with thin slices of ham, emmentaler cheese, and hunks of creamy butter.

"Where we come from, this sandwich would be treated with the same contempt normally reserved for cigarettes," Zari said. "It might even be arrested for criminal intent."

"The fat is good for you. Keeps your energy high." Mike pulled a slab of butter from his sandwich and made a show of ecstatic chewing.

For dessert they had tiny apricots and squares of bittersweet chocolate. Zari led them in a round of yoga poses followed by a series of positive affirmations that her mother had insisted she and Gus memorize as children. Mike dutifully repeated each phrase after her, the rain dripping off his hat and rolling down the sleeves of his jacket.

"'Life provides,'" he said. "I like that one."

"It's my mother's auto signature at the bottom of every e-mail." Zari fixed him with a frank look. "You're the first person in Europe I've shared my woo-woo heritage with. I figured it would be safe, since you're from California."

"Nothing like being a stranger in a strange land to appreciate shared cultural references."

She nodded. "It's funny, the fact that we're both from there makes it feel like we have everything in common. But we probably have completely divergent political views and would never get along if we met in California."

"Let's agree to disagree in advance and stay friends," he suggested.

"Deal."

They strapped on their packs and lingered under the curving branches of the hawthorn tree for a few more minutes, watching the rain fall.

"Do you want me to come with you?" he asked, turning toward her again. "I'd be happy to."

"It's several hours out of your way, and depending on what I find, I might stay in the area for another day or two. Thanks, but I'll be fine. Maybe we'll meet up again in Spain," Zari said.

"I've been bumping into the same people for weeks, so I wouldn't be surprised." Mike jammed his hat on his head. "Keep an eye out for Sue. She's walking at roughly the same pace as me, and I've shared too many evenings with her. She's American, from Minnesota. Totally harmless, but one of those people who has no filter and doesn't stop talking. She was nursing a monster case of blisters the last time I saw her. She'll be back on the trail soon."

"You've covered a lot of mileage in the past few days. I doubt she'll catch up."

"You'd be surprised. She tends to glom on to other Americans, that's why I'm mentioning her."

"I could pretend I'm Canadian."

"She'll sniff you out. It's uncanny." He slipped the loops of his poles around his wrists. "*Buen camino*. Be safe, Zari."

9

MID THE SCATTERED REMAINS of the Abbey of Belarac, Zari raised her hiking poles skyward and did her best waterlogged approximation of a victory dance. Standing between two partially sunken foundation stones, she imagined the bustle of life in this valley all those centuries ago: black-clad nuns padding silently through dim corridors to prayers, pilgrims stumbling along the valley road in search of food and shelter, the glint of scythes flashing in the fields.

In her mind she saw Mira at a long oak table, bent over a sheet of linen paper, filling in a carefully drawn italic letter with a wash of gold paint. Whatever it had once been, Mira's world was sinking into decay, like Rievaulx Abbey in Yorkshire, its secrets being swallowed up by the earth.

The storm clouds heaved, unleashing another crackle of lightning. She counted *one-one thousand, two-one thousand,* flinching at the sudden boom of thunder that followed. Her eyes caught on a dark shape moving through the rain. A tall male figure was striding swiftly toward her.

Zari's mind sifted through the possible reasons why a man would be out walking in this storm. Not just walking, she observed, but cutting straight through a meadow of soaked grass on a direct course to the spot where she stood. Perhaps he was a farmer on his way home from doing errands in the village. Or a shepherd hunting for lost sheep. Maybe she had dropped something and he was simply doing a courtesy by grimly rushing to her side through hellish weather conditions to return it. Even as she organized this list of reasonable scenarios, a dark headline throbbed in her brain: *Deranged Rapist Escapes from High-Security Prison, Heads for Pyrenees.*

She hefted one of Stéphane's trekking poles in her hand. It was light, but the point on the end was sharp enough to do some damage. Her weapons assessment was interrupted by the man's shout.

"Zari!"

The familiar voice sliced through the wind.

Wil.

"What are you doing in this storm?" he shouted. "Get out of the open."

His face was hidden in the shadow of his brown canvas hat. He stopped in front of her, planting his poles firmly in the wet earth.

"What am *I* doing here?" The pit of dread in her chest had been replaced by a snaking current of hostility. "You're the one in the wrong place."

"I came to find you."

"You canceled the plan, remember?"

"That was a mistake. Please, let's move under the trees."

"No." Somehow she managed to keep her voice calm. "I like it out here."

He dropped his eyes, rummaged in a pocket and fished out a soft square of cloth. Removing his glasses, he wiped raindrops from the lenses.

"Things did not work out with Hana as you hoped, then?" She stepped off the rock, blinking away tears.

He replaced the glasses. His eyes behind the clear lenses were pleading with her.

"I thought I could make both Hana and Filip happy again. It wasn't what I wanted, and that made it a stupid thing to do. Filip was the one who saw how unhappy I was. He told me to stop acting out of guilt. He said Hana deserved better. I deserve better, too."

"So now I'm supposed to smile and thank you?" Her muscles coiled with tension. Even her toes were curled in her boots. "This isn't how it works, Wil."

"No. You're right. I'm sorry. I didn't think about what to say when I found you. All I could think about was finding you." He bent his head for a moment. Rain dripped off the brim of his hat. "I meant everything I said to you in Bruges," he said, looking up again. "Bruges changed me, Zari. I never use this word, but it keeps coming back to me—it was magic. It was the happiest I've been in so long."

She fell silent a moment, wavering.

"How did you find me, anyway?"

"I had the itinerary you sent me. I got to Oloron Sainte-Marie this morning and hitchhiked to Sarrance. The monk at the monastery told me about your conversation."

"Wil, what do you want me to say?" She sighed. "I spent the last two months getting over you. I wasn't mad at you before, but I am now."

Rain had slithered through the neckline and sleeves of her jacket. Her undershirt stuck clammily to her chest. She watched Wil for another moment in silence. Wheeling on him, she trudged away, forging a dark path through the sodden grass. Her elation at finding the foundation stones of Belarac had vaporized.

The cool pine forest enveloped her in stillness. She found a flat boulder and leaned her pack against it, then rooted around inside for a washcloth. She rubbed her face vigorously with the rough cotton square, stopping only when her cheeks began to burn. Wil appeared in her line of sight.

"You must be cold. Let me make you a hot drink," he said.

She didn't respond.

He unbuckled his pack and sank down on his knees in the brittle pine needles. She watched him remove his glasses and wipe the lenses again, this time with a dry section of his shirt. He pulled a fleece jacket from his backpack and offered it to her. She peeled off her raincoat and slipped his jacket on, breathing in the scent of him. A glimmer of longing ignited in her heart. Irritated, she tore her gaze away and stared across the meadow.

An hour later, with a cup of hot cocoa warming her hands, Zari felt her mood lighten. She had never been able to hang onto anger long. But in this case, she sternly reminded herself, she was just setting herself up for disappointment again.

The storm thinned out, pushed west by the wind.

"Do you want to camp here?" Wil asked, settling a short distance away with his own cup.

"I don't have a tent," she said, staring up through the crowns of the trees.

"I do."

She glanced at him, at his long fingers wrapped around the cup, and the reckless delight of their night in Bruges in her tiny rented apartment came flooding back to her. A wave of heat suffused her chest at the memory. It seemed so long ago.

Sunlight pierced the clouds at last and spilled over the meadow. Zari drew in a long breath, taking in the sight of thousands of water droplets shining on the grass, reflecting the sun's glow. *Remember why you're here*, she told herself.

She pulled a small notebook from a plastic bag in her backpack and stood.

"I'm going to sketch the configuration of the foundation stones. Aggie told me when we went to Rievaulx that these places usually had buildings near the water source for washing wool and tanning leather. I want to see if I can find more stones near the water."

"Can I help?" he asked.

She hesitated. "Sure."

They searched up and down the streambed until they found two small rectangles of foundation stones half submerged in the ground on the banks of the stream.

"There once was an entire thriving world here," Zari said, her excitement creeping back. "I recreate it in my mind all the time. Nuns, villagers, sheep, grain fields, orchards. But nature has almost completely taken it over again."

Wil paced around the perimeters of the foundations.

"There's so little left," he said.

Zari nodded. "It takes imagination to fill in the gaps."

He held out an apple and she took a bite.

"Ugh, mealy."

"Mealy?"

"I don't like soft apples."

He tasted it, then flung it on the ground.

"Neither do I."

Despite herself, she laughed. His rich laughter spilled out in response, with its usual effect on her. She shook her head, sighing, taking in the sight of his lanky frame and wild sun-bleached hair.

Water churned by in the swollen stream. A single white butterfly floated above Wil's head. It dipped and fluttered, at the mercy of the breeze, drifting higher and higher until it looked like a scrap of paper scudding across the silver-blue patchwork of the sky.

"We'll camp tonight," she said, assessing him again with a measured gaze. "And maybe—*maybe*—you can walk with me tomorrow."

The joy in his eyes was unmistakable.

10

Summer, 2015
Belarac to the Ravine, France
Zari

WHEN SHE AWOKE IN the morning, Wil was already up, stirring something in a pot. She watched him tear the top off a rectangular packet and dump the contents in a cup. The fragrance of coffee mingled with the scent of chocolate.

"Mochas," she said, dragging herself out of her sleeping bag. "You are impressive."

"I spent ten years of my life eating camp food," Wil said. "You have to find ways to keep it interesting or you don't eat enough."

The sky was clear. The white peaks of the Pyrenees shimmered above the valley. A red squirrel appeared on the crest of a nearby boulder, its shiny eyes on Zari. Then the rasp of a crow broke the silence and the squirrel bolted into the woods.

"Crows. Is there anywhere they don't go?" She reached for the mug Wil held out to her.

"They are curious. And social. I like them."

"Ever since I saw that Hitchcock movie 'The Birds' as a little girl, I've had a bad feeling about crows."

"It's not just you. In the old days, people thought crows were spies." Wil picked up the topo map. "What if we skip the town of Borce and just take forest trails all the way to the pass? We'll have to camp one more night, but it should cut off some distance for us."

She stayed silent.

"I have freeze-dried meals, fruit and nuts," he added, looking through his pack. He pulled out a small gold box and held it up. "I got you this from a chocolatier in Amsterdam."

Zari widened her eyes, smiling. Her anger had completely evaporated. She sipped her mocha, listening for the crow. But all she heard was the fluttering trill of a far-off songbird.

By early afternoon her legs were shaking and she clung to her hiking poles with desperation. In places the trail was almost washed out, with scary drop-offs that she forced herself to ignore. Occasionally the forest gave way to glorious meadows bursting with wildflowers, and during those moments she breathed deeply and relaxed. But then they were in the woods again, climbing steep switchbacks and stumbling over loose rocks. Wil encouraged her by telling stories of his past adventures, trying to distract her and pass the time. Zari watched him striding ahead of her, listened to the rise and fall of his voice. The mountain sun was turning his skin almost as brown as her own. She saw the muscles under his t-shirt flex and relax, saw how he wrapped his long fingers lightly around his hiking poles, his hands loose and confident.

They stopped at the edge of a broad ravine with a stream rushing through it. Across the ravine, limestone cliffs towered above them. A lone scraggly conifer grew out of a ledge partway up the cliffs.

"Let's camp here," Wil said, raising his voice over the roar of the stream. "I'll find a site back in the woods a bit. You can rest." He disappeared into the forest.

She took off her pack and sank down on a log, staring dully at the water racing over the rocks. Shadows fell on the cliffs as twilight approached. The noise of the water pounded in her ears. She closed her eyes, breathing in the sharp, citrusy scent of pine needles.

Once the sky was well and truly dark, they lay back on a tarp in their sleeping bags. The black sky seemed to have been pierced with thousands of tiny pins. Dots of light shimmered everywhere they looked. A pale half-moon drifted weightlessly above them.

"The early pilgrims believed the stars showed the route to Compostela," said Wil. "They thought the dust made by their steps formed the Milky Way."

"Have you ever use stars as a map?"

"The North Star is always helpful," he said. "But GPS, topo maps, and compasses work better. Filip and I argued about the best way to navigate. He actually could navigate by the stars, and he even had an antique sextant that he used to sail with."

He was quiet for a moment. "An adventure today is not the same as when the first pilgrims walked the Way. So many of them died. Wolves, thieves, weather—there were a lot of dangers back then."

"Don't forget bears," Zari reminded him. "There are a few left."

She looked at him sideways, eyeing the outline of his face.

"So here's the deal, Wil," she said quietly. "I gave you a grief pass for Hana. I couldn't be angry about that—I really got it, I understood. But I can't take another disappointment from you."

He slipped her hand in his and laid it gently on his heart.

"Filip's accident turned everything dark for me. You changed that. I was laughing, I was looking at the world a different way.

I'm not sure how to say it—maybe I saw possibilities again. I thought I could make Filip happy and fix my own guilt by getting back with Hana. It was a stupid choice, because in the end I hurt all of you. I didn't want to try to explain any of this on the phone or by text or e-mail. I just decided to come find you, and try to make it right."

They lay silent, gazing overhead. Zari imagined a thread connecting each star, stitching a pattern of intersecting angles across the sky, pinning the stars in place on their velvety backdrop. Did Mira see the same pattern when she stared at the night sky? Did she believe the dust she kicked up on these mountain trails made its way into the heavens?

"I need you to understand something, Wil," she said. "I'm glad you found me, but I'm not in these mountains to talk about Hana or Filip or the mistakes of the past. I'm searching for Mira of Belarac. My wish is for her name to leap off the pages of a little girl's art history book, glowing like one of these stars, signaling: '*Look what I did. You can do it, too.*'" Zari turned to face him. "Are you in?"

He squeezed her hand. "I'm in."

There was a rustling somewhere behind them, and overhead, the rush of wings.

The moon slid lower in the sky.

11

Summer, 1503
Pyrenees Mountains
Mira

THE TRAIL THAT WOUND up the mountains to the meadow where the people met each year had not changed since Mira walked it as a child. Her bare toes sank into layers of soft rotting leaves. Overhead, the trees were crowned with lush new growth.

She had shed her novice's robes and veil. In their place she wore a flax blouse and long wool skirt. Her long hair was pulled back in a single braid. Over her shoulder was slung a satchel full of pigments and brushes. She had no intention of returning to Nay. Therefore, she must carry her livelihood with her.

Arnaud walked a few paces back. When they reached the boulder where she and Elena had encountered the wolf, she remembered how coolly Elena wielded her knife. The memory of the wolf's cold yellow eyes and curled-back lips made her pulse quicken. She hurried her pace, one hand smoothing her skirts, sliding over the bone handle of the dagger sheathed to her thigh.

The mountain folk huddled together under the great shimmering canopy of the sky on furs and blankets spread across the meadow. The last logs burned in the bonfire that the children had spent half a day constructing. Mira watched firelight dance on Elena's familiar, beloved face, listening to the story of her birth. She lay back, lulled by the sound of Elena's voice, her eyes tracking the sky in search of shooting stars.

"I won't pretend I loved you in the beginning," Elena said. "I hated the house of Oto—mostly, I hated your father. I thought of you as a parcel to be carried to Belarac. But what I didn't know was that one day you would burrow into my heart. You would become as my own flesh and blood."

"What are they like, my family?"

"The first time I laid eyes upon your father he was a boy on a war-horse, smiling at the sight of an innocent woman going up in flames. When next I met him, this was the result." She jerked up her sleeve. The mottled pucker of an old burn ran the length of her arm, glowing in the moonlight. "Child, it's too much to tell in one night."

"What of my brothers, then?"

"There's Pelegrín, your twin, and you've another brother, Alejandro, who's still just a boy. He and Pelegrín bring out what shreds of goodness exist in their father."

"My twin, Pelegrín." Mira said the words slowly, savoring them. "What kind of person is he?"

"Much like your father in his passion for war. But Pelegrín's heart is good, like yours. Somehow your mother managed to plant a seed of kindness in him. He's a man now, called to battle. He and your father have gone across the sea to the kingdom of Naples. They don't expect to be back until another winter has passed—if they return at all."

Mira pulled a wool blanket over them both.

"If they are gone, then I must go to Oto. This is my chance."

"No. When the baron's gone, the steward serves as his eyes and ears. He'd mark your every move, set his spies upon you."

"He knows nothing of me, has no reason to suspect me of any misdeed. Flora Sacazar told me she wrote to the Baroness of Oto, singing my praises. We will say I have come to paint my mother's portrait."

"After the pains we took to get you away from that place, you'd undo all we've done?"

"Death will not have me. Not yet."

"That's your youth speaking. Death is always lurking in the shadows."

Mira sat up, weighing a stone in her hand. Then she flung it into the dark. "I see you, death!" she hissed. "You cannot have me. This is my precious life and you will have to wait a very long while to put me in my grave."

The only sound was the far-off moan of some night-roaming creature.

"Either you've scared off death or woken a wolf," Elena observed. "Well done."

"If you were in my place, Elena, nothing would stop you."

"I won't argue that. But your mother's heart would break if you returned to Oto—if you put yourself in danger after all she did to keep you safe."

"It seems to me that my mother's heart is already broken. Why can I not give her a measure of happiness before death claims her or me?"

Elena's arm tightened around her. "If you must go, don't be a fool about it. Let me warn her. She'll need time to prepare."

Mira found Arnaud at dusk on the second night. They walked to the stooped oak tree where the village leaders sat on their circle of stones to right the year's injustices and hammer out changes to their peace agreement. The full moon that brightened the meadow during the feasts and dancing was now obscured by silvery clouds. Mira could barely see the outline of Arnaud's face in the darkness.

"You knew," she said softly.

"Yes. Elena carried you from the castle at Oto over the mountains to Belarac. You were hungry, so she stopped in Ronzal. My mother shared her milk with you. We were the only ones who knew, besides Elena and Mother Bèatrice. We never told a soul."

"I believe you."

They sank down on a broad, flat stone that still held a trace of the sun's warmth, and lay back in silence. The clouds blurred the trail of stars that guided pilgrims to Compostela. She thought of her childhood desire to escape Belarac, witness the roar and crash of the sea, breathe in the scent of the salty air.

"I am going to Oto," she said. "I will paint my mother's portrait."

He was silent.

"You'll not try to stop me?"

"No. But you won't make the journey alone. There's a cave up the mountain from the castle, where people hide when they need to. We'll wait there until Elena's arranged things with your mother."

"You have it all planned." The knot of fear in Mira's belly loosened.

He reached out a hand and traced the curve of her cheek. "Mira, be my wife."

The tenderness in Arnaud's voice made her eyes well with tears.

"I would disappoint you," she whispered. "I cannot knit or weave or make cheese."

"Life without you is the only disappointment I can imagine."

"Let us hope for a future together, then." She caught his hand in hers. "But the moment I walk into Castle Oto nothing will be certain for me again."

The cave was tucked in a limestone cliff above a jumble of boulders, overlooking a deep ravine. It was the size of a shepherd's cabin and smelled of wood smoke. A faint light glimmered in its far recesses.

"What is the source of that light?" Mira asked Arnaud.

"The stone in these mountains is like cheesecloth, filled with holes."

In a shadowy corner sat a wooden chest. Arnaud knelt and fiddled with the latch.

"This chest has everything a person needs to live here a while." He retrieved a small iron pot, a ceramic plate, a spoon, and two stubby tallow candles. From a small pouch he fished out a fire steel, a flint stone and a knob of touchwood.

"Why would someone live here?"

He shrugged. "Escaping the wrath of a lord. Running from a fight. Holing up after a storm."

Mira came to his side. She rooted through the chest and found a ceramic jug filled with dried beans, a carved wooden statue of the Virgin Mary, a pair of shearing blades, a dagger and a leather satchel. The satchel jingled with the dull clink of metal. Inside, she found a mallet and several iron chisels. Arnaud shrugged again under her questioning glance.

"The rule is, anyone who stays here must leave a token of thanks. There's no telling what a man has on him when he arrives at this place—or what he must leave behind."

"What will our token be?" Mira found a pile of animal furs rolled up neatly against the back wall. She unfurled two and lay them on the floor.

"We'll think of something," he said.

At daybreak on their last morning at the cave, Mira stood listening to the forest creatures stir under the warm touch of the sun. Pale light filtered through the leaves overhead.

Arnaud approached in silence and slipped his arms around her waist. She smiled, letting her weight settle against him.

"I do not know how a hollow in a cliff can feel like home, but it does," she said.

"I do," he said. "We claimed it for our own."

"Carving a mark into stone does not make it yours."

"That's not what I meant. There are other ways to claim a space."

She smiled, remembering.

He rolled up the furs they had lain on while she stamped out the last embers of the fire.

"I'll leave the quiver and bow here," he said, "in case you must hunt for your supper when you return."

"You have more confidence in my hunting skills than I."

"Elena taught you. She doesn't leave a job half-done. And Mira—keep your blade on you."

Mira nodded. She hesitated at the mouth of the cave, staring into the woods, gathering courage for the days ahead. Somewhere out there, her mother lived and breathed. All she wanted now was to meet the woman who had given birth to her and then saved her life.

12

Summer, 1503
Kingdom of Naples, Italy
Pelegrín

PELEGRÍN'S HORSE SHIFTED UNEASILY beneath him. He turned his head stiffly, encumbered by his heavy helmet, peering through the eye slit at the rows of mounted knights stretching away from him as far as he could see.

He saw his father's black war horse just ahead, its flanks covered with the black and red cloth that signaled the house of Oto. Beyond him, Gonzalo Fernández de Córdoba, the Great Captain, emerged through the half-light of dawn astride a gleaming gray horse. The scarlet of his polished leather armor was vivid against the silvery morning sky. To Pelegrín's surprise, he was bare-headed. He spurred his horse down the line, calling out the names of individual men, praising their courage and their strength.

A faint chant became audible across the broad expanse of trenches and traps of brambly vinestalks the men had spent all night constructing. They fell silent, listening. Soon the words became clear: "*Saint-Jacques! Saint-Jacques! Saint-Jacques pour la France!*"

The Great Captain held up his hands, palms facing his troops.

"Do you hear that?" he roared. "Now they have not only taken our kingdom of Naples, they have stolen our saint! Saint-Jacques is our Santiago! They call on him for aid!"

A grieved roar went up.

"This cannot be!" he bellowed. "We must remind them whose saint that is. I command you—call upon Santiago! Call upon Santiago now!"

The men obeyed. Pelegrín found himself shouting hoarsely again and again, "Santiago! Santiago! Santiago!"

The ground reverberated with the thunder of hooves as the French approached.

The sun beat down on the battlefield. Sweat soaked Pelegrín under his layers of clothing, chain mail and armor. He watched his comrades wield swords and pikes, clashing with the French mounted soldiers. The muddy soil was littered with the carcasses of fallen horses and the mangled corpses of the dead. Despite the chaos, he forced himself to focus on one sound at a time: the soft squelch of mud under his horse's hooves, the musical jingle of a silver-tooled leather harness, the dull thud of a man toppling to the earth. This practice, passed on by his father, helped him clear his mind and stay calm.

The day wore on. Pelegrín dispatched men like chess pieces, anticipating his enemies' next actions, blunting their attacks, unleashing his own. A white lather of sweat frothed on his horse's shoulders. The heat did not bother Pelegrín; he had been raised, after all, on the edge of a wilderness, where summers were achingly hot and winters transformed his world into an ice-blasted, whitewashed landscape.

Circling his mount, Pelegrín knocked a French horseman off his steed with a savage thrust of his lance. The knight lay on his back, helpless under the weight of his armor. His limbs churned like an overturned beetle's, one arm scrabbling for his sword. Pelegrín used the tip of his lance to flick the man's face plate up.

"*S'il vous plait, s'il vous plait,*" the knight gasped. His eyes were blue.

Pelegrín impaled him through the mouth with the steel blade of the lance. There was a last gurgling cry, then silence. With a sharp tug, he retrieved his lance. He turned his horse in a slow circle, seeking his next target.

At the same time his eyes darted back and forth in search of the broad-shouldered man on the black war horse. This was a moment to celebrate. But no matter where Pelegrín looked, it was no use.

For the first time all day, his father had vanished from sight.

13

Summer, 1503
Castle Oto, Aragón
Marguerite

A FTER GIVING THE SERVANTS their orders for the morning, Marguerite called Beltrán to her side. He strode across the great hall with loose-hipped confidence and stood before her, thumbs tucked in his belt, head cocked to one side to conceal his disfigurement.

"Beltrán, I have just got word that a flock of our finest sheep are trapped in a ravine in the north. Wolves pick them off by night; they weaken by day with no forage. You must take a few men and help the shepherds remove them from danger."

"With your husband and son at war, you have need of me here," he replied. "I will send some guards and a squire to sort the matter out."

"It must be you." She took a step closer. "Your task is twofold. I have just got word from the brotherhood of sheep breeders that a payment from the spring wool market awaits my husband in

Jaca. It must be carried safely back to Oto. You must do this task for the baron. I would entrust our gold to no one else."

From the pleased look on his face, she knew her flattery had hit its mark. She had long ago learned to give him orders by disguising them as something else entirely. It was a strategy that she parceled out carefully, for he was no fool.

"Very well, my lady."

"Write to me from Jaca when you have secured the gold and are ready for the return journey."

He bowed and let his good eye run the length of her body. She knew he would take her in an instant if he had the opportunity. He had never hidden his lust for her. A man whose face was so easily read could never truly be cunning. And that, she knew, was why her husband had chosen Beltrán as his steward.

14

Summer, 1503
Kingdom of Naples, Italy
Pelegrín

P ELEGRÍN STOOD QUIETLY, LETTING his eyes adjust to the dim light in the tent. A bulky figure was stretched out on his father's cot, covered with a thin wool blanket.

"I am not sleeping," a deep voice rasped irritably. "I am wounded."

Pelegrín strode to the cot and flung aside the blanket.

"Father!"

Blood seeped through a linen bandage around his father's thigh.

"A foot soldier who was quicker than most found the joint of my armor," Ramón said. "Dammed if he didn't ambush me from the left, just as that Moorish fellow did all those years ago." He grunted. "It will heal. I have known worse injuries."

Pelegrín removed his gloves and began unbuckling his armor. "Where are the pages?"

"One of them is dead. The other is God knows where."

"I have never had such a day on the battlefield." Pelegrín strained to pull the heavy breast plate over his head.

"Yes, I saw it." Ramón smiled despite his obvious discomfort. "That knight's head sailed through the air as if it were a feather."

Pelegrín hopped on one foot, attempting to remove an armored boot. Finally he managed to yank it off his leg. "What you saw was just the beginning. I killed too many soldiers to count—and three more of their best knights. All in view of the Great Captain."

He watched his father's face light up, the pain of his wounded leg momentarily forgotten.

The page entered. Seeing Pelegrín half-undressed, he rushed to assist him.

"Forgive me, my lord." He reached down to pull off Pelegrín's other boot.

"No, I will do it myself." Pelegrín waved him away. "Bring water and rags to clean my armor and wash our shirts."

The page hesitated again.

"What is it now?" Pelegrín snapped, exasperated.

"No water, and no clean linens," the boy said. "The supply line—"

"So we've gone through our reserves." Ramón eyed the page. "Are the foot soldiers getting their rations as well, or just the captains and knights?"

"Everyone is getting rations, my lord." The boy's eyes were fixed on a point somewhere under Ramón's cot. "The Great Captain makes sure of that." He bowed and slipped out the door.

"The Great Captain will make sure we get our ration, too, won't he?" Ramón added in a low voice, locking eyes with his son. He licked his lips.

"After today, Father, I believe we will top the Great Captain's list when he hands out the spoils of war," Pelegrín said, grinning.

"And tonight, after you are made comfortable, I will go out and find a woman to celebrate with."

Ramón jerked his head up. "The Great Captain forbids camp followers. You know that."

"Of course. But there are women to be had. They slip inside the tents under cover of darkness. I know where they lurk."

"You will do nothing with any ragged whore, do you hear me? Our future lies with the Great Captain. At the moment you bask in his approval. Do you know what happens when the light in his eyes goes dark?"

Pelegrín dropped his head and stared at the filthy rug under his feet.

"You will be a devout and chaste man until this war is over and we have claimed our booty. Then—and *only* then—will you reward yourself. Is that understood?"

"Yes, father."

Ramón's expression brightened. "In fact, that gives me an idea. You will approach the Great Captain tonight and ask if you can join him in prayer, in my stead. Yes, you will go to him and pray for my swift recovery and an end to this damned war."

"As you wish."

After Pelegrín had attended mass faithfully for a week, he began to take note of details. The opulence of the Great Captain's tent, for example. The dirt floor was covered in fine rugs. Carved wooden furniture had been procured from some Neapolitan mansion. There was even a portrait of the Great Captain and his family on the wall suspended from velvet rope. Sitting in a leather-backed chair, sipping wine from a silver cup, Pelegrín felt completely removed from the carnage that surrounded the army's tent city.

The Great Captain sat across from him, dressed impeccably in fine fabrics, his leather boots gleaming. The other knights said he had a tent whose sole purpose was for bathing, and Pelegrín believed it. Whatever violence the man doled out on the battle-field, by evening there was no trace of the day's brutality on his person or in his bearing.

"A beautiful family, my captain." Pelegrín gestured at the painting.

"Yes. It torments me to be away from them. My wife and daughters are the sun and stars to me. The separations we have endured are the only true pain in my life."

"But no sons—no heirs?" asked Pelegrín.

"My first child, a boy, was stillborn. His mother died giving birth to him." The Great Captain took a small sip of wine. "But that was long ago. I was little more than a boy myself. I waited many years to marry again, and when I did, I chose well. My wife has given me the great gift of two daughters, who fill my heart with joy. I have no need of sons. I have raised plenty of boys in my time."

"How is that?"

"I have fought alongside many a man who did not survive the battle. It is my duty and my privilege to take in the children of fallen comrades."

"That is honorable of you, my captain," Pelegrín said.

"It is God's will that I protect those who cannot protect themselves."

A breeze picked up. The painting trembled on its velvet cord. Pelegrín's eyes returned to the images of the two girls and their mother.

"Our house, the house of Oto, produces no girls," he ventured. "Warriors beget warriors—that is the way with us."

The Great Captain stared at him. "Your family motto, is it?"

"No—it is a gift we carry in our blood."

"It is true that you have few equals on the battlefield. Your father shows ferocity and cunning I have rarely seen in any other man."

The Great Captain stood up and crossed to a small cabinet that was stuffed with leather-bound books. He opened it and selected one.

"It is not too late for you to begin."

He handed the book to Pelegrín. Three gilded words lay on the burnished cover: *The Holy Bible*. An enormous copy of the book lay in their family chapel in Oto, but Pelegrín rarely looked at it.

"Start with Samuel. It will be enlightening for you. And then move on to Isaiah." It was clear from his tone that their visit was over.

"I am sorry if my words offended you," Pelegrín said, bewildered. "To be so skilled on the battlefield—as you yourself are—is something that can only be attained by blood."

The Great Captain's face for the first time showed a hint of impatience. "You are wrong there. It is God who arms me with strength." He gestured toward the tent door. "Good night."

"Well?" growled Ramón, shifting awkwardly on his cot. "What did he have to say?"

Pelegrín held up the book. "He told me to read this, starting with Samuel."

"That's like him. Well, you had better begin. Sit here with me and read aloud."

Pelegrín worked his way through the book of Samuel, his mind drifting back to the Great Captain's words. Surely it was just an act, this lack of concern about his failure to produce heirs. Then he read a line that jolted him into complete silence.

"Go on, Son." Ramón glanced over at him, annoyed.

"'It is God who arms me with strength and makes my way perfect.'" He showed his father the line. "This was the last thing the Great Captain said to me before he sent me away."

One night the Great Captain shared with Pelegrín a letter from his daughter Elvira. She was reading poetry from the early courts of Aragón and Castilla, had memorized all of the known constellations that had been recorded by court astronomers, and was composing several songs on the lute.

"I do not know if the world has ever seen a mind as brilliant as my Elvira's," the Great Captain remarked.

"Yes, brilliant. For a girl." Pelegrín grinned.

The Great Captain did not return the smile.

"You believe the female mind inferior to that of the male, then?"

"I do not believe it, I know it. Women are ruled by their hearts, not their minds." Pelegrín had heard his father say these words many times.

"It is natural for young people to tread only the paths that have been forged by others, particularly when those paths were laid out by our own fathers and their fathers before them. This night I suggest you consult the book of Isaiah. Within those pages, I have found, is a light that shines in the dark. You might find that it opens your eyes to things you have never seen before."

Back in his tent, Pelegrín pulled the blanket from his father's leg. The festering wound had developed an ugly smell. He ran a hand over his father's forehead.

"Your fever burns without end. I will change your bandage and ask the Great Captain's doctors to attend you again."

Ramón brushed off Pelegrín's attempt to comfort him.

"Tell me of your time with the man. What did he speak of tonight?"

Pelegrín recounted the conversation.

"The book of Isaiah? I know the passage of which he speaks. The man meant to imply you are blind, but in fact, it is he who walks in darkness. Deluded by his own faith into believing some hogwash about the mental acuity of women!" Ramón flinched, succumbing to a wave of pain. "He is bewitched by that girl of his. Let this be a lesson to you, son. A girl can charm even the strongest of men and turn him into a fool."

15

Summer, 1503
Castle Oto, Aragón
Mira

THE SAND-COLORED CASTLE OF the Oto family sat on a squat hill at the base of the Pyrenees. To the south it overlooked a narrow stream-fed valley, and to the north it abutted a scramble of giant boulders backed by limestone cliffs. Towers bristled from its high walls.

The iron crossbars that secured the castle against the outside world clanged shut behind Mira. An entire village existed within the castle gates, divided by a narrow cobbled lane that wound up the hill to the inner keep. She trudged upward, overcome with nausea at the mingled odors of humanity that assailed her: scorched meat, yeasty beer, boiled vegetables, vinegar, the nutty scent of porridge. A trickle of human excrement flowed down the lane.

She was glad for her long cloak with its deep hood, for it deflected the stares that followed her from every doorway. When she rounded a shadowy curve, she was confronted by the sight of a barefoot servant girl huddled against a wall, her skirts stained with filth, one of her cheeks bruised and puffy. Mira's resolve wavered. So this was the state of things in the house of Oto. She stopped in front of the girl, who shrank back, her eyes on the cobblestones underfoot.

"That bruise on your face—who gave it to you?" Mira asked quietly.

The girl kept silent. Under the filth and the bruise, Mira saw the pretty mountain girl she had once been.

"Do you go to Elena when you need healing?"

At the mention of Elena, the girl's watchful face relaxed. She glanced up, nodded. On impulse, Mira pulled the scallop shell necklace over her head and thrust it out.

"Here. You have more need of this than I."

The girl stared, dumbfounded, at Mira's offering.

"Go on, take it. Wear it and know the saints are watching over you."

With a faint smile, the girl took the necklace and slipped it around her neck, then melted into the shadows. Mira watched her disappear. She pulled her hood tight over her forehead and strode forward.

There was no turning back now.

16

Summer, 2015
From France to Spain, Pyrenees Mountains
Zari

THE DAY DAWNED SUNNY, with a cloudless sky. They climbed through forests that offered glimpses of distant snowy peaks and tramped across meadows frothing with wildflowers. Flocks of sheep grazed, the iron bells strung around their necks chiming a discordant melody. In one meadow they watched a brown bird with an enormous wingspan glide above them.

"Is that an eagle?" Zari asked.

"Griffon vulture," said Wil, shading his eyes with his hand.

"Seriously? That sounds like a mythological beast."

"No, they're really called that."

The bird cruised past the meadow and disappeared over the treetops.

Zari took Wil's hand and led him into the shade of an oak tree so stooped that its heavy branches nearly grazed the waving tips of the grass that grew at its base. A dozen granite boulders were half-sunk in the earth around the tree, making a loose circle that seemed almost purposeful.

"This is so private and peaceful," she said. "Perfect for napping. Bruges-style napping, that is." She unbuckled her backpack and let it slide to the ground.

Wil's eyes lit up. "I was hoping you would say that." He shed his pack and boots and began to peel off his socks. "Because I don't think any other kind of nap will work for me."

He gathered her in his arms and she slid her hands under his shirt. Heat radiated off his skin. She traced her fingers over the ridges of his spine, then drew them upward along the muscles that fanned outward to his shoulder blades. Lazily she slid her hands around the curve of his ribcage and down to his belt. With one swift movement, she unbuckled it. He put her face between his hands and kissed her, then unbuttoned her shirt with gentle precision. They sank down on the grass.

Perched on Wil's chest with the sun filtering down through the oak tree above them, she felt a soft breeze whisper across her skin. She rolled over, pulling Wil on top of her so he could feel it too. Then she lost herself in him, in the sound of their quickened breathing, in the rhythm of his heartbeat entangled with her own. When she opened her eyes, vaguely aware of the hum of bees and the silvery calls of a finch, she saw the dark shadow of the griffon vulture passing above the rutted branches of the old oak, drifting silently on an invisible current.

It only took a few more hours to reach the Col du Somport, the ancient Roman pass that took travelers from France into Spain. When they began to descend into Spain, there was a marked change in the terrain. The lushness of the mountain meadows gave way to drier, sparser vegetation. While trail markers had been rare in France, the distinctive yellow slashes that marked the Way were common now. They met two pilgrims from Montréal, who had walked from Italy to Compostela and were now making their way back. The couple told them they had saved money for years to carry out this journey, the culmination of decades of dreaming. They warned Zari and Wil of extremely hot weather in Spain and advised following the Spanish custom of siestas in the afternoons to avoid the worst of it. Both of them wore necklaces strung with shell pendants.

Walking down the trail away from the Canadian couple, Zari looked at Wil. "Good advice about the siestas," she said. "Little do they know we just did a test run."

He grinned. "I don't know if our time under the oak tree could be called a siesta."

"Sure it could. I bet half the population of Spain was conceived during siestas."

Wil's laughter echoed down the trail, startling a squirrel. It scampered across their path and disappeared under the glossy leaves of a low-slung shrub.

By early afternoon they were in Canfranc. They found an inn where they were given a shared room and told to expect two roommates. They charged their phones, tended their blisters, showered, then did laundry and hung it to dry in a small, sun-baked courtyard.

In the descending gloom, they walked to a restaurant where they were the first patrons of the evening. They were politely seated by the server, a petite woman with short dark hair whose wideset brown eyes were ringed with a latticework of fine lines. Zari plunged into Spanish and ordered the three-course menu for them.

After the server returned with a carafe of red wine, Wil poured them each a glass.

"You do speak Spanish." He raised his glass in salute.

"I'm shocked at your lack of faith in me. Although I'm not going to brag about my language skills until the food comes. If it matches what I think I ordered, then we can bask in my greatness."

He laughed, and she let the rich, warm sound wash over her.

"I love your laugh," she said. "It's the first thing I loved about you."

"Really?"

"Yes. My first impression of you was pretty terrible overall. Except for your laugh."

"Do you know the first thing I loved about you? That you make me laugh. I haven't laughed enough since Filip's accident." His eyes on hers made her wish they were not sharing a room with others tonight. He reached out and took her hand.

The first course arrived. Zari's eyes widened. Before her sat a mound of lettuce and chopped raw vegetables topped with a glistening mass of cod in a creamy vinaigrette.

"Not what you ordered?" Wil asked, suppressing a smile.

"I ordered cod salad, smart ass, but look at the size of it. And this is only the first course. How on earth do they expect me to eat the main course? And no doggy bags."

Wil was already tucking into a huge bowl of soup. Zari reached for her wine glass and settled back in her chair. The rough stone walls were decorated with paintings of medieval knights. Colorful flags hung at intervals around the room printed with coats-of-arms and names. She began to read them aloud.

"Don Felipe de Quarata, Don Pedro de Albarracín. Don Alejandro de Oto."

She jumped up and her fork clattered to the tile floor. The server and the hostess, who were engaged in conversation by the doorway, both turned to look at her.

"What's wrong?" asked Wil. He put down his spoon.

She pointed. "Don Alejandro de Oto."

Wil glanced at the flag, then looked back at her, his eyes alight.

The coat of arms was divided into six squares. The top tier showed ships; the middle one depicted castles; the bottom one, sheep. Zari pulled out her mobile and took several photos.

"Who was Alejandro de Oto?" she asked the server.

"I don't know," the woman replied.

"But was he a real person?"

"Of course. Those are all men of Aragón. You see these flags everywhere."

"How can I learn more about him?"

Without hesitating, the woman said, "San Juan de la Peña. If there is anything known about him, it will be there. But be sure to take a bus. Do not walk! It is too dangerous." She picked up the fork from the red tile floor and went back to the kitchen.

Zari returned to her seat to find Wil tucking into her codfish. He offered her his fork, apologizing.

"Have as much as you like," she said, taking a bite. "You could eat for fifteen minutes and still never see the plate."

"So—San Juan de la Peña?" he said after a moment. "Already on the agenda."

She touched her scallop shell necklace. "What luck. I think this thing really works."

17

Summer, 2015
San Juan de la Peña, Aragón
Zari

T HE BUS RUMBLED ACROSS a medieval bridge made of
sand-colored stone. Zari stared down at the gray-
green water of the River Aragón. It had escaped the
confines of ice-scoured ridges and valleys, melted its way
into the creeks that carved chutes down the mountainsides.
And now it was free, snaking through the curving foothills,
gathering heat.

"...American?" Zari turned, startled out of her reverie, and
looked across the aisle into the eyes of a middle-aged woman
who wore a yellow T-shirt with an Appalachian Mountain
Club logo stamped across her ample chest. She had short
brown hair and a pink bandanna tied around her neck.

"I heard you two talking when we boarded. Can't mistake
an American accent. Let me guess: Pacific Northwest?"

Zari shook her head. "Northern California."

"Close! Close!" The woman smiled in satisfaction. She was dressed in khaki zip-off hiking pants that she had chosen to wear as shorts, pink socks, and brown leather hiking boots with pink laces.

"Is your name Sue?" Zari asked.

The woman looked astonished. "How did you know?"

"I think we have a mutual friend. Michael from San Diego?"

"Oh, yes! We stayed in the same *albergio* last night. I tried to convince him to take the bus to the monastery with me but he insisted on walking. He just likes pain, I guess." She sighed, staring out the window at the dry landscape. Then she fixed her gaze on Zari again. "That hike to the monastery is no picnic. Everyone says it's easy to get lost, it's not well marked, it's slippery, it's steep. Why take chances when you don't have to? That's all I'm saying."

For the next hour, Wil slept and Zari played the role of a sponge absorbing Sue's deluge of observations and opinions. The bus climbed steep switchbacks. From time to time she stole a glance out the window. The compact trees with their dark leaves and reddish trunks resembled California manzanitas. Tiny blue flowers bloomed on the wild rosemary that grew along the roadside.

When the bus stopped, they emerged in front of the 'new' monastery, which was built in the seventeenth century after fire ruined the original buildings. Inside, the structure was recently renovated, with a glass and steel floor exposing the excavated rooms beneath. White plaster statues of monks stood in poses of prayer, conversation, and work.

While Wil wandered the museum with the group, Zari found the library. It was staffed by a short, elderly man with a bald head and a round, serious face. After listening to her inquiry, he led her to a bookshelf that held volumes of Aragónese history and pulled a thin book with a gray-blue cover off a shelf. The title read: *Crónica de San Juan de la Peña*. He thumbed through it to a section about the barons of Aragón. Running his finger over a page, he stopped halfway down and held the book out for Zari to see. The text explained that Ramón Fernandez, illegitimate son of King Jaime I of Aragón and his mistress Berenguela Fernandez, had been granted '*la baronie de Oto*' in the thirteenth century.

"So this man was the first Baron of Oto?" Zari asked.

He nodded.

"And what about later—the years of Queen Isabella and King Ferdinand?"

He pulled out another slim volume and handed it to her, gesturing to a nearby table. She slid into a chair. Before he could join her, a ringing telephone distracted him. She scanned the dense Spanish text, carefully turning the pages until she found it. *Barones de Oto*. Family motto: *fortes fortuna adiuvat*. She put a finger on the name Baltasar de Oto. Baltasar and his wife Madeleine had three sons, but the only one who survived to adulthood was Ramón. Ramón married Marguerite de Belay and they had two sons: Pelegrín and Alejandro. Zari's heart beat faster. Pelegrín did not marry, or if he did, it was not recorded. Alejandro married Catalin Borau de Larquier; they had three daughters. And there the history ended. There were no more Otos, apparently, ever.

The librarian, finished with his telephone conversation, reappeared at her side. She pointed to the page.

"Where did the Otos go?"

"The line died." He traced his fingertip over the text. "Look— boys, boys, boys. From before 1400 to 1500, all boys. Then, girls."

"You're right," Zari said, staring at the names. "There were no girls for generations, until those three daughters of Alejandro. But there were other Otos, right? Even if there was no longer a Baron of Oto, the family had other branches."

"Of course, but only the baronial line would appear in this book."

She took photos with her mobile of the relevant pages in both books and thanked her helper profusely. He smiled and bowed slightly at the waist.

"*Buen camino,*" he said.

The group boarded the bus again for the 'old' monastery, which was built into a natural cave at the base of the cliff. Inside, a guide informed them that the bodies of Aragón's royal families were once entombed there.

"Imagine!" Sue's braying voice echoed off the bare stone ceiling. "This place was built a thousand years ago and it still stands. I'll just never get over the history here. We can see it, feel it, breathe it. Isn't it just a marvel?"

Zari felt a surge of irritation as Sue prattled on, painfully aware of the low tones the European travelers were using for their own conversations. When they filed out of the pantheon and exited the monastery, the harsh afternoon sunlight made her eyes ache. She looked up and saw a bird circling far overhead.

Sue followed her gaze. "Oh my goodness. It's one of those griffon vultures. Guardians of the kings, they're called. From here it doesn't look like much, but did you know they have a seven-foot wingspan?"

Zari smiled, her mind caught on a memory.

Encouraged, Sue turned up the volume in her voice a notch. "It's true. They're the top of the food chain in these mountains. Their eyesight is just amazing. It's like having a zoom lens in your *eyeball.* But they weren't the top of the food chain in the old days, not even close. No guns for protection, not back then. And we're talking wolves and bears. Not to mention bandits. Can you imagine? Those were primitive times, Zari. Primitive. You know what I can't get over? The pilgrims knew the danger and they came anyway. Do you call that brave or do you call that stupid?" She didn't wait for an answer. "I know what I call it. Faith. They had faith. Their trust in God got them over these mountains." Behind her glasses, Sue's eyes were wet with tears.

"Is that what brought you to the Way, Sue? Your faith?"

"I have faith that one foot in front of the other will bring me to Compostela." Sue gave an odd, sputtering laugh. "I have faith in meeting my goals, Zari. That's what life is about. You set goals, you figure out how to achieve them, then you do it. As much as I'd like Him to, as much as I've tried, God doesn't figure into my thinking these days. I learned to live without Him early on." She lapsed into silence, ruminating over something.

Zari waited.

"I'm not bitter," Sue went on after a moment. "I've made something of myself, and I'm proud of that. But now, even when I catch myself praying, I know I don't really mean it. I just feel like a phony, to be honest. That doesn't stop me from admiring the faith of those who do believe. That's why I can't get enough of the Way, Zari. I just like being around all that *faith*."

For the first time, Zari's heart warmed to Sue.

Wil stood a short distance away chatting with other Europeans. Beyond them the sand-colored stones of the monastery glowed in the late afternoon sunlight. Zari strained to listen. It sounded like he was switching back and forth between French and German. Sue shook herself out of her melancholy mood.

"Your boyfriend is so tall. And he speaks English so well. I'll have to pick his brain on the bus ride back to Jaca. Sounds like he's had enough adventures for three lifetimes. The stories he must tell, am I right? Let's coordinate our wake-up times tomorrow so we can walk south together!" She beamed, envisioning the cozy threesome they would become.

"Not us—we're heading east."

Sue blinked. "But aren't you walking the Way?"

"We're on a pilgrimage, but we have a different goal in mind."

Sue's face fell. She stooped and rummaged through her day-pack. Finally she pulled something out.

"In that case I'll have to give you this now," she said sadly. "I give one to all my friends on the *camino*."

It was a pink bandanna.

The next morning, Zari and Wil set off from Jaca by seven, heading east. The trail was steep in parts, the earth parched and rocky. There was no shade. The buzz of insects throbbed in their ears. They walked past spindly-limbed bushes and hill-sides covered in spiky golden grass. The dark shadow of a hawk skimmed over the trail ahead of them.

In a tiny village composed of a few stone buildings capped with slate roofs, they found a café where they sat outside and ate ham sandwiches and drank orange juice. The sandwiches were much different than those in France. The bread was crustier and drier, and the cured ham was sliced paper-thin; no cheese or butter was in evidence.

They paid their bill and heaved on their packs.

"Here's my theory," Zari said. "Marguerite de Oto is the subject of the Fontbroke College portrait."

"What's your evidence?" asked Wil.

"First, and most importantly, she wears a belt that might signify the word 'Oto.'"

"There's no way to prove that," Wil pointed out.

"Agreed. There's more, though. The woman holds a book with the letter 'B' on the spine; Marguerite de Oto signed Béatrice of Belarac's mortuary roll so we know she was connected to the abbey."

"'B' stands for Belarac?"

"Why not? The portrait is on a wood panel that dates to about the same time as Béatrice's death. We know Mira illustrated the mortuary roll, so she could have painted the portrait as well. The timing works." Zari stopped on the trail and plucked a burr from her sock. "But why would a baroness of Aragón commission a nun in Béarn to paint her portrait?"

"Maybe Marguerite hired Mira to paint her portrait when they signed the mortuary roll."

Zari shook her head. "They didn't sign it at the same time. Marguerite's name was near the bottom of the roll and Mira's was at the top." She kicked a crumbly rust-red stone off the trail. "Another thing I don't understand is why there weren't any Oto girls for a hundred years. How is that genetically possible?"

"Maybe there were girls, but they died," Wil suggested. "Or maybe they weren't allowed to live."

"Infanticide?"

He nodded, offering her his water bottle. "It still happens in some parts of the world."

Zari finished off the last few swigs. They started walking again.

"What about their family motto?" she said. "'Fortune favors the bold.' The Otos weren't shy about their aspirations. No mention of God or country or loyalty there."

"You try being a baron in medieval Aragón. That world was built by swords."

Wil brandished one of his hiking poles, slicing it through the air. In the next instant the path gave way beneath him and he slid down the steep slope. He arrested his fall by crashing into a stubby bush. Zari stood frozen, her mouth open. Nimbly, he scrambled up, brushed the soil off his chest, and extended an arm to help her jump over the small landslide he had created.

"It was your sword that got you into trouble." She made a tut-tut noise with her tongue.

He clacked the poles together. "That's what all the ladies say."

18

Summer, 1503
Castle Oto, Aragón
Marguerite

MARGUERITE SLID THE LATCH of her chamber door open and slipped into the room. A young woman wearing the garb of a mountain peasant was unpacking the contents of a satchel on a low wooden table. Walking to her daughter, Marguerite felt her pulse quicken. She fought the urge to gather Mira in her arms. Instead she reached for the girl's hand.

"Has some madness taken hold of me, or am I truly touching your flesh?" she whispered. "You live and breathe."

She took in the high planes of Mira's cheeks, the coppery hair, the wide, green-gray eyes that were so like her own. The girl did favor her, more than she had anticipated. But there were also shades of Ramón in her slanting eyebrows and strong jaw, the dark gold of her skin, her tall willowy frame. She was a perfect blend of both her parents.

Mira's eyes were solemn. If she felt any joy at their reunion, it was well hidden.

"Come." Marguerite led Mira outside on the balcony.

Dark shadows moved across the cliffs beyond the castle. The ibex band radiated out over the pale limestone cliffs, springing from ledge to ledge as carelessly as if they foraged on level ground. The points of their dark horns traced patterns against the rocks.

"There must be dozens of them," Mira said, her eyes lighting up.

In the next instant the thin peal of a bugle sounded. Two of the animals fell from the rocks, impaled by arrows. The rest of the band melted away into the shadows and a pair of men climbed to the base of the cliffs to fetch the carcasses.

"I fear the ibex will one day stop returning to these rocks," Marguerite said.

"Can you not order the hunters to seek other prey?"

"They follow my husband's command."

"With him at war, you cannot command as you wish?"

Marguerite looked sideways at Mira. The bluntness of her daughter's words contradicted her sweet appearance.

"And endure his rage when he returns? My every action is reported to him."

"How can they call you the Baroness of Oto when you are spied upon in your own home, by your own servants? That makes you more a prisoner of this place than its mistress."

Marguerite sighed. "I am a woman, Mira. Your father, like most men, believes that a woman needs a lord and master, and sometimes a stick."

The servants' door swung open and a maid entered the room carrying a basket of clean linens. Marguerite turned to Mira and assumed a haughty, formal tone.

"I should like to have you paint the ibex and the cliffs in the background of my portrait. It will please my husband."

"Yes, my lady," Mira said in a tone of exaggerated deference.

Marguerite ordered the maid to fetch wine from the kitchens.

"Do you not trust her?" Mira said when the girl had left.

"There are a few who are loyal to me. But the servants in this place are beholden to their baron. I would be a fool to forget that."

Marguerite looked away, her initial rush of warm emotion evaporating. There was much of Ramón in the girl's restlessness, her quick mind, her questioning nature.

"Let us discuss the particulars of my visit. I am simply a trades-woman, come to perform a service, correct?" Mira's tone was brittle.

"No, you are my daughter and you *live*. That is the important thing. And so is the matter of keeping you safe. I have already made inquiries at convents in the north. Gascony, perhaps, will be suitable. It is far enough away. Too many rumors poison these mountains."

"A convent is not a refuge. Not to me."

Marguerite turned to face Mira, her eyes hard. "The safe course for you, the only wise course, is to live in a convent. I do not imply that you must take your vows. You do not wish to. You can live out your days in a convent as a boarder, comfortably, and continue your painting."

"I have had my fill of that life."

"But you cannot marry," Marguerite snapped. "No man of rank will have you, for you have no title and no dowry."

"I will have to set my sights on a lower-born man, then."

"Mira!"

"With my education and skills, I could attract a range of suitors." A sarcastic edge crept into Mira's voice. "A blacksmith, perhaps. No, a tanner. Or a miller? My head spins. So many choices."

"No one in the trades could ever be suitable for you. Noble blood cannot mix with that of a commoner."

"My bloodline means nothing," Mira shot back. "As far as the house of Oto is concerned, I never existed at all. I am little more than a ghost."

An urge to slap Mira made Marguerite's fingers twitch, but she stayed her hand. She motioned to Mira to follow her inside and led her to the mirror that hung near the bed. The two of them stood side by side in silence, taking in their reflections.

"See? You are no ghost, but my own flesh and blood."

Mira turned and stalked back outside.

"Listen, girl," Marguerite said, two strides behind her. "No one understands your predicament better than I. You need look no further than your own name to see the truth. When you were born I named you Miramonde because I imagined a life for you beyond the walls of a convent. My daughter will be one who sees the world, I promised myself. I had Béatrice give you a fine education. I sent Elena to you each summer so that you would learn how to survive outside the cloister if need be. When I learned you had the makings of an artist, I saw to it that your talent was nurtured. I did all of that for love of you."

Marguerite watched the fight ebb from Mira's eyes.

"What I imagined as a foolish young woman will never come to pass," she went on, more gently. "Here is the truth, Mira: it is a man's world we inhabit. As much as I wish it otherwise, women cannot enjoy the same freedom that men do. Our wings are clipped. And without the advantages of a title and a dowry, you have no choices. The only life possible for you is in a convent."

Mira bowed her head. "Please forgive me. This is not what I intended, I swear. When I journeyed here I resolved to find the woman who gave me my life two times over and show her my gratitude. Instead I have been impertinent and rude. I owe my life to you, Mother. That is a debt I can never repay."

Marguerite's anger evaporated. In its place grew a crushing sadness.

"I wish every day that we might have shared this life together. But I got comfort from knowing you lived—thrived, even—across those mountains."

Mira took her mother's hand between both of her own. "Mother Béatrice protected me. She taught me the discipline of the cloistered life, though I hated it as a child. When I grew older I understood the value of all she had done for me. But I can no longer live behind a wall. There is a place for me with the mountain folk and I intend to claim it."

"You would live among shepherds?" Marguerite was astonished. "What madness makes you want to consort with such dullards?"

"Dullards? Far from it. Some of them know Latin as well as I, and understand numbers much better."

"Who fed you these falsehoods?" Marguerite pulled her hand free from Mira's grasp.

"I speak the truth. Consider Elena. She is a mountain woman—do you believe her stupid?"

"She is wise in her way, but she is not like the rest of them."

Before Mira could speak again the door swung open.

"Ah, wine." Marguerite infused her voice with formality once more. "Young Mira, let us sip a cup and discuss the details of my portrait." She waved Mira into a chair and snapped her fingers at the maid. "We have no time to lose. Summer days are as few as they are sweet."

19

Summer, 1503
Kingdom of Naples, Italy
Pelegrín

WHEN PELEGRÍN RETURNED FROM battle one evening, he found his father lying inert on his cot, holding a sheet of parchment with a red wax seal. Ramón's cheeks were sunken. Veins bulged from his neck like lengths of twisted rope. Pelegrín wet a cloth and wiped his father's sweaty face. Then he gently removed the parchment from his grasp.

"What is this?"

"Read it." His father's voice was hoarse.

Pelegrín's eyes tracked over the script. "I have a sister?"

"According to the scribe of this letter, you do."

"It is signed, 'a friend.' Surely you do not believe the words of an anonymous coward."

"I was gone for long stretches of time." Ramón's voice hardened, gathering strength. "First during the Moorish wars in the south, then defending the northern borders from the French."

"Still, how could you have sired a daughter and not know it?"

"There was plenty of opportunity for your mother to bear a girl and spirit her away. That is a woman's way. Building their webs of spider's silk, their secret plans."

"Does this girl even exist? How can you be sure?"

"Oh yes, she exists. I saw her portrait once at a merchant's home in Zaragoza. Something in her face stirred a memory. It was mostly in the eyes." He let out a bitter laugh. "Now I know why. She has her mother's eyes. What a fool that woman made of me."

"What will you do?"

Ramón fell silent a moment. When he spoke again his voice was crisp. "She must die."

"What?" Pelegrín stood up. The parchment slid to the mud-stained carpet.

"A house of warriors is no accident, son. It must be carefully constructed. I wanted to wait for your wedding night to school you in the ways of my father, and his before him. Now I may not have that chance." Ramón found the strength to prop himself up on his elbows. "My own sister was left in the woods to die, Pelegrín. And others before her. That was always the way, since the time of the seven brothers. And it will be yours, when you sire your own children."

Pelegrín could scarcely look at his father. He reached for the bottle of poppy milk on the table next to the cot. It was nearly empty.

"Father, this drink is to blame for your strange tales. Poppy milk addles the mind. Try to sleep, and forget this matter. We will take it up again when you are well."

"These are no tales, Pelegrín! My mind is sound. I speak the truth. Since the time of the seven brothers, this has been our tradition. We are a house of warriors. That is what the kings of Aragón expect of us. But your mother tried to trick fate." Ramón's voice dropped into a dark growl. "She will pay dearly for that."

"Father, the girl lives, and so does the house of Oto. The Great Captain has taken me into his confidence and we will reap the spoils of this war. Everything is as you wanted it to be. What harm can a girl do to us? Let her live."

Ramón shook his head. "It is not your decision to make." He groaned, engulfed by a wave of pain.

Pelegrín peeled back a layer of bandages, blanching at the putrid aroma that rose from the wound.

"Sleep now, Father. Tomorrow, after I return from battle, we will discuss what is to be done about the girl."

Striding away from the tent the next morning, he comforted himself with the thought that his father would sleep off his strange thoughts and come to his senses soon enough. Perhaps tomorrow he would bring the Great Captain's physicians to his father again. There might be some remedy other than poppy milk to soothe his pain, something that did not drive him to the edge of madness.

On the battlefield that day, Pelegrín was so consumed by worries about his father's strange babblings that he narrowly missed being impaled by a French knight's lance. When he burst into the tent in the afternoon, his father lay still, eyes closed, hands clasped over his chest, a serene expression on his face.

"You are better, Father." Pelegrín said, overcome with relief. "I knew some rest would do you good."

"My leg pains me just the same. But my spirits are improved." Ramón opened his eyes and regarded his son with satisfaction. "I dictated my orders to that page. He's the son of a knight, did you know? He did as I bid him, and quickly too. Took the parchment down to the supply line and sent it with the Italians to the port. It will be on the next ship west, in Beltrán's hands soon enough."

"What?" Pelegrín asked, incredulous.

"The girl will die. Your mother will not. Only because it will hurt her far more to go on living." Ramón's wan smile faded as his son made for the door.

Pelegrín sprinted in the direction of the supply line. He arrived only to find that the Italians were well underway on their journey to the port. He ran to a group of picketed horses and launched himself onto a brown mare's back. With one sharp tug he pulled the picket stake out of the ground and dug his heels into the mare's belly.

If this madness his father spoke of was true, the Oto way would stop with him. Yes, his mother might have betrayed his father, but only because she feared her baby daughter would be cast out. He wondered what the Great Captain would think of his family's savage custom. The man doted on his daughters and cared nothing about his lack of sons. Yet he was the most respected and feared soldier in the kingdom.

His thoughts veered to the night at Castle Oto when his father had told the story of the seven brothers. Beltrán understood perfectly what his father meant when he said the problem of daughters was no longer known in the house of Oto. Now Pelegrín saw why the man had fixed him with such an odd, smug stare. Because he *knew*—and Pelegrín was too stupid, too wrapped up in his own impatient thoughts, to comprehend.

Before he had gotten half a league, a regiment of cavalry soldiers stopped him. They pulled their horses around him in a tight circle.

A voice spoke up out of the half-light. "You! Deserter!"

"I am no deserter! I mean to intercept a letter that is on its way to the harbor. Let me pass."

"You'll have to tell that to our commander. Turn around."

"You cannot give me orders. I am Pelegrín de Oto. You all know of me. I am one of the Great Captain's most loyal knights."

"That may be. But we are his loyal soldiers—and we are following his orders. Turn around."

Pelegrín considered ignoring them and taking flight. He knew such an action could invite his own death. Casting one last look at the fading light over the distant sea, he wheeled his horse around.

The horses cantered down the dusty track. One of the soldiers flanking Pelegrín whistled.

"You ride with no saddle, yet you keep your seat as handily as if you had one," he shouted.

"It is nothing to me," Pelegrín retorted. "All the men in my family ride as soon as we can walk. It is our way."

The next morning, Pelegrín was led into the Great Captain's tent with his arms bound.

"What's this?" the Great Captain said, bewildered. "One of my best knights caught deserting? Explain yourself."

Pelegrín hesitated. "To explain myself is to betray my father."

"And not to explain yourself is to court death." The Great Captain's eyes narrowed, defying him to lie.

In as few words as possible, Pelegrín relayed what had prompted his wild ride toward the sea. The Great Captain waited a few moments before replying.

"The ship you speak of has sailed. Another message to your steward will go out on the next ship. I do not know if it will reach him in time. Now I will go speak to your father and hear what he has to say."

The Great Captain left the tent and several guards stepped inside, wearing full armor, their hands on the hilts of their swords. Pelegrín's mind raced with thoughts of his father, tormented by pain and poppy milk. Perhaps Beltrán would never receive the letter he had sent. Perhaps the ship that carried it would be dashed to pieces by a storm. He glared at the guards.

When the Great Captain returned, his face was grim. "Your father is in a grave state. I fear even if my surgeons remove his leg, he will die." He gestured to one of the guards. "I will have you unbound so you can go to him. Comfort him. I will send my surgeons and my priest."

Later, they met again in Ramón's tent, standing over the dead man's body.

"I will have his body transported to Naples and buried in the tombs of the Aragónese nobles," the Great Captain said. The priest stood next to him, his lips moving soundlessly, praying for the eternal salvation of Ramón's soul.

Pelegrín stared bleakly at his father's hands. The ring that bore the Oto seal glinted in the candlelight. Outside, he heard the clatter of metal and the muffled shouts of knights calling for camp boys. Another death meant little here; the business of war went on as if nothing had happened.

"Your father was one of my best warriors. Your family has distinguished itself time and again on battlefields in every corner of our kingdom. Your service will not go unrewarded, Pelegrín."

The Great Captain pulled Ramón's ring off his finger and handed it to Pelegrín. "You are a baron now."

"Captain, I beg you for leave to cross the sea and tend to my family." Pelegrín swallowed hard. His mouth had never felt so dry. He longed for a cool drink of water from the stream above Oto.

"Your sister's life, and the life of your mother, are in God's hands. You will remain by my side until this war ends. With Santiago's aid, we will prevail. Your father helped bring us to this place. To honor his memory, you must complete the victory for him."

The Great Captain stood in the candlelight, his linen blouse impeccably clean and his thick, wavy hair pushed back neatly from his face. His eyes were kind, but his voice indicated that arguing would be useless.

20

Summer, 1503
Castle Oto, Aragón
Mira

MIRA FLUNG OPEN THE balcony shutters and slipped her paint-spattered leather apron over her head. A morning breeze drifted in, cool on her cheeks. She closed her eyes and imagined she could smell lavender, wild roses, meadow grasses, ripe apples. Opening her eyes, she glanced around her mother's chamber and sighed. Imagining did not make it so. For the time being she would have to content herself with the charred stench of yesterday's fire and the mossy aroma of damp stone.

She lifted the oak panel from the easel and turned it over. On the back Arnaud had burned his crest with an iron brand heated in fire. She traced her fingertips over it, comforted by the thought of him.

It had been a mistake to share her plan with her mother. No woman who was noble-born and bred would tolerate the idea of her daughter living among commoners. Let her write to convents if that made her happy. Once Mira left Oto, she would follow a path of her own making. She would finish what her mother had started and fulfill the promise of her name.

Marguerite stood in the center of the room in a red silk dress, regarding a pair of black velvet sleeves that lay on the bed.

"You will wear those?" Mira asked.

Marguerite nodded.

"What will you wear for ornament?"

"My ivory shell necklace. It has watched over me all these years—it is as much a part of me as my own skin. And I shall wear this." From a silver box Marguerite drew out a long strand of gold that was finished with an ornate pendant. "A belt passed down to each baroness in turn."

Mira examined the pendant, two simple circles of gold superimposed with a cross.

"It spells O-T-O," she said, tracing its curves with her fingertip. She glanced at the door to the servant's corridor and dropped her voice. "You will wear the brand of your husband?"

"I am the Baroness of Oto. Why conceal the truth?" Marguerite held up a pair of emerald earrings and a matching ring. "I shall wear these as well. His spoils from the last war against the Moors, the one that ruined them. The woman who once wore these is dead or enslaved, I am sure."

"You honor her by wearing these jewels, then."

The sound of a child's laughter rose up from the corridor. Alejandro's voice mingled with that of his nurse outside the door, fading as they continued past Marguerite's chamber to the staircase. The two women locked eyes.

"I wish—" Mira began.

"I do too. But you are a stranger to us, here to paint my portrait. It is the way it must be."

"Tell me of my brothers, then." Mira said after a moment, slipping a sleeve over her mother's outstretched arm.

"Your father has molded Pelegrín in his own image. There is no finer horseman or warrior. I pray that he survives this war across the sea. And Alejandro is a joy to us all. Full of mischief. Quick to weep but quicker to laugh."

"What if another baby comes?"

Marguerite's smile vanished.

"That will not happen."

"How can you be sure?"

"Elena helps me make it so."

"Ah. Let me guess—some brew she concocted? A poison that kills?" Mira snatched up the other sleeve from the bed. "She has a talent with such things."

"Save your judgement for the day you find yourself in need of such a brew."

"No, Mother." Mira shook her head. "That day will never come."

Over the long, bright days of summer, her mother's portrait gradually took shape. The underdrawings were completed first, and with them the scribbled words that Mira had a habit now of laying down beneath the layers of paint. "Bermejo" had been her first word, sketched out on the portrait of the Sacazar family. The merchants for whom she worked in Nay each had some token or image they wanted represented in their portraits, so the words on their paintings reflected those wishes: 'lap dog and silver urn,' for example, or 'left hand—rings.' Amadina Sacazar's portrait simply bore the word 'patience,' for that was the skill Mira had most need of during the stifling days spent toiling over the woman's image. Even when the words were obliterated with paint, they lived on in Mira's mind.

One morning in the castle's chapel, Mira knelt alone before the altar, praying. Silently she begged God to protect Marguerite and bring her peace. If only she had the collective force of many minds joined in prayer bolstering her pleas, as she had at the Abbey of Belarac. At that moment she knew what the words for her mother's portrait would be.

That afternoon she drew her name with its miniature self-portrait on the panel. Next to it, with a stick of vine charcoal, she inscribed the words 'pray for my mother.' Then she covered it all with a layer of paint. Those words, that image—they were invisible now to everyone but her. They were her secret. She would draw power from them with every brush stroke. When she left Oto the force of those hidden words would well up through the layers of paint, a silent talisman of protection for her mother, forever.

As the weeks passed Mira had employed her slender mink brushes to complete the details of eyes, lips and hair, to define the intersecting black lines that made up the patterns in the silk blouse her mother wore. She had used crushed cinnabar for the folds of the red silk dress and white lead mixed with a trace of charcoal dust for the limestone cliffs in the background. Today, she would mix yellow ochre pigment and linseed oil to create the golden belt and the Moorish jewels.

She put a hand on her hip, surveying her materials, and sighed. If only she had gold leaf dust. It would make the belt and jewelry sparkle. But there was no point in wishing for such a luxury. The truth was, thanks to Carlo Sacazar, she had been outfitted with exceptional painting supplies. There was much she owed to the man.

She wished she had never heard Amadina Sacazar's strange claims about Mother Béatrice's death, for she now wondered if Carlo believed those things too. If he knew something unsavory about the way Mother Béatrice had met her end, he was as skilled at deception as Mira had become. For he had seemed genuinely shocked and saddened when she brought the mortuary roll to Nay.

The whirl of dark thoughts in her brain was impeding her progress. There was no point in lumping Carlo in with his sister simply because they were related. They were nothing alike. She shook off her worries and turned to the jars lined up on the oak table next to the window. Uncorking a bottle of linseed oil, she poured a thin stream into a small ceramic bowl half-filled with fine yellow powder. A faint metallic clank in the servant's hallway startled her. Silently, she crossed the room, unlatched the servant's door, and flung it open.

No one was there.

It was the first morning that autumn's cool breath glided down from the mountaintops, warning of the change of seasons to come. Wrapped in her cloak, Mira threaded her way under the linens that hung near the kitchen doors, padded through the keep and followed the twisting lane to Elena's cottage. Inside, a small fire burned in the hearth and bundles of dried lavender hung on the walls. The space was furnished with a bed, a table and a chair. Arnaud's golden dog lay curled up in the corner.

"Why is he here?" Mira gestured at the dog.

"He's meant to protect you once you leave this place."

"I am in no hurry to leave," Mira said, latching the door behind her.

"You will be when you hear the news. Beltrán and his men soon ride from Jaca." Elena waved Mira into the chair. She stirred a pot of something savory that bubbled over the fire.

"How much time do I have, then?"

"A week at most," Elena said.

Mira thought a moment.

"If I am in danger from the rumors that twist through these mountains, you must be too. You were in league with my mother when she hatched the plan. You carried it out. Why do you stay on?"

"I have nothing to fear from your father or any other member of this house." Elena set the spoon on the table and straightened her shoulders.

"How can you be certain?"

"The baron and the steward leave me alone because the queen orders it."

Mira stared at Elena, astonished.

"The queen?"

"Yes, yes, Isabella the Castilian."

"She knows who you are?"

"She knows what Brother Arros told her. An upstanding Christian woman of the mountains, I believe he called me." Elena's eyes crinkled in amusement.

A patch of dry moss on a log caught fire and flared.

"Why would the queen protect you?"

"During the Moorish wars, I gathered butterwort, boxwood, willow bark, honey. Then I mixed up ointments and salves. Every summer Brother Arros sent them all to the queen in the south, for use in her infirmaries. He gave me credit for it, said it couldn't be done without me, and she put me under her protection."

"Did Mother Béatrice know this?"

Elena shook her head. "For all she knew, when she promised my services to your mother, she was sending me into a dragon's lair. I hated her for it. I thought Brother Arros was in league with her, and it near broke my heart."

Mira stood. "If this tale is true, and you are truly in no danger, I take great comfort in it. Arnaud awaits word of me in Ronzal. Will you arrange a message? I shall leave this place in three days' time, and he will be my companion for the journey I must make."

"And you'll be headed where?" Elena's face was pinched in a frown.

"Pau," Mira said. It was the first name that came to mind, the largest city in Béarn. Carlo Sacazar had spoken of it often, had praised its value as a place of commerce. "There are merchants in Pau who await me. I shall paint their portraits."

What a mountain of falsehoods she had constructed since Béatrice's death. With the telling of each one, the act of lying grew easier. She supposed it was a skill like any other, though she was not in the least proud of it.

"Is that so?" Elena's gaze was suspicious. "First I've heard of it."

"Yes," Mira said firmly. "I will have lodging and work there. It is all arranged."

When she entered her mother's room, Marguerite was already inside, dispensing orders to a maid. Mira waited until the girl left, then led her mother to the balcony.

"The steward soon returns," she said softly. "Elena told me. He shall be back within a week."

Marguerite's expression tightened. "He wrote to me from Jaca and said he would not be back until after the first frost. There was a delay with payment of our gold, that was his story."

"Now there are two stories. Which one do you trust?"

Her mother was silent a moment.

"Truth be told, neither one," she finally said. "I have found a place for you at a convent in Navarra. I must arrange a proper escort, but it shall be done, and quickly."

"Elena has already sent word to the mountain folk. In three days' time, they will come for me."

"Mira—"

"Mother, there is no one I trust more than the people of Ronzal. They will not allow any harm to come to me. Surely we can agree that the most important thing is for me to leave before Beltrán returns. The convent in Navarra can wait."

In her mother's worried eyes, she saw defeat.

21

Summer, 2015
Aragón, Spain
Zari

THE VILLAGE OF BIESCAS was perched in the green foothills of the Pyrenees. Some of its buildings were shabby
and crumbling. Others boasted immaculate stonework
and gleaming black slate roofs. Pink geraniums spilled out of
window containers, sun-drenched terraces held pots of tomatoes and herbs. The town was built along a river that wound its
way south, its milky gray waters clouded by glacial silt.

Their hotel, a sleek modern structure with rooms that boasted
floor-to-ceiling windows, clung to a hillside overlooking the
river. In the dining room, Zari and Wil ate the local specialty
of steak, eggs, tomatoes, bread crumbs and garlic cooked in a
brown glazed casserole dish. It was a variation on a traditional
meal that had been cooked by shepherds in the high mountains
for centuries. At its simplest, their server said, it was composed
of bread, garlic, wine, water and animal fat all roasted together

in an earthenware pot that sat in the glowing coals of an open fire.

The next morning, they rose early and set off with their backpacks neatly repacked, striding along narrow trails that threaded through rolling hills. The sun glared down relentlessly. By noon, the heat was oppressive. Zari tied a bandanna around her neck to protect her exposed throat. Wil, who was walking behind her, chuckled.

"That reminds me of Sue," he said.

"She gave it to me. It was her parting gift. I think the bandanna is about to make a big comeback."

"Especially pink ones."

"I wouldn't be caught dead in any other color."

"Neither would I," said Wil, his tone serious.

She turned around and began to laugh. Wil also had a pink bandanna. He had tied it skull-cap style over his blond curls.

"What?" he said. "You're not the only one Sue liked, you know."

They stopped on a low hill that looked out over a small valley to the south. A narrow stream twisted through the grass. Behind them, to the north, soared chalky gray limestone cliffs.

"I see a good lunch spot." Zari pointed at several rocks on the crown of the hill. Approaching them, she saw they all had rectangular, flat faces.

"Are these foundation stones?" asked Wil.

"Looks like it. They're lined up in formation."

They unloaded their food on one of the rocks. Wil sawed two slices off a round loaf of bread and piled them high with ham, cheese, artichoke hearts, and red-pepper spread. Zari opened a box of apple juice.

"What do you think this place was?" Wil gulped a swig of juice.

"Maybe another convent or monastery?"

"Maybe. But it seems like a good defensive spot. It could have been a castle."

Zari looked at the valley below. "Right. You could see anyone approaching from the south. These cliffs to the north would prevent an army descending on you from that direction." Turning to face the cliffs, she saw a dark shape clambering over the rocks. "Look at that! A deer?"

Wil took out his binoculars. "A mountain goat. No—three mountain goats."

Zari rummaged in the pocket of her backpack and pulled out the laminated image of the Fontbroke College portrait.

"Doesn't the background of the painting look like this place?"

"The cliffs and the peaks in the distance do look similar." Wil studied the painting. "I'm sure there are a lot of landscapes around here with the same basic features, though."

"I agree. But if this was a castle, we're in the right spot. The village of Oto is nearby. You said it has no castle."

"No—just a defensive tower from medieval days that's rented out to tourists now."

Zari picked up Wil's topographic map and traced a path from their picnic site to Oto with her fingertip. "Look. If a castle is here, it makes sense to put a tower there. The Broto Valley is the logical entry point for an army. The tower in Oto may have served as a lookout point for whoever lived here." She stood up and gazed east, toward Oto. "A signal tower makes sense. Invaders approach, a fire is lit on the tower, the smoke rises and this place goes into lock-down mode."

Wil lay back on the grass and clasped his hands behind his head.

"The buckets of tar and catapults were ready to go by the time the attackers got here," she said, imagining the onslaught of misery raining down from the parapets.

"Hmmm." Wil pulled his bandanna over his eyes. "I'm going to sleep for a while. You keep doing your detective work and give me a report when I wake up."

Zari walked the length and breadth of the foundation stones, the topo map and photocopy of the painting in hand. She wandered down toward the stream that wove through the meadow. At the far edge of the meadow, just past a copse of oak trees, the stream disappeared into a forest. Someone had thoughtfully placed several large rocks in a row through the streambed, forming a bridge of sorts.

On the other side, she headed for a cluster of boulders. She climbed one and settled on its flat top in a golden rectangle of sunlight, looking up at the delicate branches of a beech tree overhead. With her fingertips she drew patterns in the velvety moss that clung to the stone.

A crow called nearby, harsh and insistent. Zari imitated it. Silence. Then—an indignant squawk and the flapping of wings. It seemed she had either scared or offended the crow. Either way, she was now alone.

She closed her eyes, thinking of Mira. The inscription Mira had written on Béatrice de Belarac's mortuary roll praised the abbess for giving 'us' homes, food, and skills. So perhaps she had nowhere else to go. Perhaps she was an orphan, or a child born out of wedlock sent away to be raised in seclusion. At her adopted home in the convent, she might have been taught the skills of an artist by the Abbess Béatrice. But what happened next?

Why had Mira written "pray for my mother" on the Fontbroke College painting? Was it sort of a Renaissance-era sticky note? Or was the woman in the portrait—possibly Marguerite de Oto—Mira's mother?

And what about Arnaud de Luz, the man who had crafted the oak panels Mira painted on, and who also built furniture in the port town of Bayonne? Was he just a tradesman or did he have some stronger connection to her?

Zari opened her eyes and sighed. The threads that connected her to Mira through five hundred years of history were weak. She could envision dozens of scenarios, but would she ever know what really happened to Mira, who she really was?

The sound of splashing and the hollow clank of iron sheep bells startled her. A flock of sheep was clattering through the shallow streambed, their shepherd nowhere to be seen. Two dogs trotted at their heels, keeping watch for stragglers. As the herd passed her by, she watched, mesmerized, from her sunny perch on the rock. A rust-colored dog stopped and looked up. He seemed to be gauging the situation, trying to figure out where Zari fit into the scenario. He evidently decided she wasn't worth investigating and padded away. Behind him walked a man wearing rubber boots, jeans, a red-and-blue plaid shirt and a narrow-brimmed leather hat.

"*Hola*!" Zari called out. The man stopped and looked around. Spotting her, he approached. He was in his early forties, she guessed. His skin was tanned a deep brown from long days in the sun.

"*Hola.*" His voice was startlingly deep.

"Are they your sheep?" she asked.

He nodded.

"Does anyone raise merino sheep around here?"

He looked surprised. "No. Not anymore. These animals are bred for lambing. The meat is what they're valued for, not their wool."

"Merinos used to be the most important kind of sheep in Spain, right? The whole economy was based on them."

He laughed. "Depends on who you talk to. Spain wasn't always Spain, you know. It's hard to generalize about what happened in the old days."

On a whim she tugged the photocopy of the Fontbroke College portrait out of her pocket and jumped down from the boulder. She thrust it out to him.

"Look at this," she said. "Do you think the background looks like the view from the hill up there?" She pointed across the stream, up the path where Wil lay napping.

The shepherd gave her a curious look, then peered at the image. "It could be."

"I'm trying to find information about the Oto family. Have you ever heard of them?"

He shook his head, watching his animals pick their way around rocks and roots. "You're a short walk from the village of Oto. But a family called Oto—no, I haven't heard of them."

"What about this?" Impulsively she brandished her mobile, showing him the photo she had taken of Alejandro de Oto's flag. The shepherd nodded.

"I have seen that. The ships, the castles, the sheep."

Zari's heart leaped. "Where?"

"It's in the shepherd's cabin in the summer grazing meadows. Where I'm headed with my flock. You want to see it?"

She stared at him, incredulous.

"You'll have to follow me," he went on. "I'm heading there now. My animals know the way. Follow the sound of the bells."

The shepherd set off. Zari hurried back to the meadow and spotted Wil standing on the crown of the hill, shading his eyes with his hands. He waved.

"Wil!" she shouted. "We've got to go."

She jogged up the hill through the green-gold grasses and began stuffing the remains of their picnic into her backpack. He watched, mystified.

"I met a shepherd," she explained. "We have to follow him. He knows something about the Otos."

Without a word, Wil helped her finish clearing up their belongings, strapped his pack on, and charged back down the path, waving his poles over his head like a madman. She stumbled down the path after him, ragged gasps of laughter caught in her chest.

"What are you doing?" she called.

"Solving a mystery!" his voice floated back.

He disappeared into the woods, the bandanna flapping like a tiny pink flag on his head.

22

Castle Oto, Aragón
Autumn, 1503
Marguerite

It was the darkest part of the night, halfway between sundown and dawn. Marguerite was awakened by light rapping at the servant's door.

"Come!" she ordered.

The door creaked open and one of the maids crept in clutching a candle, a young woman from a village in a high mountain valley who was often targeted by the roving eye of Beltrán and had the bruises to show for it.

"You said come to you whenever I hear something important, my lady."

Marguerite went to the girl. "Tell me."

"I changed the linens in the steward's room for his return, as you told me. A guard followed me in and—" her gaze dropped to the floor, then up again. "He took me on the bed. Afterward he fell asleep and I crept into the passageway. I was dressing out there when the steward came in. First he shouted at the man for sleeping in his bed. Then he told him he'd a job to do. He said for the guard to slit the artist's throat. 'When the first cock crows to mark the dawn, enter her room from the servant's passage and put a dagger in her neck.' That's what he said."

Marguerite stared at the girl, whose eyes were huge and liquid in the wavering candlelight.

"Truly?"

The girl nodded.

"Are you certain the steward did not see you?"

"I am."

"Are you hurt?"

"They always hurt me." She averted her gaze.

Marguerite fetched the portrait from its easel and slipped it into a leather satchel.

"Run to Elena now." She thrust the satchel out to the girl. "Give her this. Tell her exactly what you have told me."

After the girl left, Marguerite lit a taper from the embers of her fire and entered the servants' passageway. She listened. When she was satisfied that no one was about, she moved cautiously down the dark hall. Steps away from Mira's chamber, she sensed a movement ahead.

"What is the lady of the house doing in the servant's passage?"

A guard appeared ahead of her, a torch in his hand.

"How dare you question your mistress?" she said sharply, backing away.

From behind, someone threw a rough cloth over her head and flung her over his shoulder. She was hauled like a sack of grain through the passageways, lugged up a twisting set of stairs. When she realized where she was being taken, she ceased struggling.

At the top of the Tower of Blood, her captor sucked in gasping breaths as his comrade fumbled with the door latch. She longed for her dagger, for the chance to slide its long silver blade between his ribs. A moment later he threw her roughly to the floor. Coiled in a ball, she tensed all her muscles, ready to spring. If she were to be ravished by her own guards, they would have a fight on their hands. But all they wanted, it seemed, were her keys. One of them wrested the iron keyring off her belt. There was the sound of a lock being turned and the shuffling steps of the guards fading away down the staircase. Then, silence.

Marguerite tore the cloth off her head and stood motionless at the arrow slit that faced south, watching the passage of the moon across the sky, marking time. When she dared wait no longer, she crouched by the door and ran her fingers along the wall until she found a loose sliver of mortar. She poked it free with a fingertip. Behind it lay a key.

Thanks to her thoroughness, the ironwork on every door in the castle was well maintained. To the servants' dismay, she frequently checked to ensure they had oiled and polished every hinge, every lock, even in the highest tower chambers. As the door silently swung open, she nodded in satisfaction.

The castle was a gilded cage, but it was her cage. And no one knew its secrets better than she.

23

Summer, 2015
Aragón, Spain
Zari

T HEY EMERGED FROM THE steep forest trail in a meadow
shaped like a shallow bowl. On three sides great snow-
crusted peaks rose up around them. There was an alpine
lake at the far end of the meadow, and the grass around it was
crowded with wildflowers of every hue.

The shepherd led them to the stone cabin. It had a wooden
door crafted from three broad planks of oak, and was constructed of rocks of all sizes and colors fitted together like pieces
of a puzzle. Matted layers of moss on the roof bloomed with
a wild bonnet of grasses and flowering plants. Inside, the one
window afforded little light. Along one wall was a wooden sleeping platform neatly laid out with a mattress, blankets, pillows, a
few books and a lantern.

"I stay here five days a week in summer," the shepherd explained.
"Then I return to the valley for two days to see my wife. She works

in the national park as a ranger in summer. I don't see her much, so I prefer to be up here with my flock and the dogs."

"Has your family always kept sheep?" Zari asked.

He nodded. "I'm the only one of my generation to stay, though. The others all left for city life. Me, I prefer the mountains."

He pointed at the wall opposite the sleeping platform. There was a rectangular stone about halfway up the wall that had a bas-relief carving on it. Drawing closer, Zari saw that it was a shield divided into six parts. Wil handed his headlamp to her. Slipping it over her head, she flicked it on.

"This is it," she said softly. "The Oto crest. Two ships, two sheep, two castles."

"But what's it doing here?" Wil asked in Spanish.

Zari turned and gave him an incredulous look. "Really?"

He shrugged, shielding his eyes from the glare of the headlamp with his hands. "Languages are easy for me—I can't help it."

"In the old days, abandoned buildings were a good source of materials," the shepherd said. "The stone probably came from one."

"It could have been that hillside where we met you, right?" Zari switched off the headlamp, turning to him. "There's an old foundation on it."

"Yes, it's possible."

"But you don't know anything about the family? Nothing at all?"

"Nothing. There is one person you could ask about it. Lucía Alvez. She lives in Broto. She's over a hundred years old. If anyone around here can tell you about those old-time stories, it's her."

Bells clanged outside the cabin. One of the dogs barked.

"I have to go tend to my animals. You are welcome to stay and look around some more, if you wish."

The shepherd pushed open the wooden door and stepped out.

After documenting the carved stone with photographs, Zari and Wil emerged into the afternoon light and watched the shepherd tramp through a patch of indigo-blue wildflowers, heading toward a loose knot of sheep on the lake's edge. The sun glared down on the water, creating the illusion of a skim of silvery ice on its surface. Zari eyed her pack. She dreaded the cinch of the straps around her sore hips.

"We can't leave this place yet. It's magical," she said. "First some stretches and energizing mantras, then back down the mountain in search of Lucía Alvez."

Wil nodded. "I'm in no hurry. Although it sounds like she doesn't have all the time in the world."

"Anyone that old knows a thing or two about keeping death at bay. I think she'll wait for us."

After a series of sun salutations, warrior poses and downward-facing dogs, they strapped on their packs and began the long descent down the mountain.

"'I call on healing light to radiate up from my feet and flow through my head and fingertips.'" Wil turned and shot her a quizzical look. "Where did your mother come up with that one?"

"She's a spiritual soul. She believes all the energy we need comes from this." Zari gestured around them at the meadow, the lake, the mountains.

"Is she a pagan?"

"She doesn't call on gods and goddesses to fix her problems, if that's what you mean. She only believes in one power: mother nature."

"So do you worship mother nature as well?" Wil shaded his eyes with a hand, watching a hawk ride a current of air.

"In places like this, I feel sure that some higher power is at work. And being here fills me with a calmness that I never feel in cities. But the affirmations—I have to admit I mock them even as I enjoy the ritual of it. I wouldn't give it up, though. Mostly it just reminds me of home."

The hawk traced a circle over them in the sky, screeching.

"We're not welcome here, it seems," Wil said.

The hawk followed them until they passed from the meadow back into the sheltering quiet of the pines and down the zig-zagging trail. Zari slipped off her sunglasses, glad for a respite from the sun's glare. From time to time she glanced overhead and searched the sky for movement.

But the hawk was gone.

24

Castle Oto, Aragón
Autumn, 1503
Mira

AN INSISTENT HAND GRIPPED Mira's shoulder. Her eyelids flew open.

"The steward is back," her mother whispered. "You must leave at once."

She scrambled out of bed. Marguerite helped her slip on her clothes and found a cloak to go over them.

"Your dagger?"

"I carry it always, as Elena taught me to do."

"Wait." Marguerite unclasped the ivory scallop shell from her neck and strung it around Mira's throat with shaking fingers. "You have more need of this than I."

"Come with me," Mira pleaded, flinging her arms around her mother's neck.

"My precious, precious girl." Marguerite gently disentangled herself. "Go. May God watch over you and keep you safe."

"Mother, no. I—"

"If you stay here everything I have done for you will be meaningless. *Go.*"

Marguerite turned her back on Mira, strode to the fireplace
and hefted the iron poker in her hands. Mira backed away. For
a moment she stood memorizing the image of her mother's
slight form outlined by the glow of the fire, staring until her
eyes blurred with tears. Then she stepped through the servants'
door and ran silently down the corridor.

Shrouded in her cloak, she followed an orange cat that moved
along the dark lane with silent grace, its tail twitching from side
to side. When she reached Elena's cottage the door opened a
crack.

"Do not stop here, but continue to the gates," Elena whispered.
"When you hear me scream, run."

"But—"

"This is your only chance. *Now.*"

A rooster crowed somewhere in the keep. Just before Mira
reached the gates, one of the entry guards emerged from the door
at the bottom of the watchtower, rubbing his eyes with the back
of a hand. She flung herself into the narrow space between the
last two cottages on the lane. In a moment, she heard a woman
cry out. The guard ran by, his chainmail vest clanking against
his sword. Mira moved quickly to the gates. A small door was
cut into the larger one so that the castle dwellers could exit
from within. She slipped through. Her skirts in her hands, she
sprinted down the steep path away from the castle.

As she descended the grassy hill and stumbled across the
meadow in the dark, all she heard was the sound of her own
breath. For a few moments she thought she had escaped unnoticed. Then the stillness was broken by frenzied shouts behind
her.

"Send the hounds out!" a voice roared. Was that him, Beltrán? Her legs churned through the tall grass, propelled by a burst of fear toward the ancient oak trees at the edge of the forest. She heard the gruff barking of dogs as they raced out the gates.

In a moment the cool quiet of the forest enveloped her. She crashed through a thicket of shrubs and fell on her knees in the stream. The icy water shocked the breath from her lungs.

Beyond the stream was a small stand of beech trees and a cluster of boulders. Mira splashed through the water, scrambled up the bank of the stream and clawed her way to the top of a large boulder. She lay flat on her back, panting. The first light of dawn filtered down through the trees.

Silently she repeated the prayer Elena had invented when she was a child, a worn, beloved talisman that she carried within her heart: "I pray for the mothers, the children, the beasts in the fields, for the sun that warms us, for the moon that lights our darkest nights, and for the starry skies that guide us."

Her prayer was interrupted by a snarling hound looming over the rim of the boulder. It snapped at her until its teeth caught on her sleeve. She yanked back her arm, but not before the hound's fangs sank into her flesh.

Tearing her dagger free from its sheath, Mira plunged it into the animal's eye. With a high shriek of pain, it released her arm and slid writhing to the forest floor. Slowly, the hound's life ebbed away.

She cradled her wounded arm, her eyes trained on the stream, awaiting the appearance of another hound. *I have nothing to defend myself with now,* she thought. A deep throaty bark echoed through the trees. There was the sound of vicious growling and a high-pitched squeal. After a moment the bloodied face of Arnaud's dog appeared in her line of sight.

Relief flooded her. She slid off the boulder, pulled her dagger from the dead hound's eye and wiped it on her cloak. Then she cut a strip of linen from her underskirt and bound it around her arm.

"Come on, then," she called to the golden dog. She struck out for the cave.

It was well past dawn, but the light of day was slow in coming. Mira squinted up through the treetops at billowing gray clouds that danced across the sky, prodded by the wind. A soft rain began to fall. She flung back the hood of her cloak, letting the cold drops burrow into her hair and tickle her scalp. Tree frogs slid out from notches in the oaks, their whispery chirps echoing through the air.

When she reached the ravine that led to the cave, she stopped to rest for a moment on the edge of the stream that coursed through it. She unwound the linen and plunged her throbbing arm into the water, watching blood float away in long red tentacles. Then she heard the silvery moan of a wolf. It was a faint sound, but there was no mistaking it. After a moment another voice joined in, sending up a wavering howl. The golden dog stopped panting. It was listening too.

She shook the water off her arm and quickly wrapped it up again. The rain-slicked leaves were slippery underfoot and the damp air burrowed into her bones. With her hand entwined in the dog's fur, she climbed up a rocky slope to a stand of beech trees. The dog disappeared ahead of her in the gathering darkness.

A final scramble and she was inside the cave. Crawling across the rough stone floor, she groped for the rolled-up furs, spread two out and lay down. The dog lumbered over and settled next to her, the heat from its great bulk seeping into her skin.

The wound on her arm ached. She resolved to keep watch for wolves, but instead she fell into a deep, dreamless sleep.

25

Summer, 2015
Aragón, Spain
Zari

THE NARROW STREETS OF Broto were lined by stone buildings capped with black slate roofs. The town was intersected by a broad, shallow river that wound through the valley. At one time a medieval bridge straddled the water, but during the Spanish civil war it had been blown up. Now a nondescript concrete bridge stood in its place.

They walked down the main street past a bar that catered to tourists. Across the street was a small grocery store.

"Let's ask in there," Zari said.

They crossed the street and went inside. Behind the deli counter was a woman with gray hair pulled back in a bun. She wore a black dress with a blue cotton housecoat over it. Behind her wire-rimmed glasses, her dark eyes skimmed over them suspiciously.

"Good afternoon, *Señora*," Zari began. "We are looking for Lucía Alvez. A shepherd told us we could find her in Broto."

The woman's mouth hardened into a thin line. Without responding, she turned and disappeared into a back room. The sound of explosive arguing commenced. Wil and Zari exchanged a glance.

In a moment, an elderly man shuffled out from the back room. He peered at them over the deli counter. "Lucía Alvez is the baker's grandmother. You have to ask at the bakery." His face was etched with deep lines and a thin layer of silvery hair was combed back from his high forehead.

"I am sorry if I said something wrong," Zari apologized.

He shook his head. "She doesn't like hearing that name, is all."

"Thank you," Wil interjected. "We'll go to the baker." He took Zari's elbow and steered her out of the store.

"This is feeling very Montague and Capulet," she remarked.

"With people that old the problem could be the Spanish Civil War," Wil said.

Zari gave him a skeptical look.

"My grandmother lived through the German occupation of Amsterdam. She saw what people will do to survive a war." Wil started walking toward the bakery.

"Like what?"

He kept his eyes focused on the street in front of them.

"Unforgivable things."

The baker directed them around back of the bakery, where on a red-tiled terrace, his grandmother rested in the shade of a broad umbrella. If Lucía Alvez was responsible for some wartime atrocity, she had reinvented herself as the most adorable old woman in Aragón. She was small and round, dressed all in black, her gray hair in braids and bound up in a bun. Her deep olive skin was a mass of soft folds.

She sat in a glider, the kind of chair mothers use to rock their babies to sleep. The upholstery was a burnished peach color in some shimmery fabric. In front of her on a low table sat a glass of red liquid.

She gestured at two simple wooden chairs with rattan seats covered by peach colored cushions.

"Sit, sit. Please, may I offer you something to drink?" Lucía grasped the arms of her chair, readying herself for the arduous process of standing up.

"No!" Wil and Zari said in unison.

She paused in her preparations. Behind her black-rimmed spectacles, her brown eyes were fixed on them.

"We just drank something," Zari explained. "And ate."

"But thank you," Wil added.

"Suit yourselves," Lucía said, settling back in her chair.

"A shepherd showed us the Oto family crest in his cabin on the mountain," Zari began. "He said you might know something about them."

"Family crest?" she repeated, cocking her head to the side.

"Yes, two ships, two sheep, two castles."

"Ah. I know it." She pushed off lightly with her small feet, which were encased in tightly laced black shoes, and set the glider into motion.

They waited.

After a few moments of silent gliding, she spoke again. "That family is gone."

There was another long silence. Finally, Zari ventured to fill it.

"Do you know anything about them, *Señora* Alvez?"

She gazed at Zari, her hands clasped in her lap. "Nothing."

Zari's heart dropped. "I'm searching for information about an artist named Mira, and I think she was connected to the Oto family."

Lucía placed both feet on the floor and the glider eased to a stop.

"Mira, you said?" There was a gleam of interest in her eyes.

Zari leaned forward, her mobile in hand.

"Yes," she said, holding up the mobile so Lucía could see the photo of the drawing Mira had made of herself, inscribed with the tiny Latin words, 'Mira drew this picture.'

The old woman craned her head, squinting. "That's from the cave. You've been there? How did you find it?" Her voice was clipped now, suspicious. She frowned at Zari.

"I—we don't know anything about a cave. This was an illustration in an old manuscript I saw in France."

Zari looked at Wil. He shook his head slightly.

"*Señora* Alvez," Zari pressed on, ignoring him. "What's in the cave?"

"It's not for me to say," Lucía said darkly, setting her glider into motion again. "The cave is not for strangers. You understand."

"Yes," Wil said. "We do." He stood up. "Let's go, Zari."

They thanked Lucía and left the cool shadows of her red-tiled terrace, heading out into the late-afternoon sun.

"The war again?" Zari asked, perplexed.

"Maybe," Wil said. "Anyway, she was upset. Let's ask her grandson about the cave."

They went back into the bakery. Sure enough, the grandson knew the way to the cave, but they would have to retrace their steps to the site of their hilltop picnic, then climb halfway up the mountain again.

"We upset your grandmother by reminding her of the cave," Zari told him. "She was not happy about it."

"Oh, she gets worked up about her memories. But they keep her alive, in my opinion. She spends all day thinking about the past. Nowadays the cave is just a cave, but it used to be a hiding place." He retrieved a piece of paper and a pencil from a drawer behind the counter, and sketched a map on it. "When you get to the end of the ravine, there's a rock wall. You have to climb it. Beyond that, you'll see a group of boulders. The cave is there."

26

W HEN MIRA AWOKE, THE dog was gone. She wrapped a fur around her shoulders and ventured to the mouth of the cave. The sound of crows chattering echoed through the trees. There was nothing to do but wait and watch the night descend.

She breathed in deeply and closed her eyes for a moment, listening to the rustle of the leaves in the breeze. Then the wind died and the crows ceased their bickering. In the silence that followed, there came a metallic clang like a hammer blow on iron.

Instinctively she drew back into the shadows. In the dark recesses of the cave she found the bow and arrows that Arnaud had left for her. She crept back to the light, her heart thudding wildly. Her mouth felt dry as sawdust.

A hound appeared at the ravine's edge. She pulled an arrow out of the quiver and nocked it in the bow. When she looked up again, the dog had disappeared. The breeze picked up. Silence had given her an advantage—but now she had lost it in the whispers of leaves, the shuffle of branches. With trembling knees, she waited.

In the next instant the dog appeared below her. Its eyes found hers. Mira drew her bow and shot it dead. Then a man strode out of the woods wearing the red leather armor of a Valencian warrior. Frantically Mira threaded another arrow into her bow and let it fly. The arrow glanced off his thick leather chest plate.

"Not bad aim, for a woman," he called.

Mira fumbled for another arrow as he bounded easily up the boulder. In an instant he was upon her.

She backed toward the wall of the cave, bracing for a blow. Instead he reached out and stroked her cheek with a gloved hand. She stiffened.

"You do resemble her a great deal." He ran a finger down her jawline. "It is the hair, more than anything. That luscious hair." He took a handful and pulled it to his face, breathing in the scent of it. "In truth, your father had planned to keep her alive. Those were his orders. But I suppose mothers cannot be expected to act rationally."

Mira pressed herself against the cave wall. "My mother is dead?"

"It is her own fault. She very nearly allowed you to escape your fate. There were rumors, of course, stories spread around winter hearths by peasants, that Oto girls occasionally trick their fate. And wonder of wonders, here is one who nearly did."

She fought to keep her eyes blank. The last light of evening sifted through the shaft in the rock. His face was covered with a sheen of oily sweat and his graying hair hung limp around his shoulders. The patch over his eye was red leather, just like his armor.

"But I'm afraid you weren't clever enough," he went on. "Your fate has found you again." He smiled. "I am in no hurry, though.

There is time for us to get acquainted." He stripped a glove off one hand and trailed his fingers along the side of her neck.

She shrank back at his touch. His sour breath sickened her.

"Let us make ourselves comfortable, shall we?" He pushed her roughly to the sleeping furs.

"Wait!" she said. "Please. I never knew my father. Please tell me a little of him first. You knew him better than any man." She bowed her head.

He hesitated. Then he stripped off his other glove.

"I suppose your father would want you to know what kind of man you betrayed before you die," he allowed. "His skill on the battlefield is exceptional, but that has always been the way with the house of Oto. Fierce warriors, valued by kings. A family of men."

His fingers found a tangle in his beard. He dug his long nails under the coarse hair to work at it. Watching him with repulsion, Mira felt her terror disperse. Anger coursed in a cool stream from her heart, steadying her mind. She heard her own pulse in her ears and was calmed by it.

"Your destiny was to die in the woods, alone, before the light of your first day." He shook his head. "Your mother dared to change your fate. That woman Elena was equally to blame."

Mira gasped. "What do you mean?"

"Oh, she got her due in the end, I assure you."

He smiled. His teeth were the color of earth. He fumbled with a soft leather bag that was slung over one shoulder and pulled out the portrait of her mother. A raw wound had been opened up on the painting's surface, an ugly splintered blister on the bodice of her red silk dress.

"She tried to hide your precious portrait under her cloak, that witch Elena. See—it stopped my first arrow." He flung the painting aside.

"No!" Mira crumpled to the ground, sobbing, her knees drawn up to her chest. One hand slid to the sheath strapped around her thigh.

The steward licked his lips, unlacing his leather chest plate.

"I always desired your mother," he said, drawing the armor over his head. "But of course, given the debt I owed your father, that was out of the question." He unbuckled his sword belt. "This, I think, is the next best thing."

He turned to lay his sword carefully by his side. In that instant Mira sprang up and jumped on his back, dagger in hand. With one savage motion she slit his throat. His warm blood gushed onto her fingers.

"*This* is the next best thing, you devil," she whispered in his ear. "For me. Not for you."

She pushed him away with a strength she did not know she possessed. The dagger clattered onto the rocks. Beltrán emitted a gurgling rasp that mingled with the sound of her own ragged breath.

Dark blood gathered in a depression on the cave floor, draining the life out of him. The pulsating gushes slowed to a trickle and then, as the evening wore on, faded entirely away. Sinking to her knees, she spread her hands wide and stared dumbly at her bloody fingers.

In the woods, a soft rain was falling.

Mira was still kneeling by the slumped body of the steward, the portrait clutched in her arms, when Arnaud climbed into the cave.

He sank to his knees beside her. "Did he hurt you?"

"I killed him before he could."

Arnaud rolled Beltrán onto his back and eyed the gaping wound in his neck. "Good blade work. Elena taught you well."

"He murdered her, Arnaud. Elena and my mother both."

"No. I'm here now because Elena told me where to find you."

"But he bragged of his attack on her!"

He pointed at the portrait. "That saved her from a fatal wound. When the guards raised the alarm once you fled the gates, he rushed off to release the hounds. Elena sent my dog out after you and made for Ronzal."

Hope rose in her. "And my mother?"

"I met a stable boy by the stream, the one Elena trusts. He said your mother's body rests under a shroud in the chapel. Could be he's lying, but I doubt that."

Mira turned away from the sight of the dead steward and stared out at the woods. "She took my place, Arnaud. She died so I could live."

Above the trees the sky turned purple, then black.

Even the crows had gone silent.

At dawn the next morning, the air was thick with the promise of a storm. Arnaud buried the body in a shallow grave and stacked rocks atop it. They hauled water from the stream and washed the blood from the cave's stone floor. Mira stacked the sleeping furs neatly and scattered the charred remains of the fire in the woods.

Thunder rumbled in the north. Raindrops splattered from the sky, exploding in every direction. They retreated inside the cave as the storm swept in and the force of the rain swelled.

"What about your brother?" Arnaud unwound the bandage on Mira's arm. "Pelegrín."

"If he is anything like our father, it would be best if we never meet."

Arnaud fetched ointment and a length of clean linen from his belongings, then tended to Mira's wound. When he finished, she moved to the cave's entrance and perched on a ledge overlooking the forest. A cold breeze ruffled her hair. Water slithered down the knobby silver trunks of the beeches and weighted the branches of pine trees so they hung at soft, defeated angles.

"Where will I go?" She did not realize she had spoken the words aloud until Arnaud answered.

"To the sea, as you've always wanted." He came to stand next to her.

"How can you jest at this moment?"

"It's no jest. The port of Bayonne crawls with merchants. You'll paint their portraits, and I'll be at your side."

She studied his face in silence.

"Will you accept me, or won't you?" he asked after a moment, his voice laced with impatience. "You've thought on it long enough."

"What will you do in Bayonne?" she retorted. "You are a man of the mountains."

"I told you, I'll make furniture. I'm skilled enough that Carlo Sacazar offered to find me a place at a wood-worker's studio in Nay."

She opened her mouth to protest.

"I know—you'll never return there," he said quickly. "But if I've the skills to find work in Nay, I can do the same in Bayonne. I can source wood from the mountains, have it shipped down the River Pau or sent overland by oxcart. You paint, I build. See?"

Mira nodded. Still, her mind stubbornly moved down the list of impediments to their alliance, finding another snag.

"But you are the first born. What about your place at the table of councilmen?"

"Tomás will take my place as first born."

Her eyes widened. "How can that be?"

"The future is my father's constant worry. His agreements with Mother Béatrice served us well, but will the new abbess work with us the same way? We'd be fools to count on it. No." Arnaud shook his head. "I can better serve my family in Bayonne than in Ronzal."

Mira thrust her arm out toward the woods. Raindrops flared against her skin like pricks of fire. Was it her imagination, or did traces of blood linger under her fingernails? Beltrán's sneering face rose up in her mind.

"What about Alejandro? He has no mother now. His father and brother are at war across the sea." Her voice broke. "I cannot abandon him."

Arnaud slipped his arm around her shoulders. "A dead sister's of no use to him. Alejandro will be looked after. After all, he's a baron's son."

She leaned into him. A movement caught her eye through the rain, a small brown bird hopping from branch to branch in a slender beech tree. It trilled a delicate, pulsating call.

"A snow finch in these woods before autumn strikes—that's odd," Arnaud observed. "They stick to the high meadows 'til winter. Could mean the snows arrive early this year."

The snow finch called again, unleashing a barrage of staccato chirps. It took flight, beating the air with its white-edged wings.

"Something comes," Arnaud said.

A crow settled in the beech tree. It rasped once, twice.

Mira picked up a small rock, weighed it in her palm and threw it hard at the crow. It missed its target and fell with a soft plunk on the forest floor. The crow cocked its head, studying her.

"I am still here!" she called. "You cannot have me yet." She was pleased at the strength in her voice.

Arnaud glanced from the crow to Mira with questioning eyes.

"I was remembering something Elena told me, that death is always waiting to snatch us away from this life," she explained. "Crows are death's messengers, she says."

"She's right."

Mira retreated into the cave and gathered their things, staring into the gloom. There was no sign of violence, of blood, of murder. Everything was neatly in its place. Soon the faint scent of wood smoke would vanish. Even the marks she and Arnaud had chiseled into the stone would blacken and fade over time. Perhaps they would become as invisible as the words she scribbled on wooden panels and covered with layers of paint, but they would never completely disappear. The thought gave her comfort.

In a moment she emerged from the darkness with her cloak on, two satchels strung over her shoulders.

Arnaud watched her with a guarded look.

"If we mean to reach the sea before winter, we must get started," she said. "It is a long way from here to Bayonne, and as you say, the snows might come early this year."

He nodded slowly, letting the full weight of Mira's words sink in. Then his face relaxed. His brown eyes shone with the old familiar warmth, lit up with the smile that was for her alone.

She held out her hand.

27

Summer, 2015
Aragón, Spain
Zari

IT TOOK A WHOLE morning to trek from the Broto Valley to the place where Zari had first seen the shepherd and his flock near the narrow stream. Before they began the climb up the mountain, they leaned against the mossy flank of a boulder and snacked on fruit. Wil tied his bandanna around his head like a sweatband. Zari reached up and tucked a few haphazard strands of his hair under the roll of cloth.

"Ready?" she asked.

"After you."

The forest was a tangle of pine, oak and beech trees. They climbed steadily through the shady understory, occasionally slipping on patches of pine needles or the slick surfaces of papery oak leaves. All around them echoed the calls of birds. Magpies, jays and crows hopped from perch to perch in the canopy above, their scolding chatter punctuated by the staccato rap of a wood-pecker and the cascading trill of a songbird.

Zari let herself slip into the reverie of hiking, savoring the quiet, unmeasured rhythm of it. During hikes as a child, she had imagined she was Helen Keller, closing her eyes and walking in the footsteps of her brother and parents, trusting their lead and her memory to keep her upright. If she was feeling dramatic she would plug her ears, since Helen was blind *and* deaf. That was usually when she fell. On these occasions, her brother would look back over his shoulder. "She's being Helen Keller again," he would report to her parents. Then her mother's far-off voice would float in. "Helen! Time to keep moving." And her father's gruff admonition would follow. "Let's go, Zari! Stop lollygagging."

She slipped on a patch of oak leaves. The Helen Keller game would never fly here. The trail wound in a series of switchbacks up the mountain. Her eyes were locked on the ground, searching for the safest footholds, spotting hazardous roots and rocks and hollows in the soil. Finally they reached a grove of beeches that led into a ravine, just as the baker had described.

They walked the length of the ravine until it dead-ended in a rock wall frothing with ferns. Zari eyed the jumble of rocks, dubious.

"Can we get up there from here?"

Wil dropped his poles and unbuckled his pack. In a moment he was at the top. He peered down from above.

"Just climb the way I did. There are plenty of good handholds."

She slipped off her pack and scrambled up the wall as fast as she could, with much less grace than Wil. She rolled onto the ground next to him, breathing hard.

"That was impressive," he said.

"I just wanted to get it over with."

She turned over on her stomach and looked up. Several misshapen boulders loomed ahead. Beyond them was a high limestone cliff.

It only took a moment to scale the boulders and then they were stepping into the cave. Wil handed Zari his headlamp. Near the back of the cave was a circle of stones. Cold embers and a pile of ash lay within it.

"The locals must still use this place," she said, poking at the embers with a stick.

She approached the rough, heat-scorched surface of the stone wall behind the fire site and worked silently by the light of the headlamp, sweeping her hands over the blackened surface. Finally, on the left side of the cave, she found it. About halfway up, an 'O' was carved into the wall. Inside the circle was Mira's self-portrait, and an inscription was etched into the stone: '*Mira de Oto pinxit*.'

"Wil." Zari sank down on her knees and ran her fingertips over the stone. "She was here." She felt shaky, saying the words aloud. "She sat here and she made that."

"Why '*pinxit*'?" Wil asked, leaning closer.

"Artists sometimes wrote that after their names when they signed paintings. It meant 'I painted this,' or 'I made this.' But what's really important is that she wrote 'Mira de Oto,' not 'Mira de Belarac.' She was one of them, Wil. She was an Oto."

A crow rasped out a harsh cry somewhere outside the cave. It sounded like it was directly overhead. Zari looked up and saw a faint wash of light filtering in high above them.

"There's a hole up there. That's why this fire circle is so far back." Wil stood and moved along the wall, tracing his hands over the stone. "I was wondering why anyone would light a fire here— without a place for the smoke to escape, it would be impossible to breathe. That explains why this is such a good cave. You could live in here for a long time." He paused. "I found something."

Zari aimed her headlamp at the wall in front of Wil. She saw the faint indentation of an upside-down V.

"Wait. Shine the light here." His finger followed the outline of a blackened and pitted letter 'A' within the upside-down V's peaked roof.

"I think I know who carved this," Zari said.

She trained the light on the wall, illuminating the letters 'D' and 'L'. Arnaud de Luz, the furniture maker from Bayonne, had carved his initials here.

"Arnaud was in this cave with her. They both left their marks on this wall. They were *together*, Wil."

The crow's scratchy call floated down into the cave.

"So if they were here at the same time, what does that mean?" Wil asked later, his voice drowsy.

They lay in front of the fire, zipped up in their sleeping bags. It was cold in the cave even with a blaze going. In the half-light thrown off by the flames, they watched smoke curl past the stone walls and disappear into the gloom high above them.

"I don't know what it means. Maybe nothing. This used to be a hiding place. Maybe they were hiding here to escape some-thing—or someone. The good news is that there's more known about Arnaud de Luz than about Mira de Oto. So maybe he can lead us to her."

"How?" Wil rolled over in his sleeping bag and ran his finger-tips lightly over her throat.

"He was from Bayonne. That's where he had his woodworking business. I can access city records and follow his traces to her."

"Aren't you running out of time?"

Zari shook her head. "As soon as I was convinced Mira was an artist, I started making inquiries about another fellowship. The problem is there's so little known about her—she was one of history's ghosts, she inhabited a gap in the record. It's hard to get support for a research project based on a few threads of evidence." She sat up in her sleeping bag and poked the fire with a stick, reshuffling the logs until a glowing ember burst into flame.

"But Vanessa kept encouraging me. She's got some deep-rooted rivalry going with Dotie Butterfield-Swinton, who promoted the idea that Bermejo painted the Fontbroke College portrait. Just the idea of pushing back against him helped get her on board. She linked me to a research center at Oxford with a history of financing risky projects. She shared the photos of the mortuary roll and the prayer book with some Oxford alums who have deep pockets and even deeper curiosity. I think Mira's mark on the wall is just the meaty evidence we needed to hook them. Now that I know what to look for, I'm confident I can unearth more of her story and her work. Laurence Ceravet has agreed to help me, so that'll open doors in France when I start digging."

"Does this mean you'll be in Europe another year?" Wil asked.

"Fingers crossed, yes."

He wrapped his arms around her and she burrowed into his neck, breathed in the smoke-tinged scent of him, kissed the warm, salty skin in the hollow of his collarbone.

Wil lay still, his eyes shut, breathing with a gentle rhythm. Despite her exhaustion, Zari fought off sleep. She sat up, watching firelight dance across the carved image of Mira's face on the stone wall. Zari wondered if she, too, had lain in her lover's arms here, watching the shadows flicker on that same smoke-scorched surface.

Cornelia van der Zee had a place in history. She was an artist of repute, with a paper trail dating back half a millennium. Not Mira de Oto. She had hidden herself from view. The words and images she drew under all those layers of paint were never meant to be seen. Yet there they were, clues—and it seemed she scattered many in her wake. It would be painstaking work, uncovering the threads that connected them. Zari had hold of one now. It was delicate as spider's silk and just as hard to see, but she felt the force of Mira's spirit tugging at the other end of the thread, willing her to stumble into the past, into the dark, into the unknown.

Did Mira wonder if anyone would find her, would one day seek her out? Did she imagine, hunched in front of that wall chiseling her image into the limestone, that eventually someone would recognize her face? The indisputable fact remained: she was here, emerging from the shroud that had hidden her for five hundred years. And Zari would follow the echo of Mira's footsteps wherever they might take her. She would let Mira lead the way.

Fitting herself against the warm angles of Wil's body, Zari closed her eyes and listened to him breathe. She remembered something Vanessa had said the day she saw the portrait for the first time at Fontbroke College. *Ars longa, vita brevis.* Life is short, but art lasts. Mira's art had not only outlasted her—in the end it made hers the only life illuminated in a family that was extinguished long ago.

One by one, Zari's thoughts untangled themselves, drifting up through cracks in the stone, spiraling out into the night. The sizzle and hiss of the fire faded. Sleep descended again.

This time, she let it claim her.

THE END

ABOUT THE AUTHOR

AMY MARONEY LIVES IN the Pacific Northwest with her husband, two daughters, and a wise old dog. She studied English literature at Boston University and public policy at Portland State University, and spent many years as a writer and editor of nonfiction. When she's not diving down research rabbit holes, she enjoys hiking, painting, drawing, dancing and reading. *The Girl from Oto* is her first novel.

For a free prelude to *The Girl from Oto*, for the full scoop on the research behind the book, and for news about the sequel, please visit www.amymaroney.com.

The support of readers means everything to an independent author's success. If you enjoyed this book, please take a moment to leave a review online or spread the word to friends and family.

ACKNOWLEDGEMENTS

FOR THE FIRST HALF of this project, when people asked me how the book was coming along, I said, "I feel like I'm pregnant with an elephant baby." An elephant pregnancy lasts about twenty-two months. After two years, the book still wasn't done, so I needed to find an animal with an even longer pregnancy. It was tough. Finally I came up with the frilled shark. The frilled shark inhabits the coldest depths of our oceans, hunting alone in the dark while its pups gestate for forty-two months. The frilled shark and I know how it feels to haul around our precious cargo for nearly four years before releasing it tenderly into the world. But that's where the similarity ends, because the gestation of this book was far from solitary. *The Girl from Oto* only exists thanks to an astounding community of family, friends, and professionals who supported me along the way.

Several years ago I was lucky enough to visit Magdalen College, Oxford, the source of my inspiration for this novel. I am deeply grateful to Magdalen College Professor Clare Harris for her support and encouragement of this project. I found my novel's setting when I visited Oto, Aragón, and stayed in a beautifully restored medieval tower overlooking the magnificent Broto Valley. Thank you, Elena and José.

I am indebted to the scholars, librarians, and art conservation professionals who generously responded to my research queries, especially Isabella von Holstein, Esther Pascua Echegaray, Jessica Stevenson-Stewart, Elizabeth Chambers, Nina Olsson, and Vanessa Wilkie.

I had an amazing group of beta readers whose insights, critiques and ideas made this book better. Special thanks to Jacqueline Jannotta Rothenberg, Jefna Cohen, Dawn Bolgioni, Marketa Rogers, Martha Koerner, Erika Ruber, Carol Greenwood and Deirdre Crossan Roman.

One of the best parts of this project was assembling a team of professionals to help me. Emma Darwin, thank you for excellent developmental editing. Andrew Brown, I love my book cover. Rebecca Brown, thanks for your kind patience and for creating the book design I wanted. Tracy Porter, you made the map-creation process dreamy.

To my parents, Jack and Sallyanne Wilson, and my brother, Jonathan Wilson, thank you for always encouraging my love of reading and writing, for modeling a tremendous work ethic and for your integrity.

To my kindred spirit Julie Cassin, you kept this project afloat. Your love for my story and my characters gave me the confidence to keep going.

To my daughters Dahlia and Nora, you inspire me every day. I am one lucky mother.

To my partner in love and life, Jonathan Maroney, your belief in me is the reason this book exists. From the first, you encouraged me to go for it. Even at the forty-two-month point, you were consistently positive and supportive. I will be forever grateful.

9 780997 521306